TAYLOR CROOK &
RYAN KIRK

PATH OF THE ETERNAL SUN

THE SENTINELS SAGA

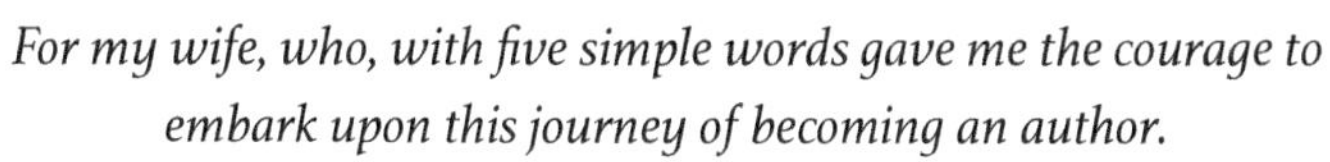

For my wife, who, with five simple words gave me the courage to embark upon this journey of becoming an author.

"You should do it, babe."

Well, here we go...

PROLOGUE

Nefia lived in the shadows, but this night held terrors she hadn't faced in years. Her head pounded with every beat of her heart.

She grimaced as the wound on her side burned. She imagined she felt the infection as it spread through her body, carried by veins that now betrayed her. If she didn't seek attention soon, the cut would fester and be the end of her.

It was a worry for later.

If there was a later.

She ran, then stumbled over an exposed root. She kept her balance, but it was a near thing.

Of all nights, *this* was the one she had to come across one of the few sentinels with half a brain left on Iru. He'd been waiting for her, stalking her like she was somehow prey.

He'd been a huge, hulking brute, head shaved bald. Clever, though, and patient. He knew the path she would take, then planted himself in the perfect location to ambush her.

Had someone within the singun turned toward the sun?

Nefia refused to believe it, but the question would have to be asked.

She blinked away the sweat from her eyes. Only this moment mattered. If she failed tonight, a traitor in their midst would be the least of their fears.

Bastard had been good with a sword, too. Most sentinels barely remembered the pointy end went in the enemy. This one had skill, and more speed than anyone that size had any right to possess. She'd intended to dance around him, her shorter swords carving great chunks of sun-cursed flesh from his body.

She'd expected an annoyance. A slight delay.

The gash in her side reminded her how wrong she'd been. The sentinel had been a master, worthy of instructing even her singun. He'd flicked aside her first attacks with a casual disregard.

In the fight, she'd lost the fat rabbit. One cut of the sentinel's sword had sliced clean through the creature. It had been its last day anyway, but it deserved a better end than dying at the hands of a sentinel. The giant had robbed the rabbit of a meaningful death.

Killing the sentinel had taken too long and cost too much. She wondered if, in whatever awaited them past the veil of death, the sentinel knew how his selfish, misguided actions had risked the fate of the world.

Nefia ran faster. She felt the disturbance ahead, the ripping of the world she knew and loved. Every second mattered.

She tripped, stumbled, and barely managed to keep her balance. Roots seemed to be everywhere.

Fear nestled in her heart.

The fight against the sentinel was nothing compared to what awaited her.

Tall pines stood guard around her, blocking the dark moon from her sight. She searched for the familiar sphere, but the trees were too thick. She hated not being able to see the sky. Through all the trials in her life, even those that happened before she took the oaths, the sight of the moon had always been a comfort to her. Not seeing it tonight twisted her insides even tighter.

She ran into a clearing, the earthy scent of pine needles filling her nose. She took one look at the clearing and almost ran the other way. She had hoped she would have more time.

It was already there, a thin slit, as though someone had gently sliced a knife through the paper-thin fabric of reality.

It wasn't the first time she'd seen it. Far from it, but every time, it made her pause, clench her fists, and grind her teeth. As a child, she'd believed that the world was solid. Knock your head against a wall and suffer a headache. Punch someone on the chin and hope your hand didn't break.

Now, though, she knew just enough to know she understood nothing. The world most people lived in and accepted as normal was just the surface of a very deep and very dark lake. There were secrets beneath that turned even the most courageous warriors into frightened children.

A darkness seeped from the slit, somehow darker than black, a color Nefia had no word for. It floated in the clearing, not subject to the same forces that pulled everything else in the world down.

Malevolence emanated from the darkness. Though it had no form, it hated.

She searched the clearing, hoping, like a child, that

there was someone else nearby who might lift this burden from her. But she had only the darkness for company.

Had it done any good, she would have drawn her swords and cut it. But she could defeat it as easily as she could kill a cloud. There was nothing to do but wait.

Wait and suffer.

As it became solid, it crawled through her mind, feeling like a dozen spiders ransacking her memories. In her training, she'd endured this once before, and it had almost broken her.

The darkness took, but even worse was what it returned. The connection flowed both ways. The realm opened itself up to her, an endless land of shadow and despair. She expected it, though, and knew it would pass. It was terrible, but not nearly as terrible as the first time.

Slowly, the shadow took form. Arms and legs that were almost human, but that ended in claws. Facial features that were almost recognizable, but twisted, as though a mockery of the human that faced it. Nefia felt as though she stared into a shattered mirror.

As soon as its form settled, she attacked, her swords dull in the moonless night.

The pain in her side flared, and though she fought through it, she knew it weakened her cuts. She was slower than she needed to be. The creature danced backward, impossibly light on its feet.

Nefia pursued, her swords cutting a path that would kill any human opponent. Even the dead sentinel on the path behind her hadn't seen these techniques.

The creature bobbed and weaved, seeming to know her moves before she made them. It slid from side to side with an ease that told Nefia there was only one way this duel would end.

A second later, it tired of dodging. It accepted a cut along its side in exchange for breaking Nefia's guard. Claws tore at her, ripping thick gashes through her good side and left arm. The arm went limp, and the sword dropped from her useless left hand.

There was no hesitation. She'd been trained better than that. From the moment the rabbit had died at the hands of the cursed sentinel, she'd known how this would end. Nefia left herself open, drawing the creature in closer. Sharpened claws ripped through her abdomen, and Nefia used the last of her strength on a final cut. Her sword passed through the creature's neck, surprising it.

They fell together. Nefia landed on her back and stared up at the hole in the trees. Though the moon was dark, she could still see it above. As it had since she was a child, it brought her a measure of peace. She was glad she could die under the watchful eyes of the moon.

There was one last task to complete. A sacrifice.

The last one she could make.

As the power coursed through her body, she twisted her head to observe the rift. A soft red glow illuminated the clearing. The rift closed, stitched together by the final gift she could offer.

By the time it closed completely, there was no pain left in her body. She stared up at the moon, smiled, and closed her eyes for good.

1

S hin pressed both her fists into the small of her back and used them as a fulcrum to arch her spine until it made a series of satisfying pops. She sighed contentedly and turned to regard the field she'd been working all day. With the setting sun warm on her face and her body aching in its familiar way, she smiled. It had been a good day.

Not one to waste time, she picked up the two buckets of stones at her feet and started towards the modest home she shared with her parents. They had finished the harvest yesterday, so today she had been "walkin' stones," as her father called it. All day she pulled out any rocks that had worked their way to the surface of the soil. That way they wouldn't damage the equipment used to till the soil before the next planting.

The stones would be put to good use. Her family couldn't afford to waste them. They would be sorted in the evenings after supper. Larger stones would be used to repair the retaining walls. Smaller ones would find their way to the stone garden behind the house.

Shin's was one of many family farms that made up the bulk of Ilos' population. Their farm was small, but they produced an assortment of vegetables that was the envy of their neighbors. It was a mark of pride that their efforts yielded as much or more than some of the larger farms nearby. Most of their crop was taken by the magistrates, as the Path demanded, but enough remained to make deals with the local ranches for beef, milk, cheese, mutton, and the other necessities.

She put the buckets down for a moment to reposition the weight when a rock passed less than a hand's width in front of her face.

The snicker of children identified the culprits despite their pathetic attempts to hide. The lazy, good-for-nothing boys down the road must have escaped their chores early to be tormenting her before supper. She turned on her heels. As she suspected, it was Semuel and his two faithful companions. They all held stones in one hand and long sticks in the other.

The glint in their eyes spoke only of trouble.

"Look, friends!" Semuel spoke loudly. "We've arrived in the nick of time. My lady, the bandits will threaten you no more."

Shin looked around, confirming the field was empty except for her and the boys.

"We're sentinels," Semuel explained. "And we've just saved your life."

"Thank you?" Shin ventured, unsure of a better response.

"Now, in exchange for our protection, we demand recompense."

Shin was certain Semuel didn't know what "recompense" meant. He was twelve, but big enough to be sixteen and intelligent enough to be eight. But he'd heard the word somewhere recently and intended to impress her.

"And what recompense would you demand?" she asked.

"We know you always keep some bread in your pockets," Semuel said. "We'll start with that."

Big as he was, he was lean. They all were. There were always too many mouths to feed and not enough food to go around. And he was right. She did always keep some bread in her pocket, for when the hunger that was her constant companion grew too great to bear.

"I've got nothing," she lied. Any food she gave to Semuel was food she wouldn't get to eat. And it wasn't like his need was any greater than hers.

"You lie," he said. "And we're sentinels. You've got to listen to us. The Path demands it."

He tossed the stone in his hand with practiced ease, giving her a threatening look. Someday, she thought, Semuel would make a good sentinel. He had the attitude about right, at least.

Shin considered the buckets on the ground for a moment. Her aim was far better than Semuel's and his lackeys'. Maybe she could buy herself enough time to get back to the edge of the field and retrieve her digging fork. Her father had made sure she knew how to use it both as a tool and a weapon, so she would be safe out in the fields alone.

She was good with it. Her father said so, and he wasn't one for false compliments.

A momentary vision of her embarrassing the young boys and standing triumphantly as they ran away flashed in her mind.

Only to be replaced by the more familiar twisting in the pit of her stomach.

She ran.

"Get her!" Semuel shouted. All hopes that the boys would tire of their game rather than give chase vanished.

The advantage she gained through surprise only lasted a few seconds, but it would be enough. Though she wasn't as big as Semuel, she was quicker. Her long, hungry strides ate up the ground in front of her until she hit the edge of the forest that surrounded her family's farm. Relief swelled in her chest as soon as the shady darkness enveloped her. She had a knack for disappearing when she needed to. She climbed a nearby tree.

"Are you just going to hide from us? You must be a filthy bandit! Innocent farm girls don't hide from honorable sentinels!"

Semuel's calls echoed through the woods but receded with every breath. The boys had long since passed her hiding spot. They would tire of the sport soon enough.

She waited about ten minutes past the point that she heard the last of Semuel's calls and then extricated herself from the tree she had nimbly ascended.

Shin slowly made her way back to the buckets of stones that those little pricks had so kindly knocked over in their chase. She refilled the buckets, careful not to leave any of the stones out, and walked back to her home.

Her shame was heavier than the buckets. She hadn't needed to run from the boys. Despite their size difference, she knew she was good enough with the digging fork in hand to fend them off.

But as always, her shame faded. She was alive and unharmed, and that was what mattered. By the time she saw warm glow from the sconces reflected in the windows and could hear her parents' laughter, her steps were light once more.

She put down the buckets of stones and opened the door with a smile already on her face.

"I hope you're hungry, Shin. Your mother made her famous mutton stew!" her father proclaimed.

"Well, I can't be late for that!" The sarcasm in her own voice matched that of her father's.

"Listen, you two, if you want something else, you make it! What else am I supposed to do with the tough old sheep that Remy sent us?" Her mother's offended tone was just as playful as Shin's and her father's.

Shin entered the house, and she and her father shared a smile. She washed up while her father helped her mother set the table. By the time she had scraped the mud from her hands, her place was set, and the savory smells coming from the stew made her stomach rumble.

The stew was thin, as it always was. The mutton was close to going bad, and the vegetables that rounded out the stew were barely slivers. But all the same, it tasted better than many of the meals she'd eaten, and it would sate her hunger, at least for a while. Her mother was a master of making their limited foodstuffs taste like a Firstborn's feast.

"Any decent stones?" Her father asked around a mouthful of bread.

"A few, probably enough to fix the western wall," Shin answered.

Before her father could respond, they all heard the unmistakable sound of war horses galloping up the path to their farm.

For the second time that day, fear coiled like a snake in the pit of her stomach.

The sentinels were coming.

2

———————

Beast looked out from the top of the steep rise and sighed heavily at the single wagon that passed below him through the trees. He tried to settle his heightened nerves by reminding himself that his mugon had pulled off hundreds of raids just like this.

But he knew in his heart this one was different.

Today, their success or failure meant everything. It represented the conclusion of his life's work. And they had little time to pull it off.

First, they had to ambush the sentinels. Then, in the blink of an eye, they had to dress as those sentinels and allow themselves to walk into an ambush. The plan was simple in design, but the slightest mistake would ruin them.

For days, Beast and his mugon had painstakingly laid out a series of unmistakable breadcrumbs for the only bandit group in Samas that had yet to join his cause. The only group strong enough to resist him.

Until today.

Today, he conquered the Red Aces.

Beside him, someone approached. Beast caught the slight familiar scent of soap.

Benji.

The man who was almost as instrumental to Beast's success as Beast himself. A skilled warrior, a brilliant tactician, and a man who seemed to know the movements of sentinels, bandits, and nobles before they even mounted their horses.

"The Red Aces set their ambush about a league down the road. They positioned themselves well. They look ready," Benji reported.

Beast chuckled grimly. "Ready for us? How can a sapling be ready for a hurricane? You give our enemies too much credit."

"Perhaps. But take care that you don't give them too little."

Beast grunted and returned his gaze to the wagon below. If any other man were to speak to him in such a way, Beast would make an example of him. Warriors needed to know who was in command. But Benji was more than just the most useful warrior under Beast's command.

He was Beast's friend.

These single wagons that travelled off the beaten path were usually stocked full of food or ore, materials desperately craved by nobles and peasants alike. The supplies within the wagon would be found in no official record. The magistrates used such wagons to fatten their own stomachs and line the pockets of well-connected guildsmen.

A secret economy, built on the backs of farmers and miners across the land, that benefitted only a few.

Guarded by the sentinels who were supposed to protect the people.

Benji's impressive network of spies found such wagons often. Unfortunately, the magistrates had grown more cautious over the past few months, and now more sentinels guarded the wagons than before. They still hadn't found a way to repel Beast's tactics, though.

And the mugon rarely left survivors to learn from their mistakes.

Beast saw one of the sentinel scouts come galloping back to the main force surrounding the wagon. Though Beast was too far away to hear, he could guess the content of the report well enough. Scouts had found the Red Aces' ambush up ahead, just as Beast had hoped. He'd even sent a few of his own mugon ahead, positioning themselves clumsily, with the Red Aces' signature armbands visible, just in case the Red Aces didn't give away their position easily enough.

True to sentinel procedures, the commander ordered the sentinels to form a defensive ring around the wagon. It would take the commander a few minutes to decide how to proceed.

Beast raised his fist in the air. Behind him, his mugon prepared for the attack.

He glanced back, and when he was satisfied that his warriors were ready, Beast hopped up and sauntered down the hill.

Blood pounded in his ears. Nearly half again as large as any man on Samas, he caught the eye of every sentinel as he moseyed toward the wagon.

The sentinels shifted their formation to address the potential threat.

"That's far enough," the commander said. His tone, confident, expected compliance. Beast, after looking at the number of nocked arrows pointed in his direction, complied.

"No need for any of that," Beast said, his arms outstretched. "I'm not here to cause any trouble."

"You wouldn't like it if it found you. You'd best turn back before I choose to make an issue of that oversized axe strapped to your back."

Beast grinned. "I guess I should say I'm not looking for trouble with *all* of you. See, I fancy myself something of a warrior and wanted to test my mettle against one of the legendary sentinels. Which of you cowards accepts my challenge?"

The commander scowled, but his eyes ran up and down Beast, trying to take his measure. Had the man heard the rumors about Beast?

Beast didn't think so. If he had, he'd have ordered the archers to release their arrows as Beast approached, the Path be damned.

But a true sentinel didn't back down from a challenge, and Beast had put the commander in a bind. The commander was no fool. He knew Beast's arrival heralded something more. He could turn Beast into a pincushion with a word, but his soldiers would look down on him, and he would lose face. If enough soldiers spoke unkindly about the incident, the sentinel might not continue his rise up the ranks.

So, what did this sentinel value more? His precious concept of honor? Or his life?

Beast was willing to bet his own life on "honor."

The commander nodded. "I accept your challenge. Should you somehow win, you will be free to leave. So says the Path. But I will offer no mercy." His voice remained calm, full of confidence.

The fool couldn't see how outclassed he was, even when Beast stood right in front of him.

His fingers tingled with excitement. "Sounds fine to me."

The commander dismounted from his horse, as did several of the sentinels.

Unfortunately, two archers remained mounted and on guard near the rear of the wagon. "Don't let down your guard," the commander ordered. "And shout if you see anything in the trees."

Beast unlimbered his massive axe, the battle-worn handle seeming to melt into his hands.

He would have to make this a show that drew the eye.

"May the sun honor this duel and shine on us as we walk the Path," the sentinel said as he bowed, his sword hand resting on the sheathed weapon's hilt.

"Sounds good," Beast said, and kicked a clump of rotten leaves and dirt into the downturned face of his enemy before charging forward and slamming his shoulder into the smaller man, sending him flying.

The observing sentinels, bound by the rules of their precious Path, remained in place despite the underhanded tactics. Surprise twisted their expressions, but none had the presence of mind to act. Rather than attack his incapacitated foe, Beast maintained his momentum and threw his massive axe at the back of one of the archers watching the surroundings. The axe lazily spun end over end in the air until it embedded into the archer's spine and knocked him off his horse, dead.

The remaining archer reacted with surprising speed. She spun, pulling on her bowstring as she twisted in the direction the attack had come from. Beast dove beneath the wagon, barely avoiding the shot. He felt the arrow cut the air where his head had been only a moment before.

Had he been alone, hiding under the wagon would have been a death sentence.

But he wasn't.

Arrows filled the air, killing several sentinels and throwing the rest into confusion. Beast watched as his mugon materialized from the shadows, slaying sentinels in the chaos.

By the time Beast shimmied out from under the wagon, the only remaining sentinel with a heartbeat was the commander. The mugon encircled him as he defiantly held his sword at the ready. When he saw Beast dusting the dirt off himself, he spat at Beast's feet.

"You have lost your honor in the face of the sun this day."

"I'll be honest, I never had much in the first place, but I'll be sure to drown my sorrows in the bosom of your wife when I see her next." Beast's smile faded. "Your honor cost you all these goods that you stole from the people of Samas. I'd say your loss is worse than mine." Beast took back his axe, offered to him by one of the mugon who'd pulled it from the back of the archer.

"These goods are not stolen! The magistrates have ordered them moved. You peddle in lies, vermin."

Beast stared at the man for a long moment and accepted, not for the first time, the true power of the oppressors from whom he and his mugon were trying to steal their freedom.

The commander believed in his orders. He had no idea his sentinels had died because they'd accepted the orders of a corrupt magistrate. And he never would, no matter what Beast said.

The power of faith.

The power of the Path.

"Kill him," Beast said and turned away.

"Are you too cowardly to do it yourself?" the sentinel sneered. "You may have no honor, but at least grant me the chance to die in combat."

"Fine." Beast's bloodlust hadn't been satiated anyway. "But I will show you no mercy."

"I accept your terms, and I will take as many of you with me as I can."

Beast grinned and hefted his weapon. The mugon moved away from the commander but kept their hands on their weapons. They didn't expect Beast to lose, but no matter the outcome of the duel, the sentinel wouldn't be leaving this road alive.

The sentinel advanced cautiously, but Beast saw his intent well enough. He couldn't read books, but people were simple. The sentinel wanted to get in close and negate the reach advantage that Beast enjoyed. Beast dropped his hands low on his axe handle and began a large arcing swing typically used to keep opponents at a distance. The sentinel darted forward, expecting to take the impact of the axe's long haft on his shoulder and then lunge with his sword. It was a beautiful attack, requiring incredible skill and unshakeable courage.

The sort of attack only a sentinel could perform.

Unfortunately, the commander was fighting one of the few men on the island who didn't fear the sentinels.

One of the few men who made killing sentinels into a sport.

Beast dropped his axe. Freed from the weapon's incredible length and weight, Beast spun away from the commander's lunge and clamped his massive hand down on the sentinel's sword arm.

The sentinel adjusted and attempted to throw punches at Beast with his free hand, but their relative positions made a clean blow nearly impossible. Beast let him fight for a moment, then seized the man's throat and lifted him into the air. He held the commander up for a few heartbeats before slamming him down onto his back.

Around the circle, Beast's mugon cheered.

Somehow the sentinel maintained his grip on his sword, so Beast placed a knee on each of the man's arms and straddled him, freeing up his massive fists to rain down blows on the commander's unprotected face.

Beast's vision went red as the sentinel's face turned into a pulpy mess. Teeth and bone embedded themselves in Beast's knuckles, and blood splattered up his arms. Eventually, the red faded, and Beast stood up.

Massive chest heaving, Beast looked around at the mugon staring back at him. They had seen his battle rage before. But they still flinched as he looked at them.

None of these warriors would ever dare betray him. Indeed, they would follow him to the ends of the earth and back. They wanted to fight with him, not against him.

"Benji, take inventory," Beast ordered. "The rest of you, you know what to do."

The mugon did. One group collected the extra horses and rode them away. Another group began unloading the wagon, Benji taking a careful but quick inventory.

Beast watched the efficiency of his mugon. The training, largely orchestrated by Benji, had worked wonders, and there was no better source of bloodlust than a lifetime of painful servitude. Not only that, but Benji's structuring of the units ensured that if anyone was caught, they could only give up one small cell.

The sentinels were dead. Now it was the Red Aces' turn.

3

———

A sheen of sweat covered Sato's body despite the cool morning air. The sun broke over the horizon behind him just as he finished the last of the forms he practiced each day. The Path of the Eternal Sun, the code all sentinels followed, demanded daily meditation and training. Many, like Sato, combined both activities into what looked like a slow-moving solo dance.

Body and mind became one. For Sato, this morning ritual was often the highlight of his day, the time before life intruded upon his perfect routines.

When he finished, Sato collected his gear and marched toward the hot springs nearby. Both Sato and his unit favored this location, camping here whenever their patrols brought them this way. The Path demanded daily sweat, but cleanliness was equally important, and for good reason. Grime weakened a warrior by inviting disease and discomfort. A true sentinel cared for their body with the same attention that they cared for their sword. Thus, rivers, lakes, and springs often served as valuable campsites.

Sato noted the reactions among the other sentinels as he

passed. All bowed and showed proper deference, but no one smiled at him the way they smiled among one another.

It was just as well. A true leader couldn't afford to become too close to his sentinels. A weak leader, poisoned by friendship, might hesitate before ordering sentinels to battle.

Still, he sometimes wished for more.

He understood that fear and authority were far from the best tools a leader should wield. Unfortunately, they were the ones he excelled at.

Not like his father, who had risen from nothing to become the Firstborn's most trusted general. His father had been the sort of man warriors couldn't help but follow, the sort of man who was born a peasant farmer and died as a close personal friend of the Firstborn. The sort of man who showed what obedience to the Path could accomplish.

After his father had passed, the Firstborn had adopted Sato as his own, an act of incredible generosity. Sato was an exemplary sentinel, and he was, in his own estimation, the best swordsman in Samas. He always followed the Path, providing an example for those who served under him.

He just couldn't inspire.

He growled at the thought that rose unbidden in his mind.

Inspiration was for children.

His warriors were sentinels. It was their calling to serve Samas and bring honor to their families. Why should he have to find ways to inspire them to do exactly what they were sworn to do?

When he'd been a younger officer, he'd been cordial with his unit. He had joined them for games of dice or leisurely swims in the lake when they weren't on duty. But at best, his presence was tolerated. They were cordial in return, because that was their duty. To this day, though, he had met but a single warrior he dared call a friend.

There were three sentinels in the spring when he arrived.

"General," one said with a nod. Sato returned the gesture and removed his clothes before sliding into the water. He wasn't surprised to find other early risers in the spring, but would have preferred solitude. No matter, they would leave soon, pretending they had soaked long enough, and then warn others away.

The sentinels, two men and a woman, waited long enough so as not to appear like they were leaving because of him, and then rose from the water to begin their day. Sato nodded politely again as they left, and then closed his eyes to prepare for the day ahead.

All too soon, his brief solitude was interrupted. He heard the soft footsteps first.

"Bandits, general, maybe twenty of them, riding towards the southern coast," a messenger, slightly out of breath, reported.

"How far away?"

"No more than a league, sir."

"Have Captain Roko ready my personal guard and meet me on the road south," Sato ordered. The man bowed crisply and took off running. Sato jumped out of the spring, dried off, and put on his armor.

Strange that the bandits would head south from here. If his memory of the surrounding area was accurate, and it was, there was no place in that direction for them to hide. They would be trapped between Sato's forces and the ocean. It wasn't like them.

In recent months, the bandit groups had gotten smarter and more organized. Instead of razing the farms on Ilos to the ground and stealing all that they could, they had started hitting supply lines between cities all over all three islands. No longer could the sentinels simply put the bulk of their forces on Ilos and patrol the farms there. Now they had to patrol all three islands in hopes of stopping the bandits before they struck.

Unfortunately, the sentinels didn't have the numbers to cover that much territory at once. They didn't even have the numbers to root out whatever nests the bandits were now using. Catching twenty of them in the open was some of the first good news Sato had received in days.

By the time he reached his horse, a sentinel had the animal prepped and the reins in hand so that Sato could hop onto the horse without breaking stride.

"Tell Hanson to take the remaining sentinels and watch the road between the port and Bulas, in case this is only a diversion," Sato ordered the sentinel who had readied his mount. Certain his orders would be obeyed, he kicked his horse into a gallop to rendezvous with his honor guard. They only numbered ten, but there were no better swords patrolling the land in all of Samas. Twenty bandits should be no problem.

Captain Roko reported as soon as they joined forces. "General. Scouts report twenty bandits on horseback. Based on their location and direction, they could be the group that made an attempt on the wagons between Bulas and Hankala. At their current pace, they should hit the coast about thirty minutes ahead of us. Even if they break east, they'll just run into the road, where I'm assuming you sent the rest of the unit?" Roko smelled something wrong as well.

Sato nodded.

Roko continued, "The scout reported that the bandits

appeared surprised when she spotted them. Perhaps it wasn't an act?"

"Then why ride south? There's nowhere for them to run." Sato posed the question to himself as much as he did to Roko.

"I suppose we'll have to ask when we catch up to them. Assuming there's anyone left to tell the tale after our swords cross," Roko said, then barked a laugh.

Sato didn't even smile. "Then let's ensure we take one alive."

4

———

Shin fought against her nerves, but they always won when the sentinels came calling. She imagined the ground rumbling beneath her feet from the pounding of the warhorses' hooves, though they were still a way down the road.

Her father, who rarely missed anything, reassured her. "They're just here to pick up the harvest. Maybe a few days early, but there's no need to fear."

Despite his air of confidence, they continued their meal in silence. The sentinels' approach grew louder and louder until Shin would have sworn there was an army of cavalry outside her door. Then the horses stopped all at once, as if each rider pulled the reins at the exact same moment. The resulting stillness was more terrifying than the advance.

Shin heard boots, so new they creaked with every step, approaching the door.

The magistrate knocked, his firm rap demanding entry.

Her father got up and answered the door with his customary, affable smile.

"Good evening, magistrate. That time again?"

"Hello, Kaius. It is. Is the harvest in the barn?" The magistrate's tone was brisk, and his face stern, but there was the hint of a smile in his eyes as he addressed her father—an effect Kaius had on most who met him.

"Of course, but wouldn't you prefer to come in for a drink first?"

"Sorry, Kaius, but I'm on duty. I have men waiting to collect your harvest."

Mother, having surreptitiously moved into the kitchen the moment the door opened, now appeared beside Kaius with a tray full of steaming bowls.

"I'm sure your men are hungry, so let me tend to them. You can rest inside and speak with my husband." Her face, weathered from years of too much sun and not enough care, still lit up the room when she smiled.

The magistrate only hesitated for as long as decency required. "The men *have* been complaining all day. Maybe your stew will finally bring me some peace." The magistrate broke into a smile, unable to resist her mother's charms.

With that, Mother brushed past the magistrate and out the door. Shin set to work putting together a bowl of stew for their guest and pouring him a glass of the wine they saved for special occasions. When she returned to the table, the magistrate sat down and thanked her. Shin bowed and sat in front of her own food but didn't resume eating until her father also sat. The magistrate stared at Father for a long moment, and then finally the dance was done.

"Kaius, I don't know how a dog-faced dirt farmer like you landed a beauty like her, but you're the luckiest man I know." The magistrate burst out laughing and clapped her father on the shoulder. Shin and Father joined in, and the scene was almost pleasant. The magistrate had been visiting their farm for years, and over that time, her father had made a friend of the man.

None of that changed the truth of what would happen if he ever discovered what they were hiding.

"You know, sir, I've said for years I don't know what she sees in me. I figure she just sticks around because Shin likes me so much," her father said with a wink in her direction.

The magistrate laughed again before digging into his stew and sipping his wine. They ate for a while, her father and the magistrate making small talk about the other farms and life in the country. Before long, the magistrate finished his meal and leaned back in his chair.

"You're a smart man, Kaius. This stew, delicious as it is, is made from what most people in the cities would throw out. Even with the tallies being raised, you've managed to keep your family fed and happy." The magistrate's tone was respectful, but something about the turn in the conversation put Shin on edge.

"Thank you, sir. The eternal sun has blessed me with a family that works just as hard as I do."

"I'm glad to hear it. It smiles upon all those who labor honestly for the good of all." The magistrate paused. "But speaking of honesty, were you aware that some of your neighbors have been hiding food and misreporting their harvests?"

Shin wasn't sure if the tightening around her father's eyes was real or imagined. "I wasn't. I'll confess I'm saddened to hear that's been happening."

The magistrate's demeanor suddenly chilled. "Do you think yourself clever?"

"Clever, sir? I've never thought so, and my wife would be the first to agree." Her father's answer was relaxed, but the magistrate's posture had shifted. It reminded Shin of a snake she'd once found in a field, coiled just before it struck.

Silence hung between the two men for a few moments. Her father smiled his affable smile, but the magistrate's face was etched in stone as he stared back at him.

Without warning, the magistrate smiled and clapped her father on the shoulder once more. The kind expression never faltered as he stood up from the table and tucked his chair back in. "As usual, Kaius, I must thank you for the generous hospitality. Now, shall we conclude this evening's business?"

Father agreed and joined the magistrate as he walked out the door. Shin nearly collapsed with relief when they left, but the pit in her stomach remained.

When Mother returned with the dishes, she saw the look on Shin's face and swept her up in a hug.

"Don't worry, dear. They won't find anything."

"But you weren't here! He mentioned the other families hiding food. I think he knows!" Shin struggled to keep her voice from rising in both volume and pitch.

Her mother held her tighter. "Shhh. Calm down, dear. Your father knows what he's doing. We hide so little food they couldn't notice. For someone in his station, it barely amounts to anything."

In time, Shin's embarrassment overwhelmed her uncertainty. By the sun, she was sixteen this year and was being comforted by her mother like a little girl. She pulled away, maybe more abruptly than necessary, and composed herself.

Her mother took no offense, and they went about cleaning up after their dinner in silence. By the time they were done, her father had returned.

"Are they gone?" her mother asked.

"Yes, with everything we expected them to take. I even put up a little fight when it was more than it should have been," he replied.

Shin felt something inside of her cracking. "Why do we have to hide anything? They're supposed to protect us! Not snatch food out of our mouths."

Her parents regarded her, surprised at her unaccustomed outburst.

It was her father who answered. "Of course they shouldn't, dear. It's not how sentinels are supposed to behave. But such is life. It does us little good to complain. It's better by far to figure out how to survive. We're together, and even though their demands increase every year, we still have enough to eat. That's what matters."

Shin growled, the sound coming from the back of her throat. She knew all of it, of course. It had been the way of life for as long as she could remember. But the injustice of it made her clench her fists and wish her father had taught her to fight with a sword instead of a digging fork.

"It's not fair," she said, embarrassed again by how petulant she sounded.

"No, it isn't, but when is life ever? You must be smarter than the predators that surround you. Just like me," her father said with a wink.

Despite herself, Shin grinned. It was hard to be upset for long around Father. He bore the weight of the world with a smile. Somewhere deep down, Shin knew that was why her mother had fallen in love with him.

That night, she watched the moon from her window as it rose over their fields. Something about it calmed the fire that flamed in her heart. Under its serene gaze, it made her feel like someday she would make a difference. She would give her parents a better life.

Somehow.

It was a dream. And she knew a dream didn't amount to much.

But it was enough.

She fell asleep with a smile on her face.

5

————

"You're still putting yourself into a compromised position."

Beast didn't share Benji's concerns. He understood that warriors of lesser skills, or all warriors, couldn't afford to take the risks that he did. "I'll be fine. I'm taking our best swords, and we only need to hold out for the few minutes it will take them to commit their forces. Then you'll be swooping in to save the day," Beast replied with a grin.

Benji shook his head slightly. They'd been together long enough that he knew he wouldn't win this argument. Once Beast's mind was made up, not even a charging army could change it.

With a wave, they parted ways and he went to meet the mugon waiting for him near the wagon. Beast was glad to have Benji leading the other forces on this operation. He couldn't think of another person he would trust with his own life.

Beast and his mugon began their march down the

treelined road, pretending to be the very sentinels they'd just ambushed.

A few miles later, he could see where the ambush would be waiting for them. The trees grew thick, and several large limbs stretched over the road. It was a perfect place for an ambush, a place he would have chosen himself if he didn't have Benji thinking one step ahead of everyone else.

The Red Aces waited until Beast and the wagon were squarely in the perfect position, then came charging through the trees. Even though he had been prepared for the attack, Beast's disdain for his enemies resulted in a burning desire to punish their insolence.

The mugon made short work of the initial ambush. The Red Aces had committed a small force to the initial assault, no more than could be hidden in the trees nearest the road. They were supposed to be a distraction to keep him from noticing the larger forces ahead.

They failed.

The Red Ace ambushers fell so quickly the mugon had plenty of time to prepare themselves for the rest of the attacking forces. Beast was pleasantly surprised to see the numbers advancing on him. If Benji's information was right, and it almost always was, it looked like the Aces had committed most of their remaining forces to this ambush. They'd gotten desperate over the past few weeks.

Once Benji and his reinforcements flanked the main force, there would be little left of these upstart bandits.

As expected, the battle around the wagon slowly turned in favor of the Red Aces. The mugon were stronger, better trained, and better fed. For every mugon that fell, at least three or four Red Aces joined them. Beast's warriors fought with such skill, the Red Aces probably thought they were actually fighting sentinels.

But some numbers couldn't be overcome. The ambushers were forcing them backwards with waves of bodies.

All except for Beast.

He carved out a large swath of the battlefield on his own as he swung his giant weapon. The mounting piles of corpses surrounding him deterred the bandits from entering his space almost as well as the whistling sound of his razor-sharp axe.

He was all that was holding the remaining mugon together.

Any moment now Benji should arrive and turn the tide.

Just as they had planned.

The mugon rallied behind Beast in a loose circle. They were fully on the defensive now. The Red Aces pressed harder. Eventually, even Beast had to retreat a few steps, careful not to trip over the corpses he'd left behind him. His incredible strength began to wane.

Any moment now.

Their attackers were malnourished and dirty, conditions that the growing strength of the mugon were at least partially responsible for, but they sensed their enemies were on their last legs and pushed harder. Beast waited impatiently for the sound of Benji's force to come crashing in.

Instead, he heard a bird call.

His heart sank. It was their signal that Benji's position had been compromised. No help was coming.

A palpable ripple of despair wound its way through the mugon fighting at his back. They knew what that call meant as well as Beast did. Without reinforcements, and soon, they'd never last.

Beast swore. Whatever held up Benji, he wasn't going to

let it crush his dream. Not when it was so close to becoming reality.

His axe slipped in his grip as blood worked its way between his hand and the leather wrap around the handle. His muscles ached and cramped.

He wouldn't die here. Not at the hands of the Red Aces, of all people.

With a primal roar, Beast charged forward, swinging his axe, and broke through the wall of attackers. Those that avoided his axe, he knocked to the ground and stomped on, bones cracking underneath his feet.

The Red Aces tried to cut him off from his allies, but Beast and his axe twisted like a tornado. Any bandit who thought they were safely behind Beast suddenly found themselves in front of him, the sole focus of his deadly attention.

Thought vanished, replaced only by rage, action, and instinct.

The surviving mugon didn't waste the opportunity Beast provided them. They pounced on the disorganized attackers, and the field was evened once more.

Beast didn't stop. He couldn't. Once the wave of rage had caught him in its swell, all he could do was ride it to the end.

They still surrounded him. The Aces, correctly viewing him as their greatest threat, focused their efforts on bringing him down.

It would be their undoing.

Beast ignored the shallow cuts that decorated his body. He felt no pain. All he knew, down to his bones, was violence. His axe was nothing more than an extension of his arm, as though he'd been born with it in hand.

Though his movements were fueled by rage, they were shaped by skill, and not one of them was wasted.

Bodies fell around him until an unlucky swing shattered the haft of the mighty axe on some fool's cowardly shield.

Beast dropped the ruined axe and tore the shield out of the hands of the poor soul in order to beat him to death with it. He threw the shield into the face of the next enemy he saw, savoring the satisfying crunch his nose made.

A true warrior needed no weapon.

He pummeled the ambushers with fists, knees, and feet. He bit at any flesh that came close to his mouth. A roar burst from deep in his chest as one last set of Aces attacked, their swords useless against Beast's sheer strength and skill.

They broke like a thin reed. He looked around, but there were no more Aces before him.

The remaining cowards had either fled or surrendered, and the battlefield was his.

Beast, the bandit king.

He smiled, licking the blood from his lips. He liked the sound of that.

6

———

The sentinels rode hard. Sato settled into the rhythm of his horse's pace, confident the warriors behind him would maintain a perfect formation. After days of eventless patrol, they finally had a chance to get some answers from the elusive bandits.

They found the bandits dug in at the southern coast, which surprised Sato. They'd known sentinels had found them, so why not run east or west?

Instead, the criminals had taken a defensive position just within a grove of trees, their backs to the water. Several archers were stationed near the edge of the grove, ready to rain arrows down on the sentinel advance while using the trees as protection.

Impressive tactics for vermin.

Not that it would do them any good.

Sato held up a hand and his honor guard dropped their gallop to a canter. Roko gave the orders. "Archers, ahead."

Two sentinels broke rank and galloped ahead, bows drawn.

Sato watched the bandits launch their first volley.

Arrows fell harmlessly around his mounted archers. None came within a dozen paces of hitting its target. The sentinels suffered no such lack of accuracy. Their first two arrows found their marks, dropping two of the bandits. As they fell, the sentinels released their next arrows. Two more bandits died.

The remaining bandit archers fired arrows in desperation, but they had no chance. Their bows, clearly fashioned by inexperienced hands, lacked the distance to reach the sentinels. The bandits pulled as hard as they could, but their arrows fell pitifully short.

For the sentinels, the danger was no greater than an afternoon of practice. They remained out of range, dropping each of the bandit archers in time. To the bandits' credit, they didn't run.

Of course, they had nowhere to run.

When the last bandits with bows fell, Sato's archers secured their weapons and returned to the ranks. They hadn't even broken a sweat.

The bulk of the bandits retreated further into the cover of the trees, a position that would prevent the sentinels from utilizing their war horses. The bandits likely thought that they had a better chance of winning this fight on foot.

They were mistaken.

Sato's sentinels dismounted and charged into the grove. Though outnumbered, the sentinels moved with brutal efficiency, cutting down their enemies with quick, effortless cuts. They fought harder when they sparred one another. Economy of movement translated into a bloody choreography in which each sentinel played their part perfectly. As their foes dwindled, the sentinels switched tactics and forced the remaining bandits into the center of a quickly closing circle.

By the time Sato dismounted and caught up to his unit, they had four bandits on their knees and stripped of their weapons. Sato regarded them briefly and then looked out at the water. In the distance, he could see what looked like one of the ferry ships used to shuttle goods and people from island to island. It must have been blown off course. No trading lanes were nearby.

Sato assumed his most authoritative voice. "By the power granted to me by the Firstborn of the sun, you are under arrest. No citizen who is not sworn as a sentinel may bear weapons. The penalty for this crime is death. So says the Path. I shall give you a choice in the manner of your death. Cooperate, and I shall grant you a warrior's death you don't deserve." He paused. "Resist and suffer."

One of the bandits spat on Sato's boots. Almost as quickly as the bloody sputum hit Sato's toe, Roko's sword flashed out and sliced the woman's ear off. She screamed briefly, but then clamped her mouth shut and glared at Sato. Fortunately, if looks could kill, he would have died a long, long time ago.

"You all have plenty of appendages to spare, but all the same, why don't you let the general ask his questions, and maybe think twice before you share any more bodily fluids with him." Roko's voice was less formal and even more intimidating for it.

Sato paused to let their situation sink in.

He looked out to the water. The ship he'd spotted earlier had moved fast and was closer now. It looked like Sato was right about it being off course, as it appeared to be tacking furiously in order to return to the shallows of the ferry lanes.

Sato turned his attention back to the bandits. "Where is your base of operations on Iru?"

They said nothing, and Sato nodded to Roko. He listened to the brief scream as another ear was removed from a different bandit.

"Same question."

Silence.

A scream.

"Same question."

Silence. Roko moved toward the last one, sword ready.

"Wait!" the only bandit that still had both ears yelled.

Sato waited.

"We don't have a base on this island, we—" The man's voice cut off as the first bandit to lose an ear plunged a hidden knife into his throat. They both died an instant later as Roko killed the woman. No peasant could carry a weapon in Sato's presence and live to tell the tale.

Sato looked between the two bandits who were still breathing. Clearly, the woman had been the backbone of this group, as both remaining men looked ready to break. Once again, Sato looked out to the ocean and saw that the ship was well on its way back to the shipping lanes. Something clicked into place. He was a fool for not seeing it earlier.

"You have your own ships," Sato stated calmly.

Both men exchanged looks of surprise before looking down at the ground.

"How many do you have?"

They were very cooperative now. "We don't know, sir. We just get instructions and go where we're told. If we need a ship, one is waiting for us. If we need horses, they will be waiting, too," one bandit answered with no hesitation. His comrade nodded along.

"No permanent base of operations either?"

"No, sir." The bandit's tone was all respect. "There are

many camps in many places, but they also move and disappear with the seasons."

A realization formed in Sato's mind. One that both frightened and excited him. "Last question: who leads you?"

They shook their heads in unison.

Roko's sword came up, but Sato raised his hand to stop him. He regarded both men for a long moment, noting the conviction in their eyes and the pride that they displayed, knowing that they would endure great pain to keep their leader safe. Sato sighed. They followed someone they were willing to die for.

How did a leader earn such devotion?

"You may have strayed from the Path, but you honor yourselves and your leader with your conviction." Sato drew his sword. "I will grant you a swift death."

In one motion, both men's heads were removed from their bodies.

Sato looked to Roko. "They have ships, and they have leadership. These bandits are much more organized than we suspected. I must ride to Bulas immediately to inform the Firstborn. You will finish the rest of the patrol." Sato gestured to the remaining corpses littering the tiny battlefield. "But first, remove the heads and tie them to the horses. Ride up and down the supply lines to make an example of those who seek to break the law. So says the Path."

7

"Remove their heads and drag them past the other farms. In death, they will serve as a final reminder to others of the cost of disobedience. So says the Path."

The magistrate's words buzzed in Shin's ears and made her head feel like it was floating away from her body. She stifled another sob, lest the sounds alert the sentinels to the tiny crawlspace between the ceiling of the farmhouse and the roof above it that served as her hiding place.

Remove their heads...

Sleep finally faded from her mind as her real life became a nightmare.

The sound of the door to her small home splintering under sentinel boots had ripped her from a peaceful slumber just minutes ago. Before she could make sense of all the stomping and crashing, her mother was dragging her from her bed and shoving her into the hiding place they had created for just such an occasion.

"We love you so much," Mother had said.

Father was right behind Mother. "Don't make a sound

and don't worry. Everything will be fine." He had been hopeful, reassuring. She believed him.

Even now, she still believed him.

She had to. Hope was her only shield against the sharp swords of the sentinels.

She couldn't see what was happening in the moonlit yard, but she heard everything. She listened to the magistrate, so cordial just a few hours before, listing off her family's crimes. Their hidden food had been found.

Her father tried to charm his persecutors, but even his silver tongue couldn't sway the magistrate or stay the swords of the sentinels who accompanied him.

She strained to hear the endless speeches of the magistrate, his torrent of words that meant nothing. And in reply, the deafening silence of her parents was sickeningly punctuated by two dull *thunks*.

It couldn't be real.

Any moment now, she would wake up and it would be morning. Mother would be making breakfast, and Father would already be in the fields.

She imagined rushing out. She would dance through the moonlight, a death-dealing shadow, dispatching sentinels one by one with nothing but the digging fork that her father had taught her to use like a spear.

It was an absurd fantasy, a desperate dream. If she emerged, she would be cut down, her lifeless body rotting in the heat of the next day's sun alongside her parents.

And now it was over, and her fear kept her rooted in place. Her only company was the shame at her cowardice.

The sounds of the sentinels galloping down the lane shook her out of her reverie. She smelled burning wood. A new fear filled her, but this one sharpened her senses and cleared her mind. She became very aware of how tightly packed she was into the ceiling of a burning building.

Shin wriggled backwards until she could reach the false panel beneath her and shoved it open. She toppled forward as the panel popped out and instinctively tucked her head forward into a roll as she hit the floor. The fall still hurt, but at least she didn't land on her head.

Shin stood, coughing through the smoke that had already drifted up to the small, loft-style top level of her home. The fire had been lit near the front door and was spreading into the kitchen. Moving more out of instinct than any conscious plan, she crawled under the railing and dropped to the main floor, as far away from the spreading flames as possible. She opened the rear window of the house and flopped into the cool night air.

"Lieutenant Walric said you'd be coming out soon."

The calm voice made Shin's heart leap into her throat. She scrambled to her feet, and one of her hands brushed against the rocks she had picked from the field. In one motion, she grabbed the first rock that came to hand and hurled it in the direction of the sentinel's voice. She heard a satisfying grunt as the man staggered back from the unexpected blow.

Shin sprinted towards the barn.

"How the—"

Her family might not be allowed swords, but that hardly made them defenseless. She was adept at hunting squirrels and rabbits with rocks. That close to the sentinel, she would have been more surprised if she'd missed.

As soon as Shin reached the darkened interior of the barn, she grabbed the digging fork she had fantasized about before, then made a direct line to a small hatch in the back wall. Her father had built it when they began hiding food from the magistrate. Much like the hidden compartment in the ceiling, her father had hoped that they would never get caught but planned for Shin's safety if they did.

Shin heard the sentinel's boots on the wooden floor of the barn as she crawled through the hatch and hoped that he didn't see the sliver of moonlight in the darkness as she closed the door softly behind her. She didn't wait to find out. She continued into the forest behind her house. Heart pounding, she forced herself to search for the landmarks that her father had made her memorize.

She'd thought he was foolish for making her do this so many times.

Now, she was grateful for his foresight. Her body followed as if by instinct. She didn't need to think.

The tree whose trunk split into an almost perfect Y. Hard left.

The boulder bisected with a line of quartz. Bear right.

The sentinel crashed through the trees behind her. Shin wasn't making any effort to be quiet, since she knew he would be able to track her through these woods no matter how careful she was. Speed was her greatest ally now.

She was almost there.

Shin followed the path until the old, grizzled oak tree stood directly in front of her. She then found the gap in the encroaching brush and squeezed herself onto the hidden path that paralleled the well-trodden one. It brought her safely to the base of a giant oak. She crawled on hands and knees to struggle through the last of the brush, and had to leave the digging fork behind. When she finally reached the tree, she paused for a moment, listening for the sounds of pursuit.

She heard the sentinel break through the trees and onto the path that led to the oak. She started climbing the tree.

"I see you, girl. You might as well come down. You can't escape me up there."

Shin didn't bother answering. Her only goal was to get high enough into the branches that he wouldn't have a clear shot if he carried a bow. He'd have to approach.

"Fine." The sentinel sounded bored and resigned, as if he was more put out by climbing the tree than having to end her life.

Shin climbed high enough that she couldn't see the sentinel. She stopped climbing, huddled in the dark, and listened for the sounds of death.

She didn't have to wait long.

First there was the crack of the thin branches, covered in leaves and twigs, that were set so carefully across the narrow deadfall. Next came the terrible screams of the sentinel being impaled on the sharpened sticks at the bottom of the six-foot hole she and her father had dug.

The screams didn't last long, and Shin didn't check on the sentinel. She wasn't sure if she could bring herself to peer down at the consequences of what she had done. She scrambled down the tree, gathered up the digging fork, then headed deeper into the woods. She moved more quietly now. There was no guessing how many sentinels had been left behind to deal with her, but she didn't want to find out. There had only been one trap. Where she had once relied on speed, her alliance now shifted—stealth and shadows were her greatest friends now.

Her father had said that if they were ever found out, the best place for her to go was Dahl. It was the only city on Ilos, and while it wasn't as large as the cities on the other islands, it was plenty large enough for her to get lost in. Any of the family farms nearby would turn her into the sentinels to save their own lives, and she couldn't blame them.

Dahl was the only place for her to make a fresh start.

She wasn't sure how long she walked numbly through the night, one foot in front of the other in a rhythmic plod that leeched away the horror of what had befallen her family. It must have been a few hours, though, because she stopped short at the edge of the forest. In the distance, she saw the main road that led to Dahl across a small field. The city itself was only a few hours down that road. She was about to break from the cover of the trees when the sounds of galloping horses made her scramble deeper into the woods.

The sentinels passed without stopping, but the sight of them made her shiver. The numbness she had felt since escaping her pursuer suddenly broke. She fell to the ground, tears falling down her cheeks as she thought of her parents. She lay there on the forest floor and cried.

When she got herself under control, she gathered up some leaves and dirt and made the softest bed that she could manage to wait out the day. She would finish her journey under the same cover of night that had helped her escape from the sentinels.

That night, she watched the moon as it set over the fields of a stranger. They were so much like the fields she had worked her whole life. The fields she had called her own.

Perhaps her life with her family hadn't been much. But it had been enough for her.

And now it was gone.

8

———

The leader of the Red Aces stood before Beast and thrust a filthy finger in his direction.

"Don't patronize me! This is no parlay!"

Spittle flew from the man's mouth and his finger shook with anger. In other circumstances, the man might have been an imposing figure. He was lean and tall, with coarse hair and a scar that cut across his left cheek. His clothing was worn, his hat splattered with blood, his boots scuffed and dirty.

Fear had stolen the man's dignity, though. Whatever power this man had once held was gone, as dead as his bandits back at the site of the failed ambush.

Beast smiled his easy smile, the one that promised either a good time, or a violent one.

In Beast's world, the two were often the same.

What was the man's name again? He hadn't paid much attention during the formal introductions. He had once led the Red Aces. Still claimed he did, of course, but that was only because he was ignoring the facts.

Beast spread his arms out expansively. "Our desires are

the same. Your Red Aces are the last meaningful group of independent bandits in all of Samas. You can claim you're free, but what does that earn you now? Look at your followers."

The bandit leader sneered, but he still glanced back at the pathetic remains of the Red Aces gathered behind him. The truth of the matter was laid bare for anyone to see.

Beast spoke calmly. Little terrified the masses as much as a calm giant towering over them. Anger and bluster were tools of lesser men. "Your men are emaciated and even beggars would refuse to wear their rotting clothing. A drunk sentinel armed with a blunt dagger could kill the rest of you without having to sober up."

Beast let his words sink in. "Now, look at us." He gestured to his own warriors, but stood just a bit taller himself, keeping most of the attention focused on him. At over six and a half feet, muscles bulging through a too-tight tunic, and a beard that grew into a neat point at the center of his chest, it was hard not to be the center of attention. His hair would hang almost to the ground if it weren't tied into a mess of different braids and ponytails. His cobalt blue eyes made it clear he was not born on this soil. A mystery, living and killing in such an isolated land.

"We are well fed, well provisioned, and strong," Beast continued. "We hide from the sentinels, not like a mouse but like a snake, so that we may strike out at will. Can you say the same?"

He paused again. Then he leaned forward, casting a shadow over the smaller leader. He repeated his question. "Can you say the same?"

For a moment, Beast thought the man might see reason. The leader wavered, his eyes comparing his own bandits to Beast's.

But some men were born fools.

The leader shook his head. "We barely have enough for ourselves, and you believe that sharing a cut of what we take is going to make our problems go away? No. We won't bow to anyone." The leader's voice grew in volume, if not conviction. He looked around to gauge his warriors' reactions. When he noticed none of them were meeting his gaze, and that some were even inching further away, his eyes widened in panic.

But only for a moment. Fear of loss quickly turned into determination. His hand dropped to the hilt of his sword.

"You don't want to do that," Beast said, hoping he would. It had been hours since he'd overcome the ambush on the road, and he was already thirsting for a worthy duel.

"Get them!" the man screamed in anger, drawing his sword.

Beast took a measured step back. Five Red Aces formed the leader's "honor guard." The remaining Red Aces survivors were all back at their camp, a mile away. All of them drew their swords, but only the leader made any motion towards Beast and his two guards.

Beast's grin was vicious. The other Red Aces wouldn't get involved. He had yet to replace his broken battle axe, but that bothered him little.

Oblivious to the fact that his men had not joined the charge, the leader raised his long sword high above his head with both hands.

Beast waited for the man to commit to his strike, then slid out of the way. The move required speed, but it was the timing, the anticipation of his enemy's movements that made Beast so deadly. One moment he was in front of the man and the next he was behind. His massive arms wrapped around the bandit leader in a crushing embrace.

His victim tried to scream, but Beast's arms forced the air from the leader's lungs. Beast reveled in the moment briefly before bringing his full strength to the task. There was a sickening crack as the man's ribs broke, puncturing lungs and other vital organs. The leader struggled for another few seconds, but his movements gradually lost their vitality.

Then he was still.

Beast dropped the lifeless husk on the ground. He turned to see the same thing he always saw when he destroyed a leader in front of his troops. Fear of their own fate. Awe at the mighty power before them. "It looks like we have some new recruits."

The Red Aces shuffled a little, then sheathed their swords and made sure to keep their hands far from the hilts.

"Sheyric," the Beast said to one of his honor guards, "have these recruits bring you and the rest of our mugon back to their camp. They'll help you explain the new situation to their comrades."

Sheyric, a man of few words, simply nodded and motioned for the Red Aces to follow him. Beast didn't bother having them remove their swords. This parlay couldn't have gone many other ways. The only real question had been if the leader would capitulate willingly or not. The Red Aces were so broken and hungry they didn't have much fight left in them. If any of the remaining Red Aces found the courage to resist, then Sheyric could cut them down without even breathing heavily. The man was a savant with his sword.

As Sheyric disappeared from the clearing, Beast sat down heavily on one of the logs around the campfire. Even after so many battles, when the rush of combat was over, weariness set in.

"That was the last of them," Benji said.

"Vermin," Beast spat derisively, "but maybe we can show them what it means to be true warriors. Come, the mugon are waiting and if they know what's good for them, they'll have my dinner ready."

Benji chuckled at Beast's gruff facade. "We've done well and have earned some rest."

"Enjoy it while you can. The recruitment might be done, but now the hard part begins."

9

———

Sato, still tired from the previous day's ride, rose before the sun and watched the daybreak as he went through his forms. His body was stiff, but that only meant he needed the movement more. When he finished his routine, he stowed his gear and returned to the saddle.

The farther he rode, the more pleased he was that he had taken the time to work what kinks he could from his body. He rode hard, pushing his body and his horse, Nightmane, right to the edge of breaking. But no further. Despite his urgency, he did no one any good if either of them got injured.

By midday, his careful pacing was rewarded as he came into view of Bulas, the capital of Samas and the home of the Firstborn. The jewel of the nation. Outside its walls, peasants toiled to earn the protection afforded them by the sentinels. The hard work of one group was rewarded by the other putting their very lives on the line. Within, though, was an oasis of peace and prosperity. A vision of what the future could become if all would learn to follow the Path.

The fields around Bulas were busy as farmers brought in

the harvest, large teams working enormous plots under the watchful eyes of their overseers. Sato grimaced as he watched the farmers labor in the dirt and the muck. Essential as they were, there was still something unclean about their lives.

At the city walls, two lines led to the gate. One was filled with farmers hauling their harvests, clutching the papers tightly in their hands that allowed them temporary access to Bulas. The other was for citizens of Bulas and sentinels. Sato rode for that line. Most days, he would have waited in the back, as was proper, but today his urgency took precedence. He weaved Nightmane forward until he was at the front of the queue. Any complaints were silenced when they saw who he was.

The sentinel at the gate recognized him and let him through without question.

Sato cantered his horse through the streets of Bulas toward the sentinel stables. When he arrived, he told the stablemaster a shoe needed attention. Then he handed the reins to a stable hand, petted Nightmane's nose, and fed him an apple he'd been saving for the end of the ride.

"Thank you, my friend. Rest well, and I'll see you soon," Sato said. He allowed himself a small smile at his long-time companion's whinny of thanks.

With Nightmane squared away, Sato walked swiftly from the stables toward Bulas Keep, where he could report to the Firstborn. As he passed through the halls of the ancient keep, sentinels on guard snapped smart salutes and opened doors for him. The stonework was immaculate, the architecture worthy of poetry. Sato, as he always did, took a moment to look around and appreciate how the perfectly ordered keep reflected the Path and the sentinels' place on it. After a brief wait for another audience to finish, he found himself inside the receiving chamber, bowing to the Firstborn of the Eternal Sun, ruler of all of Samas.

"Sato! As always, it is a pleasure, but I wasn't expecting you for another week." The Firstborn took in Sato's clothing, still dusty from the road. Among lesser officials, such an appearance would have likely earned a quick and permanent expulsion from the court. "What news requires such haste?"

"I bring an urgent report about the bandits."

The Firstborn was just beginning to show his age, but the grey at his temples and the frown lines that crinkled around his eyes as he regarded Sato did nothing to diminish the steel evident in the man's demeanor. "Too important for you to seek a bath and a fresh uniform before coming to see me?"

"Yes, sire. Apologies for neglecting a tenet of the Path but—" Before he could finish, he was cut off by an irritated sigh and a resigned smile from the Firstborn.

"Honestly, Sato, you'd think by now you'd know when I'm joking." The Firstborn laughed, a warm sound that filled the chamber.

"Sorry, sire, it's just that this information is very important." Did the Firstborn not understand this information changed everything? Sato had ridden hard for days to deliver the news.

The Firstborn ignored Sato's obvious impatience. "You have always been one of my best sentinels, Sato, but don't forget the Path requires interpretation, not just blind obedience to the letter of the law. Take tenet number three, the spirit. There is not much in this world that feeds the soul the way laughter does, don't you think?"

"I find meditation and reflection to be more nourishing,

sire," Sato responded. Through his annoyance, he forced a smile onto his face to reflect the older man's impish grin.

"Ha! See? Your tongue can be as deft as your sword." The Firstborn's eyes twinkled with undisguised mirth. "Now, tell me, what have you learned of these bandits?"

"The reason we haven't been able to find a base of operations on Iru is because there isn't one. They've built ships capable of traversing the deeper, rougher waters beyond the shipping lanes. They use them to travel between the islands without our knowledge."

The Firstborn stroked at his long beard. "You're certain? Building such ships without being discovered seems nearly impossible."

"I saw one with my own eyes, sire."

The Firstborn nodded thoughtfully and motioned for Sato to continue.

"Additionally, their command structure is unlike any I've studied. They receive instructions anonymously, carry them out, and then are resupplied and sheltered seemingly without any chain of command."

"Singun," the Firstborn interrupted quietly.

"What?"

"Such a structure is called a singun. Independent units where the left hand never knows what the right is doing. A tactic born from the legends of the sin."

"It's cowardly," Sato responded sharply. "How can one lead, if one is not seen?"

"Indeed, it certainly strays far from the tenets of the Path. Please go on."

The Firstborn's typical joviality had vanished, and Sato caught a rare glimpse of the steely demeanor that it covered. The eyes that usually danced with mirth were now a window into the mind of a peerless strategist.

Sato's news had alarmed the Firstborn. The man's mask rarely slipped, even around those closest to him.

Sato continued his report. "Given this new information, I believe we will require more sentinels and more supplies. Regular patrols will not be enough, but will need to be maintained while we form a dedicated force to address this."

The Firstborn thought for a while. Eventually, he reached his decision. "You're right about the severity of the situation. Bandits have always been a nuisance, but these recent attacks do seem to be evidence of a greater threat. However, your solution lacks imagination." He paused. "Let me ask you: do you believe our current methods of intervention will be effective against these bandits?"

Sato considered the question briefly, but the answer was easy enough. The Firstborn's question sliced to the heart of the matter. If traditional methods worked, the bandit problem would have been taken care of by now. "No, sire, I do not."

"Neither do I. We need to break the bandits' organization open, not by overwhelming force, but by cunning. Your request for more sentinels is not the answer. Bandits, for better or for worse, will always exist. But these tactics are the result of a rare level of leadership. These commanders must be our true target. You need to hunt them, and you need to kill them. A smaller group would work best. Excellent riders, as they may be required to travel long distances at short notice."

Sato nodded, making mental notes as the Firstborn spoke. Already he had a list of potential names—honorable sentinels who were almost untouchable with a blade and peerless in the saddle.

"And one more requirement," the Firstborn said, the

mirth returning to his face. "They will need to be the most cunning that you can think of."

Concern tightened his throat. "Cunning, sire?"

"You may need to draw from among those who are willing to interpret the Path... more broadly, shall we say."

His heart dropped. "Why?"

"These sentinels need to be prepared to comb through some of the seediest aspects of our nation to root our enemies out."

"Seedy, sire?"

"Indeed. These bandits aren't recruiting from noble households. Your first task will be to create a list of such sentinels and provide it to me. I'll expect it no later than tomorrow morning." He looked again at Sato's appearance. "And only after you've rested and bathed."

"Sire—these types of sentinels, I—" Sato hesitated.

"Is there a problem, Sato?" The Firstborn's look of innocence might have convinced others, but not him. "I was under the impression that you were familiar with all the sentinels under your command, be they shining examples of the sun or slightly more... dingy."

"I am, sire. That's not the problem. I'm just not sure who, among my competent commanders, would be willing to lead them." He shook his head in disgust. "No honorable officer would ever volunteer for such a duty."

The Firstborn of the Eternal Sun and leader of the nation of Samas simply smiled at Sato.

Realization dawned on Sato and he groaned.

"Oh."

10

───────

Shin woke to the fading light of dusk as it receded across the forest floor. She grumbled, her body demanding a true rest. But drifting back to sleep held no appeal. Not if it meant more of the dreams that had plagued her slumber.

Well, one dream, she thought bitterly. Just different versions of it.

In some she burst out of the house, digging fork in hand, laughing maniacally while dispatching all the sentinels, only to find that each she killed bore the face of her parents. In others, she ran out of the house and was cut down one limb at a time. The sentinels laughed as she tried to crawl to her mother and father.

The worst, though, was when she emerged from her home to find the sentinels departed and her parents' severed heads impaled on pikes in her yard.

"Why didn't you help?" her mother's head wailed.

Her father's head just smiled his affable smile, the blood-stained teeth doing their best to let his daughter know that everything would be fine.

Shin shivered at the memories and rose from her makeshift bed. Her mouth tasted bitter and her head had that light and airy quality that accompanied a lack of sleep. She opened and closed her mouth a few times to work more moisture into it. Reaching into the pocket of her trousers, she found what remained of the berries she had found the night before. She ate them greedily, but the rumbling of her stomach told her that food would have to be a priority tonight. After she filled her belly, she could worry about her future.

One thing at a time.

Shin looked around for a suitably sized stone. As the forest floor darkened with the setting sun, she realized that her chances of finding a weapon, let alone tracking prey, were quickly fading.

For a moment, Shin stood motionless as desperation welled up inside of her.

It wasn't just about being hungry. Hunger was her constant companion.

Hunting had been a task. A solid next step, a plan she could complete even as the rest of her life crumbled around her.

But the sun, the cursed eternal sun, didn't even allow her that.

Her desperation grew claws, tearing at her will until it transformed into panic. The same wracking sobs she had choked down the night before built again. She lowered herself into a crouch while she hugged her arms tight around her body. She tucked her head into her chest as she closed her eyes against the tears.

The forest faded around her, replaced by a happier memory: her earliest attempts at sewing with her mother. Mother's hands were sure, mending torn clothes until they were nearly as good as new. Beside her, Shin kept poking her fingers with the needle, drawing small drops of blood.

With a digging fork in hand, she could dance her father's forms all night without tripping once. But with a needle, all her fingers became thumbs.

She'd been younger then, more easily prone to frustration. Tears had welled up in her eyes, and she'd asked if she could quit to do something else.

Mother shook her head. "If you quit, you'll never start again. You'll never learn."

Across the room, she saw her father's smile. The real one, not the horrific caricature from her dreams. The memory gently faded, suffusing her with new strength.

She rose unsteadily to her feet and took a deep, calming breath.

There would be time to grieve her parents later. Those emotions weren't going anywhere. For now, she would call on the memories of love and support that had given her strength her whole life. She picked up her digging fork and walked to the edge of the forest. The moon was almost full now, rising in the sky and bathing the countryside in its calming silver light. Shin took her time making her way across the field. Turning an ankle now would make the relatively easy walk into the city a grueling affair.

As she picked her way across the field, she cursed her continued poor luck. Most farms had harvested their crops within the last few days. She could see the neat rows, teasing her with their barrenness, in which plenty of food would have been waiting for her just days ago. Her stomach grumbled again, and she wondered just how she was going to find something to eat once she got to the city.

She had no money, nor any friends or family there.

Shin imagined living off the land. She knew how to hunt

and knew what wild foods were safe to eat. Perhaps Dahl wasn't the place she was meant to be.

She imagined living alone in the wild, with only herself to worry about.

By the time she noticed the steady drum of hooves on packed dirt, it was almost too late. She threw herself to the ground, pressing herself into the dirt. Her breath sounded like a blacksmith's bellows in her ears, and it seemed impossible the whole countryside didn't hear her. She lay still for an agonizing amount of time before she heard the horses pass by, heading away from the city. To be safe, she waited a few minutes longer.

When the sounds of the horses finally faded into the distance, she propped herself onto her elbows and looked out to the road. As the sentinels passed out of view, her fear took on an edge of anger. The idea that they could strip everything that she loved away from her and simply carry on to the next farm infuriated her.

Alone, she might be safer.

But perhaps in Dahl she could find the means to strike back.

The road was far closer than she had thought, and she gave her head a mental shake for being so careless. Shin decided she would be better served walking through the fields that paralleled the road than by walking on it. Better to sacrifice some speed for the ability to hide at a moment's notice.

In time, the road curved and the walls of Dahl came into view. When the wind picked up, she caught the scent of salt in the air, though she couldn't yet see the water. Dahl stood on a rise in the land, the drop-off at the back of the city augmenting the already impressive walls with a natural defense. The fields below stretched out and on a clear day, one could easily make out the ocean in the distance. The main road she followed led up to the gates and then circled around the walls to the port to the east.

Shin was just beginning to puzzle out how she was going to enter the walled city when she noticed two inky blobs detach themselves from one of the grassy hills on the opposite side of the road. They were both taller than her, but had the slight frame and awkward proportions that seemed reserved for adolescent boys whose muscles had not yet caught up to the scaffolding of their bones. At first, Shin was surprised when she saw what looked like long knives sheathed at the small of their backs, but she quickly guessed what she was looking at.

Luan.

Shin had heard stories of orphaned children forming groups in the cities, arming themselves and turning to thievery to survive instead of begging. The sentinels, when they caught the luan, killed them, as was dictated by the Path. Fortunately for the luan, they knew the streets so well they were difficult to find. Luan were a constant, if small, thorn in the sentinels' side. Right now, that made them some of her favorite people in Samas.

She picked up her digging fork, then dashed across the road and into the field behind the two luan. Her progress was slow. In the open field, the only way to ensure that the two figures didn't see her was to crouch down low and scramble as quickly as she could. She followed her prey as they veered away from the road and into the shrub lands that surrounded Dahl.

When the two figures stopped to relieve themselves in a small creek that trickled out beneath the walls of Dahl, Shin took the opportunity to stand behind a larger cluster of bushes and stretch her aching legs. Though the lower half of her body was on fire, she knew she had made the right decision when she saw a small group of sentinels stationed at the gates of the city. She peeked around the bush to check on the luan.

They were gone.

How? They were too far from the walls to have slipped inside already, and she'd only taken her eyes off them for a moment.

"Didn't think it would be some lost farm girl following us."

Shin jumped, and she instinctively brought the digging fork up to defend herself.

"Would you look at that? She's got some fight in her," said another voice.

Shin's heart hammered in her chest, but she forced herself to study the two boys in front of her. They were tall and gangly, and both were trying desperately to sprout hairs on their chins. Despite the mocking tone, both had taken a step back when she raised her weapon. They each drew their crudely made weapons. Still feeling the dull ache in her thighs, Shin wondered how long they had known she'd been following them, and how foolish she must have looked attempting to stay concealed.

"Listen, we aren't looking to fight, but we need to know why you were following us," the first boy said. He had shaved his head save for a long braid down the back and appeared to be in charge.

"I need to get into the city. My parents were—" She faltered and tried again. "I'm alone and need to stay out of sight."

"Why should we trust you?" the second boy sneered. "For all we know you're spying for the sentinels." He had a small gap in his teeth and she was suddenly compelled to make it wider.

Shin jabbed at him with her digging fork, just like her father had taught her. Gap-tooth tripped over his own feet as he just barely parried the attack, losing his grip on his weapon as he did. Surprised by the suddenness of her strike, Braid hesitated a moment too long before bringing up his knife. Shin took the momentum of her parried blow and turned it into a blow with the butt end of the fork, hitting him square in the temple. He crumpled.

Before Shin could pivot back towards Gap-tooth, he wrapped his arms around her. Though her arms were pinned, she was able to move the fork so that it crossed her body diagonally. By shifting her weight and twisting, she was able to drive the fork into the ground behind Gap-tooth's ankle. With all her might, she pushed backwards, causing him to fall over the fork. He took her down with him, but she landed on top and the impact broke his grip. Shin scrambled to her feet, recovered the fork, and aimed it at Gap-tooth's chest.

"By the sun, we give! We give!" Braid was shakily getting to his feet. Shin was surprised to note that he appeared to be laughing a little. "How'd you let her take you down like that, Davin?"

"You're the one whose brain she just scrambled," Davin said as he dusted himself off. "Not like there was much there to scramble in the first place."

"Stay back!" Shin warned, still brandishing her digging fork.

"We're back, don't worry. You attacked us, remember? We were just trying to figure out why you were following us. I'm Corin, by the way."

Shin slowly lowered her weapon, suddenly embarrassed by her rash anger.

"You shouldn't have accused me of working for the sentinels," Shin said.

"Sorry," Corin said sheepishly. "I guess I wouldn't have liked that either. But we were worried with you following us like that."

Shin sighed. "I understand. You were just being careful. Would you still consider helping me?" She paused, feeling suddenly vulnerable. "I'm really not sure what I'm doing."

A look passed between the two boys. Corin spoke first. "Sure, we have a way in. It's a tight squeeze, but the trap door we built into our home isn't too far from the entrance. You'll just have to crawl through a little water." He was already heading towards the city walls as he explained.

"You're going to help me? Just like that?"

"Of course." Davin spread his hands and smiled as if it were the most obvious thing in the world.

"Why?"

"Shit happens," Corin said, "and it looks like it happened to you pretty recently. Not many other reasons why a farm girl would be out here all alone, threatening us with a digging fork. Do we need a better reason?"

Shin looked up at the moon and fought the surge of emotion that threatened to overwhelm her. She supposed it wasn't much to them. But for her, on the darkest nights of her life, the simple kindness warmed her more than the sun ever had.

11

That night, Beast's mugon feasted.

A rare treat, but one well earned.

Every significant group of bandits now answered to one man. Years of battle had led to this point, and the journey was just beginning. Today, though, was a landmark. A turning point. One Beast celebrated with ale and roasted meat.

Beast let the celebration begin without him. He visited the tents of the injured, not to provide words of comfort, but to bear witness. The injured mugon quit their groaning when he entered. He asked what he could do for them and noted their answers. When he had visited them all, he returned to the fires.

He soon found a cup in his hand, and he raised it to toast the mugon and what they had accomplished. After, one of his lieutenants raised a toast in return, which he bore with a smile. Beast mingled for a bit, but before long his stomach growled, and the frequent toasts of his mugon gave him no time to fill his belly.

They respected him and fought for him. But his mugon

were not his friends or his equals. So, when the time came, he slipped away without a sound. He found a place where he could observe the festivities without being bothered by others.

In time, a voice spoke from behind him. "Mind if I join you?"

Beast looked up at his new companion and grinned. Though his average height and easy manner led many to underestimate him, Benji was the only warrior Beast respected almost as much as himself.

The one man he did call a friend.

In battle, Beast was a force of nature. He possessed unparalleled ferocity with the skill to match. But killing sentinels was less than half the fight. Beast was the brawn and the figurehead, but the mugon owed their existence to Benji. Benji developed the training they used. Benji was the one who had thought of using ships and moving camps. And it was Benji who moved mugon, food, and supplies around Samas as though they were pieces on a chessboard.

For all that Beast had accomplished, he couldn't have done it alone.

But he'd never tell anyone else that. He gestured to the grass beside him. "Please, sit."

Benji did, delicately balancing the plate full of food as he joined Beast. "Thought you might actually join them this time."

"And never get a chance to eat?"

"You can't blame them for wanting to bask in your glory."

Beast shook his head. "This is their day."

"Not to hear them tell it. I heard you killed over a hundred Red Aces on your own."

Beast *harrumphed*. "Soon they'll be saying that I fucked the Firstborn."

"You haven't?"

Beast laughed. "Not with my dick." He looked out over the assembled warriors. A motley crew, perhaps, but they represented a change in Samas. Never had a rebellion come so far.

A comfortable silence settled between the two men, and Beast took the opportunity to dig into his meal in earnest. After a few moments, Beast sensed Benji looking at him. It was a look that Beast was used to, but one he'd never gotten from Benji. There was a first time for everything, Beast supposed.

"You've never asked," Beast said, breaking the silence.

"We always had more important things to worry about," Benji replied.

Beast gave a mental shrug. It was a night for firsts. "Go ahead."

"Do you ever wonder where you come from?"

Despite knowing the question was coming, Beast still fought to keep his hands from clenching into fists when someone brought up his past.

Few dared to do so.

"Why, Benji, as you well know, we all come from the eternal sun," Beast said, gesturing expansively to the night sky above. "We are placed on Samas with the glorious purpose of following the Path in service of the Firstborn."

Benji chuckled. For a moment, it looked like he would drop the issue, but then he summoned the courage to continue. "You don't look like the rest who walk the Path. I'm not even sure you'd fit on it."

It was Beast's turn to laugh. "I don't know where I came from, but it wasn't Samas. My first memories are a blur. I was raised by a poor family on Ilos, their about as far away from Dahl as you could get and still be on the island. As I grew older, I began helping with the chores. I was bigger than my adopted siblings, so was always tasked with the hardest jobs. At first, I thought it was because of my size, but I slowly began to realize that the pissant farmer that took me in simply favored his real children over me. When the sentinels began to squeeze more and more from them, I was the one who went hungry." Beast paused his story long enough to spit on the ground in memory of his late adopted father.

"I don't imagine you two ever mended your relationship," Benji said.

"His was the first life I took. As I continued to grow, he saw me as a liability. One night, after I had been banished to the barn to sleep amongst the cattle, I saw a lone rider approach the house. I snuck back inside and overheard the bastard negotiating the price to sell me to a high-ranking member of a mining guild."

"So, you stepped inside to calmly express your disapproval of the proposed arrangement?" Benji asked.

Beast's predatory grin made Benji recoil.

"I did step inside, but it was to strangle the life out of the rider that came to collect me. I wasn't fully grown yet, but I was still bigger than most men. My adopted father tried to pry my hands off but too late realized the futility of the attempt. I tossed the rider aside, and the coward took off running. Then I beat that farmer to a bloody pulp. Before he died, I made him tell me where I came from," Beast said with a grim smile.

"And?"

"He found me amongst the wreckage of a strange ship that had washed up on the southernmost shore of Ilos. He took me in for his wife to raise so that he would have another set of hands on his farm."

"I see," Benji said, slowly.

"Raises more questions than it answers, doesn't it? No grand plan, no manifestation of the sun bringing me to the shores of Samas for some great purpose. Just a stranger in a strange land. So, I made my own purpose."

"And now you're the Bandit King." Beast looked up to see Benji grinning at him. "Have you thought much about tomorrow? Are you going to take a few days and celebrate your accomplishment?"

Beast sipped his ale. "I had thought to spend some time settling the new arrivals. We have Red Aces to teach in our ways, and our people could use some rest. Maybe hit a few easy caravans but keep quieter than we have been."

Benji didn't say anything, but his look said enough.

"What do you propose?" Beast asked.

"The sentinels won't rest, so neither can we."

Beast waved the concern away. "They don't even know what they face yet."

"They might. One of our groups was caught trying to escape from Iru. They were all slaughtered."

"You think they spoke?"

"Not of anything that matters. They didn't know enough. But it's a mistake to underestimate the sentinels."

Beast scowled. "That is one mistake I certainly don't make."

"And I'm here to remind you of that. Our victory today gives us momentum. We need to seize it."

Beast chewed the last of the meat off a bone and put his plate down. Few rewards meant as much to him as a full meal.

Which was the whole point of the mugon. The ability to

take what one earned. A new way to live in the world, one that didn't bow to the light of the Firstborn or his corrupted sentinels.

"So, what will you do?" Benji pressed. From anyone else, Beast might have killed the messenger simply to erase the annoyance. Benji alone had the right to speak to Beast so bluntly. "You have an army now. You can't just let it sit unused."

"I'd hardly call the mugon an army," Beast said.

Benji waved aside the point as the distraction it was. "You have the advantage now, but it won't be long before the sentinels poke a hole in our defenses."

Beast grimaced. "Then we need to move to the next stage of my plan. We need land of our own. A place to defend."

"And then the sentinels will have a place to attack. For now, we live because we never stop moving."

That was the crux of the problem. To become more than bandits, they needed land. But the moment they seized land, they became an enemy the sentinels could beat. Beast gestured at his warriors. "What would you suggest? We would need lifetimes of training to defeat the sentinels on a fair battlefield."

"What if I told you there was a way?"

"If you were anyone else, I'd call you a liar." Beast eyed his friend. "But you have something, don't you?"

"I have a connection that I think you'll find useful," Benji said. He swallowed. "But I'm not sure you're going to believe me."

Beast waited.

Benji swallowed again. "I can put you in touch with the sin. And together, you can force the Firstborn, and all of Samas, to bow before you."

12

S ato sighed contentedly as he soaked in the hot springs just outside of Bulas and contemplated the Firstborn's request. He could have had some of the servants that worked in Bulas Keep prep the bath house for him, but Sato always felt cleaner when he took his baths out in nature. The short walk to the isolated springs also provided him the time and solitude needed to compile the list of sentinels that would make up his new squad. By the time he had reached the water, that part of his task was complete. Now, Sato had to wrap his head around the hard part.

How was he supposed to lead those kinds of sentinels?

Sato had trained and bled daily to earn his place as one of the Firstborn's top generals, and one of the privileges of his position was that he got the first pick of sentinels under his direct command. His honor guard, plus the men and women he led on patrols, were all strict observers of the Path. Those that he believed apt to stray, he sent to patrol the other islands under the command of his lieutenants, who needed the experience of dealing with problem soldiers.

As he went through the list of sentinels in his head, his anger grew. Every one of them had been disciplined by Sato at one point or another. In each case, they'd never been disciplined again.

As much as he wished it was due to his leadership, he didn't believe it. Not of those names. No, the reason they hadn't been disciplined further was because of the Firstborn's other requirement: cunning. They'd learned how not to get caught.

Sato sought some semblance of peace. He focused on the hot water as it loosened the knots in his muscles and imagined that it was loosening the knots in his mind as well. Once he felt his mind, body and spirit were connected once more, he rose from the spring, prepared to seek out a solution.

He toweled himself off, dressed quickly, and made his way to his chambers. The Firstborn would be waiting for him.

Sato checked his appearance in the mirror in his room. Though not given to vanity, an audience with the Firstborn was an honor most in Samas never received. Sato had skirted the edges of the Path yesterday, appearing in such a disheveled state.

Satisfied, Sato walked the labyrinthine passages through Bulas Keep to the Firstborn's receiving chambers. He expected a short wait, as was customary for those expecting to speak to the Firstborn, so he was surprised when there was no line.

One of the guards answered Sato's unspoken question. "He's not receiving visitors this morning, sir. He's training."

Sato gave a small bow of acknowledgment and turned to

leave. Patience was not his strongest virtue, but one he would need to practice today. The guard interrupted him. "The Firstborn did leave specific orders that if you were to appear, you were to join him in training."

Sato bowed again and made his way to the training hall. The guards outside let him in without comment.

Inside, Sato was almost overpowered by the scent of sweat. Though clean, the training hall of Bulas Keep was unlike any other room in the fortress. Here, generations of Firstborns had trained, sharpening their bodies in preparation for the burdens of leadership. The room was without pretense. A few simple scrolls, with the symbols of the Path, were the only decoration. Practice weapons of all kinds hung in racks around the edges of the room.

In the center of the space, the Firstborn trained with another sentinel, an expert swordsman Sato believed was almost as good as he was.

When the Firstborn spotted Sato, he dismissed his training partner and gestured to the rows of practice weapons. "Sato, it has been too long since we trained together."

A dozen objections ran through Sato's mind, but there was no denying the Firstborn. If the light of the eternal sun wanted to spar, Sato had no choice but to pick up a sword.

He tested a few wooden blades before finding one with a balance he liked. He took a few quick practice swings, then stepped onto the mat with the Firstborn.

This wasn't the first time they had sparred. The Firstborn had been a regular partner since Sato had been a young man. But Sato had never felt truly comfortable with the duels. He always held back, afraid to injure the Firstborn.

The Firstborn possessed no such hesitation. He

attacked, and Sato was forced to defend. The attack was simple to avoid, and for a moment, Sato worried the Firstborn was getting too old to be sparring at such an intensity.

But it was only a feint. After the first few passes, Sato noted the small changes in the Firstborn's stance. A subtle tightening of his grip, a slightly deeper bend in his legs, and an almost imperceptible narrowing of his old friend's eyes.

Sato braced himself.

The Firstborn exploded in a flurry of strikes at full speed. The practice sword was a blur in his hands, but Sato deftly countered each strike as he strategically gave ground. His final parry became a riposte as Sato saw the opening he was looking for and scored a blow against the eternal sun's most favored.

"Ha!" The Firstborn laughed ruefully. "I'm not sure why I thought I could surprise you. You always seem to see three moves ahead."

"Thank you, sire. I like to think I know how to read my opponent."

"Indeed, and how do you do that?"

Sato suspected that the Firstborn was now the one who was seeing a few moves ahead. He answered cautiously. "Experience and nothing more. A practiced eye can predict the outcome of a battle before the first move is even made."

"And this fight, against a new breed of bandit, would it not benefit us to look a few moves ahead?"

"Of course," Sato answered carefully.

"And yet you still come here to argue against the type of sentinels that would allow us to do that."

Sato opened his mouth to protest, but quickly shut it. The Firstborn, as was his way, had understood Sato's intent without him needing to say a word.

Again, Sato felt as if he was forced to give up ground in their verbal sparring match. "They have strayed from the Path," Sato argued. "If you would simply allow me to lead my honor guard, without the responsibility of patrols, we will sniff these bandits out and make short work of them."

"You can search all you want. But without the types of sentinels you detest, you'll never make progress. Your warriors don't think like bandits. They don't have the connections around Samas to pursue worthwhile leads." The Firstborn scoffed, "Sato, a good leader learns to use the tools afforded him. However distasteful they may seem."

Sato fought the urge to push back and instead took a calming breath so that he could consider the words of his mentor.

"The tenets of the Path dictate honor and discipline. Those are the tools we have used to succeed for generations," Sato replied, calmly this time.

"The Path dictates that all sentinels train and master the sword. Do you think you could defeat me, who has mastered the sword, with a spear?" the Firstborn asked.

"Of course," Sato answered without hesitation. False modesty was simply a polite way of lying.

"How? The Path dictates that you master the sword. The spear is never mentioned. So why do you know how to use it?"

Sato saw where the Firstborn was going, but the trap was already set. "I chose to master as many weapons as I could, to better help me serve the Path."

"As an officer, sentinels are your weapons. So, why not learn to master different types of sentinels as well?"

Sato finally understood the Firstborn's deeper intent. He meant for this assignment to broaden Sato's rigid view of the Path. Not everyone upheld the same standards he did and leading such citizens might someday be a greater part of his responsibilities. Likewise, the sentinels under his command would enjoy the benefit of serving directly under a commander who followed the Path rigidly. In time, they would grow to see the error of their ways.

"I fear sentinels of this ilk will not follow me willingly," Sato said. False bravado was no better than false modesty.

"Did we not just speak of mastering your tools?"

Sato cursed himself for a fool. He'd missed the easiest solution completely.

"Captain Roko," Sato said.

"He's always served you well and is beloved by any sentinels he commands," the Firstborn replied.

Captain Roko would be an integral addition. He could serve as an intermediary, a buffer between Sato and the others.

"Thank you, sire. Would you permit me to return to my chambers? I would like to begin selecting my unit."

"Please, go, I don't need to be embarrassed on the training floor any more today," the Firstborn said, waving him out dismissively.

"Thank you," Sato said, knowing he should react to the joking nature of the comment but too eager to begin his task to do so.

He quickly left the room and journeyed to his own chambers.

Sato couldn't claim to be pleased by the assignment, but he appreciated the deft touch the Firstborn brought to problems. It was not lost on him that this was precisely the kind of grooming that would make Sato a top choice to replace the Firstborn in time. He didn't have to like it. What kind of sentinel would he be if he only obeyed the orders he liked?

Someday, he would become Firstborn, and he would expand upon the teachings of the Path and enforce its standards to an even greater degree than his adopted father. Compromise wasn't a trait that led nations to greatness.

Sato sent a passing servant to bring messengers to his chambers. When he got to his rooms, he sat down at his desk to draft a letter for Captain Roko. It would take some time to call him back to Bulas.

Once that letter was complete, Sato wrote out the names of each of the sentinels that he would recruit and, despite himself, realized that he was eager to take advantage of the unique skillsets of the soldiers before him. Although he would have much preferred to be charged with attacking his enemy head on, there was also honor to be found here. And if he succeeded, he would be the hero who vanquished a problem that plagued Samas. His ascent to the title of Firstborn would be practically guaranteed.

A small smile crept to his lips as he once more uncorked the pot of ink on his desk, dipped his quill inside, and brought the tip down onto the paper. In the space above the list of sentinel names, he wrote two words in his neat handwriting and underlined them with one precise stroke.

Sun stalkers.

13

———————

S hin followed the two young men as they navigated the narrow passages that ran under the city. Tall as they were, the boys had to bend and stoop in certain areas, but their slight figures squeezed through the narrowest parts with ease. As the passage darkened, the boys produced small torches from their packs and lit them with a flint box. Before long, they came to a wider chamber. Her companions stretched out their muscles, and Shin did the same.

"Not a pleasant way to leave town," Shin commented.

"No, which is why we don't use it often. We're generally able to feed ourselves through other means, but it's been a tough month," Corin said, holding up the string of fish they had caught.

At the mention of food, Shin's stomach growled noisily.

"Been awhile since your last meal, I'd bet. Once we get inside, we can get you something to eat," Davin said. He walked over to the far wall, casting his torch in front of him.

Davin fished inside a crack in the rock until he pulled

out a thin rope. He gave it a deft tug and a rope ladder, concealed in the shadows above, unfurled before them.

"Follow me," Davin said. "Corin will come up last and reset the ladder."

Davin climbed nimbly up the ladder despite holding the torch in one hand. He moved with such grace Shin had trouble believing he'd been such a terrible fighter. Shin followed, only to find herself swaying uncontrollably until Corin had mercy on her and offered to hold the digging fork. Shin hesitated. Her compromised position forced her to trust these strangers. Dangling in midair she had little choice but to give up her only weapon.

When she heard a hatch being opened above, she was barely halfway up the ladder. A bright light shone down.

"We sent you for fish, not strays," an annoyed voice said as Shin struggled to pull herself up through a hole in the floor.

"I know, Mateo, but she was alone and needed help. And she can fight." Shin assumed that Mateo was the group's leader.

"We're already hungry. Will her fighting provide us with more food?" Mateo asked.

Shin pulled herself to her feet and saw Mateo sizing her up. Though close in height to the other boys, he was much larger, and likely older, than Corin and Davin. He possessed a heaviness in his chest and shoulders that showed he had been moving through manhood for a few years already, while the others were just courting it. With his arms folded across his chest, Shin saw that there was definition in his forearms that reminded her of her father. His dark eyes showed no hint of the annoyance in his tone, and Shin got the impression that he closely guarded his emotions out of habit.

"I can pull my own weight," Shin replied. Behind Mateo, a group of younger children had gathered. They were a motley collection.

"I guess we'll see," Mateo said. "What's your name?"

Shin took a full breath in what felt like the first time since the sentinels visited her home. He was allowing her to stay. Had he not, she wasn't sure what she would have done next. But now she had hope. "My name is Shin."

"Welcome home, Shin," the luan said as one. It had the feel of a ritual she had unknowingly completed.

"Thank you?" Shin said, unsure of the appropriate response. Most of the surrounding group smiled and then dispersed. Most of them really were children, probably ten and under. Corin, Davin, and Mateo were the oldest.

"Here," Corin said, handing her the digging fork. Shin took it, gave Corin a small bow, and turned back to Mateo, who was still regarding her with his arms folded.

"Is that your preferred weapon?" Mateo asked.

"Yes, my father taught me."

"A farmer?"

"He was." She frowned. How had he guessed?

As though anticipating her question, Mateo smiled and motioned for Shin to give him the digging fork.

She tossed it to him.

He caught it and in one fluid motion stepped into the exact same forms Shin had been practicing since she was old enough to hold the digging fork without stabbing herself. His technique was better than hers, though. His strikes were clean and precise, and he never once came close to losing his balance. After a final flourish, Mateo tossed the fork back to her. "My father taught me, just as his father taught him."

Before she could ask any further questions, she was interrupted by Davin and Corin's rambunctious hollering.

"That was incredible! Why haven't you ever taught us how to do that?"

"Because then you idiots would have tried to use it. You're here to pick pockets and steal bread, not brain people over the head with blunt objects. And theft is exactly what you two are going to teach Shin. If she wants to pull her own weight, she's going to need to learn how to pull some coins from some oversized purses," Mateo said. "Show her around and then get her something to eat. I could hear her stomach back when she was in the cave."

"What is this place?" Shin asked.

Corin answered. "It used to be a mill, before the top floors burned down years ago. Because it's in such a rough part of town, no one bothered to clean it up, so we moved in. Rumor has it the owners were planning on moving anyway. Fortunately for us, the fire was mostly contained above us, and didn't do much damage down here."

"So we're in the basement of a building that everyone thinks is destroyed, in a part of town that no one cares about?" Shin observed. "I'm guessing you don't get many visitors."

"Exactly. And it has the passage out of the city," Davin said, as though he was explaining the obvious to a child. "We've been here a while, but we've never had much trouble with the sentinels. Not that they're too concerned with us, what with all the problems the mugon are causing throughout Samas." There was an edge to Davin's voice, but she couldn't guess why.

"Davin, she doesn't care about any of that. She just wants to eat," Corin said.

She practically nipped at his heels as he led her toward the kitchen.

Corin deftly cleaned the fish while Davin prepared a spit over a giant fireplace that served as a multi-use cooking area. Shin saw a grill as well as some pots tucked neatly into shelving beside the fireplace. Soon, the fish were rotating on the spit and the boys were dicing vegetables and slicing bread.

"Sorry, there are no potatoes, but it's been a light month. I'm just glad we got this fish back in time for breakfast," Corin said.

"Where do you get your food? Mateo said you steal it..." Shin trailed off, hoping they would correct her.

"That's right, whenever possible. We also pickpocket all the valuables we can get our hands on. There are a few fences in town we've made arrangements with. They trade us food instead of money, which wouldn't do us that much good anyway. It would raise some eyebrows if we shopped the markets with no adults around," Corin said.

"I'll have to steal as well?" Shin asked, and Corin misunderstood the hesitation in her voice.

"Don't worry, we'll teach you how. Mateo won't put you on the streets until he knows you're good enough not to get caught. All that stuff about pulling your weight is just the way he is. He'll give you time to learn."

"Oh... good," Shin replied. She had never stolen anything in her life, and she wasn't sure if she could. Stealing was against the tenets of the Path.

And it was stealing from the sentinels that had gotten her family killed.

More company arrived and her fears were pushed aside. Soon the large room was full, maybe twenty luan in all, and breakfast was served. Everyone grabbed a plate and some food and plopped down wherever was convenient. Shin forced herself to eat slowly, but despite her best efforts, she finished her meal well before anyone else. Before she could stack her plate to be washed, though, several of the smaller luan came by and scooped a bit of their meals onto her plate so she could have seconds. She started to protest, but the kids ran away giggling. They stacked their own plates and scampered off to play.

"You looked hungry, so I asked them to share with you," Mateo said, sitting down beside her. "Don't expect it too often, though. They're much more likely to steal the food off your plate when you aren't looking."

"Thank you, for that and for taking me in. My parents—"

"It's fine," Mateo cut her off, "we can talk about them another time. For now, eat and rest. Tomorrow, those two fools will teach you about the seedier side of city life. Silly as they can be, they're good at thieving. You have to be to survive this long." He paused, as though debating whether to say what was on his mind. "And if you'd like, I could use someone to spar against. I'm a little rusty and need to practice before I start teaching Corin and Davin how to fight."

"I thought you said it was more important for them to pick pockets and steal bread?"

"For now, it is." A concerned look passed over his face. "But I worry that the time is coming where that won't be the case."

Before Shin could ask what he meant, Mateo got up and stacked his finished plate with the others. She had so many questions about Mateo, this place, and the mismatched family he led. But with her hunger satiated, Shin's eyes felt very heavy, and before she knew it, she was slumped down at the table.

Through the haze of drowsiness, she made out voices, and then someone was lifting her. She thought about resisting, but any kind of action was beyond her. Her body was placed gently onto a soft surface and her consciousness faded completely to black.

14

Beast dipped his hand into the dark waters of the ocean and watched as it split the waves.

After hours of thinking he was going to be tossed from the sun-cursed boat, the calm waters were a blessed, if boring, change. Unfortunately, the distraction only entertained him for a few moments. He jumped up and paced the length of the tiny vessel, rocking it from side to side. The skiff felt like an open-air cage on the water, limiting Beast to two steps before he had to turn around and walk the opposite direction. Benji, used to Beast's sudden bursts of energy, ignored his commander and kept the tiny boat from tipping.

Apparently, Benji was an expert sailor. A skill Beast had never known about.

One step. Two Steps. Pivot.

"Where are you taking us? We're heading south from the southernmost point of Ilos, which is as far south as you can go in Samas. There's nothing but endless ocean in this direction."

One step. Two Steps. Pivot.

"Did you think the home of the sin would ever be found on a map?" Benji asked calmly.

"Up until a week ago, I thought the sin were nothing more than a myth used to scare children," Beast answered. He looked out over the endless expanse of water. "I'm still not sure I'm wrong."

Benji ignored Beast's agitation. "Sit down, already. If you keep pacing like that, we'll be swimming the rest of the way."

Beast watched Benji for a moment and realized his pacing was causing Benji to slowly lose his battle with the tiller.

Beast hated sitting down, but he hated swimming even more.

So, he sat down carefully, settling directly in the center of the skiff. He settled for fiddling his fingers. "I don't like it," he said, and gestured to Benji's hip, where no sword hung. "They ask for too much trust for a simple meeting."

"We may be unarmed, but they are allowing us into their home. Trust is being extended by both sides."

Beast nodded, though he wasn't convinced. Approaching unarmed was asking for far more trust, in his opinion. "Remind me how it was that you were able to secure this invitation? I was under the impression that living myths don't freely toss out welcomes to strangers."

"I used to do some work for them." Benji's eyes twinkled with mirth at Beast's suspicion.

"You never thought to mention this to me?" Beast asked.

"No." There was a flat finality in Benji's tone.

"Why not?"

"I prefer my tongue in my head."

Beast nodded. If the sin were even half as dangerous as the stories implied, Benji's discretion was wise.

But being approached by them for contract work seemed dubious.

Ahead of them, the air shimmered slightly, and suddenly an island filled the horizon in front of him.

Beast had seen the horrors of combat. He'd watched countless souls leave their bodies, and he'd seen the depths of depravity humans could inflict upon one another. Through it all, he'd been implacable, a force that could not be shaken.

But to see an island appear where there had not been one only moments before, that was almost enough to cause him to jump ship and swim back to Samas as fast as his untrained stroke would carry him.

"How?" Beast asked.

"The sin call it sacrifice."

"Are all the legends true?" Beast felt no shame at the fear in his voice. He'd yet to find a warrior made of flesh and bone that intimidated him, but he didn't know how to face half-breed demon spawn or warriors that could turn into mist.

"I would hazard that the truth of the sin lies somewhere between what we understand of the natural world and the legends we've all heard." Benji said. "Would you mind pulling us in? We're approaching the shallows."

Beast nodded and deftly hopped over the side into the waist-deep water. The task focused his pent-up energy, and he had the boat dragged onto the sandy beach in no time. Benji, with his usual cat-like grace, navigated the small skiff and hopped off the bow onto the beach.

One moment, they were alone.

The next, four black-clad warriors rose from the sand like wraiths and surrounded them. Beast instinctively dropped into a fighting stance and circled slowly, doing his best to keep his eyes on all four figures at once. Benji put his back to Beast's and matched the circle.

"Weren't we invited?" Beast asked Benji.

One of the sin responded, a man to Beast's left. "Even those invited must prove themselves."

Beast smiled as his body tingled. "Good."

He leaped at the attacker to his right while watching the man who had answered his question on his left. The figure he charged reacted well. He tried to sidestep the attack, but he misjudged Beast's size. Beast simply reached out, hooked his massive arm around the smaller figure's waist, and dragged the warrior away from his allies.

The cowled sin tried to spin free of Beast's arm, but Beast easily overpowered him and pulled him into a two-handed hug. The man adjusted quickly, throwing his legs high around Beast's waist and trying to squeeze the breath from his lungs. It was a good effort, but futile. Beast dove, arcing so that the entangled man landed flat on his back. The man hit the ground with the full weight of Beast on top of him. He lost consciousness immediately.

Beast popped up and turned towards the remaining attackers. Benji deftly held off two as they pressed the attack. He was on the defensive, but his assailants weren't penetrating Benji's excellent guard. Eventually, they would wear him down, but for now Beast could concentrate on the last attacker.

Who he couldn't find anywhere.

He didn't have to wonder long as, too late, he caught a flash of movement to his right. Pain exploded in his cheek. The foot that authored the pain was attached to a small woman, who rolled out of the flying kick and hopped to her feet. Beast rubbed his cheek. "Ow."

Above the veil that covered her mouth, Beast saw her eyes widen in surprise.

"I take it that particular move usually ends most of the fights you're in?" he asked.

The woman rushed forward and threw a flurry of blows at Beast.

By the sun she was fast!

Beast blocked as many of the strikes as he could, but the ones that snuck through started to hurt. Finally, Beast caught one of her arms and pulled her straight into a punch that put her on the ground, dazed.

Beast wasted no time rushing to Benji's aid. The fight ended soon after.

"Thought you might like this part," Benji said as he spit blood from his mouth.

The sin groaned as they picked themselves up from the sand. Beast frowned. They were skilled warriors, but hardly the legends Beast expected. "You knew this was going to happen?"

"I suspected. They use these trials to test the mettle of those invited for an audience."

"And you didn't think to tell me? What if we had lost?"

"Speaking of the trials is forbidden. And anyway, it isn't the winning or losing that matters, but how we fight," Benji answered, finally catching his breath. "I lost when they first summoned me."

"Most everyone does," a woman said. "It's been many years since I have witnessed a victory."

"I don't lose many fights," Beast answered, casting around for the source of the voice.

"I can imagine," the voice whispered in his ear.

Beast spun around and jumped backwards, putting

distance between himself and the dark figure that suddenly stood beside him.

"I am Yuki," the woman said. "I lead the sin."

Beast regarded Yuki with a critical eye. She was a small woman, but the air of power around her was palpable. Her veil was lowered around her neck and her youthful smile and smooth features were at odds with what seemed to be centuries of wisdom resting behind her eyes. Her long, dark hair was tied in a braid that hung down to her lower back.

"I like to fight," the Beast answered.

"Indeed, but that is not unique or impressive. Your martial skills are considerable, but it is your actions to date that have caught my attention. Your vision of a united force of bandits should have been impossible to make a reality. And yet, against all odds, you succeeded. I believe that you and I may be able to help each other."

"I find that hard to believe. Given your abilities," Beast gestured around, at the island hidden through means he didn't understand, "I'd think my dream of putting food in the bellies of the hungry would be a little below your purview."

Yuki's gaze seemed to bore into the dark corners of his heart. "Is that all you really hope to accomplish? Because I don't believe you. You saw a vacuum of power and filled it. You saw the unfairness in a system that did not serve you and you fought against it. What you've created is not the end of your ambitions, but the beginning."

Clever woman. "So, what is the end?"

Yuki evaded his question. "Do you know why the sin were created?"

"Until today I thought it was to punish little boys and girls who didn't eat their vegetables."

Yuki laughed and shook her head slightly. "Perhaps the

legends would have it so, but our true purpose is, when necessary, to stand against the sentinels. To balance the scales. To protect our world."

Beast almost laughed at the absurdity of the statement. "You're doing a shitty job, then." But Yuki wasn't jesting. He growled. "Stand against? No. You don't 'stand against' the sentinels. You strike fast, take what you can, and then run before they have a chance to turn it into a real fight."

Yuki nodded. "And what if your tactics could evolve? What if the sin gave your warriors the skills and techniques to not just steal from the sentinels, but to fight against them?"

"They would do anything for the chance to hurt the people that have had a boot on their throats for their entire lives. But is it actually possible?"

"Of course. I will not deceive you. We can offer our training to all, but it isn't for everyone. Most will improve a little, and that will be all. But some, some will unlock a potential that has the power to change our world. Those are the warriors who will join the sin."

"Need to bolster your numbers?" Beast asked.

"If we are to hold the growing power of the sentinels in check, then we must be more... aggressive in our recruiting than we have been before."

"And what about Benji? Will you continue to allow one of your sin to work for me, now that he's brought me here?" Beast asked, expecting more of a reaction from Yuki, but she just smiled placidly.

Benji answered that. "I wondered when you would figure it out. Are you offended by my deceit?"

"You've been a good friend and an asset beyond measure since I met you. You've freely shared tactics that made my ascension possible. Tactics, I now realize, that probably came from the sin. I don't like being used as a tool, but I used you just as much."

Benji looked obviously relived. "Good, I'm glad."

Beast felt the same, but he also needed to make something else clear. "Lie to me again and I will kill you."

The relieved smile never left Benji's face, but he bowed his head slightly towards Beast. Beast had no doubt the man understood him.

Beast wondered just how much about these sin was legend and how much was truth. If this Yuki spoke true, there was value in an alliance. If his mugon could stand up to the sentinels, it would bring his dream that much closer to reality. "Now that that's settled... Show me what you can do, and we'll see if I believe my mugon should experience your training."

15

Sato pulled his eyes away from the pale moon that hung mockingly in the midday sky. He had been distracted all day trying to remember the superstitious name that the peasants had for it.

The sin moon. Sato snorted. A foolish name.

The Firstborn's mention of the mythical warriors a few days ago had been so offhand, Sato had barely registered it. Then he'd been so consumed by his new task that he hadn't thought of it again. The ghostly moon had shaken loose the small bit of memory he'd filed away and brought it to the fore again.

He shook his head. Soon he'd be jumping at shadows.

Still, fictional or not, the tactics being used by the bandits did resemble the old stories. Perhaps their leader found inspiration in the bedtime tales. Sato made a mental note to investigate some of the legends of the sin. Tactics could often be found in surprising places.

Sato turned his thoughts to the sentinels riding behind him. Six men and four women accounted for the ten names on his list that had been stationed within Bulas. They had all been surprised to be summoned by Sato, and even more surprised to be given a special assignment within a unit that Sato would personally oversee.

They'd all crossed paths before, and no one had enjoyed the experience.

Sato hadn't given the warriors any details. His only instructions were to be ready to ride in two days' time. Even now, he left them in the dark, and he could practically see the wheels turning in each of their minds.

They disgusted him.

Two of them had been moonlighting for local craftsmen to pay off gambling debts. Several had connections with fences in Versun, and he was fairly certain one or two of them were actually still drunk in the saddle. All that stood in their favor was that each of them was wily enough not to get caught a second time. And there were some decent swords among them. If he could figure out how to return them to the Path, perhaps they would become worth the air they consumed.

The remainder of his new force would meet him at a camp, Highrock, on the southern coast of Iru, that he often used while on patrol. If the ravens he'd sent were obeyed, Sato expected to see everyone within the next three days. Once there, he would have his work cut out for him. The sun stalkers were an unusual unit, but they still needed discipline if they were going to function.

And that was a problem.

He had no idea how he would teach any of these sentinels discipline. He'd have an easier time teaching a horse to walk upright on two legs.

On a whim, Sato threw up a signal and brought his horse to a clean stop.

Eight of the ten sentinels executed the common

maneuver without much embarrassment, but two men missed his signal. One skidded past the formation, almost unhorsing another sentinel. The other stopped his horse in time but was thrown headfirst over the front of his mount. Most of the other sentinels guffawed at the display.

Sato sighed. "Crispin. Alonzo. Explain why you did not heed my order."

Crispin, the one who had almost unhorsed another sentinel, spoke for them both. "Well, sir, to be fair, we did heed them. Just not in time."

Sato rubbed his forehead, upset at the sudden headache that wrapped around his skull.

"I've watched the two of you treating this ride like a pleasurable afternoon with a lover. When you ride in formation, it is your responsibility to watch the terrain and your leader."

"But we aren't on patrol! I didn't think we'd started our training yet. Besides, Alonzo is mute, sir. I have to watch him in order to communicate!" Crispin's reply sent a fresh wave of pain cascading through Sato's skull. Crispin's attempt to turn his friend's disability into an excuse for poor behavior nearly sent him over the edge. He grimaced and took a deep breath before speaking.

"When you became a sentinel, you swore an oath to walk the Path. Always. Not just when you're on patrol or heading to battle. Always. Is that understood?"

"Yes, sir!" the sentinels responded as a group. Despite their verbal acknowledgment, Sato thought he saw murder in some of their eyes.

No, this would not be an easy command.

"Very well, let us continue. We still have most of a day's ride ahead of us," Sato said.

When Crispin started to mount his horse, Sato stopped him. "Crispin! Just what do you think you're doing?"

Crispin looked around, confused. "Getting on my horse?"

"Don't. Seeing as your horse was better able to follow orders than you, I've decided to reward it with an unburdened trip. Alonzo, you too. You gentlemen will be walking to Highrock."

Unwilling to risk Sato's wrath, the two men complied and then stood off to the side of the road.

"I expect you in camp by nightfall," Sato said. Then he spurred his horse on and the remaining sentinels left his two examples to their walk.

From then on, Sato was pleased to note that any time he looked behind him, he saw a group of focused sentinels.

That most of them seemed focused on his back, no doubt imagining what it would look like riddled with daggers, was still an improvement. Before long, Highrock could be seen creeping up over the horizon.

Despite its name, Highrock wasn't a mountain camp. It was a steep hill that sprouted up in the middle of the mostly flat grasslands of southern Iru, so abruptly that it almost seemed like a mountain. The steep slope ended at a plateau about a quarter mile across that gave an excellent view of the surrounding area. Best of all, there were multiple hot springs that the sentinels could make use of.

Once they reached the camp and pitched their tents, Sato began their training. Mostly, he observed as his warriors sparred. He noted their strengths, as well as any deficient skills. Sato grudgingly admitted that a lot of the issues he saw were small and could likely be chalked up to a lack of practice due to their city postings. It was good to know that, despite the ways in which these men and women had strayed from the Path, at their core they were still sentinels. Rough around the edges, perhaps, but still the best warriors Samas had ever produced.

As the sun was setting, two exhausted figures staggered their way into camp.

Alonzo walked to Sato and bowed deeply. After holding the pose for a moment, he rose and looked Sato in the eyes. Sato nodded his acceptance of the man's apology. He then turned to Crispin.

"You want me to apologize? To beg forgiveness of the great General Sato? Would you also like me to thank you for the privilege of walking for half a day?" Crispin's road-weary face was turning red with anger.

"I suggest you amend your tone, sentinel," Sato said, his voice ice against Crispin's fire.

"I don't think I will. I sure as hell didn't want to be posted under you. None of us did. And you still haven't given us a hint what all this is for."

"Your duty is to serve the Firstborn."

"Don't quote the Path to me! I know the Path, you rigid bastard."

"Calm yourself before you say something you regret."

Crispin was on the verge of losing control.

Sato, though, already had. He didn't want them under his command any more than they wanted to be under his. But he, at least, obeyed his duty. And they should be thankful for this opportunity. They needed a strong leader to bring them back to the Path, and he had been chosen by the Firstborn personally.

Crispin didn't back down. "Fuck you. I know things. Shit that many of your noble friends wouldn't like getting out. I'm leaving. If you try to stop me, those secrets become public, and it'll be your head that the Firstborn takes as retribution."

"I challenge you!" Sato snapped, regretting his words immediately.

"Challenge? You challenge me?" Crispin asked incredulously.

Sato cursed himself for his blunder. The Path demanded Crispin accept any offer of honorable combat. A refusal would be a violation serious enough to expel him from the sentinels. But Crispin was clearly exhausted and Sato's skill with a blade was well known.

In the eyes of his new sentinels, Sato had just murdered Crispin.

And these particular sentinels might not be willing to stand squarely on the edicts of the Path and watch that happen.

Sato itched to have a sword in his hand.

The sound of galloping horses broke some of the tension. A moment later, Captain Roko rode in at the head of five sentinels. They pulled their mounts to a stop outside the ring of warriors that had gathered around Crispin and Sato.

Roko hopped off his horse.

"Sato," Roko said and saluted crisply. The captain's easy familiarity jarred the sentinels just enough to defuse some of the tension.

"Captain Roko, it's good to see you," Sato responded, using the interruption to buy himself some time.

Roko eyed the crowd. "It seems I arrived in the middle of something."

"This maniac challenged me to a duel!" Crispin cried.

Roko laughed. "This maniac is your commander. What did you do?"

Crispin stuttered, realizing coercion and blackmail of a general wasn't a good look.

Roko shook his head, then thought for a moment. "No matter. You are a sentinel under my command. As such, your failures are my own. I'll fight for you."

Sato barely kept the surprise off his face. Roko's quick thinking provided an elegant, if unusual, solution. He spoke, his voice more calm now that the threat of immediate disaster had passed. "As the subject of the challenge, you are allowed the choice of weapon. What do you choose, Roko?"

Roko dramatically turned and walked slowly to his horse.

"Practice swords!" he declared, holding the wooden weapons over his head.

The crowd was silent for a moment, and then there was a smattering of chuckles. The sentinels relaxed even further.

Sato allowed himself a smile and caught the wooden sword that Roko tossed him. Another unusual solution. But brilliant, all the same.

One Sato never would have thought of.

They put on a show for the Sun Stalkers. The wooden swords cracked against one another for several minutes before Roko finally admitted defeat.

Later that night, around the fire, Roko sat down next to Sato. "You know you'll have to address that one soon," Roko said, nodding towards Crispin. The sentinel had been sitting sullenly all night.

"I know. But I may need some help. I'm not used to sentinels like these."

Roko laughed. "You really aren't. But if what you've told me in our orders is true, we're going to need them desperately."

16

Shin's weeks passed quickly once she settled into her new life. After her first night with the luan, she threw herself into her training with Corin and Davin. The idea of becoming a thief still troubled her, but her old life was gone. This new world wasn't one that rewarded hesitation.

Besides, the illusion that she lived within an honest system was shattered the night her parents' heads were removed from their shoulders.

The first week, she practiced her budding skills on fellow luan. Corin and Davin showed her ways to slip her hand into pockets without being noticed, or bump into someone and come away with a loosely tied coin purse. Fast hands, focus, and a certain amount of daring were rewarded.

But if she faltered, even for a moment, she failed. In the beginning, she failed a lot. In time, though, her confidence grew. With confidence came success. Quite a bit of it.

She earned accolades from her trainers quickly. Every so often, she'd feel a pang of dismay as she slipped away from a luan with their purse. Her parents never would have condoned such skills. But the rush of thieving was unlike anything she'd ever experienced. Even after a training theft, it took several minutes for her heart to stop racing.

What she loved most, though, was learning to escape pursuit.

Shin was good at stealing.

She was a master at getting away.

Her first few attempts were disasters. Corin and Davin remained glued to her, no matter what she tried. Eventually, though, something clicked.

Escape wasn't just about speed and agility, although those both played a role. It was more about timing and subtle movements, of knowing when to flow with the masses of humanity inside a city and when to break away. When she felt it the first time, it was like she finally became aware of a song that had always been playing in the background. One she could dance to.

Soon, no one could catch her. Then, no one could even track her. She believed she was ready for the streets.

Only one obstacle remained.

Mateo.

"Your mind is wandering," Mateo said as Shin narrowly avoided the butt of his staff.

"And you're too slow." She snapped her staff at him but connected with nothing but air.

When they had started sparring, Shin had won occasionally. But as Mateo's muscles remembered their training, and the confidence returned to his movements, the gap in their skill became apparent.

Mateo's staff slapped against the back of her legs and sent her sprawling on the ground.

"Sorry, who's too slow?" Mateo chided.

Mateo was a riddle Shin couldn't solve. He was never unkind, but she always felt like he doubted her, no matter how hard she worked to prove him wrong. She felt like a little sister whose older brother could never quite accept her as an adult.

And yet, when they trained together, he didn't hold back. The more they sparred, the more Shin realized Mateo was a master with the staff. His skill forced Shin to learn quickly from her mistakes.

From her back, she swept a kick at his shins. He danced back nimbly, but she'd never expected to connect. His evasion gave her the space to spring to her feet, spinning her staff in a defensive form that prevented him from closing the distance while she regained her balance.

A month ago, such a combination would have been beyond her. She still couldn't beat him, but he walked away from every training session with his own bruises to match hers.

"Let's make a deal," she said.

His eyes narrowed.

"If I knock you down next, you let me tag along with Corin on his next run." She had a combination she'd been practicing on her own, one he'd never seen.

He grinned. "Fine. But if I knock you down, you promise to stop badgering me about it."

Shin spun her staff above her head, gathering momentum. She stepped forward and snapped the tip of the staff at Mateo's head.

He leaned back, letting the staff pass in front of him.

Exactly as Shin had hoped.

The moment he leaned back, she spun forward. He would expect her to keep her distance, to use the reach of her staff to protect herself from his greater size. Her hair, staff, and body spun as one, and she launched another attack at his head. He caught the lazy swing easily, but she was already sweeping out with her leg. He had no time to dodge the disguised strike, and it connected solidly.

By the sun, it should have knocked him on his ass.

Instead, he stood there, solid as a mountain, a smirk on his face.

He gave her a gentle shove, and in her shock, she tripped over her own feet and fell.

"I trust that settles the matter," he said.

She glared at him. But a promise was a promise.

Without a word, Shin stormed out of the training session and back to the quarters she shared with some of the younger luan. When she entered the room, the children, as usual, lit up. Despite her frustration with Mateo, she felt her chest lighten and soon she wore a smile of her own across her face.

"Come on, let's go get some food," she said to the little ones.

Even though she was a new member, she was one of the oldest luan, and as such she jumped into a position of caregiver and leader. She didn't mind the responsibility and was surprised at how naturally she fell into the role. The fact that Mateo relied on her so heavily within the hideout, however, only made his reluctance to allow her to contribute in other ways more frustrating.

A week passed and Shin was able to keep her promise. Barely. She worked alongside Corin and Davin, looking after the children and preparing food.

What food there was, anyway.

When she had first arrived, it was clear that food was scarce, but the luan were used to making the most out of what they had. A philosophy she knew all too well. Now, though, she noticed there was less and less to go around. Though he tried to hide it, she could tell that Mateo was skipping meals.

Finally, she decided she couldn't hold her tongue any longer. Promise or not, her new family was in trouble and she wasn't going to hide away and let everyone else deal with it.

Shin headed to Mateo's room. Corin and Davin had just headed that way and they were likely planning their next foray into the city.

She slid through the door as quietly as possible.

They noted her entrance but continued their discussion.

"Lots of trinkets, but not much food," Corin said. "Not much food anywhere, from the looks of it."

"My contacts tell me that the sentinels are getting hit harder than ever. These new mugon seem to be giving them all they can handle. Unfortunately for us, if food isn't getting to Dahl, it means less for us to grab. We can only get so much from fishing the stream," Mateo said.

"You should use the smuggler I know," Davin said. His tone made Shin think this wasn't the first time the boys had argued over the topic.

Mateo shook his head. "He has a reputation for bad deals." He sounded resigned.

"He won't backstab *me*," said Davin. "None of your usual smugglers have access to food. Mine does."

"He doesn't accept trinkets," Mateo argued. "Only coin, which we don't have. How many times do we have to have this discussion?"

Davin pointed back at Shin. "But now we have her. If all of us work together, we can get together enough coin."

"I could help," Shin said, jumping on the opportunity that Davin provided her.

"You're not ready." Mateo's tone brooked no argument, but Shin wasn't about to be deterred.

"I'm ready. They know I'm ready." Shin pointed at Corin and Davin. "I've stolen the purses off their belts countless times, and they've never even noticed."

"She's got the lightest fingers I've ever seen, and she's like a shadow out there. I think she can do it," Corin backed her up.

"It's too risky," Mateo said stubbornly.

"You don't have a choice," Shin said. "You need all the help you can get. I've been here for weeks, eating your food and not helping. Now I finally have a chance to pull my weight, and you won't let me do it. Why?"

"You aren't ready." Mateo's voice was firm. "You've only trained a fraction of the time I made these two practice before I sent them out."

Shin didn't back down. Not this time. Not when she could help her new family. She stepped right into his face "You know I am."

Mateo's nostrils flared in frustration, but Shin didn't waver. She stared at him until Mateo stepped back, giving her a small nod of acknowledgment.

He sighed heavily.

"I don't understand," Shin said.

"Look, it's just—" His voice trailed off. Then he grunted and squared his shoulders. "You still feel new around here, and I don't want to see you get hurt. More importantly, I don't want a mistake to tear down everything I've built."

"Mateo, we're desperate. When was the last time you had enough to eat? You can't sacrifice enough by yourself to help everyone here. You need to trust the tools you have at your disposal."

Mateo looked at her for a long time before sighing again. "If you're sure, I suppose I have to trust you."

"I'm sure," she replied. She tossed him the dagger she had slipped out of the sheath on his hip without his noticing.

Mateo caught the dagger by the handle with a bemused look on his face.

"Then I guess you're ready."

17

———

Beast woke to the midday light, the sun streaming through the windows of the small cabin where he'd spent the night. Yuki had disappeared shortly after he passed their test, and another sin had shown him to his temporary quarters. Exhausted from the boat trip and the fight that followed, he'd collapsed into sleep instantly.

He sat up and extended his arms out and back, stretching his massive chest, and sighed contentedly at the series of pops he heard throughout his torso. He took a long drink from the waterskin beside his bed. Then he threw on his trousers and a loose-fitting tunic and headed out the door.

Despite the hour, he was far from the last one awake in the village. Here, the day began in earnest after sunset. It was a schedule that agreed with Beast. All the things he enjoyed most in life were better after dark.

The village was a study in clean and simple structures. Every building was made of wood, rectangular, and topped with a peaked thatch roof. Only the size of each building gave any hint as to its purpose.

Beast supposed many would find the village plain or uninspired. He considered it one of the most beautiful places he'd ever seen. There was nothing wasted. Nothing extraneous. Just as he would rather have a plain axe in hand instead of a jewel-encrusted sword, he'd rather spend his days here than in any palace.

Beast made his way across the village to Yuki's small home. She had invited him to break their fast together before she began his training. He grinned as the smell of frying bacon filled his nostrils.

Despite her position, her home was no different from any of the others. He took the stairs leading up to the front door two at a time and rapped his knuckles on the front door, eager to eat.

Pain exploded through his nose and his vision flashed white as Beast went flying back down the stairs.

He shook his head to clear his blurry vision and jumped to his feet. Yuki stepped through her front door with a piece of bacon in her hand.

"By the sun, Yuki, what did you do that for?" Beast growled in a nasally voice. His nose was broken.

"That was him," Yuki said calmly as she stepped aside. A huge form darkened the entrance to her home.

Beast contained his surprise as he appraised the man walking down the stairs. He had all the features of someone from Samas, but Beast had never seen anyone from this land as heavily muscled and broad across the shoulders. Beast stood half a head taller, but the man's long arms looked as though they would negate any reach advantage Beast might have hoped for. The man smiled at Beast affably.

"I'm Hanz," the man said.

Nobody hit Beast by surprise. "Call me Beast," he said as he put his full strength into a right hook.

Hanz got a hand up, but the blow still partially landed, and Beast was happy to see the smile falter as the big man staggered backwards. Beast rushed forward and wrapped his arms around Hanz's waist. He tried to use his forward momentum to lift his opponent off the ground and slam him down hard.

Except Hanz didn't move.

He widened the base of his legs and kept himself rooted to the ground like an old tree. Instead of tackling the man, Beast had offered Hanz his back, and no fighter would refuse such a gift. Hanz's giant fists, interlocked together, landed on the back of Beast's neck, driving him to his knees.

He snarled and sprang back to his feet. His vision swam, but Hanz was too big and too close to miss. They exchanged body blows, each punch strong enough to break brick.

Beast spun away from Hanz's attempt at a tackle and kicked a foot out, tripping the giant as he charged by. He dove on top of Hanz, joyfully imagining what it would be like to wrap his hands around that thick neck.

Hanz grunted as Beast landed on him with his full weight. He pinned Hanz to the ground with one arm and lifted his other to rain down blows. But before he could complete the motion, Hanz spun on the ground like a child's top. Before he even realized the danger he was in, the arm Beast had been using to pin the man was wrapped up in Hanz's legs. With another move, Beast was on his back and Hanz was applying just enough pressure to let Beast know he could break his arm if he wanted to.

"Stop, Hanz," Yuki said calmly. "He won't submit, and he's not any good with a broken arm. Let him up."

Hanz let go of Beast, spun fluidly to his feet, and stepped

away from the battle. The moment he was free, Beast sprang to his feet and leaped towards Hanz's back with an enraged shout.

Hanz was going to die.

His war cry was cut off as he was caught in mid-air and wrapped up by arms that felt like they were made of steel.

Beast was too surprised to struggle, and the arms tossed him to the ground. His body ached and his head pounded. He looked up at Hanz, and for a moment thought he was seeing double.

He blinked, but both images remained. "There are two of you?"

"I'm Jurian," the mirror image said. Even the tone of his voice was the same.

"Hanz and Jurian are brothers. They will oversee the martial aspects of your training from here on out," Yuki explained.

"I don't need martial training," Beast said, bristling.

Yuki raised one eyebrow, challenging the claim with recent events.

"He caught me by surprise," Beast growled.

The eyebrow inched higher.

If there had been anything to punch, Beast would have smashed it. His excuses sounded pathetic, especially to him.

He'd been beaten.

He could hold onto his precious pride. Or he could learn. "Very well," he said.

Beast glared at the two giant men, but they simply smiled their identical smiles back at him.

By the sun, he wanted to knock their teeth out.

Yuki finished her bacon and licked her fingers.

Beast's stomach growled. "Well, can I at least eat before I get my ass kicked some more?"

Suddenly, the twins were at his side. He started, but there was no aggression in their body language. They pulled him toward Yuki's house. "There's lots of food! We already ate, but we'll have seconds. You have to try Hanz's eggs," Jurian said.

"I call them smashed eggs. I put cheese and bacon in there and smash them all around," Hanz chimed in.

Beast was barely able to untangle himself before the three of them hit the door at the same time. The brothers went in, leaving him alone with Yuki.

"They would be the ones helping to train my mugon, if I approve our alliance?" Beast asked.

"They're among my best," Yuki answered. "And I need your warriors to be ready. We're running out of time."

Without explaining herself further, Yuki disappeared into her home.

18

Training at Highrock went better than Sato expected. Rough as they were, the men and women he had recruited were sentinels at their core. Under his intense scrutiny, their previous training awoke. A daily routine of exercise, meditation and combat sharpened dull skills as readily as any whetstone on a blade.

"Good shooting, but focus on wheeling your mount away faster. Trust that your form and release are true, and let the arrow do what it's meant to," Sato called out to Alonzo.

The sentinel nodded his understanding and then repeated the exercise. The mighty war horse galloped forward, and Alonzo readied his bow and fired. This time the arrow didn't hit as true as it had the first attempt, but before it landed Alonzo was already turning his mount and moving out of range of the imaginary enemies.

"Excellent!" Sato called out. "The difference of an inch where your arrow hits won't matter, but the seconds you shaved off your retreat will save your life."

Alonzo gave Sato a short bow. Sato had already made note that Alonzo would make a great lieutenant.

He smiled as the next sun stalker moved forward to attempt the drill and he watched Alonzo give advice with his hands, so that the sentinel could succeed even faster than he had.

The sentinel was a natural leader.

That evening, once everyone was finished eating, Sato waited for the challenges to begin. Roko had suggested that any sun stalker brave enough to test their skills against Sato should be allowed to challenge him to a duel with practice blades. Anyone that could land a blow on Sato would be rewarded with a week off latrine duty.

So far, none had come close.

Alonzo approached, as he did every night, bowed, and signaled to Sato that he wished to challenge him.

"Wouldn't you like a night for your bruises to heal?"

The sun stalkers laughed at the good-natured joke, pretending not to notice how forced the humor must have sounded coming from Sato.

Another suggestion of Roko's.

Alonzo motioned to the makeshift training ground they'd created within the camp.

Despite his boasting, Sato was continuously impressed with Alonzo's swordsmanship. The young sentinel was a natural with the blade. But rather than resting, Sato saw him training harder than any other sun stalker.

The two men bowed to each other and readied themselves. Sato took on a traditional defensive stance, as was his custom in these sessions. The challenge was to land a blow on Sato. It might seem like this made it easier for the challengers than him, but in truth, it meant that Sato only had to prepare for and defend attacks. "Shelling up," as most sentinels called it, allowed Sato to put himself in a position to conserve energy, defending while he waited for the challengers to make mistakes and open themselves up to defeat.

As expected, Alonzo pressed the action, but Sato soon realized that most of the strikes Alonzo was using were feints. Soon, Sato was forced to give ground in order to give himself more time to read which blows were real and which were designed to keep him guessing.

Once Sato was moving, Alonzo attacked faster. Soon enough, simply shelling up wasn't an option.

Sato went on the offensive.

He read a feint and stepped in before Alonzo could throw his true strike. Alonzo's reflexes were quick, and he blocked Sato's blow, but it cost him his balance. In three precise strikes, Alonzo was disarmed and yielding.

"Very good," Sato said, his breathing heavy, "you're more dangerous every time we cross blades."

Sato extended a hand to help Alonzo up and clapped him on the shoulder.

Sato accepted a few more duels, but none were as eventful as the one with Alonzo. Only slightly winded, Sato sat down beside Roko and accepted a mug of wine.

"I think I've found our first lieutenant," he said to his old friend.

Roko watched Alonzo as he sat amongst the others, still accepting congratulations on his performance.

"A good choice," Roko replied.

"But?" Sato responded, reading his old friend's tone.

"But, if you want to get the best out of him, you'll need to make the right choice for our other lieutenant."

"I was thinking Mercer. She's not as accomplished a

sword, but she has the respect of her peers and communicates well."

"Mercer's a fine choice."

"Out with it, Roko. I'm in no mood for your riddles," Sato snapped.

"Alonzo and Crispin are a team, Sato. The stalkers see them as two sides of the same coin. If you divide them, it will only hurt them both."

Sato laughed derisively. "Promote Crispin? The man does the bare minimum and nothing more. He's the only sentinel here that hasn't challenged me. I'm closer to sending him home than promoting him. The only reason I don't is because I know it pisses him off more to be stuck with us."

Roko just shrugged at the diatribe.

Sato took a long pull of his wine and watched Crispin. The man was practically holding court among the sun stalkers, and it made Sato uncomfortable. Crispin had a reputation for manipulating situations to his own end. Sato couldn't allow that to happen here. Not with something so important.

The next few days went by without incident, but thanks to Roko's suggestion, he kept an even closer eye on Crispin. The lax sentinel did enough in training not to raise Sato's ire, but that was all. His skills were improving, but not nearly as quickly as the rest of the group. He did notice that Crispin seemed to be taking a particular interest in the duels each night, going so far as to have in-depth conversations with all those that challenged Sato, but he never came forward himself.

Sato got the sense that would soon change.

Every night Crispin watched the duels more intently, and the contingent that would circle around him once the duels were complete would grow. The air of anticipation seemed to grow with each passing night that Crispin didn't challenge.

Sato pretended to ignore it, but he wasn't sure if he was convincing anyone.

Finally, the day came. Crispin came up to Sato, bowed, and challenged the general to a duel.

Sato accepted, eager to settle the matter for good.

The air felt heavy, as though a storm was about to burst above them. His sun stalkers felt it too. Glances flew between them, and they shuffled from foot to foot as though they were the ones preparing for the duel.

Sato's eyes narrowed.

Crispin planned something.

Roko, as was custom, tended to the cook fire, depriving Sato of his greatest ally. For the first time in weeks, Sato felt alone.

Alonzo acted as judge for the match. He raised his hand, waited for confirmation from the duelists, then swung his arm down like a sword.

Sato advanced, prepared for tricks. He wouldn't stick to his pattern. Better to attack and throw Crispin off his strategy.

They passed once, Crispin avoiding Sato's combination by a whisker. The sentinel was decent with a sword, even if his discipline was deplorable.

They passed again, and this time Crispin fell.

The loss didn't seem to deter him. He stood up again, the smirk still on his face.

Alonzo readied them for the second round. Crispin acknowledged he was ready, but his stance was poor. Alonzo began the round, and Sato advanced again. Crispin didn't defend himself. Instead, he raised his left hand and snapped his fingers.

As one, every sun stalker in the ring drew their steel and stepped forward.

Sato's eyes went wide, and he spun around, looking for a gap or weakness to exploit.

Crispin's true nature revealed itself. Any promise he'd shown was just another lie to give himself this opportunity to kill the man who had wronged him. The sun stalkers, opportunists one and all, had fallen under his spell.

No matter.

Even with a wooden sword, he would show them the true strength of discipline. Of obedience to the Path.

Crispin's wooden sword struck him in the back of the knees, sending him to the dirt.

As Sato fought back to his feet, Crispin snapped his fingers again, and again the sun stalkers advanced, closing the ring until there was almost no room to move.

Sato turned his full attention toward the ring surrounding him. The one place he wouldn't survive was in the middle of them all. If he broke through the ring, he could disrupt their coordination, take them on one and two at a time, and win the day. Surely, Roko would be along in moments to help.

Crispin again took him out with another low strike to the back of the legs.

Sato fell, cursing his luck. He was supposed to become the Firstborn, to lead Samas to a brighter future. He wasn't supposed to die in the dirt, killed by the very sentinels he commanded.

He rolled over, stopping short when he almost ran face-first into the tip of Crispin's practice sword. The traitor's eyes held a hard glare, and he moved the tip of the sword until it was lodged in Sato's throat. One thrust, and Sato would slowly choke to death.

Sato snarled, and Crispin pressed a little harder, choking off the wordless protest. "Listen, you self-righteous piece of shit. Do you know why I'm the one holding your life in my hands, despite your precious purity?"

Sato leaned back, releasing enough pressure on his throat to speak. "Because you're a coward who has no honor."

Crispin shook his head. Sato thought he even saw a hint of pity in the man's eyes, like he was somehow superior to Sato. If only he had his steel, Sato would wipe that look right off his face.

Crispin resumed the pressure on Sato's neck. Sato bared his throat, daring him. He might not live to see the next sunrise, but he wouldn't lose his courage in his last moments. Let Crispin carry the stain of dishonor for the rest of his days.

Crispin shook his head again, stepped back, and pulled his sword away from Sato. Instead, he offered his hand.

Sato stared at it, wondering what trap Crispin had laid for him next.

It was only then he realized all the sun stalkers had sheathed their swords.

Still, he stared, not quite comprehending.

"You lost," Crispin said, answering his own question, "because you're so focused on the Path you can't see anything besides what you expect to see. You're too narrow-minded."

He held out his hand for one more minute, and when Sato didn't take it, he shrugged and walked away. The rest of the sun stalkers followed soon after, leaving Sato alone in the dirt.

Sato came to his feet with as much dignity as he could muster and then stumbled over to where Roko sat. Roko, who had never left the cook fire. Never before had he wanted to kill a man as much as he did Crispin.

"Well, that was interesting," Roko said with an infuriating smile.

Sato growled.

"Permission to speak freely, sir?" Roko asked.

Sato glared at him. The only reason Roko would ask permission from Sato at this point in their relationship was to provide an avenue for his sarcasm.

The captain's smile didn't falter, but he held up his hands as if to ward off the glare. "Crispin's tactics just now, though they likely skirted the lines of the Path, were successful, right?"

Sato could only manage a grunt of acknowledgement through his gritted teeth.

"Are we not trying to find a way to combat an enemy that has developed tactics that allow them to effectively defeat a superior force? Seems as though Crispin's is the type of mind that might be more useful alive than dead."

Sato was suddenly very aware of the pain in his jaw. He relaxed his teeth and took a deep breath. First the Firstborn, and now Roko?

He took another calming breath and considered Crispin. He thought back on the weeks of study and planning that the young sentinel had put into the plan that he orchestrated this night. He considered how easily he had convinced his peers to act against their commanding officer in order to demonstrate a unique tactic.

The conclusion was infuriating. Crispin, as far from the Path as he was, was brilliant.

Not only that, but he was connected like a spider at the center of a web of associates.

Not a day passed where Sato didn't hear about some long-lost relative in a distant city or a friend from an earlier age. Crispin seemed like the kind of man who would be lost at sea for a week, then run aground, and in the nearest village find a drinking companion from years ago.

And that was a skill that could land Crispin in command of the sun stalkers if Sato wasn't careful.

He sighed heavily.

"Promote him."

Roko couldn't contain his laughter.

<h1 style="text-align:center">19</h1>

S hin focused on breathing evenly as she followed her mark. The confidence she'd felt arguing with Mateo less than an hour ago had vanished.

She knew that if she returned empty-handed, he'd forgive her. If anything, he might be pleased by her choice.

But she couldn't back out now. Not after she'd dug her heels in so stubbornly.

The four of them had split up to make the most of their time. Mateo hadn't liked the idea of her alone, but she'd insisted on being treated as an equal. She wouldn't do them as much good if another luan was forced to watch over her.

The plan was simple, but risky.

Find the largest coin purses.

Steal them.

Don't get caught.

The wealthy young man she followed was a true mark. Shin was sure of it. His elaborate clothing and haughty demeanor made him either the son of a wealthy merchant or craftsman. He wore his purse openly on his belt, flaunting the oversized bag with every step. His arrogance knew no bounds, either. Shin had watched him order the sentinels that served as his bodyguards to give him more space several times. In the crowded markets, such orders made protecting him nearly impossible.

The sentinels had glared at the young man but complied. They hung back and futilely tried to keep an eye on him. Something told Shin they wouldn't lose any sleep if sudden misfortune was to befall the arrogant man.

She blended in with the after-dinner market crowds, waiting for the sun to fall. Precious time slipped away, but if she came home with that bulging coin purse, she guessed she could cover their food needs for a few weeks, at least.

Her moment arrived. She neared her mark, watching his progress and adjusting her approach. In a few moments, her target would come around the corner of a building, and the sun would be directly in the eyes of the sentinels.

Now.

The moment the blinding light hit their faces, Shin moved. In one deft motion, she stepped around the mark, sliced the leather cord with one hand and caught the purse with the other. The moment it hit her hand, it disappeared into one of her many pockets.

She walked away. No shouts followed her calm escape.

Shin breathed a sigh of relief. The hard part was over. She felt the flow of the crowd and looked for pockets into which she could step without drawing attention. The first pocket presented itself, then another, and then she was in one of the many alleys that would lead her back to safety.

She'd done it! Shin patted the bulge hidden within her shirt with a satisfied grin.

"Got something good there, luan?" The voice was laced with vitriol. A man stepped out of the shadows, his eyes hard.

Shin fought to control the sudden pounding of her heart. "Not at all," she said, as casually as she could manage.

The man smiled, and a pit formed in Shin's stomach. The few yellow teeth that made up his grin were surrounded by cracked lips and a scraggly beard. His rheumy eyes sat over a tiny pig nose. Combined with his bald head, he might have been the ugliest man Shin had ever seen.

Another man joined the first. He had the same unhealthy gaze and missing teeth. He had hair, but it hung in long greasy strands down to his shoulders.

They were both big, though.

"Well then, you won't mind if we have a look?" the bald man asked.

Shin turned to run, only to find a third man blocking the alley. Without other options, she put her back to the wall and looked for a weapon. The three men didn't waste any time advancing on her.

Shin slid down to her knees and started sobbing.

"Please, please don't hurt me!"

The men chuckled and continued forward. When they were a few steps away, Shin threw a fistful of grit from the street into the eyes of the two men. Blinded, they staggered backward, cursing, and Shin popped up from her crouched position to run past them.

Except the man behind her dove and caught her ankle.

"That was pretty clever, lovey. Unfortunately, you—"

His gloating was replaced with a sickening *thunk*, and then the filthy man's grip failed. Shin scurried away from him.

"Are you hurt?" a deep voice asked.

Shin was momentarily speechless as she looked at the

giant man blocking most of the light in the alley. He made the other ruffians look like children in comparison.

"I'm fine," she managed.

"Good, give me a moment."

The man brushed past her, incapacitating the two remaining men with what Shin could only describe as ease.

"I don't have anything," she said with her hands raised.

"Well, lucky for you I don't want to rob you," He grinned. "Because that was about as convincing as a sentinel caught in a whorehouse."

Shin stared blankly.

"Because they aren't supposed to be in there. So, if they are, it's to arrest someone."

"Ahh—"

"You're not very good at lying, is my point. And that bulge under your shirt says you do have something, were I so inclined to take it. Fortunately, I am not."

"Then why did you follow me here?"

"I didn't. I've been watching them. They've been staking out the alleys in this neighborhood for some time. Almost as if they suspected someone might be coming this way with a full purse." He shot her a meaningful look.

This alley was one that the luan favored. Not the only one in the area, but one of a few Mateo's pickpockets used to leave the market. But only the luan knew which routes they used.

"So, you're just here to help random girls in alleyways?" She redirected the conversation, so she didn't have to think about what the giant's comment implied.

"Me? I'm just here for a drink." The large man, despite his wild beard and hair, looked so kind that she couldn't help but smile.

"Well then, thanks for the help," Shin replied.

Shin watched the man as he left the alley and was surprised to see him nearly melt into the crowd. Maybe he wasn't quite as good as her, but he was several times her size. She started to thank the sun for her good fortune, but stopped herself from engaging in the old habit. The eternal sun hadn't done much for her or her family.

Shin walked toward the rendezvous point Mateo had instructed her to use, money in hand. She took her time, checking every corner and shadow for an ambush, but the rest of her return was uneventful.

She blended in with one final crowd of people and then slipped seamlessly into the mouth of the small, disused alley that led to their meeting point. Just as she started to hear hushed voices echoing against the narrow walls, an iron grip clamped across her mouth while a second pinned her arms to her sides. She was pulled into the shadows.

Before she could even struggle, Mateo's voice whispered in her ear. "Something's wrong."

She relaxed, and he let her go. She looked at him questioningly, rather than risking more words.

"I think the fence intends to betray us," Mateo whispered. "Look, there are two men in hiding."

Shin peered into the darkness ahead of her. She shook her head. She could only make out the familiar shapes of Corin and Davin speaking with the man she assumed was the fence.

"Over the fence's right shoulder, watch the shadow."

Shin kept looking. She breathed in sharply when a shadow seemed to sway slightly, like a person adjusting their feet, then melt back into the wall.

"Good, now slowly, we need to get closer."

Mateo began moving from shadow to shadow along the walls of the narrow alley. Shin followed him exactly, terrified she would give them away. When they were twenty paces away, the shadow Mateo had pointed out suddenly burst from his hiding place.

Before either Shin or Mateo could act, the shadow swung a heavy stick at Corin's head.

Corin saw the blow coming and slid away, turning so that his back was to Davin.

Shin grinned. Together, the two boys could hold off the ambush, giving her and Mateo enough time to join the fight.

Her grin faltered when Davin wrapped his arm around Corin's exposed neck. Corin's eyes went wide when his next breath failed to reach his lungs.

"Davin!" Shin shouted.

Davin turned, dragging Corin around with surprising strength. Next to the boys, the fence drew a long, wavy dagger, eyes focused on Corin.

Mateo's arm came up and down, so fast Shin barely noticed. But she certainly saw the throwing knife embedded deep in the fence's chest.

Davin's face paled as another knife appeared, as if by magic, in Mateo's hand. He let go of Corin's neck and shoved him hard at the approaching pair.

By the time Mateo had a clean look behind Corin, Davin and the shadow were gone.

Shin ran up to Corin. "Are you hurt?"

He shook his head.

"There's no time for that," Mateo said.

Shin glanced over at him. They'd won. She still had the purse, and Davin's betrayal hadn't cost them any lives.

Mateo saw her look. "If he failed here, where do you think he'll strike next?"

Her blood went cold.

"Home."

20

———

"**B**enji, what do you make of those two?" Beast asked, nodding at two disheveled men trying a little too hard to look casual.

"Judging by the way they're watching that alley, I'd say they're waiting on someone, and I doubt it's an old friend."

Beast had spent the last few days in Dahl with Benji learning both more of what the sin did from day to day, and to pick up some of the more subtle skills of the sin. How to blend in with a crowd. How to follow without being seen. How to kill without being caught. Some skills he picked up faster than others, but on the whole, he was pleased with his progress.

He considered himself the sort of man who charged through locked doors. The sin taught him that doors and locks were barriers only to those already willing to play by the rules. The sin played by different rules. Hell, they nearly existed in another world.

He was still learning the ways of this shadowy underworld, but he could certainly pick out amateurs when he saw them. The two in the alley piqued his curiosity. "I'm going to check them out."

"Want some company?"

"No, you grab us a table. I could use a little exercise. All this sneaking around has me feeling antsy."

"Fair enough, I'm thirsty anyway," Benji said. He turned and walked into the tavern.

Beast made his way towards the two men. He happily slid into the crowd, making use of his recently acquired skills, and found a place to keep an eye on his new friends while avoiding their suspicious glances.

He didn't have to wait long before he saw the two men rush into the mouth of the alley.

Beast resisted the urge to run headlong in pursuit. A few weeks ago, he would have charged in, axe in hand, eager for a fight. But Yuki and Benji had impressed upon him the importance of making stealth habitual. The only way to become a master of the shadows was to make those skills the foundation of your daily life.

Though it took him a few moments longer to reach the alley, Beast knew he'd entered without being noticed. He also knew that the men he pursued had no other allies lying in wait.

Perhaps the sin had the right of it after all.

When he entered the alley, he saw three men, large by most standards, surrounding a young girl. The trap had been sprung, and the girl was crouched down in fear.

"Please don't hurt me," she begged convincingly. Only Beast's trained eye caught the slight movement of her fist filling with sand and dirt from the ground.

In one motion, she threw the sand in the faces of her assailants and sprung forward. She almost made it, too.

"That was pretty clever, lovey. Unfortunately, you—"

Beast's fist came down with a satisfying *thunk*. As soon as he made contact with the back of the man's head, his grip loosened, and the young girl squirmed free. After checking on the girl, he dealt with the remaining men.

As was often the case, Beast was left disappointed by the ease with which he dispatched his foes. He hadn't even broken a sweat, and it was a warm day. Sighing heavily, he returned to the girl.

"I don't have anything," she said with her hands raised.

Beast grinned at the unconvincing lie and did his best to assure her that he wasn't after the coin purse that was so clearly hidden under her tunic. While he was impressed with the fight and quick thinking that the young girl had shown, he had also quickly grown bored with this whole situation. Now that the violence, such as it was, had ended, he was ready to return to Benji for that drink. Before leaving, he warned her that these men had likely known her route and were lying in wait. No sense saving her just to have her get caught again.

"So, you're just here to help random girls in alleyways?" she asked, clearly trying to turn the subject away from whatever she was up to.

She needn't have worried. He was really bored now.

"Me? I'm just here for a drink."

He didn't wait to hear her response before leaving the alley. A cold flagon of ale was all that was on his mind now.

Beast's heart sank when he saw Benji waiting for him outside of the tavern. A lithe woman with long dark hair stood next to his friend, and she didn't have the look of a new acquaintance.

"I'm not getting my drink, am I?" he asked Benji.

"Doesn't look like it. This is Raya, by the way."

She launched into her message. "I received word that a

sentinel lieutenant, Walric, was seen leaving the gates not long ago. He works directly for Dahl's magistrate, Velor, and has been on our shit list for a while. He handles a lot of the magistrate's more... unsavory tasks. If we can kill him, it will be a major blow to the local sentinels."

"Killing I can do," Beast replied.

"Of that I have no doubt, but this is a good opportunity for you to learn one of the sin's most powerful skills."

His ears perked up at that. Blending into crowds didn't satisfy Beast's baser instincts. He arched an eyebrow at Raya.

"Subtlety."

Benji couldn't quite stifle a laugh as Beast's heart sank once again.

"We need to make his death look like an accident. It's best if the sentinels in the area don't have anyone to take out their anger on. But killing this bastard is an opportunity that we can't miss. Can you do it?"

Beast snarled, "You don't think I can?"

Benji continued to struggle against his mirth.

Raya stood her ground. "It's not exactly what you're best known for, no."

The dam finally broke, and Benji laughed out loud.

"This is important," Raya said. "He's a key cog in the sentinels' operations in this area."

"I'll be fine," Beast growled. "Just tell me the plan and I'll get it done."

Raya turned and motioned for them to follow.

They made their way through Dahl and lined up with the mass of humanity that was on its way out of the city. Beast and Benji had used illegal papers to get through the gates on their way in, but leaving the city was an easier affair. Unless the sentinels had orders to prevent someone from leaving, they were far less concerned about who went out than who came in.

Before long, they were waved through the gate by two bored-looking men and were on their way down the main road out of the city.

As soon as they were away from the crowds, Raya started talking. "From what we understand, Walric is on his way to meet up with a known smuggler that operates in the area. He's alone and in a hurry."

Raya didn't elaborate as she led them off the road and across open country. She broke into a light jog, forcing Benji and Beast to match her pace. Slowly, the scrublands gave way to one of the forests that dotted so much of the countryside in Samas. After about twenty minutes, Raya stopped and motioned for them to approach. "The road he'll be taking is just beyond the trees here."

"I'm ready," Beast said, flexing his fingers and wishing he had his axe.

"I'm sure you are, but not for what we're doing here," Raya said, pulling a coiled length of thin rope from her satchel. "It has to look like an accident, remember?"

Beast gritted his teeth and nodded.

Raya continued, "Benji and I will move up ahead to where the road curves. Just after the curve, we'll secure the rope at neck level. If he comes around the corner fast enough, he should be thrown from the horse with enough force to kill him. Or injure him seriously enough that we can finish him off in a way that looks like he died from the fall."

"And why would he be galloping at..." Beast hesitated.

Benji grinned at him. "Go on, say it."

Beast sighed heavily. "At breakneck speeds."

"Enough, you two!" Raya snapped. "Beast, you're going

to wait until he passes and then startle the horse into a gallop."

"He'll be riding a war horse, trained for combat. We can't just jump out screaming and expect to spook it," Beast said.

"True," Raya said. She rummaged in her satchel and pulled out a round packet about as big as an apple. "That's why we have this."

"What's that?" Beast went to grab it, but Raya pulled it away from him.

"This will make enough light and sound to spook the horse. I promise. All you have to do is plant it somewhere close to the road, where it won't be seen. Then you hit it with a rock as the horse passes."

"Hit it with a rock?" Beast was certain this was the most complicated way to kill a person ever.

"Throw a rock at it." Raya spoke slowly, overly enunciating every word. "You don't want to be close when this thing goes off." She handed the packet to Beast. "Good luck."

With that, they were gone, and Beast stared for a moment at the packet. He didn't believe for a moment it would spook a war horse, but what did he care? At least then he could blame Raya for a foolish plan.

He found a place on the edge of the road to hide the packet. In the direction Walric was traveling from, a small clump of grass hid the packet from sight. Beast picked up a rock and found a place behind a tree where he was certain he could hit the packet.

Soon, he heard the telltale sound of a horse's hooves thudding up the dirt path. Beast readied himself. All he had to do was throw the rock well.

The sentinel came into view and Beast gripped the rock tightly.

The sentinel reached the packet, and Beast emerged from behind the tree. The alert sentinel heard the movement and wheeled his mount around.

Beast's aim was true. The ensuing flash of light and loud bang were more impressive than Beast expected, and the horse reared up on its back legs.

But that was all.

With a moment of warning, the sentinel was able to keep his mount under control.

Beast swore and leaped at the man, knocking the sentinel off his horse. The two men rolled once and then Beast was on top of the disoriented sentinel. His fists hammered into the man's face until he stopped moving and then continued until he stopped breathing.

The red in his vision slowly faded as Beast stood up. The whole exchange hadn't lasted more than a few moments.

Benji and Raya came around the corner at a full run. He looked up at them, then down at the body of the sentinel.

Raya looked around, as though worried they might be observed. "Shit." She stared down at the body. "If Velor sees this, he's going to know someone is onto his operation." She turned her glare to Beast. "You'll need to fix this. We need to make the body disappear."

Benji shook his head. "That will raise just as many questions."

Beast thought for a moment. When the answer hit him, he couldn't believe he didn't see it before. "My mugon did it."

Both Benji and Raya stared at him. Beast looked up and down the road. How would it look? He'd seen the aftermath of plenty of ambushes.

"Give me your bow," he told Raya.

She frowned but handed it to him. It felt like a child's

plaything in his hands. He held out his hand for an arrow, and Raya gave him one. He nocked it and pulled the bow back, afraid he'd snap it in half.

"Your arrow is nocked backwards," Raya said.

Benji chuckled.

Beast ignored them and walked right up to the sentinel. He hovered the point of the arrow an inch above the man's right shoulder and let go of the string.

Archers made it look so easy. The arrow hit the sentinel and punched through his armor, but at an odd angle. That was probably for the best, Beast figured. His shitty shot made the ambush look amateur.

Which, he supposed, wasn't far from the truth.

"Sword," he said, holding out his hand to Benji.

Benji gave him the sword and Beast went to work. He sliced at the man's legs. He held the sword in his left hand and made awkward stabs. The sentinel didn't bleed much, but Beast cut him enough that only the most observant would notice.

He stepped back to admire his work.

"Congratulations," Benji said. "You killed a dead man."

Beast gestured. "The mugon did it. A poor ambush by unskilled warriors."

Benji and Raya studied Beast's work. Raya shrugged. "It's not ideal, but it should keep suspicion off of us, at least for long enough." She turned to Benji and put her finger to his chest.

"Train him better."

21

———

Sato hated it when Roko was right.

The captain never let him forget it.

And in this case, the sun stalkers' daily routine was a constant reminder that the promotions he'd given had been the correct choice.

Together, Crispin and Alonzo had brought the sun stalkers closer to the vision the Firstborn had shown to Sato, faster than Sato would have believed possible.

Their methods were unusual, to say the least.

Various betting pools and competitions had sprung to life throughout the squads. Though no one claimed to know anything about them, Sato wasn't so much a fool he couldn't guess their source. Such methods were despicable. The Path demanded obedience, and discipline itself was a virtue. Sentinels were supposed to put their full heart into training, not because of reward, but because it was intrinsically valuable.

Sato had almost stopped the competitions, but Roko had asked him to wait, to see how it affected the training.

And it worked.

The squads were always trying to surpass one another. Their physical and mental discipline, at least during their daily exercises, had never been higher.

The constant gambling at night was another problem, but one Sato managed to overlook by confining himself to his tent after meals.

The pair of sentinels drove him close to the edge of madness, and yet, their results were undeniable. They were as skilled with sword and bow as all sentinels were expected to be, but their real strength was in the adaptability of their minds and tactics. More than once, squads commanded by Crispin and Alonzo had defeated squads he had commanded personally. Somehow, they always found ways to surprise him.

The time was soon coming for them to move. Training was ending, replaced by true battle.

The question that had consumed him every night was how to begin.

Which was why he had Roko, Crispin, and Alonzo in his tent while the others enjoyed their nightly distractions. The greatest pleasure of the meeting was knowing he was taking Crispin and Alonzo away from their favorite part of the day.

They were seated around a map of Samas, and Sato had just finished explaining the sun stalkers' purpose.

Crispin was stroking his chin. "Clever." He glanced over at Sato. "Not sure about putting you in charge, but otherwise, very clever."

Had those words come from any other sentinel, Sato would have assigned a week of latrine duty. Tonight, he just gritted his teeth. Roko grinned at his discomfort.

"I'll admit I'm at a loss," Sato said. "I've come up with a dozen different strategies for attacking the mugon, but all of them are variations of the same theme. We hunt them down and interrogate them, one group at a time."

Alonzo made a series of hand gestures, too quick for Sato to follow.

Crispin laughed. "He says you think too much like a sentinel."

Sato bit back his retort.

Crispin leaned over the map. "It's that rigid thinking that the mugon are taking advantage of. You'll waste all your time and resources chasing ghosts. Maybe you'll catch one here and there, but otherwise, you're not making progress."

"And what do you suggest?" Sato barely managed to keep his tone polite.

Crispin bent over the map, studying it in silence for several minutes. Then he leaned back. "Mind if Alonzo and I have a minute, sir?"

"Granted."

The two left the tent, leaving Roko and Sato alone. Roko grinned at Sato.

"You can say it," Sato said.

Roko didn't bother to get rid of the smug look on his face. "There's no need. I'm just impressed you're seeing it."

"I fear they're taking me farther from the Path than I'm dragging them toward it."

Roko sipped at his cup of tea. "You know, I've never viewed the Path as a path."

Sato invited Roko to explain further with a gesture.

"I think of the Path as more of a map. It doesn't tell us how to handle every situation. It doesn't even tell us what to do in most. Instead, it's a guide, something that shows us all the different ways to reach our destination."

Sato considered the idea. It had merit, he supposed, even if he wasn't convinced.

Before they could debate further, Crispin and Alonzo returned. From the look on their faces, they'd reached a decision.

Sato waited as Crispin shuffled from foot to foot. Then he found his spine, stood up straight, and met Sato's gaze.

"Sir, when it comes to fighting these mugon, there's no battle tactic that will win the day. You need to cut the head off."

Sato nodded. "Easy enough to say. But the cells don't know how to find the leaders."

"Which means that you don't need a new tactic or strategy. You need information."

Sato didn't speak, knowing Crispin had more to say.

"I have a friend who just might have the information you're looking for. Or, at the very least, can point us in the right direction."

"I'm guessing this friend of yours isn't a sentinel."

Alonzo grinned, and Crispin looked down at his feet. "He's a specialist in importing and exporting goods, sir. Goods of dubious legality."

Sato stared, not quite sure he believed what he'd just heard.

No wonder Crispin had been nervous about presenting his idea. He'd just as much as admitted he had connections to a criminal. Under normal circumstances, such a confession would carry serious consequences. At best, it would expel him from the sentinels. Under a strict commander like Sato, it might have earned his death.

Sato had to admit, he was tempted. Despite the development of the sun stalkers, discarding both Crispin and Alonzo would only be for the best.

He caught Roko's look. His captain no doubt knew his thoughts.

If there was another way, he might have taken it. But he'd spent weeks trying to break the mugon, and nothing had come to him. He took a deep breath, unable to believe what he was about to say.

"And you think he'll just talk to me?"

Crispin still hesitated, as though admitting his connection to criminal enterprise wasn't what had really concerned him.

"Not to you, sir, but to me. He's not very trusting of strangers."

"Shocking." Sato wondered if there was yet a way out of this. If there was, he didn't know it. At the very least, he could hear Crispin out. "Fine. Tell me your plan."

Crispin smiled. "I think you'll like it, sir. It involves you being under my command."

Roko laughed out loud.

S hin didn't think she'd ever run so far, so fast. With no concern for stealth, they ran down alleys and through streets, ignoring the shouts and questions their passage raised. Within minutes, they were at the entrance to their home.

Mateo gave the orders. "Gather the younger kids first. Corin, you lead them to the meeting point. Shin, you and I will hold off anyone who tries the front door."

Corin turned and sprinted towards the main hall.

"Just the two of us?" Shin asked, the pitch of her voice rising.

Mateo led them towards the training area. Through the walls, she heard Corin shouting at the younger children to evacuate. Mateo and she fought against the current of fleeing luan to retrieve their weapons.

"The entrance is a natural choke point. It only needs one," Mateo hesitated for a second before glancing back at Shin, "or two people to defend. We don't need to win. We just need to delay any attack long enough for the others to escape."

The objection seemed obvious. "Davin will know, though."

Mateo grimaced. "True."

Nothing she could say would comfort him. He'd been too trusting, and now paid the price.

They reached the training room, and Mateo ran to the wardrobe that housed their weapons.

"Here," he said, tossing her the digging fork that she had carried with her from her old life. He gave her a hard look. "This isn't training. If they get in, those kids die. We won't let that happen."

People were going to die.

The unspoken words rang inside Shin's head. She thought back to the sentinel she had led to the deadfall.

"I understand."

Mateo reached for the quarterstaffs that they used for training and pulled them aside. He pulled out a large bundle wrapped in animal skins. Shin had seen it before, but never had the courage to ask Mateo what it was.

Mateo unwrapped the skins and revealed a large staff, slightly longer than he was tall, made of wood that had been laboriously sanded and stained to a brown so dark it was almost black. Painted along the length of the weapon in a dark red were symbols and designs that Shin couldn't recognize. The staff ended with a thick, wicked-looking curved blade at the top that looked like it could be used to stab or slice with equal efficacy.

"It's a family heirloom," Mateo said when he noticed Shin staring at it. "Called Harmony."

For the first time, she wondered about Mateo's past. For all their time together, she knew nothing of him before he'd formed the luan. When they made it out of this, she intended to ask him.

Armed, they returned to the main hallway.

Behind them, the kids hustled through the trapdoor and down the rope ladder. But they were forced to retreat one at a time. Shin's stomach twisted in a knot. More of them should have been out by now. One of the older boys ran up to Mateo.

"Corin said there was only one person waiting at the mouth of the cave, but he took care of the intruder. He hasn't seen anyone else."

As the boy ran off, the sound of a boot smashing into the locked door echoed through the main hallway. The children jumped and screamed, and some of the smaller ones started crying.

"Stay calm and keep moving," Mateo called out in a firm voice.

The door held longer than she expected. By the time it started to splinter, the last of the children were heading down the ladder. When it finally burst open, the trapdoor was closing behind them.

Mateo didn't wait for anyone to come through. As soon as there was a space, Mateo slid the giant blade of his weapon through the door and into the chest of the first assailant. There was a low, wet-sounding grunt, and then the next bandit in line kicked the corpse of his companion through the door.

Mateo was forced to take a step back. But he gave no more ground. One more step and he would surrender the choke point. Without thinking, Shin stepped forward and to the side, then plunged the digging fork into the second man's neck. She'd practiced the strike a thousand times.

The man's eyes bulged, and blood spurted out from around the prongs of the fork. Shin held it in a death grip as blood sprayed across her face. It had a salty metallic taste that made her cringe.

She stood there, frozen.

Mateo reached out to pull the fork out of the man's neck, but was too late. The next attacker shoved the corpse forward, and the fork was wrenched out of Shin's hands. The weight of the dead man landing on it snapped the prongs.

Mateo swore and jabbed his polearm at the next assailant. Unfortunately, the woman was ready, and her sword parried the blow. Mateo pressed forward and drove her back a few paces. Shin looked at the now-useless fork.

She cursed herself for freezing and picked up the dead man's sword. The weapon felt heavy and awkward in her hand, but it was better than nothing. In such a narrow space, they couldn't really swing their swords, anyway. All she had to do was stab.

Shin readied herself to attack the next assailant as she watched Mateo parry a strike from the woman. He seemed to be winning.

Then his weapon's blade dropped as he grunted in pain.

The hilt of a throwing knife stuck out of her friend's arm. The woman came in for a killing blow, but Shin screamed and stabbed at her. The woman knocked the sword from Shin's hands disdainfully, then kicked Shin so hard she tumbled backward.

Shin tried to breathe and failed. The woman moved to strike the killing blow, but once again, blood sprayed across Shin as the blade of Mateo's weapon burst through the woman's chest. Shin rolled clumsily out of the way as the woman fell.

A shadow moved, and when she looked, she saw Davin standing in the doorway. Mateo pulled the dagger from his right shoulder. Blood spurted out, and the arm hung limply at his side, but Mateo held the dagger in his left hand and lowered himself into a fighting stance.

"Even with one arm, I can handle you, Davin," Mateo said.

"Probably. But can you take all the Red Aces?" Davin asked cheerily.

Shin's heart sank as three more men appeared behind Davin. Davin's grin grew wider at the looks on their faces. "You didn't think I'd come prepared?"

Mateo shot a quick glance at Shin. When their eyes met, he looked pointedly at the trap door and back to her.

"Why did you betray us?" Mateo asked, looking back at Davin.

"I don't think I'm going to tell you." Davin smiled wickedly and gestured to his men. "Kill them."

The gesture was a distraction. Davin's opposite hand snapped out and threw another knife. Shin couldn't believe how fast he was.

Mateo was faster.

He leaned to the side, letting the knife fly past him. In response, he threw the knife from his shoulder at the closest of the advancing men. The man fell backwards, clutching desperately at the hilt of the blade protruding from his throat.

Shin pulled the polearm from the corpse, looking for an opportunity to help.

Mateo dropped to one knee to avoid the sword stroke of the second man and drew a dagger from his belt. Davin lunged forward, drawing his own sword, and slashed down at Mateo.

Shin closed the distance and parried the blow, the jolt of steel on steel vibrating through her hands. Davin cut at her, and only the superior length of the polearm saved her.

"Imagine, you thinking you could teach me how to fight," Davin sneered.

Before Davin could attack again, Mateo appeared at her side and pressed forward. He attacked with such ferocity that, despite only having one arm and a dagger as a weapon, he beat Davin back six paces before the startled traitor held his ground.

"Shin, go! You have to protect the rest of them!" Mateo shouted.

Davin and his second ally were ready to join forces against Mateo.

He offered her a way out. But she didn't want to leave him.

She swore and sprinted towards the trap door. She flung it open and clamored down the ladder. Her last view before closing the door was of Mateo holding off two swordsmen with only one arm. Her heart sank when she saw four more men pour through the shattered doorway.

He had no chance, and she was no help.

She closed the door and left Mateo to die.

23

B enji sailed the skiff toward the island while Beast sat on a bench near the prow, looking off into the distance. As far as his eye could see, all that was before him was water. He knew it was an illusion, but his knowledge gave him no power to pierce the illusion. He drummed his fingers on the bench.

Benji hadn't pressed him for answers in almost an hour, but as they neared the island, he needed to try again. "Still not going to tell me?"

"No."

"It's about the sin, then?"

"It is."

"No question I can answer?"

If not for this damned illusion, the choice would be so simple. But the endless water before him hinted at something so much more than what anyone had yet told him. He shoved the thoughts aside and spun his body around so he was facing Benji. "Were you always there to recruit me?"

"No. I was one of several scouts sent to the islands,

hoping to recruit bandits. When I stumbled upon you, though, I asked Yuki if I could work with you instead of recruit you straightaway."

"Because I'm special?"

"Mock it if you want, but yes."

"So why change your mind after the Red Aces? Why recruit me now?"

"Because you've gone as far as you can alone."

Beast stared daggers at Benji, but his friend shrugged them off as though he were plated in armor. "Sure, you might cause a fair bit of mischief. Maybe even draw out a few generals into a large-scale battle. But that's where it ends. You don't have the numbers, and the mugon don't have the skills."

"And for the sin?"

Benji shrugged. "You've seen the island. Our mission is dangerous and our numbers dwindle. Before long, we won't be able to protect Samas."

"You've been doing a shitty job thus far."

Benji didn't rise to the insult. He gestured forward. "We're about to pass through the illusion."

Beast turned around, and just like before, the island appeared directly in front of him. It was no mirage, no trick he could discern. Whenever Beast pressed Benji, his friend gave the same enigmatic response about sacrifice.

They docked the skiff, and Beast wished Raya had returned with them. She'd claimed to have more to do around Dahl. But she'd been the only woman besides Yuki who'd spoken to him in weeks. Perhaps he could have convinced her to spend a night or two keeping his bed warm.

The sight of Yuki just beyond the docks killed any further thoughts of that nature.

Beast wobbled as he got out of the skiff, glad once again to be on solid ground. He'd dreamed of being a pirate, attacking the shipping lanes between the island of Samas, when he'd been a younger man. But only fools lived on water.

As it wasn't his nature to delay, he strode straight up to Yuki. Small as she was compared to him, she didn't retreat from his advance. "You've come to a decision, then?"

"I appreciate the training you've offered, but based on what I've seen thus far, I'm afraid that I have no interest in a further alliance."

Yuki didn't react, and Beast suspected she'd known of his decision before they'd landed. "Even after learning it is our tactics and training, provided by Benji, that have allowed you to experience so much success?"

"But that's the problem, isn't it? We already have the training, and I'm grateful. Your warriors are also skilled, but mere martial training isn't going to be enough against the sentinels. No matter how many punches and kicks they practice, they'll never match the sentinels, who have been practicing every day since they were old enough to walk."

It was a slight exaggeration, but only slight. Children born to sentinels were trained so young, but even older volunteers endured thousands of days of endless training. Beast couldn't duplicate that level of experience in the short time he had.

Neither could the sin.

An alliance added only complications and risk. The benefit he'd seen was negligible, so his choice was clear.

Yuki didn't even bother to dispute his conclusions. "So, you won't commit until you see our true power. I wondered if that might be the case."

That piqued Beast's interest. There had to be more to the

sin than what he'd seen. The legends had come from somewhere, and it wasn't because Hanz was better than Beast at wrestling. Islands also didn't just disappear when you weren't looking.

Martial training wasn't enough to defeat the sentinels in the fight Beast was seeking. But this, this might be. "Show me," he demanded.

He sensed Benji startle behind him, but ignored the reaction to his disrespect.

Yuki still didn't react, still refused to rise to his insults. She spoke quietly. "A warning, then, though I expect it'll bounce off that thick skull of yours. You've spent a lifetime obsessed by the sentinels, but the sentinels are only one part of a much larger problem, a much larger world than you've ever imagined. Not all problems can be solved by punching them harder."

"Seems to work most of the time."

Yuki shook her head. "I'm going to be delighted to show you our power. It will make putting up with your stubbornness worth every minute."

"Enough talk. Show me."

"Not now." She held up her hand. "One more day of patience is all I ask. If you feel the same when the sun rises tomorrow, I'll have Benji take you back to Samas. Meet me at the southern trailhead when the sun goes down tonight. I will show you that there are worse things in this world than facing down an army of sentinels. Now go, I have to prepare."

He would wait, because he sensed it wasn't wise to antagonize Yuki too much. But also because he wanted whatever power the sin offered. Still, he couldn't help pushing a little harder. "What do you need to prepare for? You need to bake a cake?"

Yuki didn't smile, but she didn't try to kill him, either. "Beast?"

"Yes?"

"Head to the armory. You're going to need one of those giant axes you're so fond of."

24

Sato stewed silently as he rode in a flanking position alongside Alonzo. It had been years since he'd acted as an escort for anyone lower than the Firstborn. The "merchant" he flanked was Crispin, and Sato had to admit, grudgingly, that they couldn't proceed any other way. That wasn't what rankled, though.

It was how much Crispin enjoyed playing the part of Sato's superior.

Sato sighed audibly, the one expression of frustration he allowed himself.

Crispin's contact, a smuggler named Wentz, believed Crispin dabbled in the same trading of information that he did. Alonzo, apparently, was no stranger to playing the role of Crispin's corrupt sentinel friend. Today, Sato joined Alonzo in the act.

Sato adjusted the nondescript armor he was wearing in lieu of his own and did his best to fight down the wave of nausea he felt at the part he was playing. The smell emanating from under his armor didn't help either. Rotting animals smelled better than he did now.

All part of the ridiculous disguise Crispin had insisted on him using.

"Stop fidgeting back there, you're going to give us away," Crispin hissed as they made their way to Yhin, the westernmost city on Iru.

Sato bit back a retort. He settled for resting his hand on the familiar pommel of his sword instead. Crispin had been concerned that Sato's armor would be recognized, and so he was forced to leave it behind. He took solace in the fact that he was able to keep his own sword at his side. Even though the weapon was a custom blade, made specifically for Sato by the finest blacksmith in Samas, the hilt and scabbard were plain. Let armor show status. A sword should never be sullied with flashy adornments.

Sato hadn't been on guard duty in ages but slid into the familiar rhythms easily enough. Crispin, for his part, played the role of a haughty sentinel perfectly. Even his riding style reeked of casual disregard for anyone below his station.

Sato's gaze and thoughts wandered. But both always returned to Crispin. The man's ability to be whoever he wanted was impressive, but as he watched the sentinel, a dark pit formed in his stomach. How could anyone trust a man for whom lies came so easily?

By mid-morning, they reached the gates of Yhin. They waited in the small line of people being studied by the sentinels at the gates. Sato didn't think he would be recognized, what with his face covered with grime and a bloody bandage wrapped around his head.

When their turn came, Crispin approached the guards disdainfully and handed over his false orders without even looking at them. Sato was disappointed by the cursory glance the guards gave the papers before waving the three of them through.

Their entrance should have been more difficult.

Crispin continued to lead the way. "We're almost there," he said. "Eyes sharp."

Sato bristled at the order but held his tongue. When they returned to camp, he imagined a long list of duties he'd assign the younger sentinel.

Crispin led them to one of the public stables within the city and deftly slipped a coin into the attendant's hand. The young woman gestured to another stable hand, who hurried off, and by the time the first attendant had led them to their appointed stalls, an army of help met their smallest need. Sato had never had his horses attended to so quickly.

In no time at all, the three sentinels were heading to their destination.

"All the public stables in Samas are paid for by the office of the Firstborn," Sato reminded Crispin. "It's against the law to pay for their services."

"Sure," Crispin replied, "but a well-placed coin can help speed the process. Time is of the essence."

"Indeed," Sato said. He kept his remaining thoughts about bribery to himself.

The three men came to an unassuming tavern a short walk from the stables. The sign was worn, but the exterior seemed otherwise well maintained. When they entered, Sato found the decor simple but clean and cared for.

It appealed to him greatly.

Crispin gestured for Sato and Alonzo to take up positions near the door while he sat down at an empty table. The tavern owner came around from behind the bar to take Crispin's order. Sato was too far away to hear the exchange, but he noticed Crispin pass another coin to the owner.

"Doesn't the tip normally come after the service?" Sato asked, turning to look at Alonzo.

Alonzo extended his hand palm down and then flipped it palm up while raising it a few inches into the air. Yes.

"Another bribe, then."

This time Alonzo shook his head, then rubbed his thumb and first two fingers together to indicate payment, or as Sato had more frequently seen while he gambled with Crispin, pay up.

"Payment in advance to meet his contact?" Sato asked.

Alonzo nodded.

Sato settled into the old habit of guard duty. He kept one eye on the room while Crispin was first served a drink, and then a meal. Crispin had some food and water sent over to his guards. The meat pie wasn't the best he'd ever had, but after so long in camps and on the road, Sato enjoyed the hot meal.

Two tables, each with two patrons, were of particular interest to him. At first, he'd dismissed them as part of the morning crowd. But they barely touched their drinks, and instead of friendly conversation, they sat silently, watching the room like hawks.

It was a well-protected tavern.

The four inside plus the one at the door made for a large payroll. And Sato didn't think the customers he saw were paying enough to support so many staff.

After Crispin finished his meal, the tavern owner cleared the plates and, as he was leaving, gestured with his free hand to a hallway that emerged from the back corner. Crispin nodded his thanks, left some coin on the table, and then stood up.

Sato and Alonzo fell into step behind their ward, and the three men came to a steep stairwell that led into the tavern's basement. At one end of the musty basement, an open door revealed a room that held baskets of vegetables.

Opposite the root cellar was another door, guarded by two large men.

One of the giants turned and rapped his knuckles on the door three times.

The door opened and a tall woman stood regarding them.

"Crispin! Good to see you again."

"Hella, you look lovely as always. Wentz away on business?" Crispin responded smoothly.

"Indeed. You're stuck with me, I'm afraid."

"Excellent. Aren't you going to invite me in?" Crispin asked.

"No," Hella responded flatly.

Sato resisted the urge to drop his hand to his sword, but Hella's tone had him ready for a fight.

"Hella, you wound me," Crispin said dramatically. "What have I done to earn your mistrust?"

"You? Nothin'. Him," she continued, pointing at Alonzo, "nothing. I know you and your sentinel friend. This one, though, I don't know. And he stands too straight."

Sato did everything to keep his face blank and impassive. Did she expect him to slouch?

Crispin made an exaggerated study of Sato. Then he nodded, an enormous grin spreading across his face. "I see your point. He's new to the payroll. We can leave him outside if you want. Your men can keep an eye on him while we do business."

Hella hesitated as she considered the offer. She glanced at her men and then back to Sato.

"Fine, but you keep his sword."

Crispin extended his hand without turning to look at Sato.

Sato imagined drawing his blade and killing everyone in

this hallway. The world would probably be a better place for it.

But he handed over his most precious possession.

"Look at how well he follows directions," Hella said with a smirk. Then she spun on her heel and walked back through the door.

Crispin didn't even spare a glance at Sato as he walked into the room with Alonzo in tow.

Sato eyed the guards. Without a sword or space to maneuver if it came to a fight, he didn't like the odds.

It occurred to him that he'd placed himself in an awfully precarious position.

And Crispin held his life in his greedy little hands.

25

———

By the time Shin reached the cave where the rest of the luan were hiding, she was sobbing.

Corin waited for her. "Did you bolt the trapdoor?" he asked.

Shin nodded, not trusting herself to speak. Corin put a hand on her shoulder and pulled a line which caused the rope ladder to fall to the ground. Now Mateo had no chance to escape.

But they'd bought themselves some time.

"He knew what he was doing," Corin said. "And the kids need us now."

Shin took a deep breath and turned to look at the twenty or so children that had made up the luan. She looked desperately at Corin. "What do we do now?"

"Mateo told me where to go. But how are we supposed to get away from Dahl? Who knows how many more bandits Davin brought?" Corin was frantic in his response.

Panic bubbled up inside Shin, and it was like she was back in the attic, hiding all over again. Corin was supposed to lead them out of here, but instead he was falling apart.

Strangely, his fear helped her focus.

"Corin?" She shook him. "Where did Mateo say to go?"

Above her, the sounds of steel against steel echoed through the trap door. Corin looked around wildly as the sound intensified and Shin shook him harder.

"Corin!" She snapped and he seemed to get himself under control, at least a little.

"Mateo left me a map. He told me to follow it, and then light this on fire when we get to our destination." Corin held out a large paper cylinder with what looked like a candle wick hanging out the bottom of it.

"And then what?"

"And then we wait. He said help would come."

It wasn't much, but it was a start. "First things first. We need to get out of these caves and away from Dahl. Gather up the luan. It's time to move."

Corin nodded and looked relieved to be taking orders.

Shin felt the opposite.

Within moments, though, Corin had the luan rounded up, and he led the way out. She took the rear, encouraging any stragglers to hurry.

Shin forced herself to ignore the fading sounds of the battle above as she navigated the narrow path through the cave. Part of her wanted to push the children into a sprint, and the other part wanted to go back and help Mateo. She did neither.

Somewhere behind her, Mateo, like her parents before him, died for her.

And once again, she fled.

By the time they reached the mouth of the cave, the moon, waning to almost nothing, was high in the sky. Shin made sure that all the children were out of the cave and then looked towards Corin. In the inky shadow of Dahl, dark thoughts filled her mind. She could slip away without notice. Corin could lead the luan wherever they needed to go, and she could find her own way. The whole world was open to her, now that she had the skills Mateo and the others had taught her.

She looked up at the moon once more.

Her parents had prepared for the day they were discovered. They'd built the hiding space and the deadfall. All so she could run while they confronted the sentinels.

Mateo had been injured, fighting against overwhelming odds. All so she could run while he held off the bandits.

Even in the fields, she'd run from her neighbors just in case they might turn her in.

Under the pale glow of the waning moon, she made a choice.

She was done with running.

Shin moved through the luan, speaking reassuring words to calm the frightened children, before approaching Corin.

"Does Davin know about the map?"

"No, Mateo only trusted me with it. Davin was too new. So long as we can get away from here without him catching us, we should be fine." Shin could hear the relief in Corin's words.

He needed a leader.

Shin turned to the assembled children. "I know tonight was scary, but you're all safe now. All of you were always talking about how lucky us big kids were to go outside the walls. Well, here's your chance! But we do have a big hike ahead of us. Do you think you can make it?"

Several of the luan loudly claimed they could.

The mood was ruined by a tiny voice from the back of the group. "Where's Mateo?"

Shin faltered for a moment, so Corin spoke. "He needed to take care of a few things to make sure that we were safe. I'm sure he'll be with us soon enough."

They began their journey, walking through the same fields Shin had traversed just weeks ago. Eventually, they turned away from the territory she knew, Corin following the directions on the map. Shin remained in the rear, glancing back every few steps, expecting the bandits to appear at any moment.

They hiked for a few hours before they hit a dense forest that separated them from the coast. Corin had to convince a few children there were no demons in the woods. Shin was reminded of her first night alone, after she had run from the only other home she had ever known.

They reached their destination well before the sun rose. Shin and Corin had each picked up one of the smaller children, and the young girl in Shin's arms was fast asleep.

All told, the children had impressed her. They'd heard few complaints, even when they pushed the kids to keep walking.

Their destination was a clearing, hard to find but frequently used. A fire pit was surrounded by several logs. The coast here dipped in such a way as to form a natural bay that would protect incoming boats from the wind.

And prying eyes.

The children plopped down thankfully, some falling right to sleep, and one of the older ones asked Corin if they could make a fire.

"I don't see why not," he responded. "The forest is thick enough to block the view from anyone who might be out there."

It didn't take them long to get a fire started. Once the

children were huddled around, Shin and Corin snuck to the edge of the beach with the tube Mateo had left them.

"Should we light this?" Corin asked.

Shin shrugged. "I think so."

"Alright then," he said. He placed the tube down on the square base.

He pulled the wick-like string away from the tube and Shin was surprised to see how long it was. They glanced at each other and then moved away from the tube as far as the wick would allow. Corin pulled out his flint.

"Here goes nothing," he said.

The wick immediately caught in the shower of sparks, but burned faster than any candle wick she had ever seen, sizzling and popping the whole way. When it burned to the end there was a brief pause. She expected the tube to catch on fire. Instead, she leaped back as there was a loud pop and a globe of blue fire shot straight into the air. The children all gasped as it caught their attention and watched in amazement as it climbed higher and higher.

BOOM!

All of the luan, Corin and Shin included, screamed and covered their ears when the blue ball exploded into a star of shimmering light that sizzled in the air and then faded.

Then it was over, and the only thing that hung more thickly in the air than the sudden silence was the strange, acrid smell of burning that wafted from the tube. They waited, but nothing else happened.

The excitement of the night over, the children began drifting off to sleep. One by one, their soft snores filled the air.

The building they'd lived in had been taken. But most of the family remained together.

As she listened, Shin thought that home was something more than the walls that surrounded you at night.

Eventually, even Corin fell asleep against a log.

No sleep would come for her, though. Not with her final images of Mateo so fresh in her memory.

Just as the sun was breaking the horizon to the east she saw a small, single-sailed boat tack its way into the bay. She nudged Corin awake. "Looks like it worked."

Corin grunted and rubbed the sleep from his eyes.

The two figures on the skiff waved when they were within view, and then one hopped out to drag the boat the rest of the way in. Shin and Corin stood up to meet them. As they walked onto shore, Shin could tell by the way they moved that the swords across their backs were not just for show.

"Where's Mateo?" the woman closest to them asked.

Corin and Shin shared a look but said nothing, and that was answer enough.

"I see. I'm sorry. He was a good man. We hoped when we saw his signal it meant he was ready to come home, but I guess..." She trailed off.

"You said you thought he might be ready to come home, where's home? Who are you?"

The woman considered for a moment and then shrugged as if coming to a decision. "We're the sin. Mateo was one of us." She looked around and took in the twenty or so children in the camp. "I guess we're going to need a bigger boat."

Shocked and confused, Shin's heart still swelled with relief.

26

———

The new moon hung in the sky, an ominous shadow over the horizon.

Though he'd seen it hundreds of times, tonight Beast found himself disconcerted by the sight. There was no good reason, though. Likely he was just still shaken by Yuki's odd request.

When he got to the trailhead, Yuki was waiting for him. She maintained the air of calm that seemed to cloak her permanently, but there was a sense of anticipation in her actions. As he got closer, he raised an eyebrow at her attire.

"I've never seen you dressed for combat," he said.

"This is not an evening to be taken lightly," she replied.

She was clad, head to toe, in well-fitted leather armor. The leather was ink black with no gloss. She seemed to melt into the long shadows of dusk. Wrapped around her torso was a long black chain. On one end was a smooth ball, and on the other, a wicked-looking stake about the size of her slender forearm.

"You look ready for whatever might come," Beast said.

Yuki looked at him for a moment. Then she uncoiled the

chain and, with surprisingly little effort, whipped the stake into a nearby tree with a *thunk*.

"This," she said, and with another deft motion, snapped the chain back into her hands and around her torso, "does not make me prepared for what we are about to see. I am prepared here." She tapped her temple with one finger. "Are you?"

"I am."

"Then come." Yuki started up the trail.

Beast struggled to keep up with the tiny sin leader as she picked her way along the dark trail. He had traveled the trail several times before. It was only a few miles long, but the incline was steep, and it made for a good, quick hike. When they reached the end of the trail, Beast followed Yuki into the familiar clearing and looked around. He'd never been here during the evening and there was an ominous feeling permeating the place that he couldn't put his finger on.

"You look unsettled, Beast. Are you afraid of the dark?" Yuki asked sincerely.

"Not the dark." Yuki's sincerity made Beast want to answer her as honestly as possible. "But this place doesn't feel the same during the day."

"That's very astute."

Beast looked around the clearing. It was large and as close to a perfect circle as he had seen in nature. Aside from the mouth of the trail, the entire cleaning was walled by sheer rock, almost as if someone had cut right into the wall of the valley that surrounded the sin village.

"Looks the same."

"It is important that you trust your feelings, Beast. Intuition, for the sin, is a tool that needs to be honed like any other skill."

"I'm not one of the sin, though I appreciate your

training," Beast responded, reminding her again that he would not be recruited.

"No, but you could be. I want you to join us, but all I will offer you is the truth."

"Truth?"

"Truth," she repeated.

Beast met Yuki's gaze for a few long moments before considering what she was saying.

"I doubt it will make a difference, but show me what you will," Beast said.

"Very well," Yuki said, and then whistled a familiar bird call.

Benji emerged from the trail that they had ascended carrying a medium-sized animal cage.

"Benji, it's time," Yuki said.

"Time for what?" Beast asked.

Yuki didn't answer. She retreated to the edge of the clearing so that her back was against the wall and motioned Beast to do the same. Benji placed the crate on the ground and lifted the pin on the door so that it fell open. A racoon trundled out and began munching on an apple that Benji tossed on the ground before joining Yuki and Beast.

"It's cute, but I've seen a raccoon before," Beast said.

Yuki gave him a withering glance and nodded to Benji, who closed his eyes and brought his hands together, palm to palm, and extended them directly out from his chest. Beast watched for a moment. There was a low hum and Benji's pinky started to glow red. A moment later, a red point of light appeared about seven feet off the ground in the center of the clearing. As Benji pulled his hands back to his chest, the red dot descended to the ground, leaving a crimson trail of light behind it.

"What..." Beast managed to get out before the light

began to part like a curtain and a hovering, formless darkness oozed out of it, "… the fuck is that?"

Yuki shushed him.

The raccoon became aware of the darkness and its hackles rose as it backed away. Just as Beast thought it would turn and run, the shadow floated closer to the terrified creature. Oddly, the raccoon calmed down and then froze. Its eyes were locked on the floating thing.

The formless nothing and the racoon were still for a few minutes longer and then the shadow began coalescing into a more solid misty darkness. It shrank down at first and then began to take the shape of the racoon. The paws formed first but quickly grew too thick and large. Enormous claws met the ground with razor-sharp edges. The legs extended back, skinny but too long to be proportionate, causing the sharp angles where the joints met to stick up over the large body before slanting back down and connecting. The body itself looked like a racoon's but was the size of a small bear and the fur bristled like porcupine quills. With the knee joints jutting up over the top of it, Beast was reminded of a grasshopper.

If grasshoppers were created in his nightmares.

Finally, the head took shape and Beast shuddered at the hideous pantomime before him. The large racoon head had a rictus grin plastered across its face that extended all the way to its ears. The teeth, sharp as daggers, that made up the smile, gnashed at the air. Dead eyes, pure white all the way through, cast about the clearing.

"That is a demon," Yuki said, answering his earlier question. Her voice remained remarkably calm.

The trance broke and the real racoon screamed, bolting towards the trail. The demon's dead eyes snapped towards it and gave chase, turning away from them. Beast acted on instinct and darted forward, burying his axe in the back of the demon.

The demon stiffened but made no sound. Beast pulled his axe out of the bloodless wound as the demon spun to face him. Though smaller than Beast, its long limbs gave it a reach advantage that forced him to dance backwards as the demon swiped at him. It only took a moment for Beast to get the timing down, and then he swung his axe to meet the demon's arms, lopping off one of its paws.

Again, the creature made no sound, and it continued to swing at Beast with its good paw, stumbling each time it had to put weight on the stump. Beast waited for the creature to stumble and then stepped forward, embedding his axe in the thing's head. It slumped to the ground.

Beast let go of the axe and whirled around to face Yuki and Benji.

"Are you mad? You couldn't give me some warning about that thing? I almost…"

Beast's words were cut short as Yuki's weapon flew past his head. He heard it impale into something behind him. Beast turned to see the stake pulled out of the demon's eye socket. He rolled backwards as the demon flailed wildly.

His axe was still buried in the demon's skull and the handle took turns pointing at each of the demon's attackers as its head moved back and forth to compensate for its missing eye.

"How is it not dead?" Beast demanded.

"You have to sever the head." Yuki spoke as though she were lecturing a child.

Beast grunted in anger, then jumped back to avoid the demon's blind attacks. The demon slashed again, but this time Beast caught the long arm and pulled it off balance, causing it to stumble forward on the stump of its other arm.

Beast pulled his axe free, then brought it down again, severing the back leg of the demon.

The demon tried to get up and face him, but immediately toppled over. Its remaining limbs were now all on the same side of its body. Beast took his time and carefully removed the last limbs. Still, the creature tried to rotate towards him, jaw snapping.

Beast looked on in disgust and then brought his axe down on the thing's neck. The head rolled forward, its tongue protruding through the teeth of its demonic smile.

"Demons? Demons are real? I thought that was a legend!" Beast roared at Yuki.

"You thought the sin were a legend, too. I told you our purpose was greater than just balancing the sentinels."

Before Beast could ask any more questions, the body of the demon shimmered with red light and turned back into the formless nothing it had once been. Beast took a step back as it rose into the air, but it shimmered crimson again before being pulled back into the rift. As the shadowy form disappeared, the red light ascended, closing the rift. Benji let out a long breath and slowly lowered himself to one knee. He was covered in sweat.

"I imagine you have some questions," Yuki said.

27

———————

S ato kept his face impassive as he stood in the dank cellar of the tavern. Inside he fumed. The two men that stood outside the door sneered at him, but Sato let their expressions wash over him.

If only they knew who he was.

They were barely worth his notice.

"You smell that?" the shorter of the men asked. He was stocky and thick through the chest. The tapestry of scars that crossed his exposed arms told the tale of a man familiar with violence.

The taller man sniffed the air. "I think I do."

"Smells like shit."

Sato met the man's gaze slowly and then deliberately uncrossed his arms and flexed his fingers into and out of fists a few times before crossing his arms again. He served the Firstborn directly. Only that fact kept these men alive.

Wisely, they didn't press harder.

The meeting only lasted about ten minutes before the door opened and his sentinels emerged. Crispin and Hella were chuckling.

They appeared to be good friends.

"Your business is appreciated, as always, Crispin. Now, get out. You sentinels make my customers nervous," Hella said.

"Until next time," Crispin said with a slight bow and then turned and strode towards the stairs. He started to hand Sato his sword back as he walked by.

"Not until he leaves the premises," Hella snapped before Sato could take the sword.

Alonzo's discreet hand gesture saved the moment. Sato would have acquiesced, but Alonzo's quick communication guided him differently.

"Boss, will you let me set this lady straight? You told me if I joined you, I wouldn't have to follow orders from cocky officers anymore," Sato said as derisively as he could manage.

"You watch your mouth around her, or I'm going to make sure you can't use it for a while," the short, stocky man said, stepping forward.

Hella, Crispin and Alonzo all gave the duelists space.

"Shut it, shrimp. Grown-ups are talking," Sato shot back at the man.

He had to admit, it felt good to let go of some of the frustration that had been building in him for weeks.

The stocky man responded by rushing forward, fists raised. As soon as he was in range, Sato snapped a kick, thrown with the momentum of his hips behind it, and smashed his shin into the outer calf muscle of his opponent's lead leg.

"Fuck!" the man cried out in surprise and pain before staggering back a step.

He advanced again, and as soon as he put weight on his lead leg, Sato kicked it again. The man fell on his ass.

"Stay down," Sato growled.

"Fuck yourself!" the man screamed and got to his feet.

This time, the man advanced more slowly, throwing clumsy punches all the way. Sato sidestepped easily and then rotated back, creating more space. The man advanced and, once again, Sato threw a kick. The man saw it coming and protected his injured leg. Unfortunately for him, the initial movement was a feint. Sato finished his third kick so that it landed flush against the side of the man's head.

The man collapsed in a heap. Sato didn't much care if he was dead or not.

"Impressive," Hella said.

Sato glared at her, grabbed his sword from Crispin, then stormed up the stairs. He didn't need to fake his anger. The day's events had taken him so far from the Path, he wasn't sure he would ever find his way back. This couldn't be what the Firstborn had wanted for him.

Sato was through the tavern and out the door before Crispin and Alonzo caught up with him. The men said nothing while Sato strapped his sword back on. Crispin led them down the alley and back onto one of the main roads before he turned and spoke to Sato.

"Good job, sir! I didn't think you had it in you."

"A little warning would have been nice," Sato said, his anger barely contained.

"She's never questioned anyone I brought along before. I guess you look too much like a righteous sentinel on the Path for your own good," Crispin chuckled.

Sato grabbed Crispin by the arm and dragged him into an alley.

"I AM a righteous sentinel on the Path!" Sato growled as he slammed Crispin up against the wall, "and you should be, too! I am tired of descending to your level, even as an act."

Crispin held up his hands. "No one who knows you thinks you're straying. And you got us out of there without killing anyone. Isn't preserving life part of the Path? Maybe getting that clean nose of yours a little dirty will make you a better sentinel."

"A better sentinel? You think YOU can make me a better sentinel?"

"Sometimes the ends justify the means!" The fear in the young man's eyes doused Sato's anger.

"That is dangerous thinking," Sato said quietly. He stepped away from Crispin. "First, it's something small. A petty infraction no one thinks much about. Then it's something a little worse. Pretty soon the ends always justify the means, and you look up one day to discover yourself so far from the Path that you can't even find the sun."

Crispin looked down into the dirt.

A few weeks ago, Crispin would have fought him tooth and nail.

Sato took a deep breath, releasing the last of his anger. They were all on unfamiliar terrain. Tearing Crispin down had been important. But it was just as important to build him back up again.

Someday, he wanted to be able to trust his young lieutenant.

"Tell me everything that happened inside the room," Sato said.

"I will, but let's keep moving. Hella will keep an eye on us, and it will look strange if I don't conduct my usual business."

Sato gestured to the main street. "Lead the way, boss."

The rest of the afternoon passed uneventfully as Crispin

made his rounds of the city. Merchants were his most common destination. Every stop was a show full of haggling and drama. Sometimes Crispin bought something, sometimes he didn't. But every stop ended with a small piece of paper being passed to Crispin in exchange for some coin.

As they walked, Crispin produced a rolled-up piece of yellowed parchment tied with a string and handed it to Sato.

"Apparently, this map will lead us to information on the mugon. I had to call in a lot of favors, and hand over a lot of coin to get this into our hands."

"A map? Do we know what we'll find there?" Sato asked and unrolled the parchment. The charcoal markings on it were crude and there were no written words, but Sato recognized the mountains that were depicted.

"An encampment, only there for another two days," Crispin answered.

"Can you trust her?"

"Is she trustworthy? No. Can I trust that she wouldn't lie to me on a transaction of this size? Yes. Wentz and Hella deal in information, like me. If word got out that a premium lead turned out to be a scam, then their business would be shot."

Sato looked up at the waning moon. Two more nights and it would complete its cycle and wax once more.

"If we head out first thing, we can make it to where the map indicates by tomorrow night," Sato said.

Crispin nodded. He'd been thinking the same.

Sato grinned. No more acting. It was time to bring the strength of his sun stalkers to bear.

28

Shin threw her arm over her face as light streamed into her eyes. She rolled over in her bed and pressed her face into the pillow. Staying in bed forever sounded far preferable to getting on with her life. Unfortunately, she fought a losing battle. Sleep receded and then the events of the past day hit her like a giant's fist.

Corin snored away in a nearby cot, as did most of the younger luan. They were housed in what Shin assumed was the guest lodge, huddled in pairs and triplets in cots or bedrolls spread out on the floor.

For now, they were safe.

Shin rose from her cot as quietly as she could and pulled on her shoes. The sun had been peeking over the horizon by the time they all got settled last night. She picked up Mateo's weapon, securing the strap over her shoulder so that it sat comfortably across her back.

When she poked her head out the door, squinting in the sunlight, she was surprised to find that it was well past midday. What she could see of the village was simple and orderly.

The sin village.

Somehow, Mateo had been connected to the sin.

A legend come to life.

Last night, she'd been too tired to ask questions. Today, though, they were almost all she had.

Her stomach rumbled and took her attention away from the sin village. The kids would be hungry, too, when they woke. Maybe food first, then questions.

"You sound hungry," a familiar voice said.

Shin jumped. She hadn't heard the woman approach on her right. "Starving. I'm sorry, I never got your name," Shin said to the woman that had come to pick them up the night before.

"You had a busy night. I'm Raya."

"Shin."

"Nice to meet you. We've been waiting for you to wake up. We have a meal prepared in one of our dining halls."

Corin chose that moment to join them at the door. When Shin looked back, she saw the luan were waking one another up. Apparently, they weren't planning on sleeping that long.

"Perfect! I think everyone will be up in a moment," Corin said.

Raya nodded politely. "I shall lead the way, then."

Raya walked a way down the road, giving Shin and Corin a few moments to organize the chaos created by a group of hungry children waking up in a strange place. As usual, the older children helped organize the younger ones. Food proved to be a reliable motivator.

Shin studied the village as she walked and found it more appealing with every revealed detail. The people that passed them smiled politely, and a few waved at the children.

Inside the hall there were plates of meat, cheese, fruits and bread laid out on the long communal tables. The luan, accustomed to eating in a group setting, found seats and attacked their food without preamble.

"You've done well to protect them," Raya said.

"It was all Mateo, he..." Shin's voice caught as the memory of last night's events resurfaced.

Raya bowed to Shin, giving her space. "Enjoy your meal. Jurian will be by shortly, and he can answer your questions."

"Thank you. How will I recognize him?" Shin asked. There were several sin helping with the meal.

"He's hard to miss," Raya replied. Then she left.

Shin sat down beside Corin and started to fill a plate.

"Seems pretty safe here," Corin said.

"I agree, but who knows how long the sin are willing to shelter us? We don't know anything about them. They aren't even supposed to be real! Are they willing to feed twenty growing children?"

"We can't go back to Dahl."

"Not now, but maybe later. If Davin is with the Red Aces, he'll run afoul of the sentinels soon enough."

"The sentinels or the mugon," Corin replied.

"Why would the mugon care?" Shin asked.

"The mugon took out the Red Aces when they refused to join them. The Beast killed their leader without breaking a sweat. After that, most of the remaining Aces joined the mugon. Though it seems like some must have gotten away. I'd bet the mugon won't take kindly to the Red Aces reestablishing themselves in Dahl."

"Who's the Beast?" Shin asked.

"The mugon leader. I've heard he's ten feet tall with a wild beard that hangs to his toes. He ties the skulls of his victims into his long hair and has eyes like fire," Corin said.

"Does he also shoot lightning out of his ass?" Shin asked.

Corin looked genuinely confused. Shin rolled her eyes and let it pass.

Her thoughts were interrupted when she saw a giant duck through the door of the dining hall. Shin had only ever seen one man in Samas of similar size, and that had been the man who helped her in Dahl.

Like the stranger, this giant radiated danger. Only his smile kept her from drawing Mateo's weapon from her back.

"Shin?" a deep voice boomed, causing all the luan to look up at him.

Shin raised her hand.

The huge man grinned wider and walked to her table. The children all stared and when he noticed, he started making faces and sticking out his tongue. The children laughed and made faces back. Suddenly, he seemed far less frightening.

"I'm Jurian. Are you done eating?" the man asked before popping some cheese and bread into his mouth.

"I am now," Shin said. Her questions overwhelmed her hunger.

"Come with me. I can show you around and answer any questions you might have."

Jurian extended a massive hand to help her up. When Shin took it, she was surprised at how gentle his touch was, even though her hand disappeared inside of his.

As soon as they left the dining hall, Jurian launched into a speech. "I'm sorry Yuki, our leader, couldn't meet with you, but she is recovering from a very important ritual. She wanted me to show you around, though. The hall that you're staying in is just one of our guest lodges, so we can easily convert it into permanent quarters for you and the others. Of course, if you prefer, there are several families that would be more than happy to take some of the children in. We weren't sure how they would feel about being separated."

"Wait, are we—" Shin began, but Jurian was pointing excitedly.

"That's one of our training rings. There are four around the village. Once they're old enough, the children can start training. It looks like there are a few ready right now!" Jurian said.

"But—" Shin tried again.

"Don't worry! Not everyone has to be a warrior, though we do insist that all sin at least know how to defend themselves. We have craftsmen and farmers as well. Now—"

"Jurian!" Shin shouted and grabbed his arms.

Surprised, the big man stopped and looked at her. "Yes?"

"Does this mean that we can stay? You don't mind taking us all in?"

Jurian looked genuinely confused for a moment, and then his face broke into what Shin suspected was a very customary grin.

"Of course! We wouldn't have brought you here otherwise."

Shin was so relieved that she embraced the giant.

"Shall I keep showing you around now?" he asked.

Shin laughed. She felt lighter than she had in ages.

They continued their tour. Both she and Corin were offered their own private quarters, and there was more to see than Shin expected. By the time the sun was going down, she was exhausted all over again. She asked Jurian if she could return to the lodge.

"Of course! You can take a few days to rest before

training starts. We will also ask that you contribute to the community in some way."

"I could probably figure out how to help with the farming," Shin said with a smile. How long had it been since her greatest worry was the harvest?

"Great! Yuki will be back tomorrow afternoon. You can meet her then. Nice to meet you, Shin!" Jurian said with a smile and a wave. Then he was gone.

Shin found Corin in the lodge with the rest of the luan. She delivered the good news to everyone and was mobbed by the excited children. Eventually, she extricated herself from the celebration and sighed in relief.

The luan had found a home.

She caught Corin's eye and motioned to the door. The two of them left the younger luan and she led him to their two small homes. The sin had considerately assigned them within a few doors of each other.

"That's yours," Shin said pointing, "and this is mine."

Corin nodded.

Shin took his hand and led him up the stairs to the front door of her new home. As she looked around, she was surprised to find that it felt like home. She could imagine herself living here.

She turned to Corin. For so long, home had been her mother and father as much as it had been the cozy house on their little farm. Now, Corin and the luan were her family. A family that existed because Mateo willed it.

She smiled as she imagined him dismissing any credit. He'd tell her that all he'd done was teach kids to steal and fight.

Hardly worthy of praise.

The thought of him laughing hit her harder than any

fist. Suddenly, she couldn't draw breath, and her lungs refused to expand.

He had started a family and welcomed her into it. And then, like her actual parents, had sacrificed himself for her.

Corin read her face. "Mateo…"

Shin looked at him silently and finally, after all the fighting, all the running and all the fear, let herself feel Mateo's death.

The two of them collapsed into each other's arms and cried.

29

"Questions? You bet your shriveled old ass I have questions!" Beast's battle rage was giving way to a more normal, everyday rage.

"There is nothing shriveled about me, I assure you." The tone of her voice was surprisingly sharp. "You did well. Most people panic the first time. You reacted quickly to defend yourself."

"I wouldn't give him too much credit," Benji chimed in. "Beast solves most of his problems by burying an axe in them." Benji's jibe dampened Beast's anger.

Beast looked between the two sin. "So, you're just going to stand here and pretend like everything is normal? Like a fucking demon didn't just become the world's most evil raccoon?"

Benji and Yuki glanced at each other. Yuki shrugged. "This is normal. You just weren't aware of it."

Beast struggled to wrap his head around this new reality. "So, in addition to balancing the sentinels, the sin fight demons?" The words were hard to say.

"We fight them as little as possible. We are the

gatekeepers of the rifts to their realm. In addition to the one before you, there are three such rifts in Samas, one on each island. We watch these rifts and highly trained members of the sin, like Benji, are able to use sacrifice to make sure they remain closed should the demons within attempt to get out."

"Or they open them to prove a point to unsuspecting recruits," Beast shot back, though his curiosity was cooling the anger in his words.

"Yes, that is something they do as well. It's a little complicated. Perhaps we should start at the beginning?" Yuki suggested.

"By all means."

"When the first Firstborn united Samas under the sun he enlisted two of his most trusted subjects to create two elite military forces to keep the fledgling empire safe," Yuki began.

"Shit, you really are starting at the beginning," said Beast.

Yuki ignored him. "The sentinels were responsible for protecting Samas from all threats posed by this realm, while the sin would protect it against threats from less natural forces, like these rifts. Fortunately, a rift is a difficult thing to create and use. Once we were able to identify their locations, we were able to focus our defense on those areas."

"From the demons?" Beast asked.

"No. Initially they were flesh-and-blood invaders like you and me." Yuki gave Beast an odd look. "Or you. Then something changed, and the invaders stopped. For a time, we thought the danger had passed, but then the demons came, and we had to renew our defense."

"That seems simple enough. Just make a choke point and kill them once they take form."

"We understand that now. But it was not always so. The first time we met the demons, we didn't fully grasp their nature, and they almost succeeded in burning Samas to the ground."

"Giant racoons almost destroyed the sun-chosen empire of Samas?"

Yuki sighed, which made Beast feel like a child. "Before it took form, what did you see of the demon?" Yuki asked.

"Not much," Beast admitted. "Some sort of shapeless darkness."

"Indeed, and then it took on the form of the racoon, yes?"

"Yes," Beast responded carefully.

"And most raccoons, they're fierce warriors? Feared by the animal kingdom?"

"No, not especially."

"And you still had a hard time taking one down, despite all your experience and training. Now imagine the demon took the form of something far more deadly."

"A skunk?" Beast laughed at the idea of giant skunks terrorizing the countryside with their smell.

Yuki ignored his jest again. "The demons, when they take form, don't just imitate the shape of their victims. They imprint the victim's knowledge and experiences into their own, newly formed brains. Those experiences are then perverted by the souls of the demons."

A shiver ran up Beast's spine.

"They feel only one emotion, anger, yet they can sense all the feelings that exist in our own realm. They crave them. Happiness, laughter, even sorrow, are all as foreign to them as you are to Samas."

"So they want... our emotions?"

Yuki nodded. "Once they get here, they seek a form to

take. They want to become human, and no matter what creature they first assimilate, they will hunt us. Jealousy becomes all they know, and it drives the one emotion they're familiar with."

"Anger," Beast said softly.

"Rage."

Beast thought of the ferocity with which the demon raccoon attacked him. He'd seen battle rage before, but that had been something entirely inhuman.

"They attempt to exact violence on whatever they can reach and that act of violence perverts their rage further. It imbues the demons with the only pleasure that they have ever known. Killing becomes the only thing they care about."

"How do you know all of this? I can't imagine you were able to interrogate one of these things. I mean, they can't talk, can they?"

Yuki sighed again, as if Beast was a particularly dense individual. "If that raccoon hadn't been there, if that demon had come out and seen you first, what do you think would have happened?"

Beast's mouth went dry as realization dawned on him.

"It would have turned into... me."

"That's what happened the first time the demons emerged instead of the invaders we had seen before. One by one, the group of elite warriors waiting to dispatch our enemies were caught in a trance, and when they snapped out of it, they were face to face with a demonic version of themselves. Worse still, they were linked to their foes. They could feel the torrent of emotions their alter egos were feeling. All but the most disciplined of the sin were cut down, by the skills that they themselves had honed over the years."

Beast could imagine the scene easily enough. What must it have been like to expect a human opponent, and to end up facing that? Even he wasn't sure he would have survived such a battle.

Yuki continued, "Those who were able to quiet the rage in their minds managed to escape. The founder of the sin was among them and got word to her counterpart with the sentinels of the nightmare that was growing beyond the rifts. In the months it took to put down the escaped demons, thousands were killed and the citizens of Samas lived in constant terror. Worse, because the demons took on the form of the sin, the people of Samas believed they were betrayed."

"What about the Firstborn?"

"He knew the truth," Yuki said. "They always have. But not even a proclamation of the Firstborn would change the memories of so many. To them, the sin were no longer guardians, but monsters. Enemies that had to be hunted by the sentinels. We had no choice but to fade into legend."

"And the rifts...?" Beast asked.

"Continue to be guarded by the sin. Our first leader created the village and hid the island. Only our ability to use sacrifice keeps Samas safe from the demons."

"That's what Benji used to close the rifts," Beast said, happy to be able to put at least part of this insanity together on his own.

"Yes. It is the true version of what street charlatans would call magic. Sacrifice allows those with the aptitude to alter the fabric of reality. For a cost. The greater the alteration, the greater the sacrifice required."

"So, being able to seal or open the rifts, that's why Benji's pinky is deformed?" Beast asked, feeling lost once more.

"Not exactly. The ability to control the rifts was a

powerful alteration that called for a terrible sacrifice. The sin's leader was able to circumvent the cost to a certain degree. She created the ability and spread the cost amongst all the sin, both present and future."

Beast wasn't sure he understood, but he nodded along. He got the sense Yuki's patience with his questions was almost at an end.

Yuki continued. "The cost to seal the rifts the first time was even higher. At the time, the founder of the sin believed the seal would last for all eternity. But the demons were stronger than she realized. They scratched and tore at her seams, and if left unattended, the rifts would tear open, and demons would flood our land. So, at the end of each moon cycle we open the rifts to release the pressure and then seal them once more."

"Like tonight," Beast said.

"Yes. We bring relatively harmless animals and open the rifts at a time of our choosing. It's like taking the lid off a pot of boiling water."

"So, when you think someone has an aptitude for sacrifice, you test them by making them face a demon version of themselves?" Beast asked. His intuitive guess was rewarded, and he was satisfied to see Yuki on her back foot for a change.

"That ritual is one of our most closely guarded secrets."

"Well, it stands to reason that if your elite sin are guarding the rifts, they had better know what it's like to be possessed. Plus, I've known Benji long enough to know there isn't much that frightens him. I imagine, once you've peered into this other realm, there isn't much here that seems frightening."

"Very astute," Yuki said in a tone that suggested she

wasn't terribly pleased by his observation. "I trust you'll keep that between us?"

"Sure. Last question: will the other rifts in Samas be opened tonight?" Beast asked.

"No, tonight was the first. Tomorrow night, the second will open and the last two nights from now. Then the moon will wax again. Each time we open the rifts, we risk being overcome. Were we to fail to stop the demons at all three rifts on the same night, we would doom Samas."

Beast shuddered and then nodded his agreement. He didn't envy the sin who would be receiving visits from these things the next two nights.

"So, will you consider joining us now that you've seen the evil we stand against?" Yuki asked. "If you truly want what is best for the lower classes of Samas, it isn't just about beating the sentinels. It's about protecting them from the shadows they don't even know about."

Beast looked from Yuki to Benji and then to the clearing floor, where the body of a bear-sized demon racoon had been before it disappeared into an inky mist.

He'd seen the sin as nothing more than a tool to prepare him for the sentinels.

Now, with his own eyes, he'd seen that they were so much more.

The decision was surprisingly easy.

"We'll start the training for the mugon tomorrow," he said.

30

The cart shook and bounced over the poorly maintained dirt roads on this part of Iru. Sato almost pitched forward before he was able to brace his stomach and keep himself upright. Never had the urge to swear under his breath been so strong.

By the sun, Crispin would be the death of him.

Sato was dressed in dirty rags. Clothes so dirty he wouldn't even have cleaned blood off his sword with them. They itched, and he had no trouble imagining small bugs climbing all over his skin. He'd be diseased by the end of the night, he was sure of it.

The clothes annoyed him, but it was the rope around his wrists that really made him doubt his sanity. In so many ways, it was such a small thing to simply lose the freedom of one's hands. But without them, Sato couldn't interact with the world. He couldn't wield his sword and bend it to his will. He was a helpless passenger.

And he hated it.

He hated Crispin for suggesting this foolish escapade.

But most of all, he hated himself for agreeing to give this a try.

He leaned to his right, pressing his shoulder against Roko's. "I still don't believe this will work."

Roko shrugged.

Crispin, sitting across the cart from him, hands also tied together, laughed out loud. "Relax, sir! If this doesn't work, we can always do it your way. We've got the time."

Six of the sun stalkers sat in this cart, three to a side on two rough benches. Another six were in a similar cart, trailing about twenty feet behind them. The remaining stalkers were riding in a loose guard around the cart.

Sato wished he could change places with one of the guards. At least they had freedom of movement. They got to wear the armor they had rightfully earned.

Sato closed his eyes and let his imagination run wild.

He imagined himself, sitting tall on a horse at the head of a charge of sun stalkers. His family armor reflected the sun, striking fear into the heart of his enemies. In his mind, they charged the mugon encampment, swords raised high, as they fought for the honor of the Firstborn.

His shoulders relaxed and his breath came easier.

It wouldn't be much longer. Soon enough, they would realize Crispin's plan was a failure. The encampment wasn't due to move until tomorrow night.

They'd attack at dawn, and his personally trained sun stalkers would begin to wipe the mugon off the face of Samas.

He couldn't wait.

This? What they were doing now? It was so far from the Path there was no way it could work. Crispin would lose face, and all would be right with the world.

They rode on.

It had all been Crispin's idea. The sun stalkers in the carts pretended to be farmers and peasants, caught by the sentinels for some crime. They would ride close to the mugon encampment and draw them out. The bait, said Crispin, would be too rich for them to resist.

And when the mugon came, they would find the "prisoners" were the very sentinels who hunted them.

The plan was dishonorable. It lacked even the dignity of an ambush.

But fresh off their success acquiring the mugon's location, Sato had let himself be swayed. Crispin had convinced him.

Roko had reassured him.

Never again, though.

He opened his eyes when someone kicked his foot. It was Crispin, smiling so widely Sato knew the news couldn't be good. A lone rider was silhouetted on the horizon, a looking glass to their eye.

This time, Sato swore.

The rider didn't stay long. They made their observations and then left.

At some time in his life, Sato must have strayed farther from the Path than he knew. And now he was paying the price for his failure.

The mugon attacked less than an hour later.

Sato watched with the detached eye of a commander.

Their tactics were better than he expected. They used the terrain well, concealing their movements until the last possible moment. They attacked with overwhelming numbers and force. Had the mugon been attacking what they thought they were attacking, Sato had little doubt they would have won the day.

The armored sentinels drew close to the carts. No enemy

commander would think much of the decision. They were just guards closing their thin ranks. But it kept them safe from what was to come.

Sato waited, judging the moment with cold precision.

There would be time to deal with Crispin's satisfaction later. His plan had worked, but they still needed to survive. There were more mugon than they expected. Even counting the sun stalkers in the cart, they were outnumbered at least two to one.

"Now!" Sato shouted.

He slid the rope from around his wrists, as the restraints had been nothing more than show. Crispin, a heartbeat faster than him, reached down and flung the dirty cloth from the floor of the cart. The light of the fading sun revealed six bows and enough arrows to take down a small army. Each of the sun stalkers grabbed their bow.

There was one moment when the enemy commander might have saved her mugon. If, at the moment they saw the bows and realized they'd been tricked, they'd turned tail, they might have survived.

But battles and troops had inertia. The charge had started, and once started, wouldn't be stopped. And no matter the sophistication of their tactics, the mugon were still peasants. They couldn't wheel a charge around the way sentinels could.

The first arrows flew from the carts as a wave, with every successive arrow launched as quickly as the sun stalker could nock a new one. The warriors selected for the carts had been those best with a bow. Standing still in a cart, they could hardly miss.

Nearly a dozen mugon fell to the first wave of arrows.

Against a better trained enemy, the result might have been different.

The mugon weren't fools. Sato didn't underestimate them. But they'd been spoiled by their success. They weren't used to being caught by surprise.

A few arrows came at the sun stalkers, but they missed their mark.

The mugon commander finally realized she had no chance. A bloody minute too late, but better than not at all. She sounded a retreat, and a few moments later, the remaining mugon were riding hard the other way. No doubt, they would return to the camp, pack up, and leave.

Alonzo caught Sato's attention. He pointed in a different direction, where a man was on foot.

Sato squinted. The man was quite a way away, but for some reason, he was difficult to see. It was almost as if he was a mirage, a trick of the light. If not for Alonzo, Sato wasn't sure he would have even noticed the moving figure.

Crispin followed their gaze, too.

Sato's heart beat faster. Finally, after all this time. They were making progress. It would have been nice if the "Beast" of legend had been leading the charge today, but progress was progress.

He didn't dare admit his satisfaction to Crispin. He'd never hear the end of it.

Two objectives warred in his mind, but it wasn't hard to satisfy both. He turned to Roko. "Take the sun stalkers and chase down the rest of the mugon. If you can get more information, that's good. But all I truly care about is that the cell is destroyed."

Roko nodded. "And you?"

"I'll take Crispin and Alonzo." The words almost hurt to say. But he trusted them now. They were both strong swords, and Alonzo's sharp eye might be necessary. He pointed in the direction of the fleeing shadow. "I believe that man might have answers."

Roko gave Sato a short bow. "Be safe, then."

Sato returned the bow. "You too, friend. They're wounded, but that's when they're most dangerous."

Roko knew already, and Sato had no doubt the captain would clean this part of Samas of all the vermin who terrorized it.

He had more dangerous prey to hunt.

31

I t had been two days since she awoke in the sin village, and she had yet to meet their mysterious leader Yuki. Shin didn't mind. True to her word, she had made her way to the fields outside the village and helped the farmers there. The simple act of putting her hands in the soil was a balm for her soul. She and Corin convened most nights to talk of Mateo.

Telling the children had been one of the hardest things she'd ever done. They'd done it the night before, around a campfire. Some had cried. Others had called her a liar. Still others clung to her, faces red and puffy. Corin stood with Shin, his hand on her back, as if to reassure her. She wanted to believe him. She wanted to believe they'd be okay. They had to feel the hurt to begin healing.

Sometimes, though, she wondered if the hurt was all that was left for them.

The sun was just dipping below the horizon when Shin finished her work for the day. She spoke with a few of the other farmers. They were kind enough, but all she really wanted was to soak in a hot spring and then have dinner with the luan.

She was glad for her new home. They all were, but since their flight from Dahl, their little family had become closer than ever. Corin, a good friend since the day they had met, had become like the brother that she had always wanted.

As if on cue, Corin, still sweaty from his day spent in the training grounds, joined her on the trail that led to the hot springs.

"Ugh, you smell like manure."

"If I didn't, I'd be doing something wrong. What's your excuse?" Shin asked.

"Very funny," Corin said and rolled his eyes.

"How was your training?"

"Good. Hanz forced a sword into my hand today and seems to think I have more potential with that than the spear."

"About time someone saw sense. You never were very good with a spear."

Corin gave her a sideways glance. "Can you blame me? Look at my teacher. She spends her days digging in the dirt!"

Unlike Shin, Corin had been excited to take the sin up on their offer of training. At first, Shin had thought part of it was to get out of any kind of real work. Now, she realized he just wanted to be ready the next time trouble visited.

"Hanz keeps asking when you're going to join us for training. I'm running out of excuses for him," Corin said.

"I'll come soon. For now, I could use a break."

Corin watched her for a long moment, and she thought he might push the issue. But then his face broke into a familiar smile.

"Fair enough."

One of Shin's favorite discoveries on the island had been the hot springs. She had never seen so many in one place. No matter the time of day, one could find a spring and wash up. And the sin clearly made use of them. They kept themselves almost as clean as sentinels.

Shin stripped naked and sighed contently as she sank down to her shoulders.

Corin wasn't ready to let it go. "Honestly, Shin, Hanz and Jurian have shown me so much already. I can only imagine what they'll do for you."

She looked up at the sky. He had to already suspect. "I don't know if I want to fight anymore."

Corin looked as though she'd hit him with a stick. Given his recent training, she could understand his view easily enough.

He wanted to be strong enough to fight the Davins of the world.

And all she wanted was to never fight anyone again.

"Davin killed Mateo. You don't think he deserves to die for that?" Corin asked.

"Of course he does!" Shin snapped. That Corin even felt like he had to ask infuriated her. "So do the sentinels that killed my parents, but guess what? I can't do anything about that, either. I'm not strong enough, and neither are you!"

The outburst rolled across the hot spring, and they stared silent daggers at one another.

Then Corin stood up. "So, you're just going to hide? While people like Davin get away with this shit? While those sentinels go and kill someone else's parents? The sin want us to help them fight!"

Corin didn't wait for an answer. He turned to leave, no doubt wanting to stomp away. But he tripped in the deep water, and he had to catch himself as he fell. He brushed his dirty hands off on his legs, leaving a muddy smear behind.

It shattered her anger. She did her best not to laugh. As she watched Corin's skinny butt stomp away, she kicked herself for snapping at him.

"I don't think your friend realizes how much a bare bottom undercuts the power of storming off in anger," a familiar voice said from behind Shin.

"Hi, Rua," Shin said without turning. "I think you're right."

"Come, I brought dinner. I thought we could walk the northern trail today."

Rua, an elder sin, was another bright aspect of the island. She'd met the older woman one night as she'd been trying to walk herself into a state of exhaustion. It was the only way she could sleep.

They'd talked for hours. It was one of those conversations that made it seem like they'd known each other since childhood. By the time they'd returned to Shin's home, Rua even knew the story of Shin's parents.

Since that night, their walks had become a regular occurrence. Rua had apparently known Mateo.

Rua had told her stories of Mateo when he was young, and Shin felt like she was finally starting to understand the man who'd given his life for a group of children.

Tonight, Shin looked up at her friend standing with a rice ball in each hand. "A walk sounds perfect."

"Great! Salmon or crab?" Rua asked, holding the rice balls out towards Shin.

"Crab! I'm starving."

Shin hopped out of the spring, dried herself off and quickly dressed. Before long, she was walking alongside Rua devouring the rice ball.

"This is delicious," Shin said between mouthfuls, "I could eat five more."

"Well, lucky for you, I already ate. These were both for you," Rua said with a wink.

Shin smiled and took the second rice ball greedily.

The two women walked in silence. Shin was still thinking about her argument with Corin and Rua seemed content to leave her to her thoughts. By the time they reached the northern trail, however, Shin was beginning to feel self-conscious about her silence.

"Sorry, I have a lot on my mind tonight. I'm afraid I'm not very good company," Shin said.

"Nonsense, you're always good company. Perhaps I should be apologizing. I came to find you for a walk, but maybe I should have given you some space after I saw you argue with your friend."

"No, I'm glad you came by when you did. I'm not angry with Corin. He just doesn't understand what I'm going through."

"Oh, he wasn't close with Mateo?" Rua asked.

"No, he was. He knew him longer, actually. They were very close."

"So, he wouldn't understand what it's like to be without a family?"

"No, all the luan were orphans. I don't know how he lost his parents, but I listened to mine die!" Shin felt her anger rising again.

"So, what is it that Corin doesn't understand?"

"He wants to solve everything with the sharp end of a sword!"

"Well, he is a young man and young men have a tendency to want to solve problems by fighting," Rua said, her tone one of commiseration.

"Exactly! He doesn't realize how hard it really is to fight."

"You told me that the two of you had to lead the children away from Dahl. Did Corin not fight anyone then?"

"No, he did. He killed one of the Red Aces," Shin said, a little chagrined.

"Perhaps he does understand, then."

Shin was suddenly very annoyed at how deftly Rua's questions had led her into looking foolish. She was about to tell her as much, but when she looked at her friend, smiling patiently, she realized that her feeling of foolishness was well deserved.

"Fine, you may have a point, but I'm not telling him he shouldn't fight!"

"Do you know that Mateo and I were very close?" Rua asked quietly.

"You told me you knew him." The quick change of subject once again cooled Shin's temper.

"He was a good friend of mine. Not many people know this. When he left, I was heartbroken. Yuki, our leader, approached Mateo about recruiting new members to our cause, so that we could better stand against the sentinels. Mateo believed that instead of recruiting the desperate into a life of violence, we could use our resources to help them. Mateo confided in me that he was leaving the sin to go help in his own way. Yuki, a staunch believer in allowing people to make their own choices, let him go. For a while, it seemed like his plan worked. But his peaceful hopes weren't enough."

"You think I should fight."

"It's not for me to say what you should do. But I am a member of the sin, so I know what I would do."

Shin walked in silence for a while and thought about that.

"It's easy for you to say that, Rua. You were born into a world where you were trained to fight from birth. I was born a farmer."

"Your parents didn't train you with a digging fork?" Rua asked.

"How did you know that?" Shin was taken aback. She knew she hadn't mentioned that bit.

"Who do you think taught the peasants how to fight in the first place? You didn't find it strange that Mateo's fighting style was the same as yours?"

"The sin taught us?"

"Centuries ago. Since then, families have passed it down through the generations in secret. We didn't like the idea of the sentinels being your only protection when we were forced to hide in the shadows."

"That's not the same, though. That training didn't do my parents any good when the sentinels slaughtered them," Shin spat, her anger rising again.

"Did your father and mother die fighting?"

Rua's question felt like a slap in the face and Shin's anger, ebbing and flowing all night, finally exploded.

"How dare you! You have no idea. There were too many of them! They would have been cut down!" Shin screamed.

"They were cut down," Rua replied calmly, and Shin regretted having told her about that terrible night.

"So that I could survive! I only escaped because of their sacrifice."

"You escaped because you fought back. They knew you were there, and they found you. You could have let yourself die, but you fought. On your terms. You used your surroundings, and you survived."

Emotions tore at Shin. She wanted to curl into a ball, but Rua's monologue continued.

"Shin, ask yourself, could your parents not have done the same? Could they not have used the land they knew to fight the sentinels on their terms?"

"Father got along with them. He outsmarted them for so long. He—" Shin's throat tightened, and she found that she couldn't speak.

"He played their game, Shin. He was too scared to fight back, so he tried to work their system and it cost him his life. Your mother's too."

Shin tried to throw a punch at Rua's face. The woman caught her wrist easily, but instead of countering pulled Shin into an embrace. Shin struggled, but it felt so good to have someone hold her that she gave in.

And realized Rua was right.

Her father chose not to fight. Not just that night, but any night. He had believed that he had to live within their system. Shin could choose another path if she wanted to.

After a few more moments, Shin disengaged from Rua and smiled at the woman through teary eyes.

"I'm sorry. You were right, I shouldn't have been angry with you."

"That's okay, child. I was speaking hard truths. It takes a strong person to hear them."

"Speaking of truths, I suppose I have some to speak to Corin as well. I should go find him," Shin answered.

She wouldn't let their disagreement be the seam that ripped and tore their family apart.

32

He was a second too late, and he knew it.

Pain exploded across the back of his head, and a moment later Beast was face-first in the sand. All he wanted was to lie there and collect his wits, but he knew such laziness would only be rewarded with more pain. Beast rolled onto his back and threw his legs up to defend what was coming next.

Hanz dove on top of him, trying to squish him like a bug. Having the big man above him was bad enough, but at least Beast could use his arms and legs to fight him off.

For a little while, at least.

Despite everything Beast had learned over the last few weeks of intense training with the twins, Hanz slithered through his defenses. He pinned Beast's limbs with his legs and secured a headlock that was already causing blackness to creep into the edges of Beast's vision.

Resigned to his fate, Beast tapped Hanz on his leg with his free hand and sweet, refreshing air started to flow into his lungs again.

"Better," Hanz said with his affable smile.

"I'd still be dead if you wanted me to be," Beast replied. He was angry, but only at himself. He kept his anger in check. A task made much easier with the knowledge of just what he was training to fight against.

"True, but last week he would have had your back. Your instincts are getting better," Jurian chimed in.

Having a conversation with one brother was the equivalent of having a conversation with both. The two seemed to know each other's thoughts so well that they conversed like one person.

Even though he was repeatedly getting his ass kicked by the brothers, he had taken a liking to them. The two men were so friendly that their identical smiles almost never left their faces, but their gregarious natures hid just how dangerous they were.

"There was a time when I couldn't remember the last fight I'd lost," Beast said ruefully.

"Sure, but how would that version of yourself stack up against you now?" asked Hanz.

"I'd kick my ass," Beast grinned.

"Besides," Jurian added, "on your feet you win nearly half the time. If you had ducked a second sooner, Hanz would have been at your mercy."

"Jurian is right. We have had the benefit of sparring each other our whole lives, of making each other better. Who was there to make you better before you met us?" Jurian asked.

Beast knew they were right, but it still irked him to have come across fighters who were better trained than he had ever encountered. They were also the biggest warriors that Beast had ever had to contend with. While he normally stood at least a head taller than his opponents, the brothers came up almost to his nose. They were also, astonishingly, broader across the shoulders and were almost as solidly built.

It wasn't until he started sparring with opponents who matched his size that Beast realized just how much he relied on brute strength to overpower enemies.

The twins sat down to rest, as was customary for the three of them once their training was complete. Beast, though, walked around the training grounds and supervised the newly arrived mugon that were there.

The alliance was in motion, the details supervised largely by Benji. All Beast had to do was train and encourage the others. The next fight was coming soon, but for now, they built their strength. Only after he had spoken with every group on the training grounds did he return to where the twins were resting.

"You were much more receptive to training today," Jurian said.

"I know," Beast said. Humility didn't come naturally to him, but he'd not thanked the two men properly for what he'd learned from them. "I haven't been doing enough to help you so far."

The brothers shared a look. "Seeing the rifts changes things," Hanz said.

"They lend a perspective to why we train," Jurian added.

"Perhaps there are some things you can't face on your own," Beast said, a little worried at how long the twins had gone without a smile.

"Your mugon will be ready," Jurian said, his face still serious.

Beast wanted to bristle at the reassurance. To snap at the twin mountains that of course his forces would be ready. They were *his* mugon, after all, the great bandit king's personal army. They couldn't fail.

But of course, they could.

In fact, they would, if faced with an army of demons from some strange, nightmare realm. Without this training, they wouldn't stand a chance.

"Who's that?" Beast asked, changing the subject.

The twins turned in the direction Beast had pointed.

"That's Corin," Hanz said.

"He came to us with the orphans from Dahl," Jurian finished.

Beast had noted their arrival. The sudden appearance of two dozen kids was hard to miss. Raya had informed him what had happened to them.

Beast figured the next time he was in Dahl, he'd have to visit the remaining Red Aces. But for now, he enjoyed the young man's attempt to learn the sword.

"He looks like he's never held a sword in his life," Beast chuckled.

"He was worse with a spear," Hanz grinned.

Beast nodded as he watched Corin. The young man was bloodied and bruised. He could hardly hold on to the wooden practice sword in his hands he was so exhausted. The sin training him attacked with a simple technique. Corin blocked the first two strikes but was too slow to stop the third that slammed into the meat of his thigh, sending him tumbling to the ground.

"Has he been doing this all day?" Beast asked.

The twins nodded in unison.

Beast got up and walked towards the young man. As he closed the distance, he watched Corin get knocked down and get back up three more times. Finally, and mercifully, he was able to block the final blow. Beast couldn't help but grin at the boy's whoop of celebration.

"How's that leg feel?" Beast asked.

Corin turned to look at Beast and his triumphant grin faded.

"It's fine, sir." Corin froze when he saw who he addressed. "Sir Beast."

"Beast is fine and I'm sure it's not. Come, let's soak in the hot springs. It'll help loosen those knots."

Beast laughed as Corin nodded, dumfounded.

They walked in silence, Beast noting how hard Corin tried not to show the pain in his leg. When they finally eased into the steaming water of the spring, Beast could see the relief on Corin's face.

"You know, if you had just blocked that strike the first time, your leg would be in much better shape," Beast said.

"I know. I tried, but the strikes come so fast and I haven't used a sword for long and—"

"Relax," Beast cut the young man off, "I'm giving you a hard time."

"Ah. Sure," Corin said, but didn't look much more relaxed.

"Why do you think you were finally able to block that last strike?" Beast asked.

"Practice?"

"I'm not testing you, I'm asking you. What do you think changed? I was watching you and there was nothing wrong with your technique. You always understood what you needed to do. So, what allowed you to finally do it?"

"I don't know. I just got mad at the end there. I was frustrated that I kept failing and my leg hurt so much. All I could think of was how mad I was. Then he attacked again, and I did it."

"Exactly," Beast said with a smile.

"Exactly what? I don't know what I did."

"Yes, you do. You said it already."

"Got mad?"

"Which led to you trusting your body."

"You want me to think less?" Corin was visibly confused.

"Not exactly, but yes. When you are learning a new technique, you need to think about it a lot. You need to focus on your body and the movements required to be effective. Once you're in a fight, though, you need to trust your body to do what you trained it to do. How many times did you drill that technique before your trainer started to come at you full speed?"

"Hundreds? I trained the same three motions for days."

"I promise you that your body knows how to do that now. There is no way you can consciously calculate those movements as fast as your body can make them. In a fight you need to use your focus to anticipate what your enemy wants to do next and let your training deal with what's happening in the moment."

Corin nodded as he connected what he had just done to the theory that Beast had laid out before him.

"I have a long way to go, don't I?" Corin asked.

"You're far from a natural. But you have more heart than most fighters I've seen. So long as you have someone with a practiced eye guiding your training, you'll do fine," Beast said.

"The sin are some of the greatest warriors I've ever seen. I'm sure I'll find someone."

"He's talking about himself, Corin," Yuki said from behind them, making Beast jump.

"By the sun, Yuki, you know I hate when you do that!" Beast snapped.

"I do. I have a task for you if you're willing."

"Do I have to fight any demons?" Beast asked.

"No."

"Then I'm willing," he said.

"Scouts on Ilos are late sending their raven. It's hopefully nothing, but my sin are never late. I'd rather not pull sin away from training your mugon, so I'm sending you," Yuki said.

"Because I fight like ten men?" Beast asked.

"Sure," Yuki replied, her tone as dry as always.

Then she was gone, a shadow once again.

Beast turned back to Corin. After thinking for a moment, he asked, "Want to come with?"

The young man sat up straighter. "Do you mean it?"

"I mean everything I say. I'm not sure why Yuki is worried about a raven being late, but it'll be good for you to come and watch how I work. You'll learn a lot."

"I'd love to come!"

"Good. But for now, it's time to rest. We'll have a big day in front of us tomorrow."

He couldn't help but notice Corin's grin, and it brought a smile to his own face.

It was good to be the bandit king.

33

———————

Sato, Crispin, and Alonzo pursued the shadow.

As the sun began to set, the shadow become harder to follow. Even in the light of day, it was hard to see the man's movements. Somehow, the eye seemed to slide off him whenever Sato tried to focus.

Between the three of them, though, they kept the man in sight, allowing enough distance so as not to be easily discovered themselves.

Sato wasn't sure they needed to worry. The man was in a hurry and never seemed to look behind him. He wasn't running away from the battle, but toward something else.

The three sun stalkers followed.

The mountains of Samas towered overhead.

Eventually, the shadow slowed. Sato thought he might be heading to Hankala but the city on the eastern coast of Iru was still too far away. The sun stalkers sank into the grass as they followed the warrior's furtive movements. Using hand gestures, Sato directed his lieutenants to spread out.

They snuck forward, their movement quieter than the breeze through the trees above.

Sato stopped when he saw the shadow meet with two others. Like the first, they were hard to see. Black clothing faded into the darkness of night, rendering them indistinct. But also, like the first, they had someplace to be. They spoke briefly to one another, then hurried on, moving even faster than before.

Sato frowned as the three men finally stopped their frantic trek at a seemingly random rock face that elevated the tree line they had been following.

"So now what?" Crispin asked quietly.

As if in answer, the first man turned his body sideways, like he was passing through a narrow crack, and then disappeared into the rock wall. The other two followed shortly after.

The three sentinels looked at each other in a moment of shock and then, as one, they sprang to their feet and ran towards the wall of rock.

Sato, not wanting to waste any time, set aside his incredulity and reached his hand out to the spot where he thought he saw the man disappear. His palm hit solid rock, and he slid it along the wall. After a few steps, his hand passed through the rock into an opening. It was narrow, but large enough for someone to pass through if they turned sideways. He couldn't understand how it was hidden behind the rock face.

"An illusion?" Crispin asked.

Alonzo shrugged and Sato shook his head. It was, but he had no idea how it had come to be.

"Come on," Sato said, and then turned and passed through the crack.

He tensed, preparing for a foreign sensation as he

passed through, but he felt nothing. Soon enough he was standing on what looked like an ordinary path through the mountains.

Crispin and Alonzo appeared behind him, and the three men walked carefully down the path. They dared not light torches lest they give away their position, but there was just enough light along the path for them to find their way. After a short walk, Sato noticed a strange glowing light emanating from a clearing at the end of the trail. They could see two of the men standing with their backs to them.

Sato pointed and Alonzo and motioned for them to move forward with swords drawn. Crispin, less adept at moving quietly, stayed behind. Sato and Alonzo closed the distance to the two men, who appeared to be completely engrossed in whatever was going on in the clearing. They coordinated their movements but just before they were in range to strike, the two warriors turned to face them. Faster than Sato could react, the enemy on his left fell, clutching his throat and gurgling in surprise. The second warrior fell a moment after, and Sato turned to see Crispin with a third throwing knife in hand. Crispin nodded, and the three men advanced into the clearing.

It was circular and ringed by high rock walls. To the far side stood the man they had followed. His hands extended out and were casting a strange red glow. In the center of the clearing, a red point of light, matching the glow from the man's hands, descended to the ground, leaving a vertical line of crimson behind it.

Sato had seen enough.

"Stop!" Sato said firmly and stepped farther into the clearing, flanked by Crispin and Alonzo.

The warrior looked at Sato in surprise and then his eyes

flicked down to watch a dark shape, maybe a rat, dart past the sentinels and down the trail.

"You fool!" The man drew his own sword, then froze, his eyes locked onto something Sato couldn't see.

And then he could.

At first it was just a dark shape, formless and barely visible against the night sky. Then slowly, it seemed to both expand and become more corporal. The first part that took on a real form was the feet. Black boots, like the ones the man was wearing, took shape. Then they extended and ended in three large talons.

The legs grew up from the oddly shaped feet and took on a slender, angular look that reminded Sato of insects' legs. The torso and arms formed next, and they had the same inhuman proportions. One arm ended in a long-fingered hand, but the other grew a blade where a hand should be.

The head was facing the man clad in black, but Sato could tell the jaw extended too far forward and the top of the skull extended backwards into an angular point. Instead of hair, what looked like coarse bristles grew into a grotesque imitation of the high ponytail that the man was wearing.

"What?" Crispin said. He ran out of words after that, and Sato couldn't blame him.

The monster's head whipped around as soon as it heard the sound.

Milky white eyes locked onto Crispin and the thing's mouth, all sharp teeth protruding out of its too-wide mouth, curved even farther into a rictus grin. Too fast for Crispin to react, the thing darted forward, sword-like arm raised, and closed the distance with the sentinel.

Its sword form was perfect.

34

———————

Shin found Corin the next morning. She was surprised he was awake so early.

Something in her friend had changed since she'd seen him the day before. He stood taller, and when he glared at her, it caught her completely by surprise.

The fire in his eyes made her back up a step.

"Corin—" She reached out to him.

"Coward," Corin cut her off. Even though his tone was low, the words hammered her.

"What?"

"You're a coward. He died for us, Shin. Died for you! He hardly knew you. He took you in, he taught you and then he *died* and all you want to do is farm on this island."

Shin tried and failed to form a response. Corin's words cut her thoughts into ribbons and froze them in place.

"You know what the worst part is?" Corin didn't wait for an answer. "It's that you're so much better than me. You already know how to fight. How to kill." Corin spat in response to her silence.

Shin's anger finally thawed her thoughts. "I don't want to

be a killer! I didn't even want to be a thief, but I had no choice. Sentinels are the murderers, not me!" She stared down at her hands. "I've killed. More than once! It's not my place to decide who lives or dies. I'm just a fucking farmer!"

Now Corin was the one frozen.

They stared at each other, each breathing hard.

Shin was the first to collect herself. She'd come here to make things right, not argue more. "I know that you've fought, too. I just can't deal with it like you."

The silence stretched between them.

"I see him every time I sleep," Corin said quietly.

"What? See who?"

"The Red Ace watching the cave. I guess he wasn't paying attention, but he didn't even see me until I stabbed him. I can't forget the look of shock in his eyes. The surprise and fear. I see that expression on his face every night."

"I didn't know." The words sounded weak.

"I tried to act like it didn't matter. Like because he deserved it, I didn't have to feel it. But it matters, doesn't it? It's always going to matter."

The two luan stood in silence for a moment. Shin took a tentative step forward, then embraced Corin. When they let go of one another, Shin felt both exhausted and relieved.

"I'm sorry," she said again.

"Me too, but what do we do now? I want to fight but I can't feel like this for the rest of my life."

"You won't," Beast's voice startled them both, "because it gets easier."

Shin glared at the giant man. "Where did you come from?"

Beast shrugged, then offered Corin a sword he was carrying. "Didn't mean to, but I'm here for Corin, and it was hard not to hear you two yelling at each other. At first, I thought it might be something important. Then I realized you were just whining like children."

Shin wanted to punch the bored look right off Beast's face. But Corin was quicker. "You say it like murdering another person doesn't matter."

Beast yawned. He looked like he hadn't slept at all. "Not even in the least."

Corin clenched his fist. "We're not like you. It matters to us."

Beast laughed. "Of course you're not like me! I'm the bandit king!" He flexed his enormous arms. "No one could be like me."

"You're saying I shouldn't fight?" Corin seemed confused, and Shin didn't blame him. She didn't understand Beast at all.

Beast squatted down, and Shin was reminded of how easily the man moved. For someone so large, he seemed more cat than human. "Not at all. Every morning when we wake up, we must fight to survive another day. But there are dozens of ways to fight and a hundred ways to win. Find your own way."

"It still sounds like you're telling him not to fight," Shin said, coming to Corin's defense.

Beast scratched behind his ear. "You're missing my point. I've known plenty of warriors in my time, all of whom fought for different reasons. Every one of them found their way. Not because they loved to fight, but because they had to. Maybe you'll claim to fight for justice. Maybe you'll make a vow never to kill again. I don't know. But fight."

"But how can we be the ones who decide who deserves to die?" Shin asked.

"Who cares?" Beast asked.

The question brought them up short.

Beast elaborated. "We all die, and it's all pretty damn meaningless. Why lose sleep over it?"

Shin saw the hole in that argument right away. "If it's all meaningless, why have you done all that you have? Why do you fight?"

"Because I love to. I love testing my strength against others and risking my life. I also believe that through my actions, I'm making the world a better place for those who can't fight like I can."

"That's awfully philosophical for the bloodthirsty Bandit King of Samas," Corin said.

Beast grunted. "Well, keep it to yourself. I have a reputation to uphold." He paused for a moment. "So, what do you think?"

Corin and Shin exchanged confused looks.

"What do we think of what?" Shin voiced the question for both of them.

"Can you handle whatever is necessary to be a part of this fight? Because if you can't, you had better decide now. Our enemies aren't going to hesitate, so you can't either."

Corin took her hand in his own and squeezed.

"I'm ready," Shin said.

"Me too." Corin nodded.

"Good, because you're both coming with me to Ilos. From what I've heard, the girl can handle herself better than you, and I might need some support."

"My name's Shin."

"And I'll consider remembering that, depending on how you do in the field with me. Ready your things. It's time to leave."

"Now?" Shin asked.

"Once we're in a boat I can sleep, because I didn't get any last night."

"Why not?" Corin asked.

"Grappling lessons with Raya," Beast answered. "She's a very enthusiastic instructor."

Shin decided she didn't want to know.

With that, Beast turned and left them, leaving Shin and Corin alone in their silence.

"Do you think he's right?" Corin asked, fingering the hilt of his new sword.

Shin made her choice. "I don't know, but I hope so. Even if he's wrong, you're not. I can't just keep letting people I love sacrifice themselves for me. I have to stand up."

Corin broke into his familiar boyish grin and drew his sword with a flourish. "And I'll stand right there with you!"

35

Beast stepped off the small boat and onto dry land with the same enthusiasm he maintained for the end of any sea voyage.

"By the sun, it's good to be back on solid dirt. We weren't meant to float across the water like driftwood."

"We know. You mentioned it about ten times during the trip," Shin pointed out.

"It's an important lesson for you to learn."

He didn't turn to see their expressions, but he assumed they were paying close attention as they pulled the skiff in. They were fortunate that he had taken them under his wing. His wisdom was too great not to be shared.

He looked around the beach, empty. That, at least, was a good sign. Whatever had happened to Yuki's watchers hadn't compromised the beach the sin used.

"The fire pit hasn't been used in several days," Corin said.

Beast had noticed the same but encouraged the young man. "Very observant. Keep your eye open for any other details."

Corin and Shin fell into step behind him. Whatever disagreement was between them had faded, which he appreciated. He would have thrown them both overboard in the middle of the sea had they continued their inane argument.

Some small part of him sympathized.

They had experienced a lot for being so young.

Just like Beast.

But he didn't have much patience for uncertainty. Warriors chose a path and followed it.

Their next location was a camp the sin sometimes used. Beast didn't expect to find the watchers there, but they might have left some message, or some other clue as to their fate.

After a few minutes of walking in silence, he turned to Shin. "That's a fine weapon, girl. It's a good choice for you, helps to make up for how small you are. Who showed you how to use it?"

"My father." Her face clouded over, but it passed quickly. "Well, he showed me how to fight with a digging fork, but it translated fairly well."

"Good man. Everyone should know how to defend themselves. Take some of the power from those thrice-fucked sentinels. How's that sword, Corin?"

"Better than the practice swords. It feels like it was made for me."

"Not for you, specifically, but Yuki selected one for your size and weight. Balance in a weapon is important."

By the sun, he was good at this.

"Beast?" Shin said from behind him.

Beast allowed himself his own smile at the heartfelt thanks he was about to receive from the young mind he was sculpting. He turned around and flashed Shin his most magnanimous smile. "Yes?"

She pointed deeper into the woods, where a shadow moved unnaturally.

Beast blinked. What he was seeing didn't make sense. The size of his opponent was all wrong. It barely looked human. A demon?

Beast only had time to loose the two-handed axe that he'd picked up from the sin village before a giant form came crashing from the trees to his left, sword drawn, and stopped to face Beast.

The two men froze and stared at each other.

Corin made confused noises that matched perfectly with Beast's feelings.

Beast was face-to-face with a man that looked just like him, if Beast were to shave his hair down to the scalp and remove his beard. The muscular man was also covered from head to toe in colored tattoos.

The man said something in a tongue Beast couldn't understand. It sounded like a question. From his body language, Beast assumed that the only reason he hadn't attacked outright was that he was just as confused as Beast at their similarities.

"Who the fuck are you?" Beast asked in response.

As soon as Beast spoke, the man raised his sword in attack. Beast swung his axe, but it was blocked by the man's falling sword. The power of the blow knocked the axe from Beast's hand.

No man had ever struck at him so powerfully.

Beast didn't waste a moment admiring the man's strength. He tackled the giant.

Even though the tattooed man was larger than either of the twins, Beast scrambled into a dominant position like the man was a child. The man thrashed around, trying to throw Beast off him with brute force.

He had no chance. Beast rained devastating punches into his face. His opponent tried to roll below him, and Beast slipped to his back and wrapped a massive arm around the man's neck. He rolled again, so that Beast was underneath him, but even with the weight, Beast didn't relent. He squeezed until the man stopped moving and then kept squeezing.

The man died, and Beast started to extricate himself from the lifeless limbs. He was proud of his work.

Unfortunately, four more of the giant men chose that moment to crash through the trees.

The reinforcements left him no time to finish his escape. Beast watched in horror as the closest attacker brought his sword down in a thrust that would impale the dead body lying on top of Beast before doing the same to him. There was nothing he could do about it.

And then Corin was there. His thrust was clumsy, but his sword struck true. Beast wasn't sure the young man had even been tall enough for the giant to notice.

Corin pulled out his sword as the man fell.

He didn't even see the backhanded blow that sent him flying into the bush.

"For fuck's sake," Beast shouted in rage. He threw the corpse off him and rolled away from the next attacker's blow. He scrambled to his dropped weapon and felt the sharp burn of steel tearing into the flesh of his arm as he got to his feet.

Shin engaged the last two assailants. She attacked and danced around the trees. She used the length of her weapon and her speed to keep the two men off balance. She didn't stay in place long enough to be hit, but she would also never land a significant blow.

He didn't mind. He wanted to be the one to land the killing blows anyway.

Beast whirled on his attacker and brought the axe down in a deadly arc. The bald man he was fighting brought his sword up to block the blow and Beast's axe shattered it. The force of Beast's blow was so strong that the axe continued down and sliced into the man's beardless face. Beast pulled the weapon out with a fluid motion and moved to help Shin.

Before he could take a step, a large figure, clad in a crimson robe, stepped out from the trees. He held his hands up and a familiar red glow emanated from them. Beast wasn't sure what was about to happen, but decided he wasn't interested in finding out. He grabbed the hilt of the giant's broken sword and hurled it at the robed figure. The red light winked out as the figure's hands clutched at the sword embedded in the center of his chest. He fell, lifeless, to the ground a moment later.

Beast returned his attention to Shin's attackers.

"Hey!" Beast shouted, causing the men to turn.

Shin used the moment to attack again, but the men were starting to understand her moves and blocked her easily. One said something to the other and the shorter of the two moved towards Beast.

"You're going to want to bring your friend," Beast said. His sneer faltered when the man stared at him, uncomprehending.

"Well, that's less fun," Beast muttered to himself as he brought up his axe.

Though he was smaller than his companions, the shorter man was clearly the most skilled with his blade. As

Beast pressed the attack, he noticed that the tattoos on the man's bare chest were weapons of all different kinds.

Then all he had time to notice was how fast the man was with his blade. The deep gash on Beast's arm was soon joined by dozens of others. They were small and shallow but still hurt and slowed him down.

Try as he might, Beast couldn't see any opening in the smaller man's defense. Beast was able to keep him at bay only because of his superior reach and strength.

Finally, Beast lowered his shoulder and charged, suffering a deep cut in exchange for closing the distance between them. The swordsman's blade cut to the bone of Beast's upper arm, and his axe fell from his numb hand.

But his good hand was now around the man's throat.

Beast grinned at the surprise on the man's face as he raised him into the air and squeezed his throat.

Desperately, the man tried to slice Beast with his sword, but Beast didn't give him that long. Beast felt the soft flesh of the man's throat crumple and give way under his grip. Once the man's windpipe was crushed beyond repair, Beast dropped him to the ground where he could drown in the open air.

Beast's satisfaction was short-lived.

A blow across his shoulders knocked the wind from his lungs and forced him to the ground. He picked up the axe with his good hand and, on instinct alone, spun around on his knees and threw up a block.

A massive hammer shattered the axe, and the only thing that saved Beast from a mouthful of the weapon was falling back on his knees. The strain of the odd position on Beast's massive thighs caused him to cry out, and he flopped backwards before scrambling to his feet.

Before him stood a monster of a man. He was a head

taller than Beast and just as muscled. He held a war hammer in his hand, and his face was plastered with a maniacal grin.

The only drawing on his wide chest was a war hammer identical to the one in his hands.

"How many of you are there?" Beast asked.

As expected, the giant didn't answer. Beast took the brief pause to check on Shin. She still darted in and out of the trees. Her attacker seemed frustrated, but Beast could see that her energy was flagging.

He had to finish this.

The feeling in his arm had started to come back enough that he could make a fist. He just didn't know how much strength it would have.

"I guess I'll just kill you with one hand," Beast growled.

The man kept grinning.

Beast charged the giant. The strategy had worked before, so he saw no reason to stop. The giant swung his hammer as fast as Beast swung an axe. Unfortunately for him, Beast had expected the speed. He stopped and let the blow pass less than an inch from his face.

Beast hadn't underestimated his opponent, but the war hammer-loving giant had.

Beast punched the man in the face. It was like hitting a rock wall. His fist ached.

Then the giant punched him in the face.

His world exploded in stars.

Then he saw red.

Beast bellowed, his throat raw, and answered the blow with one of his own. The two men went back and forth, landing punches, kicks, and knees to whatever part of their opponent's body they could reach. Wrapped up in his anger,

Beast didn't bother to block any of the blows the other giant threw. He couldn't feel them anyway.

Slowly, the bigger man retreated. Instead of answering each of Beast's blows with one of his own, he began blocking. Beast redoubled his attacks, and soon the man had fallen to his knees, arms at his sides while Beast landed blow after blow. With one last primal scream, he got his hand wrapped around the giant's chin. He yanked viciously, breaking the man's neck. The sound of it cracking echoed through the woods.

Beast dropped to one knee, panting. Blood in his nose blocked any air from getting through. Beast put a finger to his nostril and blew out a clot of blood. The moment of satisfaction was gone as, once the clot had cleared, one of his eyes swelled shut.

He heard heavy footsteps in front of him and looked up to see the last of the attackers, small cuts from Shin's weapon scattered across his flesh, standing before him.

Panicked, he looked around and found Shin. He was relieved to see that she was still alive, though she was struggling to get to her feet. Her face was pale.

Beast took a deep breath and tried to summon some last reserve of strength to kill his final attacker.

He couldn't find it.

Warm blood splattered Beast's face and the man before him looked down at the arrow through his chest in surprise. Then he toppled over.

"The Beast is mine," a voice said.

Beast couldn't place who the voice belonged to. He also couldn't figure out where it was coming from. He realized that his vision, even out of his good eye, was badly blurred.

"Davin?" he heard Shin say. It was half a question, half a statement.

He didn't recognize the name, but the vitriol in Shin's voice was enough to confirm that this was no savior.

"It's nice to finally put a face to the legendary name, even if that face is a little worse for wear."

Beast tried to formulate a response, but somehow a swarm of wasps had taken up residence inside his brain.

Beast spat on the man's foot. Looking down at the bloody mess he'd created, he wondered if the number of teeth he saw amongst the sputum was normal.

He never saw the blow that made his world go dark.

<h1 style="text-align:center">36</h1>

———

Sato watched the thing move forward, its inhuman speed incongruous with its very human training and form. Crispin was still frozen and hadn't even started to raise his sword. Sato reacted first, but Alonzo was closer. The sentinel parried the creature's first blow and forced it to retreat with a flurry of his own. The creature blocked Alonzo's attack without problem, then jumped backwards to create space.

The forms it used were familiar, though not quite the same as Sato's.

"How does it know our forms?" Crispin asked, finally coming to his senses.

Alonzo made the palm-down waving gesture with his hand. He had also noticed that the forms weren't quite the same.

Across the clearing, the last remaining human enemy snapped out of his trance. He threw a dagger at the creature.

Before it even struck, he was springing to attack.

The dagger embedded deep in the creature's stomach, but it seemed to feel no pain. It merely turned towards the man and raised its own sword. Sato made to join the fray, but Alonzo held him back.

It took Sato a moment, but he soon saw what Alonzo had noticed. The man and the creature weren't just evenly matched.

They were identical.

Their cuts and parries were mirror images of each other.

While their styles were the same, their abilities weren't. The creature used its oddly long legs to deliver a push kick that sent the man flying backwards. The man crashed into the rock wall surrounding the clearing, and Sato suspected broken ribs.

Crispin intercepted the creature before it could finish killing the man. They met with a flurry of steel, but Crispin was outmatched. Sato and Alonzo joined in, and the tide quickly turned. The long limbs and astounding strength of the creature allowed it to hold out longer than any human enemy would have, but even it had limits. Before long, it was overwhelmed. Crispin finished the fight by driving his sword through the thing's chest.

Crispin pulled out his sword and sheathed it in the same motion.

Rather than fall over dead, the creature backhanded Crispin with its off arm and slashed out at Alonzo with its sword, catching the sentinel across the arm as he tried to bring his own sword up. Sato cut into the thing's exposed shoulder. The cut was deep but didn't bother his enemy any more than being run through. In desperation, Sato kicked the creature with his full force, knocking it to the ground.

The mysterious man appeared out of nowhere and rammed his sword through the thing's abdomen, pinning it to the ground, before collapsing in a fit of bloody coughs.

"Remove its head," the man said, blood spurting from

his mouth between each word. Sato obeyed, but couldn't get inside the arcing swings of the creature's sword. Alonzo solved the problem by slicing the sword-fused arm clean off. Crispin, blood flowing from a gash on his forehead, held the opposite arm down at the wrist, negating the razor-sharp claws on its remaining hand.

Sato needed two swings to remove its head. It finally lay still.

"What was that thing?" Sato demanded of the black-clad man, but the red glow was once again coming from the man's hands. This close, Sato could see it was coming from his pinky finger. He wasn't sure if it was the crimson glow, but something about the man's finger seemed strange, like it wasn't quite solid.

Sato stepped back in surprise, joined by Crispin and Alonzo, as the body of the creature melted back into a black mist. The point of light from the man's hand was reflected for a moment at the bottom of the red line of light in the center of the clearing. It started to ascend, erasing the line as it did, and Sato was relieved to see the dark shape start to fade.

Suddenly the point of light slowed, blinked once and then descended, retracing the line as it did. The man coughed once more and then fell over, making gurgling sounds before finally lying still.

The dark shape was forming again. Sato stepped back and readied his sword, and then he couldn't move.

Sato's vision narrowed into a single point of red light, and as he focused on it, he started to feel weightless. He looked down to see that he was floating in a sea of nothingness. Sato panicked and looked around desperately for the point of light. When he found it, he focused on it. As he focused, it grew and extended towards him. Sato continued to focus, choosing the light over the threat of eternal nothingness. The line of light extended until it touched his forehead, right between his eyes.

His world exploded in a torrent of emotions.

First anger, then fear, and then elation. Every emotion he had ever felt swirled through his body in an endless cycle. Slowly, through it all, he felt a foreign force. A presence that was drawing the very essence of his being from his body. The more it drew, the farther out of the darkness Sato came.

Then he was in the clearing. He still couldn't move, but he heard Crispin calling his name and felt Alonzo trying to shake him. The red line still touched his forehead, and he followed it until he could see what it attached to.

It attached to the dark shadow taking form in front of him.

The idea of seeing a demonic version of himself was so revolting that he attempted to push back along the red line, but he could feel his will shoved aside contemptuously. Instinctively, he tried to attach his focus to anything.

That's when he saw the rift.

Not just the tiny tear that hung in the clearing, but the realm behind it glowing blood red. From it, he saw tendrils reaching out and into his world. One such tendril reached out to him, and he grasped for it like a drowning man would a rope. As soon as he touched it, the light guided him back to the connection between himself and the thing before him.

A demon.

The light unlocked the word in his head as if the knowledge were always his own.

Sato's panic dissipated as knowledge continued to flow into him. He couldn't stop the transfer of his essence, but he could draw from the demon and learn how to stop it. The torrent of his own emotions subsided as he was hit with a pure, unbridled rage like he'd never felt before. It took every lesson he'd learned in over two decades of meditation to push the anger aside and take what knowledge he could from the demon.

Outside his mind, he saw the demonic image of himself was formed up to his waist. Inside, he felt the knowledge of the rifts plant itself in his head. How they worked, and how to close them. They were from the man, dead before him.

A sin.

The legends weren't just tales.

The demon had almost completed taking on Sato's form. He felt the seal on the rift weakening the longer the demon was in this realm.

Sato saw the nightmare version of his own face forming in front of him and felt the demon trying to pull away from his mind. In that moment, he felt another presence desperately trying to enter his head. A presence the demon was holding back. Sato visualized entwining the two together and pulling. He felt the demon's hold on him separate, and in that moment, he was able to heave the other presence into his own.

Knowledge exploded so quickly that Sato, finally free from the trance, staggered backward. When the demon had taken over the sin, it had stolen all his knowledge, the same way it had stolen Sato's.

But the transfer happened both ways. Sato knew the other presence, then. The one that now shared his mind.

It was the knowledge of a fully trained, elite member of the sin.

Sato knew how to use the sacrifice to close the rift.

Relief swelled through him.

And then pain.

The demon, now fully corporeal, smashed its fist into Sato's face and he toppled backward.

Before it could finish what it started, Alonzo and Crispin were there, protecting Sato and driving back the demon.

Sato watched for a moment, stunned.

They risked their lives for him, without hesitation.

Crispin turned to Alonzo after driving the demon back a few steps. "So, if we take the head off, this thing will just try to turn into one of us, right? What do we do, just leave it?"

Sato found his way to his feet. "I know how to close the rift. It's just…" His voice trailed off.

"Just what? If you can close that thing, then do it!" Crispin shouted.

Sato hesitated, looked down at his pinky before his face returned to its normal mask of calm discipline.

For the Firstborn and for Samas, such a sacrifice meant nothing. He looked at his warriors. "When you see my finger start to glow, sever its head. Then stand back."

Crispin and Alonzo shared a look and nodded at Sato. He sat on the ground and put his palms together before extending them out from his chest.

He expected the pain, but the intensity of it still caught him by surprise. Sweat beaded on his forehead. A moment later, the pinky finger on his left hand slowly faded away, from the tip down, until nothing but the stump was left.

Then there was pain. Pain like nothing Sato had felt before. He felt the loss of his finger as if someone had grabbed it and ripped it free of his hand. But that wasn't the worst part. Slowly, centimeter by centimeter, a new finger grew to replace the old one. The flesh that grew felt foreign and wrong. It felt like it existed half in this world and half in another.

And as it flickered between both worlds, it throbbed painfully.

Finally, the process was complete, and his finger began to give off a crimson glow.

Alonzo and Crispin attacked. As Sato watched, he admired not just their skill but their coordination.

They were worthy sentinels.

Alonzo made the killing blow. Both men reflexively flinched away from a spurt of arterial blood that never came.

Again, the body disappeared into a black mist. The mist began to rise and fade as Sato raised his hands and the red point of light slowly ascended, taking with it the rift.

37

The point of the sword digging into her back cleared Shin's fuzzy head with impressive speed. The blow that had staggered her had been a glancing one. She shuddered at what would have happened if her giant opponent had landed a solid hit.

"I said, drop it!" a voice said from behind her, and the point of the sword dug deeper into her back.

Shin realized she was still holding onto Harmony and dropped it.

"Good," the voice behind her said, but the pressure on her back remained.

Shin watched as Davin taunted Beast.

The little weasel wouldn't be half as brave if the bandit king weren't mostly dead already. The titanic fistfight had saved her life. Beast, tearing down that mountain of a warrior with his bare hands, attracted her assailant the moment she was down and unable to catch her breath.

"Got him, boss," a voice called from the brush.

Shin's heart leaped when she saw a battered Corin being

dragged through the trees. His eyes were glassy, but when they threw him next to her, he was able to stand on his feet.

"How are you?" Shin asked.

"My head feels like Beast danced on it, but otherwise I'm fine," Corin said. He surveyed the tiny battlefield. "Did Beast kill all of them?"

"Pretty much."

"He did that?" one of the men behind them said. "He looks like a pile of ground meat to me."

The tone was boastful, but she heard the hints of fear and awe in his voice. These ambushers knew just how lucky they were that Beast had run into those strange attackers first.

"Get them moving," Davin ordered the other Red Aces. "I want to be back in Dahl before nightfall."

Davin led them through the trees, his Red Aces falling in behind and shoving Corin and Shin into motion. If she wasn't so scared, she might have laughed at the four men it took to drag Beast through the woods.

Before long, they came to one of the main roads of Ilos. Parked along the woods was a covered wagon. Davin directed his Aces to load Beast into the back, tied up with enough rope to connect two of Samas' islands. The wooden axles creaked ominously but didn't break.

"Into the back," one of their guards snapped.

Shin pulled herself into the carriage. Her world spun momentarily, and only Corin's steady hand on her back kept her from tumbling over.

"Thanks," she said.

Before Corin could respond, Shin was grabbed by rough, callused hands and pulled farther into the wagon. The two Aces inside proceeded to bind her hands and feet. They did the same to Corin and shoved them onto the splintered benches at the back of the wagon. She sneered at them as they left.

Shin sighed in relief when she saw Beast's massive chest rise and fall as he lay on the floor before them. She couldn't believe he wasn't dead. Some of those punches looked strong enough to break down trees.

Davin poked his head into the wagon. His grin was wide. "It's a wonderful surprise to see you two here. I figured you would end up with the mugon, but to have you show up with Beast?" He clasped his hands together in exaggerated delight. "I must truly be walking on the Path of the Eternal Sun."

"Fuck you." Shin wished she could think of something cleverer, but her head still hadn't cleared.

"Don't worry, Shin, I'll forgive the language. You're just mad I killed your boyfriend," Davin said, his voice sickly sweet.

Even though his hands and feet were bound, Corin stood and made to lunge towards Davin. He stopped short when Davin's sword came into his hand.

"Sit down, Corin. You couldn't hope to beat me if my hands were tied, and you were the one with the sword."

"I don't know why you're gloating, Davin. It took what— five, or was it six—Red Aces for you to kill Mateo? You couldn't have done that on your own," Shin said, as calmly as she could manage.

"True, but at least I had the foresight to bring all that help with me. Poor Mateo only had you two to rely on. Looks like Beast made the same mistake. Eventually, you'd think people would learn not to count on you two."

Shin imagined wiping the grin off his face with Harmony.

Davin's posture shifted, and the grin finally faded from

his face. "Mateo was a means to an end. You and the luan were even less than that. Now," Davin pointed at Beast with his sword, "I have what I want, and as soon as we get back to Dahl, the man that hired me will get what he wants. If you two cooperate, maybe I can convince him to be merciful with you."

Shin didn't trust Davin, but the more she knew of what he wanted, the better prepared they could be for whatever came next.

"What kind of cooperation are you looking for?"

Davin's grin returned. "There she is! Shin the survivor. My employer is trying to track down all the sin. They pop up throughout Samas like rodents, but we can't find the nest."

Shin kept her mouth shut.

"We're going to find it. We know there must be another island out there somewhere. We've even sent ships sailing south, but they find nothing. Just miles and miles of water."

Again, Shin said nothing. Davin looked to Corin but got the same response. He sighed deeply.

"Fine. I thought you might see reason, but keep your loyalty to these foolish assassins. I won't be able to help you later." With that, he turned to leave, but hesitated for a moment. "One more thing. Those big guys, the ones that looked like Beast, any idea who they were? Because they sure made life easier for me."

Shin had no answer to that.

"Me neither. Oh well, that they were here at all will still be information worth selling. Enjoy your trip."

Shin stared daggers at Davin's back as he hopped out of the wagon. The door slammed shut behind him. She heard a bolt slam home.

"That guy's a fucker," Beast said quietly.

"You're awake!" Corin said.

"Shhhh!" Beast hissed. "My head is killing me."

"What do we do now?" Shin whispered.

"Let's see where we end up first. I'm guessing somewhere with heavy locks on the doors. Once we get there, we'll need to find a way to escape. We need to warn Yuki."

"About what?" Corin asked.

"About the fact that her secret army of assassins ain't no secret."

38

—————

Beast's head pounded, but at least the pain reminded him he was still alive.

That was something, at least.

Still, it made thinking hard.

So, he thought out loud. "I fear Yuki is making plans based on the assumption that no one believes the sin are real." He thought of the demons, and the real task of the sin. "She needs to know, so that she doesn't fail."

"How are we going to warn them?" Shin asked.

Beast looked around their wagon. Even that simple movement made the world spin. As much as he hated to admit it, he was in no shape to fight. He didn't even think he could snap the bonds tying his wrists behind his back.

Yet.

Davin would regret picking this fight. He would regret it until the very last breath he took.

No one captured Beast. They either killed him or surrendered. Davin had guaranteed himself a slow and very painful death.

Eventually.

"I'm not sure," Beast admitted. "But I'll find a way."

Eventually, he noticed that Corin was staring at him.

More than people usually did.

"What?" he snapped.

"They looked like you," Corin spoke softly.

The words hit him like a bucket of cold water dumped over his head after a night of hard drinking. All his thoughts had been on escape. Partly because it was a priority but partly because he didn't want to face the reality of what he'd just seen.

They had been some big, mean fighters.

Ugly as a leper's dick, too, shaved and tattooed like that. But there was no denying the similarity.

They had been his people.

"Do you know them?" Corin asked.

Rage exploded in Beast's chest. "Know them? They tried to cave in my head with every oversized weapon they could find!"

Corin shrank back from Beast's anger, but Shin was all courage now that he was bound and dizzy. "Figured that was how most people reacted when they saw you."

Her biting sarcasm doused the fire Corin had started. He grunted, then laughed, even though it hurt. He liked her.

Beast leaned back, wishing the world would stop spinning around him. It made him nauseous. When he spoke, his voice sounded like it was coming from far away. "No, Corin. I don't know them."

He saw the question in the young man's eyes, but he was too afraid to ask. Beast snorted. Maybe someday Corin could ask Shin where to find his own balls. "I've always known I'm not from Samas, but I don't know where I'm from. I've never met anyone else like me."

"Who raised you, then?" Shin asked, as though she was trying to poke holes in his story.

"Some farmer who considered me a cheap two-legged horse that could plow his fields while he plowed his wife."

"I suppose that didn't end well for him?" Shin said. It was an echo of the question Benji had asked so long ago.

"Killed him when he tried to sell me to some miners. I think he knew I wouldn't put up with much more."

"And after?" For the first time, Shin seemed genuinely curious.

"I made my own way. Became a bandit king, in case you forgot."

"All alone?"

He saw something in her eyes then. She wanted him to be something that he wasn't. A hero, perhaps. Or a metaphor, some mirror for a choice she faced.

He didn't answer for a moment. She was one of the luan. Orphaned. But she'd told him her father had taught her to fight. He dredged his memory. She'd been proud of learning from her father.

Most likely orphaned by some sort of violence, then. And violence had taken her friend, too. The young man who'd organized the luan.

That was when he understood her.

He spoke loudly enough for the guards outside the wagon to hear him. "Alone? I'm surrounded by soldiers who adore me and women who want to bed me. I'm never alone unless I decide to be."

Corin's eyes lit up, a familiar expression growing on his face. Worship, maybe. Adoration, certainly. The young man needed someone who didn't blink in the face of doom. A hero who never backed down.

Shin saw through his bravado. She was too sharp not to.

But she was also smart enough to hear his answer to her true question.

Beast hadn't become the bandit king on his own. Hundreds had died to put him on his self-proclaimed throne, and even more had helped in other ways. He thought specifically of Benji's tireless efforts on his behalf.

Whatever future the girl chose, she didn't have to create it on her own.

"What will you do?" Shin asked.

"Introduce Davin's face to a brick wall, first," Beast said. "Then warn Yuki."

She gave him a look that cut off the rant he'd planned. He hadn't lied, but he also hadn't answered her real question.

He closed his eyes. His stomach was knotted in a way it never had been before, different from any nervousness he'd felt on the eve of battle. The appearance of others like him hit him harder than either Hanz or Jurian.

No, that wasn't it. Not exactly.

He'd always known there were others like him. It made no sense to assume he was one of a kind, despite all his vocal claims to the contrary.

Hell, it wasn't even that they'd tried to kill him. Most people did, at some point in time.

It was that he'd been a stranger to them.

He took a deep breath as a lump formed in his throat. He'd always known he wasn't from Samas. Always known he was different. But now he'd met his own people, and he wasn't like them, either.

Shit. He had more in common with the two brats sharing this wagon than he did with those who shared his blood.

That was a fucking depressing thought.

It took a minute, but when the constriction in his throat eased, he opened his eyes. Shin waited patiently for an answer.

He didn't have one for her.

"I don't know," he said.

The corner of her mouth turned up in a grin. Suddenly, their roles were reversed. "Well, I know one thing," she said.

"What?"

"Wherever we're going, I bet there's going to be plenty of people that need killing."

Beast laughed out loud.

He really liked this girl.

39

The gentle rocking of the ferry lulled Sato into a fitful, but desperately needed, sleep.

Two days of hard riding brought them from the highlands of Iru down to the port. They'd taken no rest there, though. They hopped on a ferry to Egzuki immediately and spent most of their afternoon crossing Versun. Now, on their second ferry trip of the day, Sato's energy finally ran out.

He lay down and fell asleep.

His sleep was fitful, filled with memories of demons and lives that weren't his own. His finger throbbed, a sensation he feared would never abate. The iron core he'd spent his whole life forming melted under the heat of his emotions.

He wasn't sure when he would know what was true and what was a lie.

When he opened his eyes, the island of Ilos was close. Despite his dreams, he'd rested longer than expected.

His dreams had brought answers, though. Or at least, explanations that deserved investigation. The sin had an island, south of Ilos. But some of the sin's most recent memories were of reports of the happenings on Ilos. Beast was there, as were lots of sin.

The three of them were to be the scouts, using Crispin's underground contacts in Dahl to dig up what information they could. The hunt was on, and Sato didn't plan on stopping until Beast's head decorated a pike in the middle of a field.

Crispin hadn't seemed enthusiastic about returning to Dahl. He hadn't explained his reticence, but he'd agreed to Sato's plan, eventually.

Crispin and Alonzo still slept, but now Sato woke them. "I want to be the first ones off the ferry," he said. Once, waking any of his sun stalkers had been the work of an hour. Now they were up in moments, alert and ready for action.

He missed Roko then. After the fight with the demon, the three of them had rejoined the sun stalkers, jubilant from their victory over the mugon. Sato had spoken with Roko privately, unwilling to share what he'd seen with everyone. Even Roko had struggled to believe, despite the evidence of Sato's strangely ethereal pinky.

Then Sato, Crispin, and Alonzo had been off again. As much as Sato wanted to bring the whole unit into Dahl, their only real chance of getting information from Crispin's contacts was to go alone. Roko and the others wouldn't be more than a day behind. By the time Sato had his information, they'd be outside of Dahl ready to ride.

They gathered their belongings and made their way above deck. The sun was just rising, and Sato took in a deep breath of the cool, salty air. He looked down at his pinky and shuddered.

More than anything, he wanted to seek the counsel of the Firstborn.

But with his new knowledge, even his trust of his

adopted father stood on shifting sands. According to the memories of the sin that now lived within him, the Firstborn knew of the existence of the sin. Had always known, as long as the office had existed.

It cast their last conversations in a new light.

When the Firstborn had spoken of the sin's organization, it hadn't been from a study of legend, but a knowledge of how they operated.

Did the Firstborn tolerate the sin because of the rifts? Or was he tied even more closely to them?

The thought made his stomach twist. Bile rose in his throat.

There had to be an explanation that made sense. Hopefully, at least part of that answer could be found in Dahl.

Crispin came and joined him at the bow of the ferry. "You sure you want to do this?"

Sato needed to know. He needed to have something to stand on, something to believe in. Crispin, Alonzo, and Roko had convinced him the Path was wider than he'd once thought. But it still had boundaries. The eternal sun still guided Samas.

Didn't it?

"I am."

Crispin nodded and looked as though he was about to turn away, then stopped. "It will be easiest for me to find my contacts on my own. Hella was suspicious enough of you the last time we met with her."

The sun stalker spoke easily to Sato. Like Roko did.

Surprisingly, Sato didn't mind.

"You still think Wentz is here?" Sato asked. That had been news Crispin had picked up on the journey here. Part of Sato was curious to finally meet this mysterious smuggler and dealer of information. Crispin didn't seem too excited to cross paths with him.

"As much as I can be. My contacts in Versun thought he was."

Once the ferry docked, they made their way to another tavern Crispin knew. One where he was on a first-name basis with the proprietor. They broke their fast together, and then Crispin left to do whatever it was Crispin did.

He'd arrange the meeting, and then Sato would have his answer.

Until then, there was little do. He turned to Alonzo. "I'm going to rent a room and catch a few hours of sleep. Would you like a room as well?" Sato said as he stood up from the table.

Alonzo shook his head and made some obscene gestures. His intent for the next few hours was clear.

Sato stopped him. "I don't want to know."

Alonzo winked at Sato before flashing him a mischievous grin.

"Just—try to be done by noon."

Alonzo shrugged before walking out the door.

Sato chuckled and shook his head.

Those two were like no sentinels he'd ever commanded before.

Exhausted, Sato paid for a room and eagerly headed up the stairs. He didn't even bother removing his armor before he collapsed into the bed.

A KNOCK on the door startled Sato out of his mercifully dreamless slumber. He sat up, immediately alert, and looked out the window. From what he could tell, it was a little before midday.

"Who is it?" he called, standing up and strapping his sword on.

"It's me," Crispin replied from the other side.

"Come in."

Crispin came through the door and closed it behind him. "I found Wentz and arranged a meeting with him." The sun stalker looked down at his feet, then looked up at Sato. There was a hint of desperation in his eyes. "I'm sorry, sir, but I have to ask again. Are you sure about this? If I bring you to him, I'll never be able to get information from him or his network again. Hell, I'll probably never be able to get any information from anyone again."

Sato couldn't believe it, but he felt a pang of sympathy for Crispin. It had never occurred to him what this would cost Crispin. Everything the devious sun stalker had spent years building was about to be destroyed.

Because of Sato.

"Once this is over, Wentz and his smuggling ring will be no more. There'd be no information to get anyway."

Crispin didn't look convinced, but he nodded.

Sato regarded the sentinel for a moment, then gestured for him to lead the way. Once they were down the stairs, Crispin fell in behind him and Sato nodded at Alonzo, who was waiting in the common room of the tavern.

The mute sentinel barely made eye contact with him.

The moment they stepped out the door of the inn, Sato realized something was wrong.

He dropped his hand to his sword, but a hand clamped down on his wrist. Then a small dagger pressed into his back. The hand on his wrist belonged to the short man with the scarred arms. One of Hella's guards.

His face was still bruised from where Sato's kick had landed.

The knife belonged to Crispin.

"Come along quietly, Sato, you're outnumbered," Crispin pleaded.

Sato glanced at Alonzo, whose hand rested on his sword. He and Crispin would be challenge enough. Sato knew their skills well. But there were three other thugs, including the one holding his sword arm in an iron grip. His chances were almost exactly zero.

He tried a different approach. "You can't parade a sentinel commander through the streets without consequence. The sentinels stationed here won't stand for it."

Crispin's chuckle was grim. "You might be surprised, sir."

The short man pulled Sato's sword out. Any chance of fighting his way out just vanished.

He'd been captured.

By his own sun stalkers.

40

———

Shin almost fell over as the wagon lurched to a halt. They must have reached the gates of Dahl. Hope bloomed in her chest. The sentinels would inspect the wagon, and Davin's plan would fall apart.

Muffled voices carried through the covered walls. She thought about shouting, but then she heard the laughter. In less than a minute, the wagon was moving again.

The sentinels at the gates hadn't even checked the wagon.

"That was quick," Corin said. He seemed to share Shin's disappointment. Just once, it would have been nice for the sentinels to do their duty.

"Are there any sentinels in Dahl that follow their precious Path?" Beast asked.

Corin laughed bitterly. "I've never seen one."

Shin had thought she couldn't hate the sentinels any more than she had before.

She had been wrong.

Their ride within the city hadn't lasted long. The wagon had pulled into a building, where they'd been escorted down to cells at the point of enough sharpened steel to supply a small army. Even if Beast hadn't been injured, dizzy, and bound, she wasn't sure he would have had a chance.

The bandit king, it turned out, was still human.

Now, sitting on the floor of a prison cell in some building in Dahl, she was happy to see Beast was once again exuding the deadly confidence he was famous for.

Corin, clearly less comfortable with the silence, looked around surreptitiously before whispering to the group, "Do we have a plan yet?"

Beast shook his head no.

"What are we waiting for?" Corin asked.

Beast shrugged.

Before Corin could open his mouth again, they heard the loud creaking of a door opening. Footsteps came down the stairs, and then a group of Red Aces entered, dragging someone with them. To Shin's surprise, it looked like a sentinel.

"Bold of them to snatch a sentinel off the street," Corin said quietly.

"I'm more interested in the two sentinels that helped bring him," Beast said.

Shin shared Beast's interest. The two sentinels in question walked by a man whose clothing was so fine he had to be a merchant. She wasn't surprised to see corrupt sentinels. But it was unusual to see them betraying one of their own.

The thugs threw the sentinel in the cell next to Beast.

"The least you could do is put this fucker in my cell so I can have some fun in here," Beast said to the Red Aces.

"Trust me, that would be no fun for you," the sentinel in the cell responded.

The Red Aces flashed obscene gestures at the prisoners as they left.

All three of them stared at the new arrival. Beast leaned over slowly and spit into the sentinel's cell. "Nice to have some company. Shame it's a filthy sentinel."

The two men stared death at one another.

Suddenly, Beast's demeanor changed. "I know who you are." He almost sounded friendly.

"Everyone knows who I am," the man sighed.

Shin frowned. She had no idea who the sentinel was.

Beast held up his pinkie. "Oh, no, I don't know *who* you are. I know *what* you are."

The sentinel looked confused for a moment before looking down at the pinky finger on his left hand. Shin hadn't noticed it until now, but it had a strange shadowy appearance to it.

"He's sin?" Shin asked.

The sentinel growled. "Never. I am a sentinel who stands proud in the light of the sun."

Beast rolled his eyes. "And an important one, given that you assumed I knew who you were. What's your name?"

The man considered Beast for a long moment and then spared a quick glance at Shin and Corin. Shin couldn't help the heat that rose in her face as she thought about everything the sentinels had done to her.

"My name is Sato. General to the Firstborn."

"And you're just going to volunteer that information?" Beast said incredulously.

"Deception may be the easier route to take, but it will lead me farther astray from the Path," Sato responded.

"Yeah, and if you talk like that, we wouldn't have believed you for very long anyway," Corin said under his breath.

"You speak truly, young man. I am not very good at lying, either. In the interest of speaking plainly, I assume that you are the Beast that I've heard about? Uniting the bandits into your so-called mugon?"

It was Beast's turn to take a long, considering look. "In the flesh."

Shin got the feeling the two men were engaged in a battle of words and wits. One that might very well determine their future.

"What is the Firstborn's favored doing in a cell in Dahl?" Beast asked.

"I am in charge of a unit dedicated to hunting your mugon down," Sato answered. "In the course of my duties I was betrayed by the soldiers under my command."

Beast grunted. "Sure is more straightforward, dealing with someone so honest."

"What is the leader of the mugon, the self-proclaimed bandit king, doing in a cell in Dahl accompanied by two youths?"

"We were investigating the disappearance of some sin on the island. Came across a scouting party of people that looked like me. I killed them, but they kicked the shit out of me. Then the remnants of the Red Aces, a bandit group I subdued a few months ago, captured us."

There was a hint of a grin on Sato's face. "See. Honesty is faster and cleaner."

Beast grunted again.

"It would seem we're at an impasse, then. Both of us would rather see the other die in these cells," Sato observed.

"True enough," Beast said. "But it seems to me that we should get ourselves out of these cells, kill some asshole Red Aces, and then figure it out on the outside. What do you say?"

Sato considered for another moment and then nodded. "I will kill you as soon as we are free. But until the moment we step out of Dahl, you have my aid."

"I'll make the same promise." Beast thought for a moment. "Maybe, during a visit, we can get into a fight. All I would need you to do is act like you don't like me and want me dead."

"I don't like you and I do want you dead."

"Perfect. See, even I believed that!"

Shin sensed that the two men were in fact starting to like each other very much, but she supposed that could just be a mutual respect between enemies. For her part, she would have been happy to run her spear through the sentinel's heart. She couldn't look at Sato without thinking of her parents.

Her hands started to hurt, and it wasn't until Corin pried her white-knuckled grip from the bars of their cell that she noticed what she had been doing. Sato, if he noticed her rage, pretended that he didn't and sat down cross-legged and closed his eyes.

"What now?" Corin asked Beast.

"Now we wait for an opportunity, whatever that might look like."

"An opportunity to work with a murdering piece-of-shit sentinel?" Shin asked.

Beast looked surprised at the venom in her voice.

Sato didn't react.

"Exactly," Beast said, his voice firm. "We don't get to choose our opportunities. We just have to take the ones that are offered to us. Be ready. Once the fighting starts, I'll need you both at your best."

Shin tried to nod, but another memory wouldn't let go. She wasn't sure she could promise Beast what he wanted.

"What is it?" Beast asked, reading her expression.

"In the woods," Shin wrung her hands together, "I held back again. I could have killed that man, but I hesitated. It could have cost you your life if Davin hadn't shown up."

Beast's face reddened and Shin braced herself for the explosion of rage she was sure was coming. Instead, Beast took a deep breath to compose himself.

"It takes time," he said through gritted teeth. "You'll do better next time."

Shin couldn't respond. She knew he was trying to make her feel better, but that didn't make her feel any less like a kid playing at war. She didn't belong here.

"The Path says that it is impossible to learn the will to fight. It must be found. Once found, though, that will can be trained into a force that no one can stand against," Sato said without opening his eyes.

"I don't need to learn the proverbs of monsters!" Shin screamed at Sato, who just continued to sit with his eyes closed.

As furious as she was at him for insinuating himself into her grief, she was far angrier that his words actually made her feel better.

41

Beast's heart pounded as he stared at the iron bars that formed his prison. He wasn't claustrophobic, but knowing that the door might not ever open again unmanned him in a way he would never admit to another.

He would have given almost anything to have Benji by his side. The man's cool detachment would focus his own mind.

It didn't help that when he closed his eyes, all he saw were the strangers who attacked him. Nor did it help that whenever he moved, his body screamed at him.

He'd not been beaten that badly by anyone since he was a child, too small to defend himself from his father's blows. Though he was fortunate most of his injuries were limited to bruises, it would be days before he could move without pain.

One problem at a time. They needed to get out of here.

The sentinel was thinking the same. "Don't suppose you have any solid plans for getting out of here?"

Bitterness dripped from every one of Sato's words.

Beast glared at the general but held his tongue.

He didn't recognize the man, but he recognized the name. Not only was Sato a general who reported directly to the Firstborn, he was rumored to be the best swordsman alive. Beast itched for the opportunity to fight him in a duel. It was a shame they had to wait.

He coughed, and his sore ribs reminded him that perhaps a delay wasn't the worst of ideas.

"Maybe we can dig our way out," Corin suggested.

A terrible idea, but Beast didn't have the heart to tell the young man that.

Sato scoffed. "How do you purpose we dig through solid stone?"

"At least he's making suggestions!" Shin snapped.

Beast sighed. Back on the island she had seemed so reasonable. Now, he wasn't sure he'd ever met someone who hated sentinels quite as fiercely as she did.

Sato did himself no favors, though. He aimed his next question to Beast. "Do your subordinates always speak so freely? Perhaps if they learned when to speak, it would help them to ensure what came out of their mouths wasn't quite so stupid."

"Enough!" Beast shouted. His voiced echoed through the empty basement. When the last echoes died, the cells were finally silent. "I know we want the Red Aces to believe we're at odds, but if we can't put our differences aside for a bit, then we'll die in here. Do you understand?"

"Yes," Corin said quietly.

"I should have shown more discipline. I apologize for my harsh words," Sato added.

Shin just glared.

"Do you understand?" Beast repeated, annoyed at

having to be the voice of reason. That was Benji's role, not his.

"Fine," Shin said tightly.

Beast thought quickly. "I do not have any plans for escape, yet. But we need to be ready for any opportunity. The Red Aces were a competent bandit group, but they were nothing special. If we're lucky, they'll make a mistake."

"I agree," Sato said. "Even trained soldiers get bored and let their minds wander when they pull guard duty. This scum no doubt lacks even a modicum of that focus."

Beast smirked at the ego of the sentinel general but kept his comments to himself.

"What if we aren't lucky?" Corin asked.

"Then we wait. Sato will no doubt soon have people looking for him, and we're the same."

Beast saw the look of dismay pass over Sato's face, but the sentinel said nothing. Beast wondered if Sato did have anyone who would look for him. They were in a bad place, if not. Yuki would be searching the southern coast of Ilos for them, not Dahl.

Well, there was nothing for it. Right now, he needed rest more than anything. "Now, I'm going to lie down and try to sleep off some of these bruises." Beast stretched out on the cell floor and closed his eyes.

Try as he might, though, he couldn't find any sleep. His mind kept wandering from the demons to the men that looked like him and back again. His accomplishment of uniting so many bandit groups suddenly seemed like it meant next to nothing.

The sound of the door to the basement opening roused him from his thoughts, and he stood up carefully. Sato was in his cell sitting cross-legged with his eyes closed. Beast snorted deeply, gathered up as much of the blood and snot from his broken nose as he could, and then fired it directly into the sentinel's face.

Sato shot up instantly and wiped his face.

"You..." Sato's beet-red face was contorted with anger, "cretin!"

Beast couldn't help but laugh at the mild language that was hurled at him with such vitriol.

"If these bars weren't here, I would teach you a lesson in respect," Sato said, pointing a shaking finger at Beast.

"I would welcome the attempt, Tiny, but it wouldn't be a fair fight. I think I'd let Shin have a shot first."

Shin grinned dangerously and made an obscene hand gesture when Sato looked her way.

"Calm down in here," one of the bandits said as they entered the room. "We can't have you killing each other before we're through with you."

The second bandit chuckled and put down the tray of food and water he was carrying on the floor of Sato's cell.

"This isn't over," Sato said before turning his back and moving to the other side of his cell.

Beast laughed arrogantly and folded his arms in a manner that he knew showed off his impressive muscles.

The Aces left without saying anything else, and Sato immediately crossed his cell and glared at Beast.

"How dare you defile me with your filth!" Sato said, his voice all steel.

"You knew the plan, we have to make them look like we don't like each other," Beast said, smirking.

"That doesn't mean you need to spit on me. Would hurling insults not have sufficed?"

"I wasn't sure if I could trust your ability to sell it. You said yourself that you aren't any good at deception."

"Please trust me when I say that there is no deception in my displeasure for your person," Sato growled in a low tone.

Beast nodded at what he assumed was the sentinel version of screaming in rage. "Alright, we can try it without the spit next time."

"Wonderful," Sato said, and then returned to the far side of the cell crossed-legged with his eyes closed once more. He ignored the trey of food sitting on the floor of his cell.

Beast went back to trying to sleep. Shin and Corin followed suit, finding spots on the hard floor to stretch out on. Beast eventually did find sleep, but his dreams continued to be plagued by ten-foot-tall soldiers rampaging across Samas. They burned and pillaged everything in front of them and tore through everything that he had fought to create. No matter how many times he woke, he would fall right back into the same dreams. Each dream was a little different, but one thing remained the same.

All the invaders bore his own manically grinning face.

42

The prison those traitorous moon-cursed sentinels brought him to was underground, making it hard for Sato to tell how much time had passed. When the single torch burning in the hall went out, no one came to replace it.

He slept, wakening to the natural rhythms of his body. He went through his normal morning routine of exercise and meditation. Imprisonment was no excuse for poor behavior.

Eventually, one of the Red Aces came down again with hard bread and moldy cheese. He and Beast had put on a show of arguing with each other, but the guard didn't seem terribly interested. He did at least replace the torch, which led Sato to believe that they should expect more company soon.

Sato's suspicions were confirmed shortly after.

The door at the top of the stairs creaked open and multiple pairs of feet came down the stairs.

"Friends of yours?" Beast asked him as sentinels came into view. He didn't recognize all of them, but he did recognize his lieutenants. His heart sank. Then it plummeted when the last figure made his way down the stairs.

"Magistrate Velor?"

"Good morning, Sato," Velor said with an easy smile.

Bile rose within Sato. The corruption of rank-and-file sentinels like Crispin was one thing. But a magistrate?

He clenched his fists and forced himself to take a deep breath.

Magistrate Velor's attention barely lingered on Sato for a moment. He only had eyes for the giant in the next cell.

"And you must be the infamous Beast! Your mugon have been causing all kinds of trouble in Samas. So much more organized than the old breed of bandit. I'm impressed."

"And frustrated, I imagine."

Magistrate Velor made a dismissive gesture. "You've certainly caused me significant losses. But nothing that can't be made right."

"What do you want?" Beast asked.

"What I want to know is if you'll tell me where the sin are hiding," Magistrate Velor asked.

"The sin? They're a children's fairy tale," Beast said with a wide smile. "You can probably find them under the beds of all the naughty girls and boys."

Magistrate Velor clapped his hands together and smiled. "You'll be a fun one to break, yes you will. But I'd expect no less from the legendary Beast!"

The magistrate turned back to Sato. "You, on the other hand, are a much thornier problem to solve. You're possibly the greatest sword in all of Samas. And favored by the Firstborn himself. Such a man would be a powerful ally. I would be remiss if I didn't at least offer you the opportunity to work with me." Magistrate Velor held up a large key and waved it in front of Sato's face.

Sato stared at the man silently.

"I didn't think so. You're far too rigid to see the sense in a little compromise."

"Far too much of a sentinel, you mean?" Sato asked acidly.

"Oh, I'm still a sentinel. I still do what is best for Samas, but I do so realistically. Honor might drive you, but you're a rare breed. You've never known true want, raised at the Firstborn's tit like you have been."

If the magistrate had been a step closer to the bars, Sato might have tried to kill him. Mastering his anger was one of the most difficult things he'd ever done.

"Other sentinels, Sato, need money. Money to feed their families, to pay for the education and sword schools their children require."

"Material goods are not a tenet of the Path," Sato growled.

"Grow up, Sato. You think like a child whose head is filled with stories. We are the ones who risk our lives to defend this land. We deserve recompense. The craftsmen and the merchants here in town understand. They know that if they provide a little extra, we will gladly defend them and their interests. It's how the system has always worked."

"That's not how things work in Bulas, under the watchful eye of the Firstborn," Sato said defiantly.

Magistrate Velor regarded him in disbelief. Then the man's smug face broke into a grin.

"Poor Sato." He laughed, loud to start, but then so loud it echoed in the narrow spaces of the cells. "Poor, poor Sato. You really believe that, don't you? The Firstborn really has kept you sheltered. Of course it happens in Bulas. The scale might be different, and the methods more subtle. But it happens."

Sato didn't have an argument. He didn't believe the magistrate, but he seemed to be the only one. Even Beast and the other prisoners stared at him in disbelief.

"The Firstborn would never allow such behavior," Sato argued.

Magistrate Velor leaned closer. Still not quite close enough to attack, but close. A vicious smile grew across his face. "Sato, he knows."

The ground opened up beneath Sato and swallowed him whole. Had his whole life been a lie?

"Will you join us now?" the magistrate asked. "You could even tell the Firstborn of our arrangement, and I am certain he wouldn't judge you your choice."

Sato didn't know what to say. Damnit, but he believed the magistrate.

But he couldn't abandon the Path.

He could bend. His time with the sun stalkers had taught him that. But he couldn't break. Not like this.

He would just as soon take his own life.

The magistrate made a dismissive gesture and turned to Beast. "And you? This would all be a lot easier if you bent the knee to me. Your mugon could continue their operations, but under my commands."

Beast's laughter came easily. "I'd tell you I'd fuck your skull, but your head's too small for my dick."

Unbelievably, Sato found that he respected Beast more than ever for that. The man didn't walk the Path, but he still possessed a perverse honor lacking in most sentinels, it seemed.

"Right, then." Magistrate Velor looked shaken, even though he was on the far safer side of the bars. He took a moment to compose himself. "Fortunately for us, we were able to round all of you up, so there's another easy solution. Beast, we'll need to get creative to get the information we need out of you. Sato, it seems we no longer require your services. We'll simply have these sun stalkers clear out the mugon, as they were always supposed to. Then our lives can all return to normal."

"They'll never listen to you," Sato said.

The magistrate laughed. "They won't have to. Crispin, I do believe you've earned yourself a command position. How does commander of the sun stalkers sound?"

When Crispin didn't immediately answer, the magistrate turned around to look at him.

"Well? How—"

The magistrate's question ended in a wet gurgle as Crispin's dagger punctured his heart.

"Sounds like we already have a commander," Crispin said, and shoved the magistrate to the ground.

The two sentinels standing guard at the stairs charged forward with swords drawn, but were cut down by the escort sentinels flanking Crispin and Alonzo. As quickly as it had started, it was over. It happened so fast, Sato wasn't sure what he'd just seen. "Crispin?"

"Sorry for all the deceptions, sir. You put me in a mighty tough spot, though."

Sato's mouth moved, but he found it hard to speak. Finally, he pushed out the easiest question. "What about them?" Sato asked, pointing at the remaining sentinels.

"Friends of ours from way back. I told them about you, and they've expressed some interest in being sun stalkers."

Alonzo tapped Crispin on the shoulder and pointed at the cell door. Crispin bent down and took the cell key off the magistrate's body. Seconds later, the door was open, and Alonzo handed Sato his sword.

Crispin briefed him. "There are maybe twenty men up top. I was hoping to have more sentinels join us, but this was all I could manage. Fortunately, we're fighting brawlers and street toughs, not real warriors," Crispin said. "I think we can make it."

"Difficult odds," Beast said. "Not insurmountable, if Sato's skill is as legendary as I've heard. Of course, there is a way to even those odds further."

Sato stared into Beast's eyes. The smart plan was to leave him here to rot. Or drive a sword through him.

But he'd agreed to be allies until they escaped.

He was torn. His duty was to kill Beast. It was far more important than his own personal vows.

It was also wrong.

He knew that.

And given what he'd just realized, he wasn't too eager to put his duty above his own word.

"Let them out," Sato ordered.

Crispin frowned. "Are you sure?"

"Just do it."

Crispin wouldn't let it go. "Sir, you understand that expressly goes against the orders we have?"

Sato's glare was answer enough.

Crispin grinned. "We'll make a proper sentinel out of you soon enough, sir."

Sato could do nothing but shake his head as his new allies were freed.

43

———

Shin and Corin followed Beast out of the cell and picked up swords of their own from the two dead sentinels. Corin smiled at the weapon in his hand, no doubt happy that he'd started training with swords, but Shin made a mental note to keep an eye out for a polearm of some sort. Beast seemed to read the expression on her face.

"Had any training with one of those?" he asked.

"Not really, no," Shin replied sheepishly.

Beast nodded and then took the weapon out of her hand, casting it away. "Maybe just stay behind me, then."

Shin was momentarily annoyed until she realized that he wasn't dismissing her abilities out of hand.

"Keep an eye out for a spear for me?" she asked.

"Will do," Beast said.

"Beast, you stay behind us," Sato said and immediately held up his hand to forestall any objections. "I don't doubt your skill, but you've got two warriors behind you without our training. Let us take the lead here."

Shin was expecting Beast to object, but the large man just nodded.

Once that was settled, Sato issued his commands, and the sentinels headed up the stairs. Beast, Corin and Shin weren't far behind, and she heard the chaos of battle the moment the first sentinels reached the top of the stairs. By the time they reached the top themselves, dead bodies were strewn about the floor. The sentinels moved like a single animal with multiple limbs. They were the calm center of a storm that was roiling around them, a whirlwind of steel, blood, and screams.

Once the Red Aces organized themselves, they pulled away from the deadly group of sentinels. There was a moment of calm as the two forces faced off against one another. Davin gestured at one of his men to get reinforcements, but Beast hurled the sword in his hand and caught the man square in the back before he could open the door. Beast gave a satisfied laugh and then picked up a large maul that one of the dead Aces had dropped.

Chaos broke out again.

The Red Aces, no longer surprised, fought better, but were still no match for the sentinels. The sun stalkers were simply the better warriors.

Some of the bandits decided that Beast and his two young companions would be an easier target.

They were sorely mistaken.

Any of the Aces that came at them were put down quickly and brutally. Corin didn't stab himself, but that was about the best that could be said for his swordsmanship. Thankfully, Beast was able to fend off his own attackers and help Corin at the same time.

"Beast, that one has Harmony!" Shin shouted when she saw one of the Aces trying to sneak around behind the group of sentinels.

Beast smashed the skull of an approaching bandit, then

sprinted forward to grab the thief by the back of his neck. The surprised bandit yelped in pain as Beast hauled him backwards and threw him to the ground.

"That's not yours," Beast said, flashing a manic grin before stomping the bandit's skull.

Before Shin had time to register how disgusting the sound of boot crushing a skull was, Beast was tossing her Harmony and turning back to join the fray. She snatched it out of the air.

She and Corin retreated a few steps to survey the battle. Most of the Red Aces were dead or trying to flee, but the sentinels had maneuvered themselves to block the exit. The prisoners had become the guards.

As the initial rush of battle faded, the smell of metallic blood and foul excrement filled her nostrils. She had assumed that once her weapon was back in her hands, she would join the fray, but fear still held her back. Corin stood next to her, equally motionless.

The remaining Red Aces were pinned against the wall and trying to surrender. Sato ordered them cut down.

The memory of the sentinel ordering her parents' death hit her with such a visceral impact that her body recoiled from the scene before her. Bile rose in her throat.

The Red Aces had no chance of victory. Their deaths were cruel.

She gripped Harmony so tightly that her knuckles turned white. But fear froze her tongue as thoroughly as her limbs.

Beast joined the sentinels in their slaughter.

He wasn't like them. Hell, he stood for everything they weren't. And yet he joined them in their grisly work.

A macabre torch lit in the darkest recesses of her mind

as she watched Beast join in the slaughter of defeated combatants.

They weren't helpless. They were still dangerous.

If left alive, they could cost the former prisoners their chance at escape.

They still needed to escape the city, and if the Aces were found by their allies, they could give information that would aid enemies in pursuing them. She felt ill over how quickly she could justify their actions.

And then she felt strangely free.

It wasn't until the sentinels were sheathing their weapons that she looked around the room for Davin. She couldn't find him among the dead bodies.

The slippery fucker had escaped again. But his Red Aces were destroyed. He had no more power.

It wasn't enough, but it was something.

She swore that if she ever came across him again, he wouldn't live through the encounter.

For now, though, escape came first.

"We should split up," Beast suggested. "We're less likely to draw attention than if we left as a group. We can move through the city and meet up at the gates. Once we're there, we'll have to come up with a plan, but at least it gets us moving."

The discussion was interrupted by the sound of the city bells signaling an emergency. The mismatched group headed outside cautiously to see what was going on. Shin left the hideout last and the acrid smell of smoke hit her nostrils.

"By the sun," Sato said in disbelief.

The city was burning.

44

———

Beast didn't let the surprise stop him for long. The city was in an uproar, which only served their purposes. He knew approximately where they were and had a rough idea where the smoke originated. He mapped out a rough route in his head to the gates.

Beside him, Crispin stood as still as a statue. "What the hell?" he asked. The young warrior couldn't seem to wrap his head around the sight.

"Whatever it is, let's take advantage of it. With any luck, the fire has pulled sentinels from the gates, and we can get ourselves out of Dahl," Sato said.

"Brilliant," Shin mocked. Her dislike of the sentinels colored every interaction between them. And Beast was getting tired of it. He hated the sentinels, too. But if not for Sato, they'd still be rotting in the cells below.

"Now is not the time for your disrespect," Sato snapped back.

"Perhaps I could offer an alternative?" a voice spoke from the shadows, causing the sentinels to draw their weapons.

A man stepped out, clad in black, hands raised high.

"Benji!" Beast said.

"Sorry to startle you," Benji said. "I was in town for another reason and was surprised to find you here. Yuki's been worried about you."

"I have news for her."

Benji looked at the motley crew surrounding Beast. "I imagine you do."

Beast frowned. "What are you doing here, and what are the fires about?"

Benji glanced toward the sentinels, his meaning clear.

"You can speak freely in front of them," Beast said.

Benji didn't look so sure but answered anyway. "The sin are attacking Dahl. I'm supposed to kill the magistrate. It's why I'm here. We believe he is using the building behind you as a sort of secret command post."

Sato's eyes almost bulged out of his skull. Beast laughed. "Well, in that case, I've bested you again, friend. He died not ten minutes ago."

Questions danced in Benji's gaze, but he said nothing. He was nothing if not adaptable. "Very well, then. I have another task I must take care of. I will leave you to whatever plans you had before."

"Mostly," Beast said, "our plans involved leaving Dahl."

Benji hesitated, then glanced at Shin and Corin. "They know the best way out. I entered the same way the luan bypassed the city gate." The younger warriors looked surprised that Benji knew that fact.

Beast considered for a moment. "Can you help me escort them to the exit? I don't want to leave Shin and Corin behind, and I gave my word I would help the sentinels escape. Then I'll join you on whatever your task is."

Benji gave the whole group a hard look. Then he nodded. "Very well."

He led them through the alleys and back ways of Dahl. He navigated the narrow passages and dark corners with an ease that spoke of tremendous familiarity. Shin, Corin, and Beast followed close behind, with Sato and his sentinels bringing up the rear.

They reached the ruins of a burned-out mill within a few minutes, and without problem.

"Here we are," Benji said.

Shin and Corin looked at the building as though it were haunted.

Beast remembered the stories of their escape from Dahl. Their friend had died here.

They'd have to put the ghosts of their past to rest, eventually. Shin especially. Beast couldn't help her with that.

Benji pointed. "Shin and Corin can lead you the rest of the way. There will be sin waiting in the caves below. Ask to speak with Yuki."

The two young luan nodded and seemed to take heart from the presence of one another.

Sato, however, seemed less than enthused. "You're going to tell me to leave the city, just when it is being attacked?"

Beast turned to the sentinel. Sato's right hand hovered near the hilt of his sword, and Beast could tell the sentinel was eager to draw his steel. The ones behind him looked like they would follow his lead.

An impressive man, to show so little fear in opposing Beast, even after he had seen Beast fight. Most men would be pissing their pants by now. Or worse.

As much as Beast wanted to test his mettle against the sentinel, now didn't seem the time. Benji was practically hopping from one foot to the other in his eagerness to be someplace else, and he wasn't a man who got excited about much. "I promised you I would be your ally until we escaped the city. I am a man of my word. If you stay, what side will you fight on? The sin, who seek to cleanse the city of the sentinels who have so corrupted this place? Or the sentinels, who bask in the heart of it all?"

The righteous sentinel had no answer to the question.

"Escape," Beast said. "Tell Yuki that I've promised you safe passage. I do not know if it will be honored, but I believe it will. Our purposes, at least for now, align."

Sato's eyes traveled around the group. Beast could see him flapping like a flag caught in the wind, blowing one way and then the next. The man had spent his whole life in service to Samas. How would such a man choose?

Finally, Sato nodded. "When we meet again, I expect a duel."

"You are one of the few sentinels to whom I would grant one."

Sato motioned to the other sentinels. They passed by Benji and Beast to join Shin and Corin.

Beast couldn't help but share a few last words of wisdom for the young warriors. He met the gaze of each of them in turn. "Fight. There aren't many lessons I can teach you, but that, at least, is one. No matter what obstacles come. No matter what shit life pours over your head. Fight. Fight until you can't anymore, and then dig deep and fight some more. It's the only way to bend the world to your will."

They stood up straighter at that. Then they led the sentinels into the old mill.

Beast hoped they straightened out their feelings. Now that his life and well-being weren't tied to their answers, he figured they could take as much time as they wanted.

"Nice speech," Benji said. "Didn't know you even knew that many words."

"Fuck you, too."

Benji chuckled. "That's the Beast I remember."

"So why are you really here?"

"Yuki sensed something unusual not long after you left. Something that made her worry enough to launch a plan we've only ever talked about before. She wants us to secure Dahl within the next day. Two at the most. She says we're out of time. Says there's another enemy out there, far worse than the sentinels."

"The demons?"

Benji shook his head. "Something else. She claims that Samas is about to be invaded."

The next time they met, Beast felt like he was going to have even more questions than usual for her. And maybe this time, she'd even answer a few of them honestly. But for now, he would accompany his friend. "So, what do we need to do? Kill a bunch of sentinels?"

Benji grinned. "Even better. We need to open the gate and let our friends in."

45

———

Sato was grateful for the close confines of the cave that ran under the walls of Dahl. The damp stone gave him something to brace himself against as the world spun around him.

A dozen small decisions, each seeming right at the time.

But now, he was running from Dahl as though the sentinels within were his enemies. Straight into the arms of the sin. People that, two weeks ago, he hadn't even believed existed.

There was no doubt the sin they'd met, Benji, had mischief and murder planned for the city. The fact Beast had decided to accompany his friend seemed evidence enough of that.

Was he still on the Path?

There was no single decision he could point to that had been against the tenets.

Yet here he was, and it certainly didn't feel like he walked the Path.

Shin and Corin were leading him out of Dahl, hopefully toward his sun stalkers.

He wasn't sure if he could take another step. His breaths didn't seem to reach his lungs. He stopped and doubled over, sweat dripping from his forehead.

"Sir?" Crispin was beside him.

Crispin.

A traitor, and worse.

Who'd risked everything to save Sato. Not because he had to, but because he'd wanted to.

Of all the sentinels in Samas, it was Crispin who displayed the loyalty Sato had always sought.

That fact lit a fire that cleared away the fog of doubt in his mind.

Sato wasn't sure of much. But for the first time, he had a unit filled with warriors who followed him not because the Path demanded it, but because they'd chosen to. When everything else twisted itself into knots, that loyalty was his lighthouse.

He would fight for them, if nothing else.

He stood up straight. Met Crispin's questioning gaze. "I'm good."

And he meant it.

The caves were small, more suitable for children than for full-grown adults. It was probably a good thing Beast hadn't joined them. If he had, he probably would have gotten stuck.

Although, Sato thought, that might have made everything he'd recently gone through worth it.

They came across two of the black-clad sin. Sato let Shin and Corin speak for the party. Their word carried much more weight, in this moment, than one of the Firstborn's top generals.

Corin broke away from the conversation and came to the sentinels. Although Shin was clearly the leader between the two of them, she wasn't going to approach Sato unless she had to.

The girl hated him, though he wasn't quite sure why. He was certain their paths had never crossed before.

"They'll escort us out of Dahl," Corin said. "They've promised you safe passage, at least until you meet with a commander."

Sato nodded. It was a generous gesture, and no more than he had hoped for.

A few minutes later, they were out of Dahl and hurrying out of bow range. Once safe, their pace slowed. Sato found that he breathed easier out here, away from the walls of that cursed place. The city rotted from the inside. It was as close to the opposite of Bulas as he could imagine.

With the immediate danger past, Sato began to think of everything that had happened. He had questions, and the sentinel walking beside him had some of the answers.

"How much of this did you know?" Sato asked Crispin.

"You mean Magistrate Velor?" Crispin grimaced. "He found me a long time ago. Once I started to demonstrate talents that were outside the tenets of the Path, he used Wentz to reach out to me. I'd been working for him for years before you recruited me."

Sato hesitated before asking the next question. He didn't want to know, and yet he had to know the answer. "Why did you do it? You could have just warned me about Wentz and Velor. We could have gone in with the sun stalkers."

"It was too late, Sato. The minute we stepped into Dahl, Wentz was onto us. Your face is too recognizable. You never would have survived if you brought the sun stalkers into the city. You would have found an arrow in your throat before you'd even prepared for battle."

"So why the deception?"

"Would you have listened to me if I told you everything, and told you to stay clear of Dahl?"

Sato admitted he wouldn't have.

"Velor's greed was his downfall. He thought there was a small chance that you might choose to join him. He'd heard about the sun stalkers and wondered if your adherence to the Path had grown more flexible. At the very least, he believed capturing you alive worth the risk. You are, after all, the Firstborn's favorite. Knowing you would be safe, at least for a few days, I decided on this approach."

Sato supposed Crispin's strategy had worked, but he didn't understand. "If this corruption has spread to the other magistrates, then what need would he have for me?"

"They're all constantly competing for power and wealth. Velor would have used an alliance with you to further his own ends above the others."

Sato considered the younger sentinel's words.

Samas was not what he had grown up believing it was.

But Crispin was far more of a sentinel than he'd believed him to be.

He stepped ahead of Crispin, then stopped. He bowed deeply to Crispin, then to Alonzo. "Thank you."

Crispin nodded, but Sato thought he saw the man's eyes glistening in the moonlight.

THIS LEG of their journey ended just beyond the sight of the walls. One moment, they were a small party walking through the grass. The next, they were surrounded by dark figures.

"General Sato, I am honored to meet you," a small but imposing woman said with a bow.

"You must be the leader of the sin," Sato said, certain his appraisal was correct. The inner strength radiating from the woman was incredible.

"I am. My name is Yuki, and I have a proposition for you."

"Help you take over Dahl?" Sato responded.

She gave him a small smile. A smile that told him she knew far more about everything happening than he did. "You may call it a conquest, but perhaps a liberation is more apt? I've been informed that Magistrate Velor had you in his cells. That you were captured in broad daylight, and that not a single sentinel walked the Path to defend you. After all that, do you still believe the citizens of Dahl are best served by the sentinels currently stationed there?"

She raised fair points, but his stomach churned at the idea of fighting against sentinels. "You expect me to believe that acting against my own order could be anything but treason?"

"I suppose it's a matter of perspective," Yuki replied without taking her eyes off Sato. "In this case, treason against the sentinels in Dahl is actually in service of Samas."

He glared at her. He didn't like the way she manipulated words, and it solidified his resistance. "I won't allow my sun stalkers to fight other sentinels."

"You're not really in a position to bargain," Yuki said.

They stared at each other for several long seconds.

"What if I told you the sentinels in Dahl are not our true enemy?"

"You twist words until you could convince a child that killing their parents was honorable and just. Speak plainly."

If his words had any effect on her, he couldn't see them.

"I am speaking plainly. We will kill the sentinels in Dahl.

Perhaps you would agree they deserve their fate." She gestured toward his pinkie. "But you have seen our true enemy."

"You're besieging Dahl to fight demons?" He didn't believe her in the least.

"No," she said. "To fight the Maramans."

Sato almost threw up his hands. "Who are the Maramans?"

"You've met Beast. He's one of them, even if he was raised here. Imagine a whole people of such strength. A people who have made weapons of the very demons you've fought."

Sato's world froze in place. Beast and the demons. The two most terrifying foes he'd faced in the past few weeks. "You speak true?"

Yuki nodded. "They come, even now. The sin don't take Dahl because of some sense of justice. We take Dahl because we need thick walls between us and the force that is somewhere out there."

Sato wasn't sure he could bring himself to believe.

It seemed too convenient a justification.

"A different proposition, then," Yuki said. "I will guarantee safe passage to your sun stalkers. Rough waters delayed their arrival, but they come. By the time you reach them and return, Dahl will be ours. The gates will always be open to you and those under your command. No harm will come to you, so long as none comes to us. You may see with your own eyes and then choose."

Sato wasn't sure he liked it. But she was asking nothing specific of him and promising safe return in exchange. For now, it was enough. "I agree."

Sato made to leave, but she stopped him.

"Sato, please hurry." He thought he saw the first hint of true emotion in her eyes then. And it was worry. "We don't have much time."

46

Shin sat in the tall grass. When Rua had revealed herself as Yuki, she'd suddenly gotten very dizzy.

The whole time, the friend she had confided all her secrets in was leader of the sin.

Who had been lying to her.

She wasn't close enough to hear what Sato and Yuki spoke of. She didn't much care.

Corin sat beside her. He didn't know what bothered her, but he was by her side, anyway. She took some small comfort in her friend's presence.

Returning to the old mill had taken more from her than she'd expected. The blood had dried in the corridor where Mateo had fought his final defense of the luan, but there was no doubt about where he died. They had walked right through the choke point where he made his last stand.

She kept expecting him to appear, to come around the corner and flash one of his smiles at her.

He never did.

But she'd made it through the corridor. She'd stepped on his dried blood. She'd led them out of Dahl.

Now, with Yuki's betrayal, the one support aside from Corin that she thought she had was pulled from her.

Sato and Yuki finished their discussion. Somehow, both looked like they had lost. But Sato led his sentinels away, and none of the sin made to stop them.

Hopefully, he would fall on his sword as he tripped over an exposed root.

She turned her attention to Rua.

Yuki.

The woman who'd masqueraded as her friend.

She and Hanz were talking together as they approached where Shin sat. She overheard the end of their conversation. Hanz seemed concerned. "The mugon are in position. As soon as Benji and his singun get the gates open, we'll be there. But are you sure we want to just walk through their front door?"

"That many sin within their walls will cause so much havoc that the front door will be the least of their concerns," Yuki replied.

Hanz nodded in acceptance and then read the look between Yuki and Shin. "I'll update Jurian. Corin, why don't you head over and help the camp attendants?"

Corin gave Shin a questioning look, and she nodded. She would be fine. He gave her one more embrace, then wandered towards the young sin who were dealing with the more mundane realities of a military camp.

Shin turned her attention to Yuki. "I thought you were my friend," she said, wincing at how petulant she sounded.

"I apologize for the deception. I needed you to open up to me. I didn't believe you would do so if you thought of me as an authority figure. Your walls were up from the moment you arrived at the village."

"So you lied?" Shin snapped back. "You weren't worried

that abusing my trust might build those walls even higher?"

"Perhaps, but I became Rua to serve a greater purpose. What you've already accomplished is remarkable. You and Corin held the luan together after Mateo's death. You led them to rescue. You have within you the ability to lead, to matter in the conflict to come. But fear haunts your every step. Had I allowed you to continue to wallow in fear, to hide from the horrors that had befallen you, then you never would have come out to face them," Yuki said, not unkindly despite her directness.

Shin wanted to be angry with the woman, but her anger was spent. Yuki spoke true. She had been regressing. Spending her days farming had been so much easier than standing up and facing the world. Corin had tried to reach her, but she had pushed him away.

"Why did you have to lie, though? I trusted you," Shin said, still trying to hold onto some anger.

"I couldn't tell you what you needed to do. You had to discover it for yourself. Had you known I was the leader of the sin, would you not have questioned my words? As I said, your walls were up. I took on the guise of someone unassuming to help bring them down. I may have deceived you, but there was truth in that deception. You did find a friend in me, and I hope that one day you can see that again."

Part of her worried that this was simply Yuki manipulating her once more. She finally decided there was too much truth to what she said, and that Yuki had read her so well, that whatever her deceptions, they had been necessary.

"Fine, but I will miss the long talks I had with my friend, Rua," Shin said.

"That friend is not gone, I assure you," Yuki said. "I am

still here if you need to talk."

Shin sat in silence for a moment. She had so few friends. Why push one of them away?

"I'll think about it," Shin said with a small smile.

The two women sat in companionable silence for a few moments and Shin's mind started to return to the same thing that had plagued it since her fight with those giants in the forest.

"All of this," Shin gestured towards Dahl and the sin forces that surrounded it, "this assault on Dahl, it's about more than the sentinels, isn't it?"

"Your intuition serves you well. Tell me, quickly, what happened to my sin, to you and Beast."

Shin did, retelling their story as quickly as she could. Yuki nodded along, as though she'd already guessed most of the story.

When Shin was finished, she said, "You are right. This is about more than the sentinels. It is about those giants you fought. You saw the power of Beast's people, the Maramans, when you fought them. Now imagine an army of them sweeping across Samas."

Shin shuddered at the thought of the Maramans arriving at their shores in force. She knew from experience that the sentinels would leave the peasants to fend for themselves. They would defend their interests and let the rest of Samas burn.

"So, we remove the sentinels and defend Samas ourselves?" Shin asked.

"Your hate blinds you, child. The sin are not a conquering army that can sweep its enemies away. Even here, at a relatively small sentinel outpost, we rely on stealth and surprise to weaken our enemies before we attack. We had to bolster our numbers with Beast's mugon to ensure we can hold the city. You saw the ferocity with which the scouting party fought. Do you truly believe the sin could stand alone against something like that?"

Shin's mood darkened with each word Yuki spoke. She knew where Yuki was leading her, but her mind recoiled against it, nevertheless. She sighed when she could no longer resist the truth.

"You intend to ally with the sentinels." The words felt ashy in her mouth.

"We intend to try. There is a corruption amongst the sentinels that we must first cleanse. Once that is done, the sin and sentinels will be united, as they once were, as allies and we can, hopefully, stand against the Maramans."

"But they're already coming! If that was a scouting party we fought, then the rest are on the way," Shin said, fear in her voice.

"Events are moving faster than I anticipated, but we have no choice but to prepare as quickly as we can."

Shin studied Yuki momentarily and realized that the woman was thinking ten steps ahead of everyone else. Relief swelled in her chest that Samas had a champion like Yuki to stand against its enemies. Had it been Shin in Yuki's place, she wouldn't have been able to see past her anger with the sentinels to even consider a plan like this one.

In fact, Shin was still struggling.

"Does this mean I don't get to fight any sentinels?" she asked through gritted teeth.

Yuki's normally serene smile seemed to take on a hint of malice. "No, child, there are plenty of sentinels like the ones that killed your parents who still need to be dealt with."

Shin nodded and flashed a smile that was tinged with violence.

"Good."

47

———

Beast and Benji hid behind a building as they waited for a patrol of sentinels to pass them by. They'd been targeting several such patrols, attacking from the shadows and then disappearing again to draw them from the walls. They killed a few, but at this point it was more important to sow chaos.

"So, remind me of your master plan?" Beast asked.

"Pull enough sentinels from the wall that we can attack the main gate and open it."

Beast shot his friend an incredulous look. "That's it?"

"You don't like it?"

"You're supposed to be a master strategist. That's not any better than a plan I would have come up with."

Benji laughed. "You would have just found the biggest and heaviest weapon and charged in directly. Trust me, this is better."

They moved closer to the gate. Beast heard other engagements in the distance. Other sin had entered Dahl and were employing the same tactics amongst the confused sentinels.

They reached a blacksmith's forge that backed up to the wall of the city, where they found Raya and four sin engaged with a sentinel patrol. As skilled as the sin were, the battleground wasn't ideal. In direct combat, the sentinels were equally effective. One of the sin had been cut down.

Beast and Benji joined the fray and fought to turn the tide. Beast took out two before they even realized he was among them. Only three sentinels remained, and the sin closed in for the kill.

Before they could end their enemies, the door to the forge burst open and the blacksmith charged out with a scream. The man, short but with the broad shoulders of a smith, was clad in heavy steel armor and wielded his hammer in one hand, a torch in the other. The sin and sentinels alike were surprised by the would-be hero's appearance.

The blacksmith, far braver than he was skilled, continued his charge into the sin, swinging his hammer wildly. He ran directly at Raya, currently trapped between two sentinels. She wasn't as mobile as the others because she was wearing a bulky leather pack strapped to her back.

Beast stepped in front of the man and thrust his club, head first, into him. The crack of wood on steel reverberated through Beast's arms. The club splintered, and the man's momentum was stopped as he was knocked onto his ass.

Unfortunately, the torch he was wielding flew out of his hands. Beast watched it arc high overhead and land squarely on the pack that Raya carried. Beast wouldn't have thought anything of it, but the reaction that the rest of the sin had as the pack started to smoke made him realize that something was wrong.

Raya threw the pack off, then turned and sprinted towards a nearby building. Beast caught a glimpse of her as she threw herself headlong through the window, and then Benji was pulling him to the ground.

The sentinels stood, dumbfounded by recent events, as the air itself exploded.

The sentinels were knocked backwards and riddled with debris. The sin were far from unscathed, but as they staggered to their feet, it appeared that none of them were seriously injured. The blacksmith took a moment to collect his wits and then staggered away. The sin let him go.

Beast shook his head to try to clear the high-pitched ringing from his ears but only succeeded in making himself dizzy. His arms were covered in tiny cuts from the glass.

Benji gestured away from the explosion. They needed to get away from here.

Beast nodded, and they were off. Slowly, the ringing in his ears lessened enough that he thought conversation would be possible.

"Why are we still heading towards the gates?" Beast asked. The commotion from the explosion would have every sentinel in the city here in minutes, and they were too close to the gates.

"No choice. We need to let our forces in," Benji replied.

Finally, they came into view of the gates. Sentinels with bows stood on the ramparts and more with weapons at the ready stood below. The wrought-iron doors were shut and two massive iron bars were locked in place. Beast wasn't sure if the doors or the thick stone walls would be harder to get through.

There were more sentinels than Beast expected. Surely, by now, most of them had been drawn off by the sin assault. And yet the gate seemed to be fully guarded.

Beast ducked back around the corner as arrows glanced off the stone of the building he hid behind.

Beast swore, then turned to Benji. "There are far too many sentinels for us to fight."

Benji frowned, then shoved Beast to the side so that he could risk a glance out. He grunted, then also took shelter as a couple of ambitious archers tried to use his face for target practice.

"I thought you were supposed to pull the sentinels away with the fires." Beast looked off in the distance. Now that he thought about it, the fires seemed to be burning out of control. The sentinels weren't chasing the bait the sin had started.

Benji, as usual, seemed a step ahead of Beast. "They knew we were coming." He swore under his breath.

"So, what do we do?"

Benji took a deep breath and looked around. His eyes settled on Beast's weapon. "Are you particularly attached to that broken club?"

"No, but I'd rather not be empty-handed."

"You can use my sword. What I'm about to do will take a lot out of me," Benji said, and took the club from Beast. "Maybe too much."

Benji handed his sword over to Beast.

Beast raised an eyebrow but kept any questions to himself once he saw the red glow begin around Benji's hand. That glow meant that any answers he got he wouldn't understand anyway.

Benji closed his eyes and sweat broke out on his forehead as the red glow moved from his hand up to encompass his entire arm. After a moment, it suffused the broken weapon so that the entire surface glowed with a pulsing red light. Finally, Benji opened his eyes.

"Think you can throw this all the way to the gate?" Benji asked, handing Beast the club.

Beast gingerly took the club and then peeked around the corner of the building, gauging the distance.

"I'll need to take a few steps into the open, but I can get it there," he replied. "Those archers will turn me into a pincushion if they see me, though."

Benji gestured to one of the few remaining sin, who produced a leather pouch. "Smoke," he said. "They won't be able to see you, but you won't be able to see the doors."

"No problem." Beast directed his attention to the sin with the pouch. "Can you put that thing halfway between here and the cart?"

"Easily," the sin said with a nod.

Beast took a deep breath, stood up, and motioned for the sin to throw the pouch.

The sin deftly lit the device with the flint box and then tossed it exactly where Beast wanted it. Moments later, there was an intense hissing sound and the entire road filled with black smoke. Cries of alarm went up from the sentinels, and several launched arrows blindly into the smoke. Beast waited a moment for the archers to stop their fire, then ran into the street. He held his breath in the smoke and released the club in an overhand toss. The weapon disappeared into the haze, red light trailing behind it, and then Beast heard the dull thud of wood smacking against iron.

Beast retreated to the safety of the corner.

Benji raised his glowing arm with his hand open. His friend looked as worried as he'd ever been. Then Benji growled and closed his fist.

For the second time that night, Beast's world exploded. The black smoke was blown away by fire and rushing air. The crack of stone and gate drove nails into his ears. Even around the corner, Beast was knocked flat on his ass. He coughed as dust filled his lungs. "By the sun! Why didn't you just do that in the first place?"

"The cost is… high," Benji said in an exhausted voice.

When Beast looked down at his friend slumped against the wall of the building, he was lost for words. Where Benji's left arm had been, there was now only a stump. Benji's tired eyes looked up at him.

"At least it isn't your sword arm," Beast said.

Benji let out a weak laugh.

"You're right, my friend. I'm still a better swordsman than you, even with only one arm. I'm in no shape to fight now, though." He nodded at the other sin, crawling to their feet. "They'll keep me safe. You join the others."

Through the open gate, sin poured in.

They danced nimbly over the destruction, ignoring the bodies and stone at their feet. Benji's sacrifice hadn't just destroyed the gate, it had killed almost half the sentinels.

The sin clashed with the survivors, still dazed from the explosion. Beast's mugon followed the sin, and despite the recent sacrifice of his friend, Beast's heart lifted to see his warriors here, finally striking a blow that mattered against the Firstborn.

Beast drew Benji's sword. It felt more like a knife in his hands, but it would do.

There were some sentinels that needed killing.

48

"I want you to accompany me," Yuki told Shin. Around them, Shin saw the sin beginning to form up into loose groups. Something was about to happen. Not wanting to be left behind, she nodded, and followed Yuki to a place near the rear of the line.

Soon the entire column was marching toward Dahl.

"We're just walking up to the gates? I thought the sin were all about stealth and surprise?" Shin asked.

"We are. This is part of the distraction. We have sin inside as we speak, silently cutting down our enemies. Soon, they will open the gates for us, and we will rush in to clean up the remaining sentinels, if any still live."

Shin nodded but remained silent. She didn't understand, but she'd also never commanded a battle.

Suddenly, she felt an odd tug at her mind. As if something was being summoned and wanted her to know it. She didn't think she'd felt anything like that before.

"Did you feel that?" Shin asked Yuki.

The look Yuki gave Shin was so full of surprise, it made

Shin realize just how little emotion she normally showed. "You can?" Yuki asked.

"Yes, like something pulling at my mind. Beckoning me."

"That, dear child, is called sacrifice. It is the greatest gift that the sin can wield. Not many are attuned to it. There are few sensitive enough to feel what you do now."

She looked at Dahl. Towards the incessant tugging that was growing stronger. It almost felt like a physical pull.

"What does it mean?" she asked.

"There is much that you would need to learn before I could begin to answer that question fully. For the moment, though, it means that something has gone wrong."

"Gone wrong?" Shin asked.

"If all had gone according to plan, there should have been no need to use sacrifice, but the chaos of battle rarely respects even the best laid plans. Whatever happened, it appears Benji has decided the need is great enough for him to use his talents."

"I don't understand. What is sacrifice?" Shin asked.

"Sacrifice is an ability that only the most attuned of the sin can use. It allows us to sacrifice a piece of ourselves, physical, emotional or mental, depending on the cost, in order to bend the reality of this world to our needs."

"So, you can show me how to do this?" Shin asked.

"It's a bit more complex than that. There is a ceremony that you must undertake first. It is unpleasant. Tonight, though, I can help you to feel what it is like to pull the threads that weave the workings into our world. Preparation like this can help with the jarring nature of the process of awakening your abilities."

Shin wanted to ask about the ceremony but something in the way Yuki spoke led her to believe that she wouldn't get any answers tonight, anyway. Instead, she simply followed Yuki as the leader trailed the sin forces that were marching briskly on the gates.

Before Shin could say anything else, the march halted and the singun were arrayed before the gates of Dahl. Shin saw sentinels on the ramparts. They stood with their bows at the ready, but the sin remained well out of range of their weapons. The gate was busy, though, with sentinels running to and fro.

Shin was about to ask what they were waiting for when Yuki gently put a hand on her arm.

"Calm your mind and focus on my touch," she said.

Shin nodded and took a deep breath. At first, she only felt the firm, callused grip of the elder warrior's hand on her flesh. Then the tugging returned, more insistent. At first, she tried to focus on the feeling and each time it would slip away, like trying to squeeze a wet fish too hard. She relaxed her focus, allowing the feeling to dance at the edge of her consciousness, and it coalesced into something she could focus on.

"Good," Yuki murmured, "stay relaxed."

Now a second presence joined her mind. Yuki, she knew intuitively. Together, they followed the thread.

The working was being weaved within the city walls, but in her mind, it might as well have been right beside her. The threads were being pulled into their reality from somewhere else. She couldn't understand anything except that it was a place that wasn't here. At first, she was so amazed by the weavings of the threads that she only focused on that. Soon, though, a feeling of dread permeated her mind. Wherever these threads were coming from, it was a terrible place. A place of anger and jealousy and a deep, insatiable need.

"Yuki, I don't want to see anymore," Shin said and tried to pull out of the iron grip.

Yuki only squeezed tighter, but a calming pulse came from her mind and Shin knew that, however unpleasant it was, she was safe.

The weaver of the threads, presumably Benji, continued his work until the spell was woven. Shin couldn't understand what it was, but she could feel it finish taking form. Then, she felt Benji tie off the weave and cut the threads coming from the other place with his mind. The spell was ready and waiting.

"That was the weaving of sacrifice. This particular working will be activated when Benji triggers it. Once that's done, the sacrifice will be demanded," Yuki said, still holding Shin's arm.

"By who?" Shin asked, knowing she feared the answer.

"Not who—what. We pull our power from another place. You felt it. It is not a place that gives without exacting a toll."

Shin swallowed hard and then she felt an incredible pressure on her mind. A moment later, the gates blew off their hinges. Iron, stone, wood and blood mixed in with a cloud of dust that billowed outwards. Once it cleared, there was a gaping hole where the doors had been and most of the stone to either side was reduced to rubble.

"That pressure you felt was the sacrifice demanded. Because we were simply observing, feeling another's work, we felt none of the pain. Know that when you use sacrifice, the cost is much higher." Yuki let go of her arm.

Hanz and Jurian ordered the sin forward without waiting for instruction from Yuki. The sin disappeared silently into the smoky destruction that used to be a gate. The mugon followed closely behind, their hard training paying off. The lack of sound was unnerving.

"It's so quiet," she observed.

"That silence means that we are fighting on our terms. It means we have a chance," Yuki said. "A good lesson if you are to join our ranks."

Shin's heart skipped a beat at that. Only days ago, she had been farming in the sin village, thinking she could hide from the fears that plagued her. Beast and Corin had encouraged her to find her will to fight once more, but now that Yuki was giving her a clear path to do so it was all feeling very real.

"You think I can do... this?" Shin asked and pointed toward the assault.

"This, and maybe much more. Once you are trained."

"Good," Shin said with a conviction she had struggled to find since the night her parents died.

It frightened her to think about how close she had been to simply giving up and hiding. She could never have forgiven herself if she had grown old, only to look back in regret on the things she had never fought to save.

Shin turned to look at the sin leader as her forces stormed the city and its disoriented defenders.

"Are you sure you desire this path?" Yuki asked her.

Finally, the silence broke as sounds of battle and screams of pain rang out in the distance. The cloying dust had made its way to where they were sitting and drifted into Shin's eyes and nose. Though all her senses were assaulted, she calmly looked into the eyes of the person that could teach her how to orchestrate the same kind of chaos.

"Yes."

49

Near the end of the battle for the gate, two giant figures emerged, engaging the few sentinels that remained on their feet. What was left of the resistance at the gate was swept away by the giant twins. Hanz and Jurian stopped before Beast, and they had a brief discussion.

"I never thought I would say this, but it's actually good to see your ugly faces," Beast said.

The twins chuckled in unison, the effect unnerving.

"It is good to see you, too, little one," Hanz said. He noted Benji's sword in Beast's hand. He shook his head and clucked like a mother hen. "No, no, no. No good. A sword like that's not meant for little one."

Hanz pulled out a knife, tiny in his enormous hands. He held it out to Beast. "This is more suitable for one of your ability."

Beast took the knife, holding onto the sides of the blade between thumb and forefinger. "I cut my food with a longer blade than this."

"It's perfect for you," Jurian chimed in.

Beast shook his head, but he was never one to say no to a weapon. He stashed the knife at his hip. "What next?"

Hanz nodded toward the center of Dahl. "We finish taking the city. Most of the sentinels are defeated, but some remain. The sin hunt from the shadows, but there will be some pockets of resistance that require a blunter approach. Your help would be appreciated."

Beast agreed, eager to smash more sentinel heads. "Benji is injured."

Jurian shook his head. "Not injured. Honored. But your point is understood, and you should have no fear on that part. He will be cared for."

"Good. Give me a moment with him, and then I'll help you."

Beast went over to where his friend was propped up against the wall of a building. Several sin hovered around Benji, making preparations to carry him off. Beast squatted down next to him. When he looked at Benji's missing arm he felt his stomach twist inside. "I wish I'd found a better way."

Benji growled and raised his remaining hand. Beast took it, and Benji pulled Beast close, surprising him with his strength. "*This* is why we will beat the sentinels. Do you understand? They sit on top of the world and take from those below, claiming it is their right. While among the sin, those of us who lead are the most prepared to sacrifice." He pulled Beast even closer. "Do you understand?"

Beast squeezed Benji's hand. Somehow, he knew that no matter how hard he squeezed, his friend's hand was one he would never be able to crush. "I understand."

"Good. Now go kill some sentinels for me."

Benji pushed Beast away.

Beast took one last look at his friend. "Be well, Benji."

Benji waved him away. "I'll be fine. Go!"

Beast called his mugon to his side, and they went hunting for any sentinels that resisted the fall of Dahl.

Unlike the brave but foolish blacksmith, most citizens of Dahl seemed content to hide in their homes and wait for the danger to pass. Beast and his mugon walked through empty streets, nearly as silent as the open plains.

Here and there, they heard running footsteps. Likely sentinels fleeing for their lives.

More than once, those footsteps ended suddenly as a sin finished the kill.

After a few minutes, they encountered their first real pocket of resistance. A group of six sentinels had gathered and waited for them in the street ahead. Beast and his mugon charged into battle.

If not for Beast, it might have been a close fight. The mugon had the numbers on their side, and a few weeks of training with the sin.

But they were still just skilled peasants.

Not warriors trained in the art of combat from a young age.

In any fight, each sentinel was tactically worth at least two or three mugon, but Beast easily destroyed that battlefield math. He threw himself into the thick of the fight, chopping at sentinels with Benji's sword.

To his surprise, the weapon proved almost as effective as his axe. Its blade was sharper than anything he'd ever fought with, slicing even through armor without much problem.

Or maybe he was just so strong it didn't matter.

He lost two mugon, each killed when they attempted to duel a single sentinel. But all the sentinels died.

The brief engagement did nothing except whet his

appetite for more. They wandered the streets, but no more sentinels appeared.

Dahl was the largest city on Ilos, but it still wasn't that big. The sentinels had been overrun.

Beast left his mugon with one of the sin commanders, then returned to the front gate.

There, he found exactly the person he was looking for.

Yuki stood among the carnage, giving quiet orders and listening to reports. Shin was close to her, watching everything with those sharp eyes of hers. He looked around but didn't see Benji anywhere. Hopefully, his friend was already getting the care he deserved. If not for him, the sin wouldn't have taken Dahl.

At least they wouldn't have taken Dahl as easily as they did.

Yuki finished with the group of sin gathered around her, then motioned for Beast. "I spoke with Benji. He asked me to check on you. He was afraid you'd be overrun by sentiment."

"I'm fine," Beast growled.

"We needed Dahl, and as quickly and bloodlessly as possible. His sacrifice made that happen."

Beast didn't need Yuki explaining what he already knew, so he changed the subject. "What happens now?"

"We solidify our position. More sin are on the way. Some are working with the late Magistrate Velor's staff. We're coordinating food and supplies. We're trying to arrange to get people out of Dahl as quickly as possible."

"Why?"

She gave him a sharp look. "Because the people you fought a few days ago were just a scouting party. They're your people, the Maramans. And their invasion is near."

Her words struck him, but perhaps not in the way she expected. "You knew? You knew where I was from?"

"I did."

"And you didn't think to tell me?"

"I didn't think it mattered. You're no fool. You knew you aren't from Samas. You are the bandit king, not some mere Maraman outcast child who somehow found your way to our shores."

Beast gritted his teeth. Now was not the time. "How do you know it's an invasion?"

"They have individuals who can manipulate reality, as do we. I can sense some of their workings, and they're close. I don't know if we have days or hours, but we need to move fast."

"What do you need from me?"

"Organize your mugon. We brought a lot of them over, and Benji sent out orders to all of them operating on Ilos before we began our trek. We need to be prepared for whatever is coming our way."

Beast nodded, more than eager to be away from Yuki. He supposed he understood her manipulations, but they didn't sit well with him. Straight and direct was best. He had the suspicion she'd lived so long with secrets and lies she didn't know any other way of being.

Fortunately, he was able to push her out of his mind quickly enough. His mugon were here, and every meeting felt like a reunion. The conquest of Dahl had put some steel in their spines. They'd always been brave warriors, but now they stood a bit taller. The fire in their eyes was a bit brighter.

They weren't just ambushing sentinels anymore. They weren't just stealing back what had already belonged to them.

The taking of Dahl had meaning.

Beast organized them as well as he was able, though he wasn't as skilled at it as Benji. But one didn't spend as much time with Benji as he had and not pick up a few skills. By the time the sun rose, Beast had his mugon situated.

Which was a good thing.

Because as the sun rose above the horizon, black sails appeared on the water. Perhaps a dozen of them, ships never seen by any living soul on Samas.

The Maramans had arrived in force.

50

———

Sato was surprised to find that not only had Yuki offered him safe passage, she had also ensured that he would have horses to speed his way. If the old woman thought it would somehow affect his final judgment, she was sorely mistaken.

But still, having the horses made his life easier. Soon enough, Dahl and all the problems it represented were behind him.

He and the other sentinels made good time, and they made the trek in silence. Sato had too much on his mind, and the others didn't seem to be in much of a mood to talk.

After a league of riding, Sato finally gave it up. He could think for a lifetime about the events of the day. He wasn't sure he would ever come to a satisfying conclusion. Only two facts held any weight in his mind.

First, and perhaps most troubling, was that he'd been wrong about the world. He felt a fool, and when he thought too long on the matter, his cheeks began to flush with shame at all that he had once believed. How could the

Firstborn's favored one be so naive? Or was that why he'd been so favored? He was someone the Firstborn could shape, like a piece of clay before it had been fired.

Those thoughts inevitably led him down dark alleys he would rather not travel.

So, he didn't and instead focused on the second fact. Crispin had come for him.

The young sentinel had every chance in the world to betray him, to return to the ways that had once been his whole life. But in that moment, he'd gone against everything he knew to help his commander.

Sato wasn't sure what that meant.

But he knew he would never abuse that trust.

He also knew that the Path, though perhaps imperfect, was not something to be ignored. It had, possibly in ways Sato could never guess, transformed Crispin.

Up ahead, Crispin burped loud enough to be heard over the sound of the horses at a run.

Perhaps not transformed, then.

They reached the scheduled rendezvous point with the other sun stalkers just as the sun was rising. The whole ride, Sato had never looked back, not wanting to see what had become of Dahl. There was little he could have done.

Truly, there was little he could have done.

If he kept repeating it, perhaps he would someday believe it was true.

Friends took their horses, and the camp leaped into motion. Sato and the others were later than they'd planned, and there was much to discuss. He turned to Crispin before they parted ways. "I imagine that when you tell the story, you're going to be quite the hero?"

Crispin grinned. "I'll tell them all I saved you when you

only had seconds left to live. Might even make a comment about you pissing your pants."

Sato raised an eyebrow at that. "And I suppose there will be no mention of the fact it was your initial betrayal that put me in that prison cell?"

"They won't hear it from me." Crispin leaned in conspiratorially. "Tell you what. If you make no mention of it to anyone but Roko, I won't tell anyone about you shitting your pants in terror."

Sato laughed at the man's gall. "Only one of those is true."

"Truth belongs to whoever tells it first and loudest," Crispin said. "And the good captain looks like he's about to explode with nerves."

Sato glanced over and saw that it was true. Roko was practically beside himself. "I guess you've got a deal, then."

While Crispin regaled the rest of the sun stalkers with his mostly fictional adventures, Sato and Roko sat down by themselves. Sato told Roko everything that had happened since they'd last parted. By the time he finished the story, the sun was well above the horizon.

Roko sat and looked up at the clouds when Sato finished. "You've changed a lot since we started this journey."

"I was a fool."

Roko shrugged. "I don't believe that. But your view of the world was narrow."

"Did you know?"

"About the corruption?"

Sato nodded.

"I knew that it existed. Few sentinels can abide by every single tenet of the Path every moment of their lives. They wield tremendous power, which will always lend itself to abuses. That's human nature. I didn't realize the rot had spread so deep."

That was what Sato had hoped Roko would say. His friend, as always, was reliable. "I don't know what to do next," he confessed.

"Lay out your options," Roko suggested. "Let's discuss them."

"My first idea is to do nothing. The sun stalkers weren't created to solve a problem this large. We return to the Firstborn and enlist his help. And I confront the Firstborn over what I've seen."

"A safe plan," Roko said. "Responsible, and the only one you would have seen a few months ago."

Sato agreed. "But by the time I do that, whatever is happening here on Ilos will be over. If Yuki spoke true, there might already be an invasion force with a beachhead. Again, alone, there seems to be little we can do. We're too small. Which leaves us no option but to cooperate with Yuki."

"You seem decided," Roko said. "So, what's the problem?"

"I'd be working with the sin, who have spent their whole existence fighting against everything I believe in."

"Have they?" Roko asked.

Sato frowned.

"Again, if what Yuki says is true, they're killing corrupt soldiers who are making life miserable for many on Samas. They plan to defend against an invasion. It seems to me these are all things you would do, too."

Sato tore a patch of grass from the ground. Everything Roko said made sense. But it was all backwards.

"They'll never follow me if I ask this of them," Sato said,

gesturing to the assembled sun stalkers. Perhaps it was a weak excuse, but one he believed to be true.

"Try them," Roko suggested.

Sato glared at Roko, who simply urged him forward. Grumbling, Sato got to his feet and went to the sun stalkers. By now, all of them had the basic idea of what had happened in Dahl. By now, Sato expected that the city had fallen to the sin.

The circle of warriors quieted as he neared. He took the measure of each sun stalker, predicting how they might react. When there was no sound but the cackling of the firewood, Sato spoke. "I trust by now that Crispin has told you all about what has happened in Dahl. We were granted the right of safe passage, and I intend to take us back to Dahl. Our fellow sentinels may be dead, but the city itself is still in danger."

"You want us to work with the sin, sir?" There was doubt in the voice, and rightfully so. For most of these warriors, the sin were still nothing but villains out of legends.

"I do," Sato said. "But this is not an order I can give. What I will ask is far beyond what is required of your oaths. It's been an honor to be your commander. I must return to Dahl to see what is happening and help as I may. Any volunteers are welcome to join me. The rest can return to Bulas with Roko."

There was a long silence around the fire, and not a single person moved a muscle. Sato's heart sank. He'd hoped to get at least a handful of men and women to join him.

It was Crispin who spoke up. "Hell, sir. We're all going with you. It's already decided. We were just waiting for you to ask."

Laughter echoed around the fire. Sato caught whispered

comments about the pickpocketing skills they could learn from the sin. Others wanted to learn how to turn invisible.

Impossible. Every one of them.

Sato bowed deeply, and once again, the ring was silent.

He turned on his heel and left, not wanting them to see the expressions of relief and gratitude on his face.

51

Shin was tired. She hadn't slept well in Magistrate Velor's cells, and since their escape, she'd been on the move constantly.

Now that she didn't have anything specific to do, she was wandering the streets. The sun was falling, and the sin were trying to restore something resembling order as quickly as possible. It was all well and good until Shin came upon Yuki, presiding over a group of captured sentinels.

Shin's nostrils flared. Even though Yuki had told her she was planning on recruiting the sentinels to their cause, seeing it in action turned her stomach. The only good sentinel was a dead sentinel.

She almost left the scene behind, but then she overheard Yuki speaking to them and her anger rooted her to the spot.

"Those who choose to help defend Dahl will do so under the command of the sin. If you can't handle that, there is plenty of room in the cells."

Shin's hands balled into fists. Even in her anger, though, she couldn't confront Yuki so publicly. The sin leader had shown her kindness, and even forbearance, but she had a hard time imagining that she would escape unpunished for interrupting Yuki now.

She waited, stewing in her own anger, while Yuki finished up with the sentinels. Half were led, bound, into the same building where she had been recently imprisoned. The other half were allowed to stand and be released. Their weapons were returned to them, and they split up under the watchful eye of sin commanders.

The process complete, Yuki glanced over and saw Shin glaring. The older woman made no invitation, but Shin's feet were moving of their own accord. She stomped forward. "You should have killed them," she said.

Of course, her anger had no effect on Yuki. Even as Rua, the woman had been impossible to get a rise out of. "Would that have been your solution?"

"I wouldn't have even hesitated." The venom in her voice surprised even her. She hated the sentinels, yes, but it wasn't until just now she realized how much.

It made her doubt, just for a moment.

Vengeance and murder were two different things. She just wasn't quite sure where the line was anymore.

"They all deserve death," Yuki said, snapping Shin's attention back to the present. "Each of them is guilty. Most were actively working against the citizens of Samas. They took too much in taxes and gave too little in return. Even the best of them, who remained closest to the Path, are guilty of knowing the situation and doing nothing to remedy it."

"So why not kill them?"

"Because it is inefficient. Criminals or not, I have a larger problem on my hands, and a sentinel is a trained warrior without equal. Even a handful might be enough to change the tide of battle in our favor."

Yuki's cold logic clashed against Shin's anger. But no anger stood a chance against Yuki.

Before Shin could decide what to do next, alarm bells began ringing throughout town.

Yuki didn't seem surprised. She glanced at Harmony, strapped to Shin's back. "Mateo died so that you could live and escape. How will you use that gift today?"

Shin's emotions tore her in half. This whole journey, the reason she was standing before Yuki, fell squarely on the sentinels. They destroyed her life, and she was being asked to work with them when all she wanted to do was stop them from destroying more lives.

And yet, impossibly, they were the lesser of two evils.

As horrible as the sentinels were, they weren't invaders. Shin couldn't guess what the Maramans intended, but she suspected it wasn't good.

In that moment, she felt the last of her childhood, already tattered and broken, fall away. This fight wasn't about her and Yuki or her and the sentinels. She couldn't afford to indulge personal hatred. The Maramans wanted Samas. If they succeeded, it wouldn't just be the sentinels and the magistrates who suffered. It would be the farmers, the woodcutters, and the bricklayers. It would be hundreds, if not thousands, of families just like hers.

She couldn't allow that to happen. She was just one person, but she could help.

The thought of fighting yet again made her knees tremble.

But she wouldn't let fear hold her back again. "I'll fight."

"Good. Go find Beast. Knowing him, he'll be somewhere near the front gates or up on the wall. He isn't going to miss this battle. You'll work best under his command."

That was an order she had no problem following. She

liked the enormous man, especially after watching him crushing the Red Aces above their cells. And she wouldn't be useful among the sin. Their ways were not yet her own.

She ran toward the front gate. As Yuki had guessed, Beast was there, ordering his mugon to strengthen the impromptu barricade at the shattered gate. His mugon filled the gap with everything they could find. It was ugly, but hopefully it would hold.

Beast saw her as she neared and waved her to him.

"Yuki ordered me to join you."

"Do you mean to use that thing, or hide in a corner?" Beast gestured to Mateo's weapon, now her own.

"I plan on using it."

The grin that broke out on his face was vicious. He heard the determination in her voice. "Good. I can't keep saving your life all the time." He nodded toward the wall. "Come with me. I want to get a better idea of what we'll be facing."

She ran up the stairs with him, and the sight that greeted her almost froze her in her tracks.

At the entrance to the bay, several ships were blockading the port. They were bigger than anything she had seen before. Nothing from Samas stood a chance against ships of that size. She pointed to them, unable to speak.

Beast followed her finger. "It looks like they don't want any help to come."

They walked a little farther down the wall, so that they could see more of the harbor. Shin watched, mouth agape, as a steady stream of Maramans set up their camp. Normally there would have been at least a small unit of sentinels guarding the harbor, but Shin had heard everyone had been recalled inside the walls of Dahl prior to the sin arriving.

It was then Shin realized just how much trouble they faced. Dahl wasn't designed to be defended against an attack like this. Shin didn't know much history, but she didn't think Samas had ever been invaded by foreigners.

She studied the preparations with interest. The Maramans had erected one large tent. Shin assumed it housed someone important, and in front of it the Maramans were setting up sharpened stakes. Others kept a constant watch around the temporary structure.

The bulk of their forces, however, were already marching towards the walls of Dahl.

They made a wide circle from the beach, keeping out of arrow range. When they saw the broken front gate, they formed up into a column that could only have one purpose. Shields rose, protecting the column and making it look like an armored snake. Beast swore softly, then turned to her. "Back down, then. It'll be a fight at the gates."

"Wouldn't it be better to help the others with bows?" Shin gestured to the archers taking up stations along the wall, the sin commanders directing the warriors.

"Can you shoot a bow?"

Shin shook her head.

"Neither can I. So, unless you want me to dangle you from your ankles down the wall while you stab at Maramans with your pointy stick, I suggest we go down and help defend the gate where we'll be useful. Besides," Beast pointed to a woman in sentinel armor, "that woman was one of the sentinels who guarded these gates for years. She's much better suited to the task than I."

Shin couldn't bring herself to argue against Beast. If he trusted a sentinel, there was nothing she could say or do that would change his mind.

She followed him down to the gate, putting herself front

and center of what was certainly going to become the most violent part of the battle. With Beast by her side, she could almost convince herself it wasn't the worst decision she'd ever made.

The waiting was the worst. It gnawed away at her confidence. Every few seconds, she would look behind her into the empty streets of Dahl. Every citizen that hadn't taken up arms was hiding deep in their homes. If she believed there was any safety in running, she would have. But there was nowhere to go.

Up above, the archers valiantly tried to defend against an opposing force many times their number. One by one, the archers fell, many of them with enormous spears in their chests. Shin was certain she didn't even have the strength to throw one of those high enough to reach the top of the walls. The Maramans made sport of such a feat.

When the first Maraman climbed over the top of the barricade, Beast was there to cut him down. He wielded Benji's sword, a two-handed weapon in its owner's hands, with one giant fist. His first cut took off the Maraman's arm. The second cleaved his skull in half.

The second Maraman met a similar fate, but the third one was either clever or suicidal. He climbed over the top of the barricade and launched himself at Beast, tackling him to the ground. They wrestled for a few moments, enormous muscles bulging against one another. Beast won the fight, but in the time it took him, more Maramans had climbed over the barricade, and the other mugon weren't as effective as Beast. With every passing moment, more Maramans clambered over the barricade, and soon they had pushed the defenders back far enough that some of the giants could dismantle the barrier while others fought.

As always, Beast was in the center of the storm, Benji's sword cutting a swath of destruction everywhere it went.

But he was slowly being overwhelmed. The Maramans focused on Beast, even to the point of ignoring many of the mugon.

Her last vision of Mateo flashed through her mind. Fighting to defend her, just like Beast did now.

She wouldn't let herself continue to live in regret.

Something inside her snapped, and she charged toward Beast, Harmony in front of her. She wasn't a master, not by any means. But she knew enough.

Because she was smaller and her weapon had more reach, the first Maraman she fought didn't even see her coming. He was dancing just outside of Beast's range, waiting for an opening to strike, eyes only on the bandit king.

Shin stabbed out, and her aim was true. The giant man crumpled to the ground, surprise frozen on his face.

She waited for the pang of guilt.

For once, it never came.

She chose another target and dove into the heart of the battle.

52

Beast caught the massive club swung by an attacking Maraman with his off-hand and drove his sword through the neck of another. Before he removed his sword, he kicked the Maraman with the club, knocking him backwards and wrenching the club away. By the time the Maraman moved forward again, Beast had freed his sword and was able to bury it in the face of the now weaponless attacker.

Then Shin was there, killing the Maraman closest to Beast and breaking the circle that had been closing in on him. Beast made short work of the remaining attackers. He was impressed to see Shin dance back into the fray. To tell the truth, he'd expected her to go find a corner to hide in once the battle began.

She had hate enough for a whole nation, but that didn't necessarily equate to courage.

Beast surveyed the battlefield. The time to call the retreat hadn't arrived, but it was close. As he looked around, he saw Shin, not far from him, deftly cut down another attacker. The girl had some spine after all. The deaths barely seemed to register with her as she moved on to her next target, and Beast felt a swell of pride in his chest. Maybe his words had helped.

Then Beast's moment of peace came to an end. A Maraman came at him from his left. Beast saw the attacker and parried his sword strike. He laughed manically as he rejoined the fray. He cut down his attacker in a few strokes and then a particularly heavily tattooed Maraman caught his eye. He fought his way towards the bloody giant and flashed a deadly grin as the man turned to face him.

The tattooed Maraman rushed him, a bearded axe in each hand, and tried to overwhelm Beast with a flurry of strikes. Beast simply stepped from side to side, moving backwards, until an errant strike buried one of the axes in the shoulder of a Maraman engaged with a mugon. Beast stepped in and ran Benji's sword through the fool's heart.

All those tattoos and not a bit of skill to match.

The Maraman who took the axe in the shoulder turned, bumping the lifeless body before Beast could pull the sword out. The weight of the falling giant snapped Benji's blade in half. Beast looked at the jagged metal that remained for a moment before burying it in the face of the wounded Maraman beside him.

"Benji's not going to be happy about this," Beast said to himself. Benji had used the same sword for years.

"I won't tell him if you don't," Shin said.

Beast's sidestepping had taken him right beside his young ward.

"Deal!" Beast said and picked up the two axes that he'd so recently dodged.

"These tattoos don't look half bad. Maybe you should get some," Shin continued.

Beast recognized the boisterous tone as Shin's outlet for battlefield nerves. "And sully this perfect canvas? No way!"

The mugon at his side fought bravely but, Beast hated to admit, would have been overwhelmed were it not for the sentinels that bolstered their ranks. The discipline and skill that his one-time enemies showed was a reminder of exactly why the mugon had always avoided open conflict.

Beast continued to fight but kept an eye on the ebb and flow of the battle. They engaged their enemies in the narrow gap where the gate used to be to negate their numbers, but they were slowly being forced back. Beast used the natural rhythm of the battle to spring their trap.

He signaled the retreat.

As planned, the mugon broke and ran in disorganized chaos. The sentinels, along with Beast, retreated as well, but with a deadly efficiency. They closed ranks and held the Maraman push at bay just long enough to keep most of the mugon safe, but not so much as to tip their hand. It was as artistic a maneuver as Beast had ever seen.

Once they reached the streets of Dahl, the mugon separated into groups, the bulk of which were led by Beast. As the Maramans committed to what they thought was a rout of their enemies, the sin entered the fray.

Unseen hands whittled away at the Maramans. Shadows coalesced long enough to strike before once again disappearing. Arrows, darts, and sharpened discs of metal struck from dark alleys and shuttered windows. Smoke appeared from nowhere, cutting Maramans off from their allies, and by the time it cleared, only dead invaders remained.

All the while, Beast and his mugon continued to draw their attackers deeper into the city. Any time Beast saw a heavily tattooed Maraman, he would hunt them. In time, he realized he was hunting down their chain of command. The more heavily tattooed warriors were the ones most often issuing commands. Whenever he killed one, those under the leader lost their cohesion and could be killed easier.

The Maramans weren't fools, though. Eventually, they realized the city was nothing but a trap, and ordered a retreat of their own.

"Let them run!" Beast bellowed.

The sin would continue to hunt the Maramans as they fled, so there was no need to risk any more mugon in open conflict. Whatever happened next, Beast had a feeling that he would need as many warriors as he could muster.

"Did we win?" Shin asked him.

"For now. This is far from over, though I doubt they'll be too keen to come inside again anytime soon. You handled yourself well."

Before Beast could issue more orders, a familiar face appeared beside him, coalescing from the shadows.

"Beast, Yuki needs you," Raya said.

"Are you sure it's not you that needs me?" Beast asked with a wink.

Raya smiled briefly before her face returned to stone. "Maybe if we survive. For now, go see Yuki."

Beast grinned, then hurried in the direction that Raya pointed. Yuki was in the magistrate's tower overlooking the city. Before he had even reached the gates of the magistrate's compound, Yuki called down from the window.

"Too late! Ready yourself!"

Beast, confused, looked towards the walls where Yuki was pointing. The sun rose over the ramparts and backlit a nightmare. Impossibly, he saw a huge, clawed hand dig into the rocks of the ramparts and then a distorted demon-version of a Maraman pulled itself over the crenellations.

"Fuck," Beast whispered to himself and then bellowed, "Mugon! To me!"

53

Sato and his sun stalkers made good time back to Dahl. Not so fast that they would arrive at the city with horse and sentinel exhausted, but hopefully fast enough to make some sort of difference.

He knew it was too late to help the sentinels within the walls, but his unease was due to more than just that. It was even more than the enigmatic warnings the old lady had given him. Somewhere, in the very darkest recesses of his mind, he sensed a wrongness. As much as he wished it otherwise, the night when he, Crispin, and Alonzo had fought against the demon had changed him. What he saw, heard, and touched were no longer all of reality.

This world was deeper and more mysterious than he knew.

He *felt* the force approaching Dahl. Which made no sense. He dared not utter a word to any of his sun stalkers about his feeling. But he feared what he would find when they arrived.

Even with his premonition, when the walls came into view, he pulled his horse to a stop in surprise. Fires burned unchecked throughout the city, sending smoke billowing into the air. Smoke rose from the harbor beyond the city as well. Ships were burning.

All that meant little, though, when Sato saw the invasion force assembled outside Dahl. Every soldier was as big as Beast, and several even larger. He heard the curses from his sun stalkers and was tempted to join them.

So, these were the Maramans Yuki had warned him about.

On his land. The land of Samas, home of the Firstborn and blessed by the eternal sun.

They would pay in blood for every step they took.

For the moment, the scene was calm. The Maramans surrounded the city, but they didn't advance upon the sturdy walls. Given the hole that had once been the gate, and the smoke from inside the city, Sato assumed the Maramans had launched an assault that had been repelled. But there were still dozens of warriors.

On the opposite side of Dahl, below the high walls perched on the cliff that overlooked the bay, was another encampment of Maramans. Judging by the large tents and the defensive structures, Sato assumed he could find the Maraman commanders there. Looking past the camp, he could just make out strange, black-sailed ships.

Sato scratched at his chin. He'd seen Beast fight, which was the only point of comparison he had to these invaders. But if Beast was representative of these people, they were a considerable force.

Roko pulled his horse next to Sato's. "A smaller force than I expected."

"I think they struck already and were driven back. I'd guess they took heavy losses in the process."

Roko nodded. "Thoughts?"

"They're between us and Dahl. Their camp seems too well-defended for us to attack. Our best course of action is to charge the Maramans in the fields."

"We could let the two sides fight it out and come in to pick up the pieces. I doubt there are many sentinels left in Dahl."

Sato had considered the same. It certainly seemed like a convenient solution, except for one problem. "If we do that, it's the people inside Dahl who suffer. If we can end this with one decisive strike outside the walls, it would be a worthy action."

"I don't see any mounts," Roko said.

Sato grinned. His old friend was thinking the same as him. "It doesn't matter how fierce those warriors are if we're mounted and they're not." He stretched. "It's about time I get to fight a familiar battle. Something I'm actually trained for."

"Bit out of practice, aren't you, sir?" Roko asked.

"Never," Sato replied.

He wheeled his horse around and gathered his sun stalkers. They weren't a large group, but Sato believed they would be enough to make a difference. It was time for them to make their name.

He outlined his plan, giving the sun stalkers a chance to ask questions. The tactics, though, were straightforward, a pleasant change from their more recent battles. Enormous or not, those invaders were going to fall.

Sato had just lined up his cavalry for the charge when an overwhelming pressure grabbed hold of his mind. It twisted and tugged, making him gasp for breath. He collapsed forward, barely catching himself from falling out of his saddle.

Roko shouted at him, but Sato heard nothing. His mind felt like it was being torn apart from the inside.

He'd sensed something like this before.

A rift was opening.

He groaned and squeezed his eyes shut, imagining a wall between his mind and the rift. It wasn't perfect, but the pain in his temples subsided to a dull ache. He sat up straight on his horse and waved off Roko's concern.

He felt it. It called to him from the encampment. A group of crimson-robed Maramans were standing in a semi-circle with their arms raised. The glow from their hands matched their robes. Above them, a giant point of light was pulsing.

The largest rift he'd ever seen.

Sato almost changed his orders. Attacking the camp was a suicidal charge, but those crimson robes represented the greater threat. But then the canvas of the tents parted. Enormous demons, each a grotesque pantomime of the already giant Maramans, stepped into the sunlight. There were at nearly a dozen, each of them with chains that ran from a collar on their necks to a Maraman handler.

Fighting a much smaller one of those had almost killed Sato, Crispin, and Alonzo working together.

Each stood as still as a statue, something he'd never seen them do before.

The Maramans had some level of control over the demons. He could have guessed it from his observations alone, but more than that, he felt it in his bones.

Once they were all assembled, the handlers snapped the chains and the collars popped off.

The demons broke ranks, all of them at once.

They charged the walls of Dahl, even as the warning bells pealed for help. Only a few bodies rushed to the walls, though. Perhaps the sin and sentinels had pushed back the first assault, but it looked like it had cost them dearly.

The demons tore up the fields outside Dahl and hit the wall like hammers. The thick barriers didn't even slow them down. They climbed it as though it were flat ground, their claws leaving enormous craters in the stone. Within a few heartbeats, they had climbed up and over the walls and were inside Dahl.

Sato didn't even think the eternal sun could protect those inside now.

The scene had frozen him, but as soon as the demons disappeared, his reason returned.

He turned around so his warriors could hear him. "We advance! Kill everyone. We can't let the Maramans flank the defenders inside Dahl. Once they're dealt with, we'll attack the encampment. If we can kill the ones controlling those demons, we might be able to stop them."

He wasn't sure if any of it was true. He wanted it to be true, though. In his limited experience, killing humans, even Maramans, had to be easier than fighting those beasts. He raised his sword, waiting for others to join him.

For a long moment, no one moved. Fighting humans, even enormous ones like the Maramans, was something they had trained to do. But most of his sentinels hadn't even heard of the demons. He could hardly blame them if they ran.

Alonzo raised his sword first, and that was all it took. Nearly two dozen swords joined Sato's.

The sight caused a lump to form in Sato's throat. They knew, and still they followed him.

He turned and brought his sword down. His sentinels charged.

For the first time in months, the world felt right to Sato.

This was what he was meant to do. He wanted to lead a charge of well-trained sentinels against the enemies of Samas. It was clean and pure, the most perfect expression of his dedication to the Path.

His sun stalkers never crashed into the waiting Maramans. Once within bow range, they wheeled around and picked off the invaders, filling them with arrows until even their giant bodies fell.

A few spears came flying their way, but on horseback and at range, they were easily avoided.

They circled out of range of the spears twice, drawing the Maramans further from Dahl, before turning and launching another storm of arrows.

The Maramans never had a chance.

When the last body finally stopped twitching, Sato circled their horses.

He looked at his assembled warriors with pride. Their months of hard training had paid off handsomely.

Soon, he would lead them back to Bulas and present them to the Firstborn, and he would be suitably impressed.

He congratulated his sun stalkers. But before he could issue further orders, he saw a few faces drop in the circle. The ones facing Dahl. He turned to see the problem, and then his expression mirrored that of his unit.

One of the demons had emerged from the ruined gates, and was now charging for them as quickly as it could run.

54

S hin heard the screams first. It took her a few moments for her tired mind to even register the sound. The moment Beast left with Raya, she'd stumbled through a doorway and collapsed in exhaustion, and apparently had fallen briefly asleep. Sunlight streamed through the open window of the abandoned building she'd been sleeping in, and the screams were coming from far away. She couldn't have been asleep for more than a few minutes.

For one last moment, she basked in the confusion, a blanket of sleep still covering her thoughts.

Then the reality of the moment hit her, leaving her wide awake.

She sat up and grabbed Harmony. She looked out the window but saw nothing. The fires didn't seem any more intense than before, and she couldn't hear the clash of steel on steel that she'd come to associate with battle.

She stuck her head out the window, trying to understand. The screams were louder, of every pitch she could imagine. It sounded like a massacre, but one without the familiar sounds of combat.

She ran into the street before she could even question the wisdom of her choice. Her feet flew down the narrow alleys as she sought the source of the disturbance.

The screams pointed her in the right direction, and a trail of bodies led her to the battle.

After watching for a moment, she decided that slaughter was a better term.

The group of victims was mixed. A woman wailed in a corner, holding what appeared to be the torso and head of a man. Children whimpered in the other corner, and mugon died by the handfuls.

She didn't know what killed them. It was large and looked vaguely like a Maraman, but it was all wrong. It was too tall and too wide, and the proportions were off, as though a child had drawn a human and then gotten bored halfway through and switched to drawing a monster.

But by the sun, it could kill.

Sharp claws slashed through warriors, leaving only parts of bodies behind. It spun and backhanded one mugon woman so hard her head flew right off.

Shin would have run, but it didn't give her a chance. It finished the last of the mugon and sprinted at her.

She took a step back and stumbled. The butt of Harmony struck and lodged in the street behind her, and the blade went clean through the beast's chest as it charged. Her weapon bent under the strain but didn't break. Shin held onto it for dear life as the beast sought to free itself. If not for the back end of the weapon being stuck, Shin was certain she would have been thrown through a wall.

Finally, the creature retreated, the blade slowly revealing itself as the monster pulled itself free.

The wound barely bled, and it closed as Shin watched in horrified silence.

Behind the monster, a sentinel came sprinting around the corner.

Shin's relief at seeing help arrive overwhelmed her hatred and she almost let out a cheer, but the look on the woman's face killed the sound before it could leave her lips.

Another creature skidded into view.

She hadn't been running to help. She'd been running from her own demon.

Fortunately for the sentinel, the demon between them was still focused on Shin. It looked angry, though she imagined it always looked angry. Her accidental stab might not have killed it, but it had certainly earned its attention.

To the sentinel's credit, she seized the opportunity. She launched herself at the demon as it raised its claws to tear Shin to shreds. It was a race between sentinel and demon, and this time, the sentinel won. She swung her sword in midair. The precise strike and razor-sharp steel separated the creature's head from its shoulders.

The creature dissolved, slowly melting into a dark smoke. Shin found her way to her feet, eyes locked on the smoke.

The sentinel, though, didn't have time for talk. She saw the people huddled in the corners and shouted at the demon that had been chasing her. She spared Shin a quick look to make sure she was well, then ran away. The other demon followed.

Shin had never seen such bravery.

It pained her that it was from a sentinel.

Her attention returned to the smoke. Taking their heads killed them. That was good to know.

Then there were no more thoughts. Her world shifted

into a kaleidoscope of memories that weren't her own. Light and darkness warred within her, trying to steal something very important to her. She dropped to her knees as the shadow before her began to take shape again. Long legs and strong arms, familiar and yet strange. She saw another place, full of shadow and rage.

She knew where these demons came from. Knew what they wanted.

When she blinked open her eyes, she now stared at the demonic mirror version of herself.

It wasn't her. Anyone with eyes could tell as much. It had some of her features, some similarities. But the long claws and beady eyes were the hallmarks of demons.

She brought Harmony up, then froze. Where was this fear coming from? She thought she'd purged this weakness when the Maramans had charged into Dahl. She'd cut down several and felt nothing. But now she stared at a perverted image of herself and hesitated.

Shin cursed as, once again, the scared child inside her came out. All she wanted to do was run. To hide. To let someone else fight for her.

The demon gave her no chance. It attacked, using her own forms.

Instinct kicked in. She blocked and dodged, giving up ground with every exchange. Harmony's longer reach kept the demon at bay, but she wouldn't be able to retreat forever.

The demon fought as though fighting was the only thing it knew. Rage drove it. Consumed it. Made it fearless.

For one twisted moment, she admired it. She wanted to be more like it and wished their places were reversed. She lunged at it, not because she saw an opening, but because her admiring thoughts twisted her mind into knots, and she wanted to be rid of the fear that controlled her.

It knocked her lunge aside with contemptuous ease.

Shin never even saw the leg that snapped out and caught her in the side. Her whole body lifted off the ground and crashed into the building on her left. She thrust her weapon out at the creature as it waddled toward her, only to realize Harmony was no longer in her hands. She looked desperately for it, only to find it in the middle of the street.

It grinned at her, pointed teeth dripping with saliva.

"Fuuuuuck," she groaned.

The kick had broken a rib. Maybe two.

The demon raised its claw to finish her, and she closed her eyes, not wanting to witness her own end.

She'd fought a version of herself that had overcome its fear. It lived to fight.

And it would kill the weaker version of her without a second thought.

Shin rolled away as the claws came down. Flame erupted in her chest as her cracked ribs shifted under her weight. The claws struck a building, sending rubble crashing down on top of the demon. She took the moment the collapse gave her and pushed herself to her feet.

Light, shadow, and pressure fought a war within her mind.

What she could see, touch, and hear was only the surface of a battle happening on many levels. Lines of light connected these demons to some sort of source, far away. At times, she could see the lines.

She wasn't the only one fighting the demons, and when the other sin sent back the demons, they were using some sort of sacrifice.

One such sending was close. She felt it, more clearly than the others. Thanks to her brief instruction with Yuki, she even knew whose sacrifice it was.

Benji.

A man she'd barely known, but someone Beast respected. A sin who had reported directly to Yuki. His sending back of the demon affected her. It unlocked an understanding.

Yuki had told her that because she could sense sacrifice, she could also use it.

Once, Shin had thought she would have to endure years of training under Yuki's tutelage.

But that wasn't necessary.

Sacrifice was something natural, built into the fabric of reality. It was as natural as breathing.

The Shin-shaped demon burst out from under the rubble. It was faster and stronger than any human.

All she had to do was take off its head.

Somewhere, deep within her body, she already knew how to do it. A red glow emanated from her stomach. The power burned, demanding release.

She even knew what sacrifice would be demanded from her.

It wasn't something she could choose, she learned. It was a cosmic scale, operating on a principle she didn't understand. She could exert her will, and the universe would exact its cost. In this case, memories.

Mateo.

The demon stepped forward, ready to charge.

She treasured several of the memories. The first time she'd met him, when he welcomed her among the luan without question. The sense of relief she had, not just for finding a place she could sleep and be fed, but for finding someone who cared enough about her to offer aid. Their training sessions together. Her whole world focused on their weapons and their bodies.

His anger at her forcing herself into their thieving.

She smiled at how hard she had pushed and how he had eventually caved.

And their final defense of the luan.

He'd fought brilliantly. Even the most skilled sentinel couldn't have done better.

Every memory of him hurt. Sorrow and regret colored every thought of him. Even now, staring at her demon face to face, the pain of his memory almost brought her to her knees.

If that was all it took to kill the demon, it was a price she would gladly pay.

Hardly a sacrifice at all.

She offered up his memories, and the power was granted to her.

The demon leaped at her, blocking out the sun as it raised its claw for the killing blow.

Shin released her will. In her mind, she envisioned a tether, invisible and unbreakable, attached to Harmony, a weapon that... someone had gifted her. The memory was already gone. The link to the weapon was in place as soon as she imagined it. When she opened her hand, Harmony came spinning through the air. In one motion, she caught it and took the head off the demon.

She held Harmony high. The mist began to reform. She didn't know how to send it back, but it didn't matter. She would keep killing it until one of the other sin came to send it back to its realm.

Her name was Shin, and she would cower no more.

55

The first towering demon that cleared the wall and started running towards them was the closest Beast had ever come to true fear. The demonic mirror image of a Maraman warrior charged forward with the strange weapon-fused arm that some of the demons had. The creature was taller, stronger, and pointier than anything Beast had ever faced.

Beast charged straight at it.

He knew that his mugon, and likely even the sentinels, wouldn't know how to react to the creatures. If he showed any hesitation at all, his forces would surely break. Upon seeing him, the demon grinned viciously, and a long, black tongue slithered from its mouth in anticipation of its first victim.

It was the first thing Beast cleaved off.

The demon didn't seem to notice as it swung its sword arm at Beast. Fortunately, Beast had never stopped moving. The two axes in his hands were a blur of sharpened steel. Beast hacked at the demon's joints to remove its deadly limbs. He dodged and slid away from dangerous cuts as he continued his grisly work.

In his peripheral vision, he noticed more demons spilling over the walls and, to his great relief, saw his mugon join the fight. He just avoided a cut from the demon's sword arm and returned his full attention to the monstrosity before him. Before the demon could bring the weapon around again, Beast sliced the arm clean off. The demon, thrown off balance by the loss of limb, staggered slightly and Beast took advantage.

With his full fury, he hacked a leg off and then kicked the demon to the ground. Before it could recover, Beast pinned its remaining arm with a knee and then hacked its head off in a few rapid blows. He roared as his body experienced the rush of victory against a strong opponent.

Too late, he realized his mistake.

As the physical form beneath him faded away and was replaced by a dark shadow, Beast closed his eyed and cursed.

"Open your eyes, you giant fool, you're in the middle of a fight."

Benji's light tone caused Beast's eyes to snap open. He saw his friend, one arm gone, extending his remaining limb. He grimaced, and sweat beaded down his forehead, but the shadow shot over the walls. A minute later, Benji slumped to the ground, exhausted.

"About time you joined us," Beast chided. "How long does it take to recover from losing one little arm?" He found it hard to keep his voice steady. He picked his friend up and helped him to stand.

"Can I have my sword back?" Benji fired back with a raised eyebrow.

Beast looked down at the axes in his hands. "I might

have broken it inside of a Maraman."

"Of course you did," Benji sighed. "Well, let's go kill some more demons."

Beast smiled widely at his friend. "It's good to see you, Benji, but you shouldn't be here. Find some place to lie low and stay safe."

Benji arched an eyebrow, taking in the destruction of Dahl. Beast supposed he had a point. There weren't many safe places in the city. "I think I'll find a way to fight."

The thought of Benji fighting made Beast feel ill. The man had sacrificed enough for one day. But he'd never deny a warrior's desire. He nodded. "Well, don't die, then. I would be put out for at least an afternoon."

The corner of Benji's mouth turned up in a smile. "We couldn't have that."

Beast turned his attention to the rest of the battle. He didn't like what he saw.

The sin, trained in fighting demons, were practically overrun. Beast saw more dead mugon than alive. He recognized their faces and knew their names, each death making his limbs a little heavier than the last. The defenders fought with all their heart, but the martial skill of the demons mixed with their otherworldly strength was too powerful a combination. If there was any bright side to the situation, it was that the sentinels died side by side with warriors who had been enemies a day ago.

Slowly, the defenders were figuring out they had to take the demons' heads. But it only succeeded in shrinking the demons to more Samasian proportions as they regenerated. Only the sin could send the demons back for good.

"Stay behind me and get ready to send those things back to where they came from," Beast said, knowing that he shouldn't ask what had happened.

"I'll do what I can," Benji said. "But sending them back is no easy feat."

Beast sprang into motion. There were days he felt as though he'd been born with an axe in his hand, and today he put the lessons from a lifetime of struggle to good use. He took off limbs with every swing. When he could, he took off heads. He didn't wait around to see what Benji did. He killed, then was onto the next.

The demons reminded him that for all his strength, he was still only human. When they reformed, they had the training of sentinels, the stealth of the sin, and the determination of the mugon. Cuts decorated every part of his body, and with every swing, his speed decreased just a little.

One demon kicked him hard in the chest, its razor-clawed feet slicing through muscle as Beast stumbled backward.

He was near his limits.

The demons had yet to be pushed to theirs. He'd taken, what? Three, maybe four heads? But everywhere he turned there was another demon, slaughtering a friend from the past years of campaigning.

His mugon had fought too hard for something to call their own.

This shouldn't even be their fight.

Since he was a child, his best friends had been named rage and pride. Today, at the end of the world, they picked him up when he was weak. It was his friends who were dying.

No more.

Red seeped into the corners of his vision. Exhaustion fell away. He roared and threw himself back into battle. He still hadn't healed from the pummeling the Maramans had given him, but it didn't matter. His scars told the tale of his victories.

After several swings, he took another head. He knew he'd been cut, and badly, but pain had disappeared along with his exhaustion. He turned to the next demon, spinning until he found one. It had taken on the form of a twisted sentinel and was seeking to escape the area and run deeper into the city.

Beast charged, catching up to the creature in six long strides. Almost his whole world was red, and he swung the axe in his right hand with a fearsome strength. The axe buried itself into the demon sentinel's back. It turned, yanking the axe out of Beast's hand. He didn't even see the sword hand as it carved a new gash across his stomach.

Beast swung with his other axe, aiming for the neck. His axe never landed. The demon punched him, a single blow that picked him off his feet and sent him crashing into a house behind him.

His battle rage vanished, as quickly as a flash of lightning. Exhaustion crashed over him, and his wounds screamed for attention. He tried to stand, but his body wouldn't answer.

The demon didn't even bother with him. It just ran deeper into the city, hungry for lives to take. Beast couldn't even summon the strength to shout a curse after it.

Benji stumbled and fell next to him. His friend looked as terrible as Beast felt. He had new wounds and a hollowed look to his eyes. Benji's breath came hard, and blood trickled from the corner of his lip.

"I can't stop them," Beast said. "I can't."

Broken as he was, he never would have admitted the truth to anyone but Benji. At the end, even rage and pride abandoned him. Only Benji remained.

Benji coughed up blood. "I think I can."

Beast laughed, and the laughing made everything hurt. "You can barely move."

Benji looked over. There was a look in his eyes that Beast understood but refused to acknowledge. He shook his head.

"You did well with the girl. I saw her fight against the Maramans. Her skill was always there, but I think you helped her master her fear."

"I'm a natural leader, Benji. Inspiration drips from every word," Beast said.

Benji laughed, then wrapped his remaining arm around his torso. "Fuck, that hurts."

"Don't do it. We'll find another way."

"This is the way. Yuki could do it, or maybe Raya." Benji looked down at his injuries. Beast had seen how much blood was pumping from his friend. Benji left the rest of the argument unspoken. He took a deep, shuddering breath. "You mock, but you speak true. You're an excellent warrior. But Samas has plenty of those. What it doesn't have enough of is people who inspire. Who make others want to be more than they thought they could be."

"Blood loss is making you talk nonsense, old friend."

Benji gestured around the area. "These mugon of yours? They died as warriors. Not on their knees, like the sentinels would expect. But with steel in their hands. They only found their courage because of you. Just like the girl."

Beast didn't like the earnestness in Benji's voice. He changed the subject. "Ready to keep going?"

"I'm not going anywhere, friend. We both know that. But I can do what I need from here. Fortunately, our Maraman friends have opened up a rather large rift that I think I can take advantage of."

"Benji—"

"Just, stay by my side, will you?"

"What are you doing?" Beast asked.

"What needs to be done."

Beast looked at his friend for a long time and then nodded. He didn't trust himself to speak.

"The last few years of my life have been my favorite," Benji said, his voice distant. "Thank you."

Beast fought to master himself. He clasped his friend's hand in his own. "Couldn't have done it without you."

The sin smiled, took a deep breath, and closed his eyes. The red glow surrounded him again, but otherwise there was no evidence of his efforts. After a time, sweat began to bead on Benji's forehand and his skin drained of all color. He began shivering violently and Beast gripped his friend's hand tighter.

He wasn't sure if it was just in his mind, but Beast thought the shivering lessened.

Above him, a cloud of crimson light formed and began to spin. With each rotation, it drew inky blobs of mist towards it. Soon, the crimson light was full of black forms, some mist and some demons, and the spinning accelerated. The cyclone of light moved out over the walls of Dahl, towards the beach, and out of sight.

Then, with a final gasp, Benji slumped forward and was still.

Beast gathered his friend in his arms and held him. All around, he could hear the din of battle fade. The silence that followed combat was always eerie, but today it seemed to hold a palpable emptiness. Beast didn't know how much time passed before he felt a hand on his shoulder.

"Beast, we need you," Raya's voice said gently.

Beast nodded and laid down his friend.

Then he said goodbye to him for the last time.

56

"RUN!" Sato shouted. Not that his sun stalkers needed much encouragement. They wheeled their horses and kicked them into a gallop. They kicked up dust, blocking the sight behind them for a moment.

But only for a moment.

Then the demon tore through, gaining rapidly on them. Even the horses at full gallop couldn't outrun it.

Sato had believed the demon he fought back on Iru was the most terrifying sight he would see in his life. This demon, larger and stronger, chasing down his horse with ease, was worse.

He felt the demon, like a sickness in his mind.

There was no running from the creature. That was obvious within seconds.

Certainty settled over his heart, erasing fear and indecision. He gestured to Roko. His hand signs passed on his strategy. Roko looked doubtful but nodded.

Sato pulled his horse to a stop and jumped off. It

spooked as soon as he was off, but he didn't mind. It had done enough.

There was a commotion behind him, and Crispin and Alonzo were suddenly beside him. Their horses, too, left as the demon bore down on them.

"Thought I ordered you to circle the demon and turn it into a pincushion while I fought it," Sato said.

Alonzo just shrugged.

"Never was too good at following orders," Crispin said.

"No shit," Sato replied.

Crispin's eyes went wide at the language. "General?"

"A parting gift, if it comes to that." He gestured to the demon. "We just need to kill it. I'll send it back."

There wasn't time for anything else. The demon had eyes only for Sato, and the rage radiating from it was palpable. It leaped at them from over a dozen paces away, and the three sentinels scattered as it landed, leaving a crater where they had just stood.

They attacked it from all angles.

Sword met claw, and more than once, Sato was forced to retreat, to give up space against the unpredictable forms of the demon. It fought not like a sin or a sentinel, but a Maraman, a style uniquely suited to the demon as it already relied on incredible size, strength, and speed.

As they fought, the remaining sun stalkers circled the battle, launching arrows into the demon whenever an opening presented itself.

The creature never reacted when it was struck, and the three sentinels kept moving, never giving the demon a clear path to retaliate.

But they also weren't killing it. For all the wounds and all the arrows jutting at every angle, they couldn't bring it down.

It was Crispin, of course, who was foolish enough to find the solution. He charged the creature, shouting at the top of his lungs. When the demon swiped at him, he slid underneath the it. His sword flashed twice, cutting through both ankles.

The creature fell, and Crispin learned the full extent of his foolishness. The demon landed on top of Crispin with such force Sato was certain his sentinel was dead.

A dozen new arrows punched into the demon. Sato struck, promising himself that he wouldn't let Crispin's sacrifice be in vain. He made one cut through the creature's neck, and the battle was over.

The demon dissolved into smoke, and Sato fell to his knees. Alonzo was by his side less than a heartbeat later.

"You crying for me, sir?" Crispin croaked.

A grin broke out on Alonzo's face, and Sato shook his head. He wiped his face quickly.

Alonzo helped his friend up. Crispin didn't look like he was in terrible shape, but he wasn't moving too fast either.

Roko and the others rode closer, bringing the escaped horses. Sato jumped up onto Nightmane. Alonzo and Crispin were quite a bit slower. Soon, though, they were all mounted.

"Is it over?" Roko asked.

Sato closed his eyes. "Soon."

He operated mostly on instinct and the distant memory of closing the first rift. He felt warmth in his shadowy pinky and knew it was glowing red. He found memories that weren't his, but which showed him to send back the evil that had escaped. He let the memories guide him and soon he was going through the same motions that he used to send the demon back before.

The demon fought him, and Sato was so tired, he could barely keep his focus.

He wasn't sure how long he could hold out.

Then, Sato felt another sacrifice, much more complex than anything Sato's limited knowledge could understand. He felt the demon being pulled away from his grasp and he willingly let go of it. As it faded, the presence of the demon disappeared.

Sato opened his eyes, expecting to feel relief, but shook his head in confusion. The wrongness that he had felt on the ride to Dahl was still present. If anything, it was growing.

It hadn't been the demons at all. This close to the city, now that he could spare the attention, he could tell it came from behind Dahl. From the beachfront. He turned to his sun stalkers. "One last fight remains."

No disappointment showed on Roko's face, though he was certain Roko felt it.

They were all exhausted, but none uttered even the slightest complaint. He had them line up their horses. They followed as he led them on one last charge.

His stomach fell further as he rode. The rifts had been bad enough, but this felt like someone had taken everything good and right about the world and tore it into pieces.

They rounded Dahl, and Sato caught view of the camp once again. There was one last contingent of Maramans, almost naked except for loincloths, covered from head to toe in tattoos. They had built a barricade that would stop Sato's cavalry in its tracks. Sharpened stakes had been dug deep, thick enough to easily impale a horse. Four demons, long-limbed and grotesque, sat statue-still behind the stakes. A reserve force, or someone's twisted idea of an honor guard.

· · ·

Behind them, Sato saw a handful of Maramans wearing crimson hooded robes. They hid between a wall of wooden shields. The evil was emanating from them.

Their work was easy enough for him to sense.

Not a rift, but a portal, enormous.

The air shimmered as their work came close to its conclusion.

Sato knew one thing. He didn't want to see what would come through that portal.

Sato kicked faithful Nightmane into one last gallop. He didn't see a way past the Maraman defenses. Not in the time they had. The defenders shifted smoothly, anticipating the attack.

And the summoners were... *changing*. Now that he was closer, he saw them aging before his eyes. Every second added a decade to their appearance. Skin sagged and wrinkles deepened. Hair greyed and fell out in clumps.

The portal began to solidify. He was too late. The sacrifice was almost complete.

But Sato had to try.

The Path demanded no less.

Not a single sun stalker even slowed his horse. One final charge, and then they could enjoy a final rest.

The Maramans released the demons. Four of those monstrosities would shatter Sato's charge before they even had to deal with the stakes, the shields, and the warriors.

Their charge was doomed, but at least they would die with honor.

Then, a crimson glow creeped over the battlefield. At first, Sato thought something was happening with the portal, but the light was coming from the wrong angle. He looked over his shoulder to find its source. His mouth gaped open as he watched Yuki float down from the walls of Dahl with her arms spread wide. Red tendrils trailed from her fingers and attached to rifts that opened on either side of her. Sato realized then that she wasn't floating, but that the tendrils were lowering her. She quickly positioned herself between his charge and the Maramans.

Sato motioned to his sun stalkers, and they wheeled their mounts with a precision that would have done the Firstborn's honor guard proud. He wasn't sure what Yuki was planning, but he didn't think it involved being run down from behind.

The small woman strode into the battle with the demons like she was making a grand entrance at a ball. Hands outstretched, the red glow of sacrifice surround her. The demons swung their heads in her direction and charged. Before they could take two steps, rifts opened all around them and red tendrils shot out, grasping the writhing demons, and lifting them into the air by their arms and necks.

Once the demons were entangled, Yuki closed both of her fists and the tendrils around their necks tightened and pulled the heads off the monsters. The moment the demon bodies disappeared, the tendrils turned into rifts that sucked in the formless mist and then closed so quickly that Sato could barely see or sense them.

To say Sato's understanding of sacrifice was limited felt like an incredible understatement, but even he could appreciate just how difficult it was to create one rift. The demonstration of power that Yuki displayed by opening so many at once was unbelievable.

The red-clad Maramans redoubled their effort with the portal and Sato sensed the ominous wrongness increase in scale. Yuki cast her arms out again and more rifts appeared, each one shooting out tendrils that wrapped around the edges of the portal and tried to squeeze it shut.

Yuki's power was enormous, but Sato could feel her struggle against the combined strength of the Maramans.

"Yuki! The shields!" Sato shouted.

It took her a moment, but Yuki redirected some the tendrils to wrench the shields free from the Maramans defending the summoners. The moment they were gone, Sato ordered his sun stalkers to open fire.

A flurry of arrows tore through the now parchment-thin skin of the Maramans. Their tattooed defenders scrambled to help. Some threw their bodies in front of the arrows and others attempted to scramble around the stakes they had stuck in the ground to reach Sato's mounted cavalry.

The few that made it close to the sentinels were filled with arrows before they could even throw a spear.

With most of the Maramans dead, Yuki slammed the portal shut in a matter of moments. The closing created an explosion of sound and force that knocked the sentinels clean from their mounts. Sato hit the ground hard, and for a moment, his world went black.

When he came to, Crispin was pulling him out of the sand. All around him, the other sun stalkers were rising like corpses from the beach.

Crispin brushed the sand off his armor. "Is it over now, sir?"

Sato looked for any sign of the portal, but it was gone. The wrongness that had bothered him from the beginning of the day had also vanished.

He nodded and embraced Crispin. The surprised sentinel returned the gesture with impressive strength.

"It is."

57

Shin didn't think she was more than a block or two away when she felt Benji's enormous sacrifice.

Close as she was and attuned as she was to the battle of wills shaping the siege of Dahl, it felt as though she was standing next to him. She felt every strand of the weaving, and it was beautiful. Then she felt the true nature of Benji's sacrifice, the cost it demanded.

The newly formed Shin demon was one of the first to be caught. It scratched and tore at the street, but all its strength was useless against the power of Benji's sacrifice. Above her, a maelstrom of crimson light and demon forms was spinning and moving away. It passed over the walls of Dahl and Shin slumped to the ground in relief.

They'd pushed back the Maramans, and they'd pushed back the demons. A single glance at her surroundings told her how steep the cost had been. The streets were covered in blood and viscera. A silence fell over the city, broken only by the moans of the injured and dying.

Beyond the walls, a sickness grew. Some part of Shin knew she should go and help, but she also knew that particular conflict was beyond her. The power gathering beyond the walls was enormous, and she could feel the realm, seeking to expand its territory. Rage, hate, and jealousy flooded through her, just because she was too close.

She wasn't sure how long she stood there, but after a time she began wandering the city. Searching for a familiar face. She wouldn't die without fighting, but she also hoped she wouldn't have to die alone.

The power she felt next caused her legs to fold beneath her. She'd never felt anything like it before.

It was Yuki, revealing the full extent of what she could do. Shin stopped and let herself feel the battle beyond the walls. She felt the effects of Yuki's sacrifice, the way she tore through the enemies of Samas. And it brought her joy.

Then Shin focused on the portal, on one woman's sacrifice against a group of Maramans. Shin studied every moment, memorizing what she could. There was a deep learning here if she could understand it.

An explosion of sound and fury hammered her chest, even through the thick walls of Dahl. She could only imagine what it had been like to be nearby. But here, in Dahl, all she knew was that the battle was over.

Yuki had finished it. For what cost, Shin couldn't say. She was a little surprised to find that she was disappointed. Harmony rested on her back, but she swore she could hear it singing a gentle song, whispering for more blood. She found she wanted that, too. But there were no more Maramans or demons to kill.

She wandered toward the front gate. On her way, she found Beast, who looked even more lost than most. She saw a sight she never thought she'd live to experience. The enormous man had tears running down his cheeks.

He didn't need to tell her. She'd experienced Benji's

sacrifice, too, and guessed the big man had been close when it happened.

For all his muscle, his heart was soft.

He'd helped her. Maybe one day, he would let her help him harden his heart, to prepare him for what was yet to come. She didn't think the realm would be denied so easily.

They just looked at each other, and then Beast turned and led her toward the gate. She followed, taking stock of what the city had suffered.

Buildings had been destroyed, and the number of bodies was beyond count. Given the vicious nature of the demons, Shin suspected they would never know exactly how many had died here today. Too many.

Shin swore to herself that it wouldn't happen again. Not so long as she had strength in her body and Harmony by her side. Together, they would protect the innocent from the ravages of both the sentinels and the Maramans.

But it was Beast who kept her attention most of all. The giant man stumbled slowly but refused all aid. No doubt, he had fought valiantly. The wounds that ran from his forehead to his shins attested to that. She could barely believe he still walked.

They walked out the front gate and made their way around Dahl. She looked up at the holes in the wall where the demons had climbed. Far from discouraging her, they gave her hope. The demons were the strongest enemy Samas had ever faced, and they'd won.

Ahead of her, Beast stumbled and almost fell again. She rushed forward and helped support him, and for once, he didn't push her away.

She looked up and saw the suffering written on every line in Beast's face. Grief didn't fit him, and she felt like she needed to say something. "He was a good man," she offered.

The words rang hollowly in her ears, but Beast nodded. "The best," he accepted.

She got the sense that it didn't really matter what she said. Her words couldn't truly reach Beast, not where he was. The loss of Benji was a wound only time could heal, and even that was questionable.

They finally came to a place where they could look down on the beach. It was a mess of bodies, blood, and flame. A group of cavalry were trying to recapture and calm their mounts. Heavily tattooed Maramans lay all around them, riddled with arrows. Shin saw Sato, and for the first time since her parents had died, didn't feel any anger at him. She wasn't sure she could summon any anger at all right now.

She and Beast walked down to the beach together.

Survivors.

Victors.

58

Beast tried to summon the usual exhilaration he felt in victory, but there was nothing but a void in his heart. He took some comfort in Shin walking by his side, but he still felt hollow.

His eyes scanned the strange battlefield that was the beaches below Dahl. He saw Sato and his sentinels tearing through the Maraman tents and pulling up makeshift stakes that had been driven into the ground. They appeared to be salvaging what they could and killing any wounded Maramans they came across. Even wounded, his countrymen fought to the death.

His attention drifted towards the elderly-looking Maramans in their crimson robes. Judging from their location amidst the defenses, Beast had to assume they were somehow important. The color of their robes suggested they had something to do with the demons that Benji had given his life to destroy. It reminded him of the color that had surrounded Benji when he made his final sacrifice.

He started walking towards them with deadly purpose.

When he closed the distance, he was pleased to see that

some of the wrinkled husks were still breathing and looking about in fear. One of them reached a hand towards Beast but whether it was to ask for help or ward him away, Beast wasn't sure.

Nor did he care.

With a swift kick, he knocked the Maraman flat and then stomped down on his skull. The wet crunch he heard was both sickening and intensely satisfying. He moved onto the next figure. This one was dead, riddled with arrows, but he brought his boot down anyway. His rage grew with each skull he stomped. Before long, he was screaming like a wild animal as he crushed the life out of the bastards that killed his friend.

A red haze clouded his vision, but as he moved to kill the final living Maraman Yuki stepped in front of him. Somehow, just the sight of the small woman was enough to restore his calm.

"Feel better?" she asked, her voice as dry as the husks he'd been stomping.

"I will in a moment. Could you step aside, please?"

"I indulged your revenge with the others, but I'm afraid I need one of them alive."

For a moment Beast imagined his fist rearranging the placid mask that was Yuki's face, but as quickly as the image came it was gone, replaced by Benji's indulgent smile. The one he used when he had to calm Beast's temper.

"Fine, my boots were getting ruined, anyway."

"Thank you, Beast. Whatever this was, there is more to come, and we need whatever information we can get."

"They don't speak our language," Beast said.

"No, but I have other methods. Their connection to sacrifice is something I can use. You should rest, Beast. I know it was a hard day."

Beast brought his fist up. A hard day? She didn't begin to have the slightest clue. Something in her eyes stopped him, though. The last of his anger faded again. His wounds needed attention, and soon. Movement out of the corner of his eye brought up another question, though.

"What are we doing about them?" Beast asked as he pointed at Sato and his sun stalkers.

"I believe them to be our newest allies in this fight."

"How do you figure that?"

"I gave Sato the opportunity to help us, and he took it. He could have waited until we were weakened or destroyed by the Maramans and then swept in and finished off whoever was left. Instead, he stood with us, for the good of Samas."

"The only good sentinel is a dead sentinel," Beast answered.

"I'm beginning to see why you get along so well with Shin," Yuki said. Even she was starting to sound tired. "My more pressing problem, though, is you."

"What do you mean?"

"You've seen the faces of all our foes. You are still the leader of the mugon, who were instrumental in this battle. What will you do, now that you know all that you do?"

His first instinct was to tell her to go back to her island of sin and rot.

But Benji's memory put a stop to that. He'd been Beast's friend, but he'd been a sworn sin, too. Beast checked his impulse.

A hard truth formed in Beast's mind. He knew, just like with Sato, that Yuki needed Beast to come to this decision on his own. That since they met, she'd been manipulating him so he would think he was coming to this conclusion on his own.

But that knowledge didn't make the choice any less clear.

He'd been fighting a truth that had been staring him in the face for a while now. He'd built the mugon into a fighting force, but when he wasn't looking, the fight had changed.

This wasn't supposed to be their battle. He had planned to join forces with the sin to overthrow the sentinels and then—what? Take his forces and lead them somewhere else?

Now, seeing what the Maramans were capable of, his previous goals felt somehow petty. Hell, if the Maramans had their way, who knew what would become of Samas?

His mugon were the people he lived to protect. The farmers, peasants, and craftspeople who'd been driven to desperation by the greed of the sentinels.

They called him the Bandit King.

But in Dahl, he'd learned that he wasn't enough. If not for the sacrifices performed by Yuki and Benji, they'd all be dead. His pride had abandoned him in that city, and he found that it still hadn't returned.

If he really cared about his people, he had to admit that there was a better leader for his warriors. Someone prepared to lead them in the fight to come.

And he was looking right at her.

Beast dropped to one knee, bowing his head.

"I pledge my service, and that of all willing mugon, to you and to the sin."

59

S ato watched the giant man take the knee before Yuki, and emotions flooded him too quickly for him to pick apart. Though he'd never say so out loud, he liked the big man. Beast lived in a simpler world, driven by pure desire.

Their paths would cross again. Of that, Sato had no doubt. He wasn't sure if they would cross as allies or enemies. He wasn't even sure which he would prefer. Though there was respect, he also hated most of what Beast stood for. Besides being a sentinel-killer, his desires led him far from the Path. He was chaos personified and had no place on Samas, just like all other Maramans.

As he watched Yuki and Beast formalize their alliance, he knew the islands he called home were in for a period of change. The sin and the mugon were now firmly entrenched on Ilos, and there wasn't anything he could do about it.

Almost all the sentinels on the island had been stationed in Dahl, and there were precious few left. His small force couldn't fight against the sin. Of that he was certain. At this moment, Yuki could give the order to kill him, and there wasn't much he could do.

So, he remained quiet and considered. Given the level of corruption among the sentinels that he'd witnessed in his short time here, Sato wouldn't be surprised if most of the farmers and peasants weren't glad for the change.

And therein was the heart of the problem. When the sentinels strayed too far from the Path, it allowed forces like the sin and the mugon to rise. Had the sentinels behaved as they should, none of this would have come to pass.

Sato knew that adherence to the Path was the answer. It meant something different to him than it had a couple of months ago, but it was still the answer. The problem was, he knew he couldn't make that argument here and now. None of the peasants here had even seen what true adherence looked like. No one would believe him.

Once Yuki was finished with Beast, she came over to him. She shuffled slowly over the sand and sat down next to him, her every movement deliberate. Sato thought she was trying to sell the old lady bit too hard. He'd just seen her float from a wall and unleashed destruction on a scale he couldn't have ever imagined. She wasn't going to earn any sympathy from him for her age.

"You have the look of a man deep in thought," Yuki said.

His first instinct was to push her away. She was the head of the sin. Everything he stood against. A couple of months ago, he probably would have even tried to kill her.

But the Firstborn's plan to expand his horizons had worked, perhaps too well. He accepted her invitation to conversation. He gestured to the barricades where the last of the Maramans had fought. "This was only the beginning, wasn't it?"

She didn't answer at first. "It's not, really. The Maramans

have visited these shores before, though not for some time. It is, instead, a continuation of a battle that has been going on for many generations."

Sato digested her answer and what it meant. "The Firstborn knows of them, doesn't he?"

"He does."

Though he'd expected the answer, it still hit him hard. Again, before his time with the sun stalkers, he wouldn't have even accepted such an accusation. But even Magistrate Velor had implied that the Firstborn was aware of at least some of the corruption within his lands. If he had kept such a secret from Sato, why wouldn't he keep others?

"I would offer you an alliance," Yuki said.

He appreciated that she didn't try to manipulate his thoughts through some labyrinthine discussion. Straightforward was best, especially when the world around him was in chaos. "What is the nature of the alliance you have in mind?"

"Non-interference, as well as the right to ask for additional aid when necessary."

Sato scoffed. "That's hardly an alliance."

"You would give me more?"

Sato wouldn't, but it seemed impolite to say so.

"Believe me or not, Sato, but your life is one the sin have been watching." At his look, she gave that smile of hers that was meant to comfort but only left him cold inside. "Not just you, but most people who are important to Samas. I know you, and I think I know what pulls you forward."

She spread out her hands, encompassing the whole beach. "This is not the beginning, but it is a beginning. The sin will rise to take their rightful place on Samas again."

"You mean to rule?" he interrupted.

"Not at all. I mean to serve, just as we have here. We cut

out the cancerous sentinels and defended Dahl against an invading force. We are the other side of the scale, Sato. The justice that operates in the shadows, while the sentinels work under the blessing of the sun. I won't ask that we become fast friends. I know such is not in your nature. All I ask is that you allow us to continue on the path we have made for ourselves."

Sato considered the offer. There was always the chance that if he refused, he wouldn't leave Dahl alive. He'd seen Yuki's power firsthand, and as of right now, he had no answer to it.

But the sin were also a tool. She spoke true. They had killed the corrupt sentinels and led the defense of the city. If Sato only had his sun stalkers, he wouldn't have accomplished either. Eventually, he would have to expel the sin from Samas again, but for now, they served his purposes.

He turned the offer over, examining his own logic. Then he nodded. "I can agree to those terms."

Yuki didn't burden him with additional unwanted conversation. She acknowledged his acceptance and stood up. When she walked away, her movements were smooth and even.

Before Sato could even form a coherent thought, Crispin had plopped down next to him. "Hell of a day, eh, sir?"

"Indeed," Sato replied dryly.

"You thinking about courting her, sir? She's quite a looker, and she's the only woman who isn't a sentinel who has spoken more than a dozen words to you since I've met you."

Sato's eyes slowly tracked over to his lieutenant. "Even my sense of humor has limits, Crispin."

"Of course it does, sir. I've never doubted that for a minute." Crispin's eyes twinkled. "I came to ask for orders."

"Is that a first for you?"

Crispin laughed. "You know, sir, it might be. A truly momentous day."

"They're ready to go?"

"And eager. We all have the sense we aren't going to be much wanted in these parts for a while. We all want to know what you have planned."

"For now, back to Egzuki," Sato said. "I think everyone has earned a bit of a break, don't you?"

"Couldn't agree more, sir. There's a gambling den there I think you'd like, and Alonzo has a woman who will break your heart to look at. Maybe we can even—" Sato cut Crispin off with a look. "Yes, sir. Right away, sir."

Crispin beat a retreat, and Sato looked out over the battlefield one more time.

He'd always had grand ambitions. But if the last few days had taught him anything, it was that Samas wasn't the gem he thought it was. But it could be. If people found the Path once again.

He stood up. Egzuki would be a good place for him to gather his resources and prepare for what would come next.

It was time for him to become the Firstborn of Samas.

60

———————

While Beast moved among his surviving mugon, Shin once again found herself without anything to do. She walked along the beach, slowly circling the final battlefield.

Then Rua was beside her, and they were walking just as they had on the island of the sin.

Except it wasn't Rua.

It was Yuki.

"I felt your sacrifice," the old woman said.

Shin nodded. "One of the demons took on my form. It managed to disarm me. But after feeling Benji using sacrifice nearby, I knew what to do."

"It's an impressive talent you have," Yuki said. "I've long believed that more people are capable of sacrifice than we expect, but it is very rare for someone to pick it up so intuitively."

"It all felt very natural."

"It can," Yuki said, "but that is not always true. The portals and the rifts are also products of sacrifice, and you've felt how nature rebels against those."

They walked in silence for a bit, but then Shin pushed the conversation forward. She was too tired after everything to be polite. "What do you want, Yuki?"

"Who says I want anything?"

"You're the leader of the sin, who just finished one of their most important battles. You have other important tasks to be doing. You earned Beast's loyalty and just spoke with the Firstborn's top general. I hardly rank highly enough for your time now. Which means you have something to ask."

"Clever."

Yuki stepped in front of Shin, stopping her. "I know that you're upset about my deception earlier. I understand if forgiveness isn't easy to come by. But the truth is, now I need your help."

"You do?" Shin didn't believe her.

Yuki nodded. "No more lies. Not from me. That is the first promise I give you."

Shin's eyes narrowed. That was no small promise, given Yuki's normal behavior. "Go on."

"You know, now, how sacrifice works. How the cost is always determined. I've been alive for a very long time, Shin, and I'm running out of things to sacrifice. What you saw from me, today, would be nearly impossible for me to do again. I only have one more sacrifice I can make, and you can guess well enough what that is."

"What does any of that have to do with me?"

"You have a talent," Yuki said. "I can train you to do what I do. And you can carry on my legacy."

"You want me to become the leader of the sin?"

"Possibly, someday. But what really matters to me is developing your power."

Shin thought of the destruction she'd witnessed, of the power she'd felt. It wasn't even a question. "Of course."

Yuki shook her head. "I'm glad you're eager, but I want you to understand. I'm very literally asking you for a lifetime of sacrifice. By accepting, it will eventually cost you everything."

Shin just shrugged. "I already told you I accept."

Yuki studied her hard for a moment, then nodded. "Fair enough."

Off in the distance, Shin saw Corin running toward her, hand waving. He looked like he'd come through the battle unscathed, and she was grateful. But when she looked at him, she felt a darkness in the back of her mind, like a word on the tip of her tongue. He reminded her of something, but of what, she couldn't say.

Yuki turned away. "Now, as you yourself said, there is a lot more for me to attend to. We will talk soon." Yuki started to leave, then turned back. "Out of curiosity, what did you sacrifice to defeat the demon you were fighting?"

Shin thought for a few moments. She knew she'd given something up. But for the life of her, she couldn't remember what. She shrugged again.

"I don't know. Nothing much, I guess."

EPILOGUE

Emperor Kordano watched through the eyes of the surviving summoner and smiled cruelly. He was concerned that the lost child of Maramas would kill them all, but the old one, true to form, was arrogant enough to take a prisoner. However great her skill in calling the realm, it was no match for his own.

He chuckled softly as he watched the lost one take the knee before her. His long hair and beard were an affront to Maramas. His unmarked skin a sign of just how weak he had become so far from his own people.

But perhaps he could be brought back into the fold.

The summoner looked around the battlefield and Kordano took in the scene of their defeat. The Samasians had proven stronger than he'd expected. They had grown much since the Maramans had first attempted to conquer their lands.

The Maramans had grown too since his ancestors' times.

"You are smiling, my emperor. Did you not say we had been defeated?" General Gordak asked.

"Defeat means many things, general, so long as you are prepared. We've learned much with this skirmish. Their skill in calling the realm has improved as a people, but they're still no match for us. Their warriors, while small, are formidable. They mustn't be taken lightly. And, most importantly, we drew the old one out of hiding."

"Is that best? You said that her skill rivals your own."

The emperor smiled. Few men would speak so plainly to him, but Gordak had earned leniency and much more. "Her power is done. We may have failed in opening a gateway today, but she will not be able to stand against us next time."

"And the year that it will take for the next fleet to arrive? Will they not have time to prepare?"

The emperor considered that question for a moment. Gordak had counselled patience when Kordano had sent their first juggernaut across the ocean. It had taken six months to create the first ocean-faring vessel and would take another year to build two more that could house the full force of the Maraman army. Had they waited and sent all three, perhaps the Samasians would have been overwhelmed. Kordano had believed that one juggernaut was enough to establish a foothold and open a portal that would bring the Maraman forces to Samas without the risk of an ocean voyage.

He had been wrong.

"I took a risk in rushing our forces across the sea. A risk that failed. I am no fool, however, and as always have made contingencies."

"My lord?"

"There are four rifts in Samas, Gordak. The old one and her little cult have managed them for centuries."

"Yes, my lord, the original passages created by your predecessor. The ones that the old one poisoned against us."

"Good, Gordak, you know your history. Though it's a bit of an oversimplification. The first demons were created in those paths. The truly rabid ones. The ones that no one can control. As we speak, I have sent summoners there to tear those rifts asunder. In the year it takes for our forces to arrive, whatever resistance Samas has will be busy fighting the very demons they created to keep us out."

"Do you think they will be able to overwhelm the old one and her people?"

"I do not underestimate our enemies. The sin will probably hold out against the demons until we arrive, but then they'll be fighting a war on two fronts."

General Gordak nodded his understanding. Even he knew not to push the limits of the emperor's indulgence. "With your permission, my lord, I will take my leave. I have preparations to make before my voyage."

"Go, Gordak, and do be careful."

Gordak clapped a fist to his breast in salute and left the room.

The emperor smiled and returned to watching the Samasians through the eyes of the summoner. They had led him to a cell and left him alone. Soon enough they would return to interrogate him. Kordano had no illusions about how long the summoner would hold out. He was almost dead as it was, but whatever information he could glean was power.

"You were reckless with my gifts. Let's hope your next attack doesn't fail," a voice whispered in Kordano's mind.

"For an eternal being, your patience is terribly short," Kordano answered aloud, even though he didn't need to.

"My patience is eternal. My tolerance for failure has limits. Mind you don't test them."

"Calm yourself, demon. Soon enough Samas will be

mine and then you can have your corporeal form. I do not fail."

In his mind, he heard the demon's whispered laughter.

THANKS FOR READING!

Thanks again for reading! In this era of unlimited entertainment choices, it means the world to us that you chose to spend your time in Samas, and we hope that you'll join us again soon.

If you'd like to learn more about Ryan or Taylor you can check them out here:

Taylor: www.taylorcrook.ca

Be the first to get your hands on Taylor's solo work, sign up for monthly newsletters or just check out some short stories.

Ryan: www.waterstonemedia.net

You can purchase all of Ryan's extensive library as well as sign up for monthly newsletters to keep up with everything he is doing. Ryan has also created a membership program with all kinds of incredible benefits.

If you enjoyed the book, reviews are the lifeblood of independent publishing, and we would be grateful for your feedback.

AUTHOR'S NOTE

I have found that any journcy worth taking is made better when the experience is shared. The time that I've spent writing this book has only strengthened that belief. Sharing the reins of this story with Ryan has only served to improve it at every turn and resulted in a friendship that spans hundreds of kilometers (or 869 miles for you Americans.) Being able to share that magical moment when we knew our book was complete was a uniquely remarkable experience.

One that, as it turns out, pales in comparison with getting to share this story with all of you. Creating something is wonderful but it wouldn't mean a thing without readers. We put a story out into the world and you keep it alive and growing.

So thank you for taking this journey with us. It's only beginning and we can't wait to take you the rest of the way.

Taylor Crook

January 2022

ALSO BY RYAN KIRK

Saga of the Broken Gods

Band of Broken Gods

Last Sword in the West

Last Sword in the West

Eyes of the Hidden World

A Sword Named Vengeance

Oblivion's Gate

The Gate Beyond Oblivion

The Gates of Memory

The Gate to Redemption

Relentless

Relentless Souls

Heart of Defiance

Their Spirit Unbroken

The Nightblade Series

Nightblade

World's Edge

The Wind and the Void

Blades of the Fallen

Nightblade's Vengeance

Nightblade's Honor

Nightblade's End

Standalone Novels

Blades of Shadow

The Primal Series

Primal Dawn

Primal Darkness

Primal Destiny

ABOUT TAYLOR

Taylor Crook is a fantasy author living in Hamilton, Ontario with his beautiful wife and two German Shepherds. Before taking on a writing career his life was shaped by nearly two decades in the restaurant industry. Long nights in bustling dining rooms have proven to be an invaluable and beloved step on a journey that led to finally achieving the dream of being a published author. When he's not writing, Taylor enjoys basketball, drumming, video games and, the hobby that started it all, reading. His favourite activity, though, is anything that he gets to do with his wife.

www.taylorcrook.ca

 twitter.com/TaylorC68001927

 instagram.com/taylorcrookwrites

ABOUT RYAN

Ryan Kirk is the bestselling author of the *Nightblade* series of books. When he isn't writing, you can probably find him playing disc golf or hiking through the woods.

www.ryankirkauthor.com
www.waterstonemedia.net
contact@waterstonemedia.net

 facebook.com/waterstonemedia
 twitter.com/waterstonebooks
 instagram.com/waterstonebooks